King Dido

Also from Five Leaves

Rosie Hogarth

With Hope, Farewell

The War Baby

So We Live: the novels of Alexander Baron
edited by Susie Thomas, Andrew Whitehead and Ken Worpole

King Dido

Alexander Baron

Introduction by
Ken Worpole

Five Leaves Publications

King Dido
Alexander Baron

Published by Five Leaves Publications in 2019
14a Long Row, Nottingham NG1 2DH
www.fiveleaves.co.uk
www.fiveleavesbookshop.co.uk

Copyright © Alexander Baron, 1969
The Estate of Alexander Baron, 2009/2019
Introduction © Ken Worpole, 2009/2019

ISBN 978-1-910170-68-7

Printed in Great Britain

Introduction

I

Alexander Baron was born in 1917 to Jewish parents who had separately grown up in Bethnal Green and Spitalfields prior to marriage and setting up home in Hackney. The new family started with one room in Abersham Road, then two rooms in Sandringham Road, before settling in a small terraced house in Foulden Road, Stoke Newington, the subsequent locus of many of Baron's most lyrical evocations of street life and community. His father, Barnet Bernstein, was a fur cutter, a "very prim and correct chap"; his mother, a former factory worker in the docks. Baron's mother never worked after she married and had children. In later life Baron remembered her, by then an avid bookworm, "sitting reading *Pride and Prejudice* — which she discovered in the public library. A couple of neighbours came in and said, 'Good lor', look at 'er, a schoolteacher.' His father, he recalled, read books of popular science such as *This Wonderful World* by Sir James Jeans, one of the great popular intellectuals of the time.

Baron attended Shacklewell Lane Primary School, which was then considered "rough", though he later described his years there as "the happiest time of my life." At the age of eleven he won a Junior County Scholarship to attend Hackney Downs Grammar School (also known as The Grocers' Company's School), subsequently made famous as the place where the young Harold Pinter was first encouraged to write. In 1954 Pinter adopted the stage name of David Baron, the surname possibly adopted from that of his by now already famous namesake who had anglicised his name from Bernstein to

Baron soon after the war. Another Hackney Downs pupil of this era, Henry Cohen also published two well received novels, *Scamp* (1950) and *Rain on the Pavements* (1951), writing under the pen name of Roland Camberton. Baron's post-war reputation was the first to establish the reputation of the school as a place where the imaginative life flourished, and indeed was encouraged. I was lucky to teach in the English Department there between 1969 and 1973, and some of that seriousness about literature and enthusiasm for creative writing still survived.

As an adult, Baron never spoke about Hackney Downs with quite the same animation and affection reserved for his primary school years and the pavement games of Foulden Road. This street life later mutated into a youthful political activism on the left, along with a fellow crowd of young Jewish and non-Jewish idealists, much of it conducted at street corners and open air meetings, often in and around Ridley Road in competition — sometimes violently so — with Oswald Mosley's fascist Blackshirts. He left school to work for the London County Council and increasing political involvement in the Labour Party, despite the offer of a place at King's College, London. "For God's sake, let's get out and get a job instead," he later recalled saying to a friend when they were offered the prospect of university education.

Nevertheless, he remained grateful to Hackney Downs School for the attention and encouragement he received for his writing, though, again, he also believed that this skill had come as much from his own parents' enthusiasm for the pleasures of reading. From a very early age, he was a story-teller. "In the street when I was a small kid, I used to tell stories. I wasn't very good at a punch-up. Story-telling gave me status. I could sit down on the kerb, with the others all around me, and tell them a story. I drew the material from the masses of books I read."

There were also escapes into the countryside. "My dad was a great one for the open air, parks and so on. He'd come home from work and say, 'How about some fresh air?' And we'd get the bus to Wormley. Walk through the side lanes and feel we were in the country, and then come home about ten o'clock." This appreciation of easy access to the countryside — not always shared in East London immigrant Jewish life, with its residual suspicion of rural atavism and enmity — is powerfully evoked in Baron's epiphany, "Strangers to Death", the prologue to his 1953 collection of short stories set during the Second World War, *The Human Kind*. This lovely recollection of a brief idyll is, alas, only a prelude to the disasters of war:

> "Every Saturday morning from early spring to late autumn, a crowd of young people would meet at the street corner. The cyclists, with rucksacks on their backs, tin mugs and kettles, all a-rattle, tied with string to their crossbars, and cheap little tents slung under the saddles, would stream away along the Cambridge road to their camping-site by the River Lea."

This collection was made into a Hollywood film in the early 1960s, under the title, *The Victors*, co-written and directed by the blacklisted screenwriter Carl Foreman. Until the outbreak of war, Baron's writing was restricted to campaigning journalism for the Labour League of Youth, where he worked alongside Ted Willis, later Lord Willis, a prime mover in the establishment of Unity Theatre, and more famously the script-writer for *Dixon of Dock Green* and other stage and television plays. It is likely that this friendship stimulated Baron's later, and highly successful, move into screenwriting and television drama.

At the outbreak of war Baron joined the Pioneer Corps as a sapper, and was involved in several of the most ferocious battles involving British troops, in Sicily and at the Normandy landings. In a letter to me he once wrote that, "I always carried at least one small volume (*Golden Treasury* in Sicily, *Oxford Book of French Verse* in Normandy) and we were dished out Penguins from time to time. It was six years without books but full of experience."

The story of Baron's entry into the world of the novel is best told by himself:

> I had no time to think about writing novels before July 1940, when I was called up. I was in the army until the spring of 1946. All the time, through those years, I was seeking experience. And knowing exactly what I wanted to do: I wanted to write a novel about the war. When I came out of the army, I was interviewed by a committee. They said, "What do you want to do? And how can we help you?" And I said, "I want a typewriter." There was a twelve month waiting list, yet they got me a portable typewriter straight away and I just went home.
>
> I was quite ill for the first two years after the war. I went back to live with my parents. And then, as I got better, I began to stay more and more with my friends. I fell in love with Paris. I'd gone over there for the first time.
>
> For two years, after the war, I lived in Hackney. I never got into real journalism. I was a member of the NUJ. Ted Willis, a man of many enterprises, started a theatre magazine which was very successful in its time, in the profession. He made me the editor. I used to work in the office until — at least — half-past eight at night. Then go home, have supper.
>
> After the war, the first novels to get published were all by officers. Either by officers or people who'd come through *Penguin New Writing*, which was a great influence at the time. Stories were by the kind of intellectuals to whom the army was an agony. They wrote about it as an awful experience, sleeping with thirty-five ruffians. The officers didn't seem to have the Robert Graves touch. Graves, Sassoon, knew the Tommies were the men getting the rough end of the stick.
>
> I read those books and I thought that nobody was writing about the ordinary soldiers. Soldiers were the nation in arms, they were the whole people. They were the young men of the nation. Obviously, I was on the left then. My writing was also therapeutic. I wasn't in the thick of the war all the time — but I was in some fairly big actions. Leading a troop on D-Day, all that. Towards the end of the war I had two fairly hectic concussions. I was pretty ill at this period. And it may be that writing this novel, *From the City, From the Plough*, really put me on my feet.

It would be hard to over-estimate the impact of *From the City, From the Plough*, when it was published in 1948. The novel was unanimously praised and sold over half of a million copies. Baron — who died in 1999 — was, as John Williams wrote in his obituary of the writer, "the greatest British novelist of the last war". This first novel was also one of his finest, creating the basis of his subsequent literary reputation.

II

Nearly seventy years after the events it describes, *From the City, From the Plough* remains a gripping and poignant book, though there is a barely suppressed anger beneath the surface at the tragic enormity of everything to do with war. All of the author's sympathies and affections are for the assorted anxious young men from all walks of life who make up 5th Battalion of the Wessex Regiment, training on the south coast and waiting for D-Day. Baron wrote sympathetically of the officers too, equally anxious and missing their families, though often being older they also waited for news of their own adult children fighting and sometimes dying in other theatres of war.

Amongst the men are the Swedebashers (the farming lads from the West Country and rural Wales), the Doggy Boys (the city boys unendingly pre-occupied with dog-racing and gambling), and various loners and misfits who, for the most part, treat each other with an embarrassed comradely respect due to others whose support in battle may well be a matter of life and death. In the course of the first half of the novel we get to know some of these men intimately, often through their quiet conversations late at night after lights out, as their reserve breaks down and they tentatively reach out to each other in fear of the horrors to come.

The more these people are individualised — and Baron was adroit at swift and vivid characterisation — the greater is the shock when, within hours of landing on the Normandy beaches, most of them are dead. They have been drowned, blown to pieces by grenades, crushed by tanks, their limbless, eviscerated corpses left lying in the cornfields and orchards. The sheer horror of close quarters fighting and the constant need for terrifying sacrificial sorties to keep the enemy pinned down, is nowhere better described than in Baron's tender, but heart-breaking novel. It is not too much to suggest that rather than simply expressing the democratic mood of the post-war social settlement, novels such as *From the City, From the Plough*, helped shape it. Baron's quiet humanism and common decency became, for a brief period, the language of popular politics and everyday life. This was not to last.

There were other novels and collections of short stories set in the Second World War to come, as well as historical novels, and novels about the Spanish Civil War, which Baron himself had volunteered to join in 1938. "I like several of our friends in the Labour League of Youth was very much involved with Spain. Virtually every boy in our crowd volunteered. But the people in charge of recruiting, the communists, sent us home." It has been suggested that Baron was more useful politically in London, writing and campaigning. In another of his Second World War novels, *With Hope, Farewell* (1952), Baron told the story of a Jewish fighter pilot. On publication this caused some public disbelief, though as he told me, the Jewish comic writer Denis Norden had been a fighter pilot, and on several occasions Jewish flying officers with DFCs (Distinguished Flying Crosses) had turned up at Ridley Road after the war when there was a concerted campaign to put a stop to Mosley's gatherings there. In general though, Baron eschewed the opportunity to put the specifically Jewish experience, either of London's East End or of the war, in his writings. There were two reasons for this. Firstly, because he said that he "always had a personal rebellion against the idea of a separate Jewish identity. My father and both my grandfathers were free-thinkers and so am I." Secondly, because he saw his respectable, free-thinking Hackney childhood as being beyond the classic Jewish East End, even though both parents had once belonged to it.

In later life he changed his mind on this, publishing *The Lowlife* in 1963. This was the story of one of the last of the *luftmenschen*, the elderly Jewish gamblers and street philosophers, who once filled the pavements of Whitechapel, Mare Street and Stoke Newington of a summer's evening to put the world to rights, exchange news of casual work in the rag trade, and discuss the evening's dog-racing at Haringey, Clapton or Walthamstow. "I had to write a Jewish novel," he told me. "I had to get something off my chest."

That something was not the common account of poverty and politics, or the religious impulse to radicalism, which characterised much Jewish writing about London, but was a celebration of a more tangential aspect of Jewish life, the bohemian, sometimes semi-criminal sub-culture of the eponymous "lowlife": a common Jewish expression for a gambler, workshy intellectual or bookworm, or habitué of basement jazz clubs and Soho drinking dens. In short, a latter-day boulevardier or flâneur. The novel also portrayed, with only a gentle hint of satirical intent, the security and satisfaction afforded the post-war generation of upwardly mobile Jews who were steadily moving northwards and westwards, via Stoke Newington, into suburbia and professional respectability. It is a great novel of cultural transition, capturing the pleasures and anxieties of a generation caught between two worlds, and of one particular character unwilling to adapt or change.

It is also geographically specific. "Physically, *The Lowlife* is Foulden Road, completely. I've always had a great love for Foulden Road." In this and other London novels, such as *Rosie Hogarth* (1951), the evocation of place is extraordinarily detailed and specific. More than anything, Baron was a London novelist when he was not writing about war. "I have always loved London. From childhood I used to roam about. Nobody was afraid of the traffic. I don't know if Londoners still love London. A city should be accumulated memory." Foulden Road is simply renamed Ingram's Terrace, where Harryboy Boas rents a room, and sorties out daily to walk the streets, or call in at the barber's shop and the bookmaker's. Very occasionally he visits his sister and her family in Finchley where he is guaranteed a good meal as well as the inevitable lecture on getting a proper job and settling down. It is a warm, humorous novel, with a tragic back-story, but it succeeds overwhelmingly as a novel of a place and a way of life that was shortly to disappear. Three years later there was a sequel, *Strip Jack Naked*, rather less successful as far as the critics were concerned, though even then Baron had still not got Hackney out of his system. A couple of years later he returned to an area he knew well from his childhood, Hare Marsh, on the fringes of Shoreditch and Bethnal Green. This was the setting for *King Dido*, published in 1969.

III

Today, just north of Bethnal Green Road, is to be found a series of monumental brick and terracotta tenements clustered round a Victorian bandstand in Arnold Circus. The pioneering Boundary Street Estate, designed by London County Council architects in an Arts & Crafts style, was erected on the rubble of the "Old Nichol", once London's most notorious slum. Of the appalling poverty which previously existed there was little doubt, and it came to fame as a result of Arthur Morrison's 1896 bestseller, *A Child of the Jago*, a work which early on captured Baron's literary imagination, and which he decided to emulate in spirit — but with a very different interpretation — towards the end of his fiction-writing career.

Baron's interest had been awakened in this particular part of east London from childhood. His mother had grown up in Hare Marsh, just off Cheshire Street. "I visited the area often to see my grandparents. And I think, from what I notice now, that fiction absorbs the power of legend and folklore. Local myths contributed so much to the formation of my novels. The final clash between the actual police inspector who ruled the area and a villain who thought he had the upper hand took place in Spitalfields. The story was told to me, as a very small boy, on the knee of my grandfather who lived in Spitalfields."

A Child of the Jago was a hard act to follow as it had then, and retains today, the aura of a fictional classic, representing a turning point in late Victorian literary realism. Published in the last years of the 19th century, it quickly became the definitive "slum novel", and not without reason. It was deftly written, fast-paced, had a strong sense of geographical accuracy, employed an authentic slang, and displayed strong enough roots in Dickensian melodrama to keep the reader gripped. However, even Morrison never regarded it as a novel of working class life, but more pointedly as a novel of semi-criminal life located in a ghetto of its own making, lawless and defiant of all social and political conventions. Four years earlier, Israel Zangwill had written and published his collection of inter-linked short stories and vignettes of Jewish life in Whitechapel, *Children of the Ghetto* (1892), which had also enjoyed critical success and to some extent paved the way for Morrison's novel.

It was presumed in *A Child of the Jago* that there could exist a neighbourhood without any connections to the social and political changes unfolding in the wider world, and it was this insistence on the total moral isolation of the "Jago" that caused a number of critics to qualify their otherwise wholesale approval of the novel. There is no doubt, for example, that the narrative voice issuing from this netherworld is sympathetic to the then current eugenicist arguments, suggesting that it would be better if such desperate communities were wiped off the face of the map. In reality, more than 10,000 children from the district were transported to new lives in the colonies over the years. Did the pig make the sty, or did the sty make the pig? This formulation of the problem was posed by many social reformers in this period when attention was turned to the plight of the people inhabiting the worst of Britain's city slums. On at least two occasions in Morrison's novel ostensibly sympathetic characters — including Father Sturt, modelled on the real life High Anglican priest Father Jay of Holy Trinity, Shoreditch — describe the inhabitants of the Jago as breeding like rats — and with little more worth to the world.

More recently the historian Sarah Wise has devoted a whole book to de-mythologising the story of the "Old Nichol", the slum on which Morrison's Jago was based. While admiring the pace and skill of the novel, Wise strongly objects to its "obnoxious moralising and sneering arch tone"; she also highlights, with much evidence, the fallacious basis for much of the story's implied realism of detail. For example, while murder seems commonplace in the Jago, in reality there was only one murder in the Old Nichol between 1885 and 1895, the period when the novel was set. The Jago inhabitants are portrayed as illiterate bruisers prone to drunkenness and rape, whereas, according to Wise, the area was rich in clubs and societies, and many read the newspapers and commented upon political events as a matter of course. And where Morrison portrays the clergy as selfless paragons, Wise evidences on occasions a priestly predilection for incense, frocks, boxing and rough trade.

King Dido, while exhibiting the same narrative energy as *A Child of the Jago*, nevertheless eschews the moralising and reform-mechanics of "the social novel". It is a taut revenge tragedy about a man who tries to break free of his surroundings but is doomed by his own pride. It is as geographically specific as Morrison's work, and though in *King Dido* Hare Marsh becomes Rabbit Marsh, nearly all the other streets mentioned in the novel — Brick Lane, Curtain Road, Kingsland Road, City Road, Old Street — are real. The novel is expertly plotted, full of twists and turns, and unexpected reversals and surprises. If it has a weakness, and this is one shared with Morrison and Dickens before him, it is that sometimes the attempt at transcribing "Cockney" speech comes across as owing more to the melodrama and the chapbook than the more heterogeneous babel of the living street.

It is significant that at least one critic has mis-remembered the novel as being about Jewish gangs; it is not. The origins of the principal character, Dido Peach, and his family, are, it is suggested, connected to Romany antecedents. Dido has clear linguistic affinities with *didicoi*, a common slang word for Romany people; otherwise it was commonly a woman's name with regal aspirations. This is an interesting device for suggesting the "otherness" of Dido Peach, which in different writers' hands might have become an allusion to Jewish origins or suppressed homosexuality. Queen Dido ruled Carthage. King Dido rules a scrap of Bethnal Green.

Dido Peach dominates the novel from start to finish. There is something of a Heathcliff figure about him: elemental, willing to pull the heavens down about him rather than compromise or seek redemption. In this violent, expressive novel, Baron created a complex, mysterious figure whom it is hard to like — perhaps impossible to like — but who represents some kind of vital force in the back streets of Bethnal Green, only matched, and in the end defeated, by the equally frightening Metropolitan Police Inspector Merry, his archetypal class nemesis.

The reader is told many things about Dido that go towards explaining him, but never quite enough. He is described as strong-jawed, brutal in aspect, with the bearing of a "Teuton warrior"; he is always clean-shaven, always wears highly polished boots, and is as meticulous "as a Guardsman". He is also, at the age of thirty, celibate, and unable to express his emotions in any way whatsoever: his feelings were "an enclosed violence" we learn early on. And it is this inflexibility that leads to his destruction. For, having "challenged power" in the neighbourhood when he fights and vanquishes one of the local villains, he inadvertently sets himself up as the target of both the criminals and the police. Never a man to walk away from a fight, his early innocent actions are interpreted by others as deliberately provocative, and so he enmeshes himself further in the tangled net of local criminal and corrupt police power. Lacking imagination, he cannot see the traps that are being laid for him. By contrast, Inspector Merry has "a chess-master's grasp on life, quite naturally seeing several moves ahead, patiently sure of the larger results that would flow in future from presents acts apparently insignificant."

There are obvious literary precursors to this almost diabolical relationship between a relatively innocent, but wronged fugitive, and a tenacious detective, notably in Victor Hugo's *Les Miserables* where the escaped convict Jean Valjean is ruthlessly hunted down by Inspector Javert. Baron's Inspector Merry is also within that tradition of the Victorian detective exemplified by Dickens' Inspector Bucket in *Bleak House*, or the intrepid Mr Whicher most recently canonised in Kate Summerscale's remarkable history. On several occasions Merry refers to himself as God, as far as the people in Rabbit Marsh are concerned, and even Dido is not surprised when at every turn Merry is ahead of him, for it "was taken for granted that Merry knew everything." Not only is the detective all-seeing but he possesses an assured psychological instinct for human fallibility, and even when deliberately instigating the framing of a criminal, he "always brought his subject to the correct boiling point. He could not see that he falsified or invented anything. He believed that he was merely by informed experiment demonstrating the properties of his subject."

As with *A Child of the Jago*, it is the women who bear the brunt of poverty and violence. Dido's mother is a pious Christian, a former domestic servant who has learned to speak the "prim English" required of such posts, and who labours to keep her three sons respectable, but hardly dare open her mouth unless spoken to. Her fears are that Dido will "inherit the sins of the father", a common Victorian trope. It is revealed early on that her deceased husband had proved to be a violent and abusive drunk. Grace, the orphaned waitress who is raped by Dido and then quickly married by him, is an intriguing mixture of the naïve, the put upon, and latterly, towards the end of the novel, the desperately calculating.

Dido is a lost man amongst women. He idealises his mother, but time and again betrays her; he is incapable of showing any affection for his young wife, and yet he would love to be a decent husband. More than anything, *King Dido* is an unusually penetrating exploration of a frustrated, violent and uncomprehending masculine world, in which women are cast as victims and drudges. Where there is poverty, the novel suggests, there can be little or no love or familial affection. In this brute world, sympathy for others is only a sign of weakness. By the end of the novel Dido is a man with "nothing laid on his conscience", even though he is responsible for the deaths of four people, including a child, whose slum hovel he had deliberately set on fire as an act of revenge.

There are, though, two moments in the novel in which Baron allows Dido to lift his eyes from his own existential predicament. The first is when, anxiously waiting in Tommy Long's stables to settle scores with one of his worst enemies, he sees a Jewish sabbath meal being prepared in the Burskys' kitchen. Despite the poverty of the family, on this and all other ritual occasions, the single room becomes a temple, where a clean table is laid, prayers are said, food is taken, and sanctuary and peace reign. It raises in Dido's mind, "drifts of longing which he could not follow." The second occasion is more commonplace though no less affecting, and occurs when he sees his newborn daughter, whose innocent gaze returns his and transfixes him: "pure life, unspoiled by experience." Yet neither potentially transforming moment is powerful enough to deflect him from self-destruction, and King Dido ends with his sovereignty and kingdom in ruins.

Ken Worpole

Ken Worpole is a writer who has lived and worked in Hackney for most of his life. His study of early 20th century radical and working class fiction, Dockers and Detectives, *is also published by Five Leaves.*

NOTES

[1] Nearly all biographical and autobiographical details in this introduction are taken from a long, tape-recorded interview I conducted with Alexander Baron in his home on 7th June 1983.

[2] The anglicisation of surnames was common, indeed encouraged, amongst Jewish immigrants. It is surprising that Baron retained his original surname throughout the war, as I always understood that Jews were encouraged, on enlisting, to register under an anglicised surname. This was what my own father-in-law told me had happened to him. The reasons for doing so were obvious.

[3] John Williams, *Obituaries: Alexander Baron*, The *Guardian*, 8 December 1999.

[4] I am grateful to Iain Sinclair for providing me with the transcript of an interview he made with Baron for a film called *The Cardinal & The Corpse* by Sinclair and Chris Petit. Hare Marsh was a street in Bethnal Green where Baron's mother lived, just off Cheshire Street. It is still there today.

[5] Sarah Wise, *The Blackest Streets: The Life and Death of a Victorian Slum*, London, 2008.

[6] There is a good account of the Victorian admiration of the tenacious police detective in Kate Summerscale's recent, *The Suspicions of Mr Whicher*, London, 2008.

Chapter 1

In June 1911, the Coronation ceremonies of King George the Fifth, who had been on the throne for a year, were celebrated throughout Britain by two days of public holiday. Stands to accommodate fifty thousand people were built on the routes of the two State processions. A hundred and twelve gated barriers were erected in the central areas of London to keep the crowds under control. At night the facades of public buildings were outlined against the darkness by coloured lights that streamed like a continuous firework display. Twelve thousand policemen were drafted into the West End to keep order.

The new King, the Sailor King, was immensely popular, his trim beard and honest firm gaze looking out from so many cliff-high portraits in coloured lights, and from tens of thousands of photographs in windows, an exemplar of the national respectability, as was his sedate and stately Queen. Their Majesties had presided at a brilliant Derby. A great Pageant of London was in the offing. Two thousand five hundred beacons were to be lit from hilltop to hilltop throughout the country, as on that night over three hundred years before when the Spanish Armada had been sighted. Among the throng of great ones from abroad were fourteen Grand Dukes or Archdukes and fifteen Crown Princes; and in the central streets were to be seen a host of picturesque representatives of the world-wide Empire come to pay homage. How fitting it all seemed, the universal tribute to the Imperium on which the sun never set, the pride and high spirits of a nation breathing an air of power, prosperity and peace.

"Rich and poor alike," wrote the leader-writers; and truly the excitement was no less in the East End slums of London than in Mayfair and Westminster. The great breweries and emporia of the Whitechapel Road put up their chains of electric lights. The schoolchildren had a week's holiday and swarmed shrieking and sportive in the streets. Families tramped westward to see the sights and others crammed the penny buses. Even the old folk in the workhouse were promised an egg for breakfast on Coronation Day, along with their usual cocoa, and such other wonders as jelly for tea, sweets, tobacco and entertainments.

Rabbit Marsh, in Bethnal Green, acquired its name at the end of the seventeenth century, when it was a green and pleasant country place on the outskirts of London city. Artisans came here to picnic, practise their sports and trap the rabbits and other small game which abounded. Here, as in other parts of the East End, a cluster of Huguenot weavers had settled and had built for themselves a row of neat houses. The houses, surrounded by well-kept gardens and vegetable allotments, were three stories high, two floors for habitation and the top floors laid out in long weaving-rooms with big windows. Within a hundred years the industrial revolution and the growth of the London docks had turned the whole eastern quarter into an immense slum which had overrun Bethnal Green. Rabbit Marsh was swallowed up with the rest. Gone were the rabbits and the gardens. The houses were filthy, overcrowded tenements.

In 1911, although the crowding was less abominable and the old, Hogarthian bedlam had vanished, the street was still a slum, the roadway narrow and cobbled, the houses black and decayed, many of the ground floors turned into miserable shops and workshops.

Rabbit Marsh, God knows, had little enough to celebrate, and on Coronation Night one might have thought that it had turned its back on the national occasion. There were no fairy lamps. No bonfire blazed. Unlike more prosperous streets (for poverty has an infinitude of strata) there was no street party with benches set out laden with beer, lemonade and sandwiches, children scampering in excited swarms, families dancing to the jangle of barrel-organs. Such corporate efforts called for a level of community spirit that did not exist in Rabbit Marsh, where each family guarded its crusts and looked warily upon all the others.

When darkness had thickened between its walls it lay almost silent, the occasional gas-lamp casting no more than an uncertain stain of yellow light upon the cobbles for a few yards, leaving a patch of blackness before the light of the next lamp was reached. Hardly a glimmer showed through the shutters over the ground-floor windows. From time to time a few dark-clad figures scurried (seen from above, like so many rats) down the street and vanished into a doorway.

Yet in its own way Rabbit Marsh was celebrating. To the labourers and unemployed, who with their families formed the majority of the inhabitants, all festivities were consummated in one form: the booze-up. And on this night there was one window from which light streamed. It was at the end of the street, and it belonged to a public house; not one of those magnificent pubs of the main thoroughfares with resplendent panelling and counters, ornate glasswork, shining brass, blazing lights and music; but a dingy dram-shop, distinguished from its neighbours only by a surround of green tiles. This was "The Railway", so called because of the railway line which ran behind high brick walls on an embankment behind Rabbit Marsh. This was the doorway which swallowed almost all the occasional groups that hurried down the street. From here came the vague, ugly bray of noise that alone marred the silence of the dark street.

Number 34 Rabbit Marsh stood three doors from an alley which led to the railway. In this alley a steep flight of steps ascended to a bridge over the railway track. Another flight of steps at right-angles led down to a narrow street called Jenner Street which backed on to Rabbit Marsh and faced the railway.

In the first-floor back room of Number 34, a man sat under the faintly snoring gas-mantle. He was dressed in his best clothes, a suit of thick navy serge; but he had as yet put no collar on and he was in his socks. One of his boots was in front of him, on a last fitted into a post which he held between his knees. With great concentration and deliberateness he was nailing iron rims on to the sole.

He was thirty years old, short and square. His fair hair was cut to a stubble with a fringe in front. He was clean-shaven and his cheeks were shiny from the razor. His face was a frame of strong, brutal bones, so hard, the set of his jaw so aggressive, that it brought to mind Teuton warriors, shouts, swinging of axes, berserk; an impression contradicted by the grey eyes, their gaze level and patient. His name was Dido Peach.

His two brothers stood by the door watching him, Chas, aged eighteen, and Shonny, fourteen years old. Neither of them spoke and there was no sound but the tap of the hammer and the throaty burning of the gaslight.

Dido put down the hammer. He took the boot off the last and stooped to put it down next to the other. He pulled the boots on to his feet and started to lace them up.

"I'm coming," said Shonny. He and Chas were like two dolls of identical appearance but different sizes, both so different from their brother that they might have been of a different race; two young gypsies with cheeks like red apples, eyes like black berries and shining black hair. Both were dressed in their best clothes.

Dido went on lacing his shoes as he looked up. He did not speak. There was nothing in his direct gaze but the same "No" that is presented by an obstructing wall.

Chas said to his younger brother, "You stay with mum."

Shonny said, "I'm coming."

"You're stayin' 'ere."

"I'm not a kid."

"You'll be in the way. You got no more weight than a new chick."

Dido stamped his feet gently in the boots, then stood up. "You're both staying."

Chas said, "You can't tell me." He looked into Dido's level gaze. He said, "'E's a big feller."

Dido turned to the door. Chas said, to his back, "'E could 'ave 'is mates with 'im."

Dido shook his head and opened the door. He beckoned them to go out and they obeyed. He took his cloth cap from a hook on the door, crossed the room, wrapped something in the cap and went after his brothers. The wooden staircase was uncovered and their footsteps echoed as they went down. Chas said, "I'm not 'avin' it. Fancy a drink, I can go in the pub if I want."

"I'm not frightened," Shonny said. "I'm coming."

Dido reached the ground-floor corridor and opened the door of the back kitchen. "Do as you're told, both of you."

They followed him in. Their mother sat at the table by the back window. She looked up from the paper she had been reading. She wore steel-rimmed spectacles. She was small and pinched, and her fair hair had become a tarnished grey, worn in a drab bun. Her plain black dress made her look like a parson's housekeeper rather than an inhabitant of Rabbit Marsh. She said, "You're not going out?"

Dido answered, "I am. Not them."

"We —" This came from Chas. He broke off as Dido, very close to him, turned on him. Dido's face frightened him. Dido turned to Shonny. "You too. Not another word."

He jerked with his thumb towards the table. "Go on."

They hesitated. "Give 'em their cocoa," he said to his mother. And to them, again, "Go on."

They moved like daunted animals towards the rear of the room. Dido, standing by the door which led into the shop, watched like their tamer.

His mother said, "Dido, I don't want you to go."

He said, "You read your *Christian Weekly,* mother."

"I'm telling you. I'm your mother."

"That's right." Now it was towards the shop that his

thumb motioned. "And I know what he done to you. In there."

"Dirty beast," his mother said. "That's all he is. A dirty beast. Have nothing to do with him. Nothing to do with any of 'em."

"He done it on the floor. In front of you." He opened the door to the corridor.

"Dido —" He paused as his mother spoke again. She said, "You're wearing your chapel suit."

He looked at her mildly. "It's the King's Coronation."

Her eyes were vague and puzzled behind the glasses, and her voice was vague, as if the talk had scattered her wits. "You got no collar and tie on."

"That's right. Give them two their cocoa."

He went out and in a moment they heard the heavy slam of the street door.

Poverty has many strata and Rabbit Marsh was far from being at the lowest. It was a paradise compared with the sinister back alleys of Spitalfields where lived a strange population of down-and-outs, men and women with meth-bloated faces and the eyes of dead fish who might have come straight out of Hogarth prints. It was respectable compared with the back streets of Hoxton where gangs reigned and roaring drunkenness prevailed. In Rabbit Marsh, people worked when they could, not only those who subsisted as scavengers, but those who followed regular, almost aristocratic, occupations — the porters, draymen, cleaners, stable hands and others who worked in the immense railway goods yards that covered acres of the district; the dockers and costers; the sprinkling of foreign immigrants, mostly Jews, who kept to themselves and worked long hours at bench or last; and the keepers of small shops.

Mrs Peach's shop always had its shutters up. She ran a rag business and the shop was her depot. It was crammed almost to the ceiling with bundles of rags of every colour and material. She bought from people who earned their wretched livelihoods going round the streets buying old rags or rummaging for them in dustbins. The pick of her purchases she sold to second-hand-clothes shops; others, carefully sorted by material, she sold to slum tailors for use as paddings or linings; the rubbish went for doll stuffing, or for pulping into paper. She had scraped a living in this way since her husband died ten years ago.

Shonny, who had left school only recently, stayed at home and ran all over the East End with a hand-barrow, delivering. Mrs Peach toiled like a slave, sorting the foul rags and boiling them in the yard. Only a few of her purchasers wanted clean rags, but she could not abide filth in the spotless home that she kept. Although the woodwork of the houses teemed with bugs and rats infested the yards, she always had clean windows and curtains, and she was not the only one in the street. She had put up bright, flowered wallpapers at her own expense in the kitchen, the hall, and the two rooms on the first floor, in one of which she slept and the other of which was occupied by her three sons. The top floor was tenanted by two families. She could afford the luxury of wallpaper, for although her own earnings were small, Dido was in regular work as a sorter on the Poplar scrap-iron wharf and Chas worked in a timber yard along the Regent's Canal.

Rabbit Marsh was respectable; and it would have been left to itself, if it had not been for its Sunday market. The traders of Rabbit Marsh scratched such meagre livings from the surrounding poverty that they were only enabled to survive by what they took on Sunday mornings, when thousands of people from all over the north-east of London surged through the Bethnal Green streets on the lookout for bargains.

The market brought money. And because of the money they lived under the rule of Ginger Murchison.

A stone's throw from Rabbit Marsh was Bethnal Green Road, wide as a boulevard through the maze of slums. On the other side of Bethnal Green Road, towards Shoreditch, lay the area once known as the Old Nicol, a thieves' kitchen so notorious, dangerous and insanitary that it had been demolished by the authorities. But its clans of roughs, who for generations had lived by terror and easy pickings, only scattered into the surrounding streets. The Murchison family, with its hangers-on, had come to settle in a courtyard named Jaggs Place, in the block that backed on to Rabbit Marsh on the opposite side to the railway. Lying in the right angle formed by Rabbit Marsh and Brick Lane, both of which streets had Sunday markets, it was an ideal base for the Murchisons. For several years they had thieved off the stalls, put their hands whenever they fancied into the tills of the shops and blackmailed the artisans with the threat of destroying their workshops.

They had never had any trouble with the people. It was as if a ruling dynasty had been driven from its hereditary lands and settled, knights in fearsome mail with lances and long swords, upon some neighbouring province, where the peasantry, weary with toil, weakened by privation and bitterly taught by past punishments, accepted a new authority as they might accept the coming of plague, hail or drought. And in fact this was the attitude of Rabbit Marsh. Wherever they came from, descendants of dispossessed country folk, refugees from foreign persecution or Irish famine, seekers after work on many brutal waterfronts or in many pitiless streets, often-evicted tenants, they accepted that there must be victims and victimisers, that someone must assume authority over them and take tribute from them; someone much nearer and more plainly visible than the monarch whose coronation was being celebrated tonight. Perhaps they celebrated that monarch's coronation because he was so remote, and therefore beneficent. Perhaps they celebrated because one of the few pleasures of the downtrodden is to tread upon others, and in their poverty they felt themselves lords of the British Empire. Certainly they had no objection to drinking the King's health. They would drink anyone's health. The King did them no harm. His policemen were almost as remote as he was, walking majestically down the street, occasionally collaring a drunk if he became a nuisance but otherwise only the wardens of a distant and non-interfering power. The King was not the visible ruler of Rabbit Marsh. The King took no taxes from Rabbit Marsh. It was too poor. Rabbit Marsh paid its taxes to the Murchisons. The Murchisons ruled.

No one knew why the Murchisons had always left the Peaches alone. Probably the little shop, its tall shutters always up, had simply escaped their notice. It was just a gloomy cavern crammed with bundles. There was no counter, no cash-drawer or till. The Peaches did not put a stall out on Sunday mornings.

But nothing in a realm is too insignificant for the eye of the ruler, or the eyes of his stewards. A week ago one of the tribe, a boy known in the street only as Cockeye, a grandson of Ginger Murchison, had come into the shop. He was a wizened, sickly creature, but a demon of impudence and cruelty, compensating for his squint, his scrawniness and his ugliness by the unbridled use of his family's power. He came into the shop and said to Mrs Peach, "'Alf a dollar."

She had never been asked before. Silently she put her hand into her apron, brought out her purse and found half-a-crown.

"'Ow much yer got there?"

She looked at him in a vague and fearful way. What reeled through her mind then was not fear of him but fear of her sons, who were brave. She did not want them to be brave. She knew what life was. She was submissive. She wanted her sons to be submissive, to remain unnoticed, to survive.

"You 'eard me. Show us."

And then, to her horror, she heard the iron-rimmed wheels of the barrow clatter to a stop outside. Shonny came in. She said, "Take the barrow round the yard, Shonny."

There was a stable yard down the street where they left the barrow for sixpence a week. But Shonny stood there looking at Cockeye and Cockeye spoke again. "Show us that purse."

"'Ere," Shonny said, "that's my ma."

"Fuck your ma!"

Shonny grabbed Cockeye's collar with one hand and the back of his jacket with the other, and swung him out of the shop. Cockeye flew across the pavement, fell over the end of the barrow and landed on his back in a pile of horse-dung. He started to scramble up. Shonny, back at the handles of the barrow, ran the barrow at him. Cockeye lurched up and away. Shonny ran at him again. Cockeye retreated again. "I'll kill you," he shouted. People were in the doorways, watching. "I'll cripple you."

Shonny, with the barrow, took a step forward. Cockeye loped off. From the comer, before he vanished, he shouted again, "I'll fucking kill you."

Shonny put the barrow back in the kerb. His mother was standing on the doorstep of the shop. He watched the wisps of thought wandering across her eyes. His own expression was patient. This was a situation to which he and his brothers had been accustomed since childhood. In time she would grasp at one idea, not because it was the best but because she was desperate. She said, "You won't tell your brothers?"

"No, mum."

"I suppose you will tell them."

He did not answer. She said, "No trouble, you see?"

"No, mum."

"I don't want no trouble."

"No, mum."

"Not with you boys."

"Cup o' tea, mum?"

Her eyes were on him, puzzled, groping within her own mind. "I knew you'd forget."

"Forget what?"

"I told you."

"What did you tell me?"

Her voice weak with humility, "I can't remember." She sought. "I told you last night. Something."

He uttered a high, boy's laugh. "I never forgot. You told me git seed for the canary."

"I knew I told you something. Last night."

"I got it this mornin'. It's be'ind the ornaments. Cleaned the cage out, I did, too."

He followed her into the kitchen. The room was furnished with a deal table covered by a sheet of oilcloth with a blue check pattern, three bentwood chairs, and a black sofa, its leatherette much cracked by use, against one wall. There was a blackleaded kitchen range and grate and over it a mantelpiece and a big mirror in an elaborate walnut frame with many shelves. These shelves, like the mantelshelf, were laden with framed family photographs and with china souvenirs of trips to the seaside. Against the wall separating the room from the shop was a gas stove. The shallow alcove between the chimney-breast and the window had a cupboard in its lower half and shelves of crockery above. On the wall Mrs Peach had hung a framed print, in colours, The Light of the World, showing the Saviour in a nimbus of rays. In the frame of the mirror she had stuck a coloured plate of the new King and Queen. The canary watched, beady-eyed and silent, from its cage hanging from a bracket between the sofa and the hall door.

Shonny went out to the yard to fill the kettle. An outside tap and an outside water-closet served the whole house. From other yards came the clucking of poultry. In most of the yards people, many of whose families a few generations back were from Kent or Essex, kept hens, dogs and rabbits, and most had singing birds indoors.

He told his brothers, of course. Chas looked quickly at Dido for a lead. Dido, busy polishing his boots, which he always kept shining, grunted, "Comes round here again, let me know."

Nothing happened for a week. The brothers, vigilant at first, let the incident sink out of mind. Cockeye and other Murchison brats made all sorts of trouble around the district. Their elders took little interest in their fortunes or misfortunes; but from time to time, moved by no more than a whim, or a surge of pent-up savagery, they would march forth in defence of their young, a phalanx of outraged family virtue; to raid another street, or to terrorise a schoolmaster who had used the cane upon one of theirs. And now, because of some whining complaint from Cockeye, Ginger himself, the Old Man of the tribe, noticed the existence of the little rag-shop in Rabbit Marsh. There must have moved in his mind the idea (or rather one of those spurts of primitive heat that took the place of ideas) that his authority had been belittled. The lord must uphold the least of his minions.

This morning Mrs Peach had heard the shop doorbell jangle on its loop of wire. She had come out from the kitchen to see a man in the doorway so big that he seemed to fill it. She did not recognise him against the light but when he advanced into the shop she knew that Ginger Murchison had come to deal with her.

Without a word she went into the kitchen, took a little one-piece cruet set from the mantelshelf (a souvenir from Southend, the words in gilt upon it among wreaths of roses), removed the lid from the mustard pot and took out a small gold coin. She returned to the shop and without a word held the coin out to Ginger Murchison. The fluttering of her heart could be heard in her murmur, "Half a sovereign."

She was a small woman. To her Ginger, as he looked thoughtfully around the shop, seeming to make a valuation, was a giant. He reached out, took the half- sovereign gently, unbuttoned his jacket and put it into a waistcoat pocket. Deliberately he buttoned up again. He straightened his bowler hat upon his head as if about to leave. Then, with the same deliberate movements, he undid his flies, exposed himself before her and urinated at the foot of a pile of rags. He buttoned up, stood over her for another moment, relaxed and quite benevolent, then with a leisurely tread left the shop.

Mrs Peach stood with her head bowed for a little while, shaking, her fingers laced together in front of her. Then she went to the yard for a bucket of water, washed the shop floor, took the sodden bundle of rags out to the yard and dumped it in a zinc bath to be boiled. She washed at the tap, went back into the kitchen and sat on the sofa, shrivelled with fear. She meant to say nothing and hope for the best. But there had been witnesses from the street. There almost always were in Rabbit Marsh. Dido, trudging home from work at seven o'clock that evening, had been stopped a dozen times. "Ginger Murchison was in your shop. 'E pissed on the floor. In front o' your ma."

He had followed his usual routine; eaten his supper in silence, stripped to the waist and gone out to the yard to scrub himself, and then gone to the bedroom to dress. Meanwhile he had sent Shonny to the Jew cobbler's shop for six pennorth of iron plates. He had dressed in his good serge suit and hammered the plates on to his boots. He had laced on the boots and put something inside his cap and now he was walking down the street to "The Railway", the folded cap in his right hand, the iron on his boots making a cold, hard noise on the cobbles.

Chapter 2

There was a door at each end of the green-tiled front of the public house, one to the only bar that it possessed, the other to the small jug-and-bottle department, from which the bar was separated by a plain wooden partition.

Dido went into the bar. It was crowded and full of noise. There was no singing, only a cacophony of London slum voices, quacking, raucous, ugly; and, since everyone was trying to talk above the din, deafeningly loud. He pushed his way to the bar, not looking about him, and only saying "Evening" a couple of times. He had no friends in the street. He knew everyone, as everyone knew him, but Dido Peach was marked out as a silent man, a man who kept to himself, who was enough of a hermit to have no dealings either with the bookies or the women of the neighbourhood. He often came in for a pint but he never stood or was offered one.

He said "Evening" to the publican, ordered his pint, and drank it in occasional sips, taking no notice of his surroundings. The slightest of glances as he came in had already told him what he wanted to know.

Apart from the wooden bench that ran along the wall beneath the window the only seat in the pub was a high-backed chair in the far corner by the counter. This was occupied by a man who was well over six feet tall and was fat in proportion. He wore a good serge suit; apart from Dido and the publican's, the only respectable suit in the pub; with a waistcoat, a gold watch on a heavy chain, and a silk choker. His narrow bowler hat, with a brim that dipped fore and aft, was tilted back, so that some of his hair could be seen; not — although this man was Ginger Murchison — ginger, but an indeterminate greying colour shot with strawy streaks. For Ginger, so named from his earliest childhood, was now sixty-five years old.

He sipped his drink peaceably, a big, solid man, respectable to look at, a landlord, one might have said, having a drink among the tenants of his houses. He was alone. His reputation was enough to protect him; not only as the leader of a gang, but as a man strong and cunning enough to have survived the fights of fifty years without a mark on his face. In any case, the Rabbit Marsh people wanted only an easy life, and had never challenged his power. A few toadied round him, trying to entertain him like court jesters, perhaps in the hope of some future favour or emolument. His red, jowled face hardly seemed to hear them, moving only in the faintest of smiles at the mouth. Some others, when they bought their own rounds, ordered a pint for him and set it down by him, saying nothing and neither expecting nor receiving any acknowledgement. Others affected to ignore him, though none really did.

A few people were glancing at Dido, and small groups could be seen conferring within the din. Somebody spoke to Meek, the publican. Meek came and spoke to Dido. "Busy night, Dido."

Dido nodded, half-turned away from the bar.

"Wouldn't mind a Coronation every year."

Dido made an 'uh-huh,' of acknowledgement in his throat, not opening his mouth.

"You keepin' all right?"

"So-so."

"Dido—" The publican leaned forward. "Don't want no trouble."

All he had from Dido was a side-glance that said nothing.

"Not tonight," the publican said. "Don't want no trouble tonight."

Dido sipped his ale. The publican said, "Here, have another one."

"No thanks."

"On the house."

Dido shook his head. Meek laid a hand on his sleeve across the counter. "Dido, we don't want no trouble. Not with him. Never been any trouble with him. Not down this street."

Dido left the counter but he did not go to the door. He walked to Ginger Murchison and stopped in front of him. He said, "You."

Ginger looked up. He said, "I got a name. It starts with Mister."

Dido said, "Come outside."

Ginger did not stir.

Dido said, "Mister."

"That's better." Ginger heaved down on the arms of his chair and with the resigned grunt of a fat man stood up and followed Dido to the door. The conversation did not die away. It changed tone. It became the sound of people pretending to carry on their many conversations.

When the door closed behind them the din soared and the sound in it was a compound of eagerness and panic. They were excited by any free entertainment, including fights; but this fight might bring them trouble, and it had come too suddenly for them to do anything to avoid it. They surged out into the street, and their only hope was that Ginger would lay Dido out quickly. The business settled, they would buy the victor drinks, flatter and appease him, so that when he lumbered on his way to visit his subjects in another pub in another street, he would be without anger against Rabbit Marsh.

Dido and Ginger stood a few yards apart, relaxed, as if each was waiting for a bus, appearing not to look at each other; though each was aware of the other's every movement. The pub had emptied and the crowd on the pavement quietened. Ginger heaved a long, pitying sigh. He handed his bowler hat to someone, took off his watch and chain and dropped them into the bowler hat, and, now watching Dido intently, unbuckled from beneath his waistcoat a black leather belt. The belt was thick but supple, three inches wide, with a buckle like a slab of armour plate. Ginger folded the belt into thirds, the buckle at the far end; his eyes never leaving Dido. But Dido did not interfere.

On the embankment behind the street a goods train was passing. It rattled on and on. The two men waited as if for it to go. When the sound of the trucks had died to a faint clatter in the distance Ginger walked towards Dido.

Dido's left and right hands came apart. His left hand clutched his cap, now empty. In his right hand was the claw hammer he had been using in the bedroom. Ginger paused. Then his hand swung, and the belt shot out to its full length, Dido leaping clear to barely miss the hurtling buckle. Ginger gathered in the buckle, so that the belt was a flexible, steel-headed truncheon again. Again and again he struck at Dido; and Dido, small and lithe, ducked, darted, retreated.

Ginger paused. He let the belt drop to its full length, then with an astonishing speed for his bulk he rushed at Dido, the belt lashing to right and left. Dido went backwards fast; and as he did so, someone stuck a foot out. He fell headlong back, the belt came down on him and the thump of the buckle into his flesh was so loud that against one male shout of, "Do 'im, Ginger", there was a medley of women's cries and gasps.

Ginger was attacking with the speed of a wild beast, his boot driving in and the belt whistling down again. Dido, arms wrapped round his head, squirmed away and avoided an onslaught that would have been lethal. In a blink, he was on his feet, gasping.

He scurried backwards, and as he did so he glimpsed his two brothers on the pavement. With them was Tommy Long, a little coster with whom he was on speaking terms. Ginger came in again and Dido, eyes on him, saw no-one else. To avoid being driven to the wall he retreated down the street.

Ginger bore down on him, his eyes showing the faintest smile of victory in his heavy, brooding face. He had his challenger on the run. Dido waited. He ignored his brothers' shouts of warning. He waited and as the belt lashed down at him he deliberately stepped forward beneath it and took it, deliberately, on his left arm, the buckle curling round him to dig into the back of his shoulder. And in that second, his will shutting out the awful pain, he drove upwards with his right hand and smashed the hammer into Ginger's jaw. He heard the bone break and the man's hoarse yell of agony but the belt lashed again and he took it and this time he kicked with all his force, steel-capped boot going into the big man's kneecap. And Ginger lurched away, one leg buckling, face distorted by the broken jaw, bellowing like a wounded beast, the belt still lashing, but out of control.

And while the people murmured on the pavement, obeying the imperative to keep out of a fight, yet fearful of the consequences if they failed to help their overlord, Dido lunged at the crippled, lurching man, catching him on the side of the head with the hammer, hitting him again, bringing the great bulk of him thumping down, and going in with steel-shod boots to kick, kick, kick.

At last he stopped. Ginger lay still. Blood ran between the cobbles around his head. Chas came forward, knelt and listened. He stood up and said to the struckstill crowd, "'E ain't croaked."

They murmured again. Their world had fallen to pieces and they did not know how it would be ordered again. Chas said to his brother, "You all right?"

Dido was panting, almost doubled up as he hugged his left shoulder where it had taken, by his intent, the blow. The back of his suit was covered with dirt. He ignored Chas and managed to say to Shonny, "Get the barrow."

He and Chas waited, and so did the crowd, till Shonny came back with the barrow. Dido took his hand away from his hurt shoulder and gestured, "Lift 'im on."

His brothers strained to lift the inert Ginger on to the barrow. Dido gasped, sharply, to the crowd, "'Elp 'em." He looked round. — "Tommy!" Reluctantly, Tommy Long stepped off the pavement.

Dido pointed to another man. "And you!"

The man obeyed. They and the two boys lifted the body. It rolled on to the barrow. Dido walked to one of the onlookers and took from him the bowler hat, with the watch and chain in it. These, with Ginger's belt, he placed in the barrow. Then he made another sign and his brothers started to trundle the barrow away down the street. He limped after them.

The crowd watched till they had turned the corner. The conversation gradually grew louder and more animated. People drifted back into the pub. Others went home.

The Peach brothers took the barrow to the corner of the next street, down which Jaggs Place lay. Here they tipped the unconscious man on to the pavement. They put his belongings down next to him. Then they returned to Rabbit Marsh, put the barrow away and went home.

A little while after they had gone a man came along the deserted street. He saw the recumbent body and crossed towards it. He stooped and examined it. He was a plump man with plump, smooth cheeks. He was a couple of inches under six feet in height. He wore a soberly cut grey overcoat, a trilby hat and small, lightweight boots highly polished. He drew something from an inside pocket, put it to his lips, and the blast of a police whistle shrilled.

His name was Merry. He was an inspector in the detective force of the Metropolitan Police. Tonight, when most of his colleagues both in uniform and plain clothes had been drafted to central London for Coronation duties, he had been making a round of his area.

He knew Ginger and he guessed what manner of drama had taken place. He had not interfered with Ginger in the past. He did not regard petty extortions of the Murchison kind as crime, but as part of the normal life of the riff-raff over whom he, Merry, watched. They could do what they liked to each other as long as they did not infringe what Merry regarded as law and order.

Merry knew everything that happened in the area, and he watched it as he might watch the murderous existence of insects under glass. Tomorrow he would know who had felled Ginger; for like Ginger, he had his toadies. But he knew that those who would whisper to him would not give evidence in court. Even if he wished to, he could not arrest the assailant; but he did not wish to. Unless, of course, Ginger died.

Already he had a notion of the future course of that unknown man's life; at a moment when Dido, the man in question, was lying on his bed, after Chas had painfully undressed him and put plasters on the two lacerated wounds made by the buckle. Dido was aware of little but the violent throb of pain. His only clear thought was that he would be unfit for work tomorrow.

A crowd gathered. The police came, and then an ambulance. Merry went with the injured man to hospital; and when he learned that Ginger was not likely to die, he gave little more thought to the affair. It would lead to consequences, of course, and on those consequences he would keep an eye. It was even his way sometimes to direct them with a discreet touch here or there; not interfering, of course, but making sure that events ran his way. Not the way of justice, which was one of those abstractions that he never thought about; but the way of Inspector Merry, an ambitious man, a man of authority.

Chapter 3

"It was him that gave your names," Mrs Peach used to say, pointing to the photograph of her dead husband on the mantelpiece. "He said they ran in his family."

And when, once, Dido grunted, "Romany," for this was the only explanation he could think of for his own Christian name and that of his youngest brother, she was indignant. To her gypsies were not respectable. She said, "He came from respectable people."

Dido, a damped-down derision in his voice, "Him respectable?"

"His people were."

She had grown up in domestic service and consequently spoke a decent English. She had been a maid in a tradesman's house in Dalston when Dido's father, then in enviable regular work as a gasfitter, had come to the house and charmed her. He had been a handsome young man. His photograph, which showed him older, fuller of face, with a spiked moustache, was that of a full-blooded and attractive man. His Mediterranean swarthiness and thick, gleaming black hair had indeed suggested a gypsy ancestry. The two younger boys looked like him. Dido alone, blond and Saxon, took after their mother.

The little fair-haired housemaid, lonely, excited into something she called love, had thought she was coming into great good fortune when she married this man with a skill and a guaranteed job. She was soon disillusioned. It took the day of her wedding to teach her that he was a mad drinker and a few weeks after to discover that he was a ceaseless pursuer of other women. He lost his job a little later, and many other jobs after that.

When she tried timidly to plead with him he shouted at her and the day came when he hit her. After that he hit her more and more often, until, as his decline hastened and his rancour against life grew, he would strike her without provocation, enraged simply by her weakness and passivity, furious perhaps at the continual contrast between her (in bed a limp thing, like some little creature hunted almost to death, paralysed with terror) and the innumerable brazen women he grabbed, coupled with and forgot as he lurched from pub to pub in the back streets.

It became a mercy when he spent more time away than at home. She had five children to bring up — there was a daughter, now decently married to a market gardener along the Lea, and there had been another boy who died in infancy of diphtheria. To make ends meet she started the little rag business, at the suggestion of the Methodist minister whose chapel she attended every Sunday, as she had since childhood. When her children were small she took them with her every week, a little procession of scrubbed, neat infants. When they were older she went alone; but as a demonstration of regard for her and of the respectability she had taught them to treasure, her sons went with her at Christmas and Easter, a solemn parade in best clothes along Rabbit Marsh — a family demonstration of apartness.

It was a small miracle that, with no other help from the chapel than occasional coals, blankets and cast-off clothes, she brought her children up in cleanliness and decency, always warm, always with a meal, if it was no more than bread and cocoa, always with boots on their feet; for the business brought in little. The children knew it. Living among the barefoot, ragged-arsed, pallid, dirty children of Rabbit Marsh, they were in no danger of taking their status for granted. All their lives they felt gratifyingly different from the rest. For this they loved their mother and, when then father occasionally appeared, looked at him with shame and hatred.

For he did come home sometimes. He came when he was penniless, to bully money out of his wife. He came when he was cold, hungry or ill, to creep like a dog into the bed, never whining but growling and glowering, till he had regained his strength. He came when he was injured, for another thing that his wife had learned early in their marriage was that he fancied himself as a fighting man, and as time went on he got into more and more fights. He always lost. Losing only increased his combative rage. The older, the flabbier, the more drunk and muddleheaded he became, the more ferociously he fought, and the more disastrous the consequences. Nothing deterred him. His ear was pulped, his face scarred, his head split time and again; perhaps his brain was damaged, by injuries or by his excesses, for he fought on like a wild beast. Ten years ago, when drunk, he had fallen headlong under a brewer's dray, and a wheel over his head had finished him and his wife's martyrdom.

It was impossible to know how she took this relief, for she just sighed and looked vacantly about her when she was told, and never showed any other reaction. She had always been quiet and passive, and her absentmindedness grew as the years went on. It was as if, utterly startled in her girlhood by the bitter shock of her marriage, she had never gathered in her scattered wits.

It was an irony that Dido's readiness to fight, which may have come from his father, was inflamed by his disgust for his father. The first time he tried to defend his mother from the savage drunkard was when he was twelve years old and he was knocked across the room for his pains. This did not deter him from flying to his mother's defence every time she was attacked. After many a cruel beating he was able to give a good account of himself, and at the age of seventeen, to thrash his father. After that, when the wastrel came home, Mrs Peach at least did not have to fear bodily violence.

And it was because of his fierce attachment to his mother that he came often to use his fists outside the house. Workless men filled the East End and converged like wolf packs whenever there were jobs going. They fought each other like hungry beasts for work outside the wharves, outside warehouses, to shovel snow in the winter, anything for a crust. The greater part of them were not savages or drunkards like Dido's father. They were men with human love and responsibility in their hearts to drive them mad because they knew that hungry children waited for them to come home. They fought better than Dido's father and Dido, who from the day he left school at the age of twelve was determined never to come home one single week without a pay packet to help his mother, fought for work, learned to win and always brought money home. Now, valued for his intelligence and strength, he had a regular post of responsibility on the wharf at Poplar.

It made a strange contrast in him; the ruthless, savage streak buried in him, the animal craft and ferocity; and the outward self to maintain which he had been forced to act in this way — the outward self of respectability. He ruled his brothers quietly but with a fist of iron. As during their childhood they were always scrubbed and dressed tidily. Under Dido's rule they all worked regularly and hard and gave most of their wages to their mother. Dido permitted Chas, as he permitted himself, an occasional drink but they never wasted their time or money in the pub. He taught the boys that the women of these parts were loose and dirty. He was haunted by a vision of his father's paramours.

Yet though he worshipped his mother he was a silent worshipper; like some tough, taciturn man who steps into a church to make a genuflexion then strides vigorously on his way. There was nothing of the mother's boy about him. He was not the sort who would hand the sandwich plate around; or serve as sidesman at the chapel; nor would he look at any of the "nice girls" his mother brought home from chapel "for a cup of tea". She was fifty-four, the gold washed out of her hair, her skin white, with the tissue-paper look and the innumerable fine lines of exhaustion. She feared her death, that would leave him uncared-for; or worse still, her own helpless infirmity. She prayed for a good wife for him, another decent and capable woman to take over the cares of the household.

Dido was a silent man. He looked neither to the right nor to the left, not at women, not at his workmates, not at neighbours. There was a strange intensity in his face as if ceaseless thoughts churned inside him, but what they were no-one could know. He could not express himself. Even with his mother, to whom alone he was close, he could only exchange brief remarks.

Imagine a narrow ravine whose floor consists of worn cobbles running between pavements of uneven flags. Such was Rabbit Marsh. The June sunshine gilded it as pitilessly as theatre lights show up the dirt on a bare stage. The walls of corroded brick were black with railway soot. The air was impregnated with the acrid smell and taste of soot. The rows of windows in the house fronts were mostly bare oblongs of glass which stared blind, black and grimy against the sunlight; only a few were curtained, the best with coarse lace, others with multicoloured patched rags.

The windows of the shops at the base of these dark cliffs, each divided in its own pattern of small panes, were no less dirty, and the paltry goods within them were few, faded and grubby with age. The paintwork of the shops had long faded to a dingy dark uniformity and the names over them were barely discernible. Most of them had their shutters up, locked by great bars of rusty iron, as did the workshops, for the Coronation holiday lasted into the next day.

That was all the street was; two narrowly facing rows of such buildings, leaning forward with age, cleft by an alley here and there or pierced at the base by a porch leading into a yard; the line of parapets against the mocking blue purity of a bright and infinite sky broken only in the centre where a tenement block reared like a prison five stories high divided by three open iron staircases. The poorest of Rabbit Marsh lived here and it was known as the Bug Hole.

On working days an endless procession of railway wagons passed down the street, and filled it with the noise of steel-bound wheels on the cobbles and the clash of great horses' hooves. No wagons passed today, but there was noise in plenty on this holiday morning. The street always swarmed with small children, dirty and bare-bottomed; even the babies were put out to take the air in orange crates. Today their numbers were swelled by the liberated schoolchildren, crowding round marbles contests, pulling each other about in soapbox chariots, or playing rowdily at hopscotch, Release or the violent Jimmy-Knacker. The eternal loafers leaned against the front wall of the pub as if they were paid to hold it up or puffed their clay pipes at the street corners. The women screamed conversations from window to window, in doorways and on the pavement. A few families set off in their best clothes to see the sights in town and a sedate minority brought out chairs and sat quietly in the sun.

Dido Peach sat on the kitchen sofa. He was unshaven and in his shirtsleeves. He could not put his jacket on, for his left arm was discoloured purple and blue and hugely swollen from elbow to shoulder. Pain throbbed in the muscle behind the shoulder. The dressing was brown with dried blood. His hand was pressed to his ribs, where pain stabbed each time he breathed.

His brothers finished their breakfast, eyed him anxiously across the table. Shonny said, "I been to the doctor's shop. 'E ain't there today."

"'Ave to go to the 'ospital," Chas said. Dido removed his hand from his chest, reached out for his mug of tea, sipped, and said, "All right I tell you."

His mother said, "I told you, Dido."

"Never you mind."

"Leave well alone I say. I always said."

"You look after the house. I'll look after you."

She said, "Oh, dear. I was always afraid."

"I'll look after you."

"Those Murchisons," she said.

"Look after them, too."

Chas said, "You wanna look out they don't look after you. And us two." He indicated his younger brother.

"I can manage them."

"You can't sit there with that arm," Chas said. "'Ave to go to the 'ospital."

"Like this?" Dido touched the blond bristles on his cheek.

"Be blowed to that. Your arm I'm worried about."

"See me like this? Them?" Dido gestured towards the street. "Be seen like this?"

"I'll shave yer."

A half-hour later, shaved by his brother, his jacket pulled on despite much agony, Dido walked out of the house accompanied by Chas. His clothes were brushed. He was spruce and stiffly upright.

He had ordered Shonny to stay at home. It was only now, as he walked with his jaw clenched against pain, that the meaning came to him of what he had set in motion. He was as aware as Chas that vengeance from the Murchisons was to be expected. He did not yet know what he was going to do, but he knew that he must watch every step that he and his brothers took; more, that their home and their mother must not for a moment be left unguarded.

He knew that he was being watched all the way down the street and he walked without flinching. At every step the thrust of pain at his lungs was an agony. He nodded to a few, said "Mornin'" to one or two and walked past the rest ignoring them, head up, eyes fierce.

At the hospital he learned that he had three cracked ribs, which were taped. A wound an inch deep in his triceps, caused by the edge of the buckle, was cleaned, stitched and dressed. The swelling would subside with rest and hot bathing. The doctor told him that he must stay off for a week and then come back to the hospital for further instructions.

He said, "Can't do that. Living to earn."

"If you don't look after yourself," the doctor said, "you'll be off work all the longer."

On the way back Chas said, "Don't worry. We can manage on my money."

"You won't be going in either."

"Why not? I'm not the one that's crocked."

"Murchisons."

"I wondered about them. I said, didn't I?"

"Look," Dido said. "I can't manage 'em. Not like this. Not on my own."

"It ain't much better the three of us. Shonny's only a nipper."

"We'll manage."

"How?"

Dido walked in silence for a few paces. Then he stopped and checked his brother. "Start with, you keep quiet about this."

"This?"

"This arm. All this. I'm fit, see?" The comprehension was slow to appear in his brother's eye. He muttered, almost angrily. "Don't you see? I done Ginger, didn't I? I could do any of 'em. Long as they think I'm fit. They got to think I'm fit. All of 'em. Everyone. Got to think I can fight."

"Well, you can't 'ardly move your arm. People'll see."

"You leave that to me."

When they turned into Rabbit Marsh his walk was entirely normal. No-one could tell from the swing of his arms that one of them was hurt. This time he nodded more genially to the neighbours, who were more numerous on the pavement now that the sunshine was warmer. Blakers, the tobacconist, in whose shop he bought his occasional ounce of pipe tobacco, called "Mornin', Dido."

"Mr Blakers." Dido went across to him and, an unprecedented gesture that was meant for the many eyes that watched him, picked up Blakers' youngest, a nine-year-old, and raised him up into the air. "What cheer, Holey? Glad when you go back to school?"

He did not even hear the child's "No, mister" as he put him down; any more than a monarch hears the answer to the routine remarks he makes as he passes among his subjects; or a politician the words of the voters among whom he canvasses. But Dido was not soliciting support. A solitary, threatened man, he was only bolstering the protective legend of his own invulnerability.

Blakers said, "Right turn-up for the book last night."

People were gathering round.

"Over and done with."

"I don' know," Blakers said.

Coglin, a railway vanman, said, "'E must 'a creased you a bit with that belt."

"'Ardly a mark." In spite of the dropped aspirate Dido's speech was clear and curt. It cut like a knife through the horrible distortions of English speech that came from his neighbours' lips. Mrs Peach spoke the prim English of a trained domestic servant. Her sons' utterance was more touched by the Cockney, but thanks to her they all talked intelligently and articulately; especially Dido. Nor did any of them punctuate their speech with the blurts of obscenity, as mindless as hiccups and almost as frequent, that were common to all around them, small children not excluded.

Chas said, "'E's like leather, our Dido. 'Ardly a mark on 'im. I seen 'im."

"Caught you a fair crack, that belt," Blakers said.

Dido flexed his arms, "See any difference?"

People murmured; and in the sound of their voices there was the first note of calculating flattery. "'E's a one, old Dido." "Take more than a belt to stop old Dido." "Dido, 'ide like a bloody elephant, 'e's got."

"All the same," Blakers said, "you wanna watch out. They been out this mornin', the Murchisons."

"Down 'ere?"

"Nah. Down Brick Lane. Prowlin', like."

A woman called, "You done the old man up properly. Bust his jaw in about six places."

"Stove 'is face in like a bleed'n matchbox, I 'eard," another female voice interjected with relish. "'E ain't come round yet. Smashed up all over."

"You put 'im out all right," Coglin said.

"'E won't drink 'is pint round 'ere much before Christmas."

"'E won't be missed," Chas said.

Dido said, "'E can stay out."

"'Ere," Blakers said, "I told you. You wanna watch out. Them five boys are terrors. There's still them boys."

"Five of 'em."

"Terrors, they are."

"There's 'undred fit men down this street," Dido said. "You —" He gestured at Coglin. "Work on the vans. Strong as an ox, you are. Lot more like you."

"What abaht it?"

"Keep that lot out for good."

Blakers said, "The Murchisons?"

"You wanna go on payin' 'alf a sovereign a week?"

"I don't want no trouble," Blakers said.

"No fuckin' trouble," Coglin echoed. "That's right. Never 'ad no trouble."

"Not till now," a woman said, her voice and demeanour accusing.

"Not till you done your nut." This was Meek, the publican, who had been drawn from his doorway by the voices.

"Done your nut properly," said the woman. "Never stopped to think, did you? Never a thought of others."

"Nothing to be frightened of," Dido said. "'Andle that lot."

Meek, "Who? You?"

"No-one else game?"

"You mind your business," Meek said, "I'll mind mine."

There was an assenting chorus. Dido said, "All canary, are you?"

"You be fuckin' brave," Coglin said. "You show us."

"That's right." The woman grew more aggressive at each intervention. "It's you and the Murchisons, ain' it? No one else. You be brave."

Chas said, "And you'll let 'em go on thievin' an' wipin' their boots on you."

"Don' 'urt me, it don't," Blakers answered. "Bit of peace, all I want. Don't you go making trouble for us."

"Not less you can look arter us," interjected the woman.

More cries of agreement. "Oo's gonna look arter us, eh?" This was another woman, stout, shrill and scornful, "You?" She uttered a brassy laugh.

"'Im?" This was the first woman. "I'd like to see him look arter 'imself. Agin that lot."

The faces were all grinning and hostile. Dido cast a grim, quick look around him. Then, contemptuously, "Don't you worry."

He pushed through them, once more not looking at them, and Chas followed. Behind him the laughter rose, and the derisive voices.

All the boys stayed at home that night. The shop window had stout shutters and the door was thick and massively bolted. But they did not know what kind of assault to expect, or when. Dido sat in the shop till late, puffing his short pipe. He had challenged power. He had created a situation that he had not wished for and he had been left alone, with his brothers, to face it.

They dared not go to work when the holiday was over. Dido and Chas took turns to stay in the shop and neither went far from it alone. Shonny scurried about the streets with his barrow and on his return each time would report what he had seen or heard of the Murchisons.

Dido calculated the odds against him. Ginger had two sons who, with the husbands of his two daughters and a nineteen-year-old nephew, were the core of the tribe. The five terrors. Around them were a swarm of youngsters, children, parasites and gutter-rats who on occasion had been known to march with them. In the past there had been massive raids on other streets and battles that remained legendary. But these were of the past. And they had always been internecine, feuding conflicts, clashes between hooligan clans. The truth was that for many years the East End had been by steady degrees growing more peaceable. Mazes of black decaying houses there still were, warrened courts and alleys crammed with the hungry and desperate. There was still drunkenness, unemployment, crime in plenty. But schools, drains, hospitals, churchmen and social workers despised but persistent, broad new main streets that clove through the brick jungles, public baths, housing schemes, and better policing, had all had their effect. The street battles were no more than legend; none had occurred for years. The hangers-on might prowl when their protectors made it possible to do so, but the times had tamed them. As the people of Rabbit Marsh stood aloof, fearful of the Murchisons, so the neighbours of the Murchisons would stand aloof, fearful of the remote but ever-present law. He, Chas and Shonny need only fear the five younger Murchisons.

They were being watched all the time. They were left alone because they only emerged by day, and night was the chosen time.

After a week the confinement to shop and kitchen and the presence of their mother, silent, frightened and reproachful, became intolerable to Chas. He announced that he was going to the music-hall for an hour or two. Dido said, "Better not."

Chas said, "Frightened of that lot? They're scared stiff without their old man."

Dido watched him put his jacket and cap on; then, as he opened the door, said, "I'll go with you."

They went to the Cambridge, in Spitalfields. At eleven o'clock they were coming home along Brick Lane. The cobbles were blanched by moonlight but they walked in the middle of the road and kept an eye on the doorways on both sides.

Ahead of them, only fifty yards from the corner of their street, was the railway bridge which spanned the break in the embankment. It was wide, supported by massive girders. Dim gas lamps cast a little light beneath it, but the wide gates of stables lay in deep recesses on both sides, and were dark.

Dido and Chas walked into the cavern of the bridge and their footsteps began to echo. They were alert now. They were half-way before the clatter of boots came and their enemies rushed out from the darkness. They started to run but two of the Murchisons converged ahead of them. They could see the gleam of knives in upraised hands.

Ignoring the three behind them, they hurled themselves at the two who barred their way. Chas grappled with one. Dido, a foot of gas-pipe suddenly in his hand, struck the knife from the other's hand. Shouts. Dido struck with the pipe at the head of his brother's antagonist and moved back-to-back with Chas as the others closed in. And as the bodies came in to overwhelm them, eyes and knives gleaming, a whistle shrilled, deafening among its echoes under the bridge.

The response of the Murchisons was reflex. They scattered and bolted down Brick Lane. Two policemen were at the other end, one coming at a run with truncheon drawn, the other blowing his whistle. Behind them, hands in the pockets of his overcoat, stood the plain-clothes inspector.

He signed to the policeman to stop whistling. He said, "Won't need that."

The policeman said, "All right, Mr Merry," and followed him to where the other uniformed man waited with the Peach brothers.

Merry said, "Right, Peach. I'll have you two."

Dido did not ask how he knew their names. It was taken for granted that Mr Merry knew everything.

Merry took the piping. "Offensive weapon."

Dido, still breathless, gasped, "They 'ad knives."

"Who had?" Mr Merry indicated the empty street.

Dido and Chas spent the night in a cell at Bethnal Green Police Station. Next morning they were in front of the magistrate at Old Street.

"You are charged with creating a breach of the peace," the magistrate said. "You are very lucky. You —" he was addressing Dido "— carried a length of gas piping. This might have laid you open to the much more serious charge of assault or affray."

Dido remained silent.

The magistrate said, "No doubt the police decided not to charge you with affray, since your antagonists ran off, and it is usual to charge both parties in such cases. I take into consideration the fact that you are first offenders and men of respectable background —" Inspector Merry, who watched the proceedings impassively, had given his evidence with impartiality, in the level, mechanical accents of a man who had no further concern with the outcome "— but I take a serious view of hooligan behaviour. You, Dido Peach, who possessed the weapon, will pay a fine of five pounds or go to prison for one month. You, Charles Peach, will pay twenty shillings or go to prison for a week."

Mrs Peach was in court with Shonny. She paid the fines. The two elder brothers had now been away from work for a week, and the outlay almost exhausted the family's savings.

The abortive attack, like the earlier fight, precipitated unforeseen results.

In the first place the Peach boys feared more trouble, and still dared not go to work. The last of their money dwindled and they did not know what to do next.

In the second place, the Murchisons mysteriously avoided Rabbit Marsh from now on.

Thirdly, the attitude of the Rabbit Marsh population to the situation underwent a change that increased from day to day during the next week.

All they knew was that the Peach boys, so it was said, had put to flight the Murchisons and cracked the pate of one of them, who had subsequently been glimpsed with head bandaged. Police whistles had been heard, but no importance was ascribed to this. It was merely known that the rozzers had come in time to pinch the Peach boys who had been up in court and now had the prestige of a conviction.

At first the neighbours merely waited in apprehension. Then, when the Murchisons did not appear in the street, there began to stir an idea that their exactions might have ended. Those who had accepted them now began to talk against them with increasing rancour and indignation. Those who had toadied to them now reviled them with a boldness that grew with each day of immunity. Scepticism about their acceptance of defeat turned to wonderment or anxious calculation, then to triumph. After three days it seemed weeks since the Murchisons had been driven off. After a week it seemed an age, a bygone age.

At the same speed the people came to see the Peaches in a new light. They had been begged not to make trouble. Now they were praised for it. Their actions had been feared, now they were admired. Those who had shunned them for fear of involvement began to make up to them. They were coming to be regarded as deliverers; particularly by the tradesmen who found themselves better off at the end of the week by the money and goods which in previous times would have been taken by the Murchisons.

Chas was the first to benefit from the new era. He was walking past Blakers' shop when the proprietor hailed him, "What cheer, Chas."

"What cheer."

"Not working yet?"

"Not yet."

"Making sure you've seen *them* off, eh?"

"Them?"

"Them bastard Murchisons."

"Oh. Yes. Them."

"Reckon you've seen 'em off by the looks of it."

"Looks like it."

"Won't show their noses round here, eh?"

"Better not."

"You're right they better not. Not while you boys are on the lookout."

"We're on the lookout, never you fear."

"It's a blessing all right. Shot of that lot at last. Thanks to you boys. 'Ere, Chas, you ain't been in for your fags lately."

"'Aven't I?" Chas already had to watch his pocket-money.

"Don't you fancy a Wood no more?"

"Fancy one when I fancy one."

"'Ere, Chas. Come in. Come on in." Chas hesitated, then followed Blakers into the shop. Blakers handed him a packet of twenty Woodbines. "Reckon you got to give a present now and agin to an old customer."

"What for?"

"You're a good feller, Chas. Eh? You put 'em in your pocket. 'Ave a smoke on me. Know my friends, I do."

Chas looked at him for a moment, then dropped the cigarettes into his pocket. "Ta."

As he went out, Blakers said, "Any time you're passin', Chas. You don't 'ave to go short of a fag. You look arter me, I'll look arter you."

It was cheaper than propitiating the Murchisons.

Puzzlement at this experience in Chas's mind turned, after digestion, into pleasure, then to pride, in his strength, in his exploits, in the status of himself and his brothers. Blakers' offering seemed only right and proper. Chas believed, as the neighbours believed, that he had shared in a victory. He, too, eighteen years old and easily influenced by a surrounding atmosphere, saw himself as a deliverer and entitled to a deliverer's dues.

So day by day he collected more tributes; until the next rent-day when Mrs Peach looked in the jar where she kept her money and said, "Whatever shall I tell the landlord?"

Dido looked up from a plate heaped with bacon and fried bread. "Tell 'im to wait."

Chas threw a half-sovereign on the table and said, "Pay 'im." Dido said, "You never 'ung on to that for two weeks."

"Oo said I did?"

"Where you get it?"

"Never you mind."

"I said where you get it?"

Chas said, "Arkell."

Arkell kept the goldfish shop.

"You been workin' for 'im?"

"No."

"What for, then?"

"Present."

"What 'e give you a present for?"

"What you think?"

"I'm askin' *you*"

"'E's got the Murchisons off 'is back, 'asn' 'e?"

"Give you money for that, did 'e?"

"Only right, ain' it?"

"Anyone else?"

"Where'd you think that bacon come from you're scoffin' away?"

Dido finished his bacon and tea, and went out in silence. He walked down the street and went into Arkell's shop. Arkell was a bent man of sixty with a long, wrinkled face and scanty white hair. Dido said, "Mornin'."

"Mornin', Dido."

"You give my Chas 'alf a sovereign?"

"Yes. No 'arm, was it?"

Dido's eyes on him were thoughtful, but with a hard glint in them. Arkell said, "Enough, wasn' it?"

"You don't reckon we're after charity?"

"Oo said charity?"

"You give my Chas 'alf a sovereign."

"'E's off work, isn' 'e? You as well. You reckon the Murchisons'll come back if you two go back to work?"

"Might do."

"They might do. That's what I mean."

"Mean what?"

"Can't take chances, can yer?"

"They come back, we'll knock off work agen."

"Talk sense, Dido. No offence. I mean. No use you goin' after 'em once they done something to your shop or your Shonny. Or your ma."

"They better not."

"That's what I'm tellin' you. It's too late to bash 'em once they done the 'arm."

"I don't need tellin' that. It's why I'm still off work."

"Well, then."

"Well, then what?"

"We need lookin' after as well. The 'ole lot of us. You got 'em off us. It's up to you to see they don't come back. You can't go back to work yet a while."

"Not for a bit."

"Well, then, you got to live. I don't mind 'elpin' out. A lot of us don't. What's a neighbour for? You look arter us. One good turn deserves another."

Dido stood for some seconds looking at the other man. These seconds were a turning point in Dido's life. At last he said, "Fair enough. Fair enough," and, as he went out, "Mornin'."

Dido was a proud and intense man. In those few seconds his pride had been on the point of flaring up into rage, against the offerers of humiliating gifts, against his brother who had been petty enough to accept them. But at the white-heat of his pride (hidden behind that impassive face) there had struck into it a perception of the gifts as tribute. In a flash, like a chemical reaction, the whole make-up of his mind had changed. The taste of homage, the recognition that others are dependent and servile, the glimpse of power, these things do not offend pride but inflame it.

"Fair enough." A different Dido strode away down the street.

Neither the Peaches nor their neighbours knew why they lived in peace.

After the arrest of the Peach boys Mr Merry paid a visit to Jaggs Place. Mr Merry was a man with his own — not schemes, for he was nothing so petty as a schemer — his own vision of the working-out of things. Life must be ordered in such and such a way. People were devious and nasty little creatures who could not be trusted and who must therefore be manipulated both in their own interests and the interests of an overall maintenance of all things in their ordained orbits that Mr Merry called law and order. To this he was dedicated. Without giving the matter a thought he had a placid confidence in his own right and ability to order the game of peoples' lives. Considerations of his own future came into it, for he was newly appointed; and moreover was a supernumary, since the detective force in the Division already had its establishment of one inspector; but these were so tacit, so undisturbed beneath the surface of his mind, and so justified by what he accepted as his own proper place in the scheme, that he would have been startled and contemptuous of anyone who confronted him with the accusation of impure motives.

Mr Merry did not play chess; nevertheless he had a chess-master's grasp on life, quite naturally seeing several moves ahead, patiently sure of the larger results that would flow in the future from present acts apparently insignificant.

From the moment that Ginger Murchison had been brought down, the Murchisons, while watching for their enemies, were themselves watched by Mr Merry. He did not interfere when they laid their ambush, and he did not use it as a chance to take them in, for it suited him to wait for greater things. He arrested the Peach boys because it accorded with his plans but he saw to it that the charges were not serious. He wanted them to be marked by the law, but it suited him that they should remain at liberty.

However, it did not suit his plans for the feud to be quickly consummated. An hour after the abortive ambush he returned to Brick Lane, pounced on the skulking Cockeye and sent him with a message to the oldest of the Murchison brothers, Harry.

Harry was tall and skeletal, with a skin pale as the underside of a toadstool and sunken, melancholy eyes. Not only was he Crown Prince by age, but by the reputation of having done a "real stretch", which none of the others had. He was thirty, and had served five years penal servitude for house-breaking, an activity which he had tried as a matter of youthful independence when he was twenty-three, and which he had forsworn when his father represented to him how much safer it was to share in the family trade of extortion, with which the police, content to see no evil and hear no evil for the time it took them to pace unhurriedly out of sight in each slum street, did not interfere.

He found Mr Merry sitting at the back table of an almost empty coffee shop, a mug of strong tea in front of him. "Sit down, Harry."

Harry sat down. "What can I do for yer, Mr Merry?"

"Had a quiet evening?"

"Been at 'ome with the missus."

"Have you now? Quite a home-lover."

"She can swear to it, Mr Merry."

"Mm. So can a dozen others, I dare say."

"All them that seen me."

"I dare say. Very anxious to prove you had a quiet evening, Harry. Why?"

"Dunno why you sent for me. Told you where I was. That's all."

"Quite." Mr Merry leaned across the table. "Harry —" His voice dropped, becoming positively friendly. "I think it's time you and I came to a little understanding."

"Understanding?"

"That's it."

The two men looked at each other. Harry felt himself on

familiar ground. The conversation had taken a turn in accord with local custom. Remote the police might appear, majestic when in uniform; there was one widespread mode of contact. He chuckled. "I got you, Mr Merry."

"Have you, Harry? I'm glad."

"I play ball with you, eh, you play ball with me."

"You were seen this evening, you know. By myself and two constables. Where's your knife, Harry?"

"What knife?"

"The chiv. Hidden it? Wouldn't do you any good against me and two constables in the witness box. Not with your record."

"Ah, go on, Mr Merry —" Harry was grinning. "You know what a short memory you got."

"Have I now?"

Harry took a hand out of his pocket and laid it on the table.

"'Aven't you?" He shifted his hand slightly.

"It's the best way, Harry, isn't it? Best way to deal with the law."

"Ah!" Harry chuckled. "Never 'ad no trouble. Always understood each other, us and the coppers."

Mr Merry's right hand shot out and clamped Harry's down on the table. He turned his head and called, "Weldon."

A tall man in a sailor's reefer jacket was reading a newspaper at the other end of the shop. He put it down and came to them. Harry glared at Merry, then at the man. "Weldon," Mr Merry said, "what do you see?"

Weldon said, "Banknotes, inspector. Two five-pound notes."

"You git," Harry said. "You rotten lousy bleedin' swindlin' git."

The mildness of his voice unchanged, Mr Merry said, "Can you identify this man, constable?"

"Yes, sir. Harry Murchison, 5, Jaggs Place."

"Thank you, constable." Mr Merry was still grasping Harry's hand. "You can go now, constable."

"Right, sir." Weldon went out, his police issue boots clumping on the plank floor.

Mr Merry released Harry's hand. "Now, Harry, just put it away."

Harry, glowering and bewildered, shoved the notes into his pocket.

"You know what you could get for that, Harry," said Mr Merry. "Attempting to bribe an officer of the law."

Harry muttered, "What's all this?"

"A little understanding," said Mr Merry. "No witnesses now. Just a little understanding between us two."

Harry was silent. He was rubbing his hand, which still ached from the terrible grip. Mr Merry said, "From now on, Harry, you'll play ball with me. Just that. Never mind who I play ball with."

Harry said, "I don't git you."

"You don't have to. Just do as you're told. Now listen to me. This is for you and your brothers, your cousin, your nephews, your women and brats, your thieving pals, the whole lot of you. Keep out of Rabbit Marsh."

"Rabbit Marsh?"

"Don't come the innocent. Rabbit Marsh. Keep out of Rabbit Marsh and leave the Peach boys alone."

Harry was sullen and silent.

"The word was, leave them alone. I think you know me now, Harry."

No answer.

"I said, I think you know me. Do you? Answer me now."

The plump, suburban man in trilby hat and light smart overcoat sat across the table and looked at Harry. His eyes were calm, his voice mild, neat and suburban. Harry was utterly daunted by him. "Yes, Mr Merry."

"Don't think you can catch them somewhere else. Or set someone else on to do it. Or sneak down there by night. Or get a hundred and fifty people to swear an alibi. Because I'll have you for it."

"What 'appens if someone else —?"

"If someone else does them, it'll be your misfortune. Because I shan't ask questions. I shall stick it on you. Look at me. Look at me I say. I swear on the Book I'll stick it on you."

"What's the idea —?"

"Never mind the questions. I'm telling you, that's all. I want no more trouble down Rabbit Marsh. That's the form. From me. And you'll do as you're told."

Harry scowled at him. "They squared you first, did they?"

"One more word and I'll fix you, Harry Murchison. One more word, one bit of trouble from you and I'll have you breaking stones on the Moor till your kids have forgotten what you look like. I can do it, you know."

"Can yer?"

Mr Merry reached out and dropped a hand, gently this time, on Harry's sleeve. His voice became soft again, but menacing. "Look at me, Harry. I can do it. I can do anything I like to you. Not God in his heaven can save you from me, because I'm down here and He isn't."

After a moment, "All right."

"You've got the word. Keep out of Rabbit Marsh. Leave those boys alone."

"You can go now, Harry."

As Harry stood up, Mr Merry spoke again. "There's other places you can make a living. I won't tread on your heels. I'm an easy man with those that understand me. Just you do as I said."

Harry grinned. Once more the language of his familiar world was being spoken. He was used to the police letting well alone, and now he thought he saw what this policeman was after. He would be left alone as long as he preyed outside this copper's parish. He said, "I understand yer, guv'nor. No trouble. Not on your beat. I promise yer."

Mr Merry watched him go; then left his cold cup of tea and went his own way.

The Peach Boys were now accustomed to be spoken of as "holy terrors", a title of honour in their world, and their gratification swelled.

That it should go to the heads of Chas and Shonny was inevitable. To understand why Dido, the proud and taciturn man of more mature years should also be seduced by this shabby glory, one must understand how vulnerable a self-determined solitary is to the offer of friendship and flattery; one must ponder upon his celibacy at the age of thirty, in a milieu where most coupled young.

The very intensity of his character made him exult in his new status with an intensity undreamed of by his easy-going young brothers; though he affected to ignore it and maintained his old, stern demeanour.

The Peach brothers were like workers of primitive "magic" who are astonished at what they seem to have achieved but believe in it because the evidence of their own eyes is not to be denied. The tribe believes in it too, and offers them gifts and leadership. So chieftains and kings once came into being, in return for their protective powers. Dido, Chas and even young Shonny found it daily more natural to accept gifts. Daily their air of authority grew, and the confidence with which they gave the assurance that there would be no more trouble as long as they were about.

Even though their enemies had been driven off, a return to work was not to be thought of as long as menace lurked in the darkness without.

Chapter 4

In the same stable yard where the Peaches left their barrow, Tommy Long kept his pony and cart. He lived in a room over the entry with his wife and four children. He was less than five feet high, thin as an urchin, with a face like a grey chip above his dirty choker and ragged jacket.

The pony, a sturdy, barrel-chested little beast, was the pride of his life. He had bought it, together with the cart, with compensation money he had received after an accident which had ended his career as a docker. Thus equipped he had gone into business as an itinerant merchant in old rags and lumber. A bizarre assortment of his purchases was stacked in an empty stall in the stable.

On a fine morning in July he was grooming his pony; and Dido was helping him.

"Yer can't git away from it," he said. "I wouldn' 'a got my compensation else."

Dido, busy with the curry-comb, seemed preoccupied with the pony's glossy coat.

"I couldn't prove nuffin," Tommy said. "Not on me own. Gaffer swore it was my fault. It was the union. The union, mate. I wouldn' 'a got a penny compensation wivaht the union."

Dido stood back to admire his own handiwork as if he had not even heard Tommy.

"Yer can't git away from it," Tommy said. "What's the workin' man wivaht 'is union?"

Without looking at him, Dido said, in a voice of disgust, "Workin' man!"

"The workin' man, mate. What's you an' me but bloody workin' men?"

Dido used his foot to push a bucket noisily under a tap.

He turned on the tap and water rushed. "You speak for yourself."

"Why? Wha' d'ye call your bleetn' self? Work on the wharf, don't yer?"

"I did."

"Be goin' back there, won't yer?"

"Depends."

"It's got to end one way or another, 'asn' it? You an' the Murchisons? Can't go on for ever."

"Depends on them."

"They don't seem in no 'urry. You got it cushy, you 'ave."

"Think so?"

"Must be 'alf a dozen shopkeepers payin' their dropsy to you 'stead o' the Murchisons. If that ain't cushy I don' know what is."

"Like to change places?" Dido set the bucket down in front of the pony, who drank contentedly.

"Well," Tommy said. "I ain't talkin' abaht that. You asked for it."

"That's right. An' I got it."

Tommy took time to consider while he filled the pony's nosebag. "All the sime," he said at last. "You'll be goin' back to work one o' these dies."

"Makes no odds to me."

"Then you're a workin' man," Tommy said triumphantly.

"Tell you what I am."

"What?"

"Dido Peach. An' I'll tell you what your workin' man is."

"What?"

"Same as every other man. Dirt."

"Much obliged, mate."

"Dirt. Anyone can tread on 'em. They want to be trod on. They stood round that night and yelled for Ginger to pulverise me."

"I give you a yell," Tommy said. "I 'eard you."

"Couldn't do no more," Tommy said. "If I stood alongside Little Tich, 'e'd look like Jack Johnson."

"If Ginger 'ad done for me that night you'd 'ave 'ad all your bones broken. Just for opening your mouth."

"Too true I would, mate."

"An' you still will if the Murchisons come back."

"Gawd," Tommy said, "don't talk abaht that!"

"Right," Dido said. "Then don't you talk about me goin' back to the wharf."

Without another glance at Tommy, but with a friendly pat on the rump for the pony, he walked out of the yard.

It is hard to convey the effect of freedom on those who hitherto have risen daily in the dark, tramped for miles to do heavy work and tramped home too weary for anything but sleep. This had been Dido's life for eighteen years and Chas's for four. For six days in every week they had risen at five-thirty, lit the fire in the kitchen, washed in the yard or gone out into rain or snow to bring water indoors. They had trudged each day to and from their distant places of work in all weathers.

Once a week, on Sunday mornings, they enjoyed the bliss of a "lay-in". Sunday was not a day of rest in Rabbit Marsh. From eight in the morning the stalls went up, and by nine o'clock the weekly market had filled the street with a mass of people. The Peaches kept no stall and Sunday morning was all the sweeter for the hubbub that rose from the street while they lounged half-dressed about the house. They had a big fried breakfast, then brought out the entire family stock of footwear to be polished to perfection, a ritual established since childhood. Dido boiled up water and all of them enjoyed the profound, unhurried pleasure of a hot-water wash-down. Dido shaved carefully in front of the mantelpiece mirror, Chas flattered himself with a scrape of his smooth cheeks, and all the three sons put on their best suits. The two older sons pushed through the crowds to the pub for the one pint permitted by Dido, listening to the din of talk but rarely joining in; while they waited for their mother to come home from chapel. The hours of Sunday were glittering gold coins to be grandly spent.

Now all their days were their own. Prisoners of their situation, they could not go to work, but "could not" meant "need not". Dido's response to the situation was a pointer to the man's nature. Chas left to himself would have given himself up to the enjoyment of unlimited holiday. He soon learned that if he lay in bed too long Dido came up and whipped the blankets off. If at nine o'clock he was still unkempt, a curt word from his brother sent him about his business with soap, comb and razor. Dido performed his own daily toilet meticulously and before leaving the house inspected himself in the mirror as minutely as a Guardsman about to walk out of barracks.

Dido showed the same military concern for the proper occupation of their time. Shonny continued working for his mother. Chas was set to work in the yard. Before he could go out each day he had to heat up the boiler, carry out the bundles of dirty rags his mother had bought the previous day and boil them thoroughly, poking them during the process with a long paddle. Afterwards he ran them through a big mangle.

Dido even tried to make him take over the weekly scrubbing of the stairs but Mrs Peach suddenly showed a flare-up of spirit and refused to permit it. She was so used to toiling for her menfolk that it had somehow become transmuted from a degradation to an honoured part of her woman's status. To put the scrubbing on to Chas would demean both her boy and her. She was also so bewildered at the rapid turn of events that, although she could neither comment nor intervene, she had an unexpressed fear that the gift of leisure would demoralise her altogether. On her knees, scrubbing, she could scrub the thoughts and fears out of herself.

But it was also of Dido's nature that he did nothing in the house himself. He did not enjoy idleness. On the contrary, such energies gnawed both in his mind and his muscles that he always had to be occupied, if possible strenuously. Pride, however, inextricable from these energies and perhaps their source, burned always through him; and it was natural to him that he should be head of the family. He must look after his mother but must perform no menial act within her home. He must regulate the lives of his brothers but always remain above their level. It was his due to sit upright at table while his mother in humble attitude set his food before him; always, of course, the first to be served.

He made a routine for himself. He walked out at nine in the morning and looked in from door to door. Life in Rabbit Marsh was lived on three levels. Like a little kingdom, it had its social classes. The traders and artisans were its upper crust. Some prospered, some lived on such a knife-edge of poverty that they would have done better to go out to work. Status was the supreme possession of all this class. To them all the others came to buy the necessities of life, to plead for credit in hard times; they sometimes had work to give; and, being credited as business people, they were dispensers of advice to neighbours who were so terrified of all authority that even a typewritten letter was taken as a ukase that one dare not defy. Below the trading class were the regular labourers; and below these were the drifters — the pathetic sellers of matches and bootlaces, the hopeless seekers after odd jobs, the parasites upon charity organisations, the unemployed and other flotsam, who lived in the attics or in the Bug Hole. These were the ugly dregs of the street, the children pasty and barefoot, the men imprinted with the cunning that is required for survival in the gutter struggle, the women ageing quickly into shrivelled hags or mountainous termagants. They fought and drank and many of them had the scaly, bloated red faces of meth drinkers. Yet in spite of their misery they were not criminal. Crime seemed to confine itself to a number of well-known thieves' kitchens like Jaggs Place. The people of Rabbit Marsh counted themselves as law-abiding.

From all these three groups Dido now received greetings which were overtly those of friendly equals, but which were as respectful in tone as those of feudal vassals. For most he had only a brief nod. But among the handful of traders whose paid protector he had become, he had a regular morning round.

He went from the stable yard into a cabinet-maker's workshop. With the shutters always up, it was a den of gloom, lit by a shaft of sunshine from the open door and by the fire of chips and sawdust which burned even in the hottest weather. He sat on a bench, enjoying the smell of bubbling glue, the tang of resin and the strong-scented sawdust that impregnated the air. He sat, legs swinging, listening to the talk of the cabinet-makers, only throwing a brief phrase in now and again. When tea was brewed by an urchin just out of school who spent the rest of his time sweeping the floor or sandpapering, Dido accepted a mug. After a while one of the men went out on an errand. Dido took off his jacket, went across to the bench and started to drive the man's plane efficiently, concentratedly and with untiring strength. Dido was one of those men who had the gift of doing any job as if they had been trained to it alone.

When he left, he looked in to see Arkell. He contented himself with a "Mornin'," and listened to Arkell's conversation while he looked past him at the shelves on which stood rows of tanks in which tiny, painted fish glided through green water, and bowls through whose bulging glass hundreds of goldfish stared with magnified eyes.

His next call was on the Jew cobbler, Barsky. The few Jews in Rabbit Marsh lived their own life and were left alone by their neighbours, whose dislike of the alien was often expressed violently in conversation but never seemed to direct itself against individuals. Dido felt so much apart himself and was so strongly possessed by bitterness against the weakness and meanness of mankind in general, that he felt no special urge to hostility against one section of it.

In any case, Barsky was a man he felt inexplicably at ease with. The Jew was in his early forties, a broad, muscular man of middle height, with black hair bordering the bald crown of his head, a nose like the end of a small potato stuck over a thick black military moustache in the middle of a round, humorous face and keen eyes that scrutinised from under thick black brows. He had been a Russian soldier for several years, and from the occasional brief anecdotes he had given of his experiences, Dido reckoned that the man had been through a harder school even than his own. Certainly Barsky was as tough and taciturn as Dido.

The shop was crowded with great sheets of hide whose strong smell, and the rust-smell from heaps of iron lasts, filled it. A bell like the bell at Number 34 chinked as Dido came in and slipped into the small space between the hides and the bartered counter. Dido said his "Mornin'".

Barsky sat on a small round stool in the far corner, wearing an apron, holding with his left hand a piece of leather jammed against his chest while his right hand cut out a sole with a curved cobbler's knife. He only grunted, and did not look up until he had finished.

"Weather keepin' nice." It was only with this man who outdid him in reserve, that Dido could be compelled to take the lead in talking.

The Jew gave a double-grunt of assent, not unfriendly, and turned the sheet of leather to cut out another sole.

"Boys all right?" This was Dido again.

"They work." Barsky had two sons, aged fifteen and seventeen. Both were apprenticed to a cabinet-maker. His English was guttural but more strong and intelligible than the English the native Cockneys spoke.

Dido said, "Give us."

He reached out. Barsky gave him a piece of leather, a curved knife and a paper pattern. Dido set the leather against his chest and started to cut out a pair of soles around the pattern. Dido said, "Busy?"

"So long I make a crust I don't grumble." Barsky looked up. "And you?"

"Me?"

"You busy?"

Sly humour glinted in Barsky's eyes. Dido felt no rancour.

"You're keepin' me busy," he said.

"I'll keep you busy. Plenty more soles."

They worked in silence for a while. Then Barsky pushed the door to the kitchen ajar and called out in his own language. His wife opened the door wide and answered in Yiddish before she nodded to Dido and said, "Good *morgen*."

She was bony, with worried eyes and hollow white cheeks. She had a weak, querulous voice. "Is the mama all right?"

"Keepin' well, thank you. You all right?"

"Gott sei dank."

Dido stood up. He said, "Be goin' now. Mornin'. Mornin', lady."

Barsky's wife said, "Wait."

She went out of sight into the kitchen and came back. She held out to him a small bowl in which were four eggs. She said, jerking with her head towards the back yard, "From the hens."

The Barskys were the only shop-people in the street who had never yet offered him anything. He said, "Ah, don't matter."

"For the mother," she said.

"Ah," he said. "Ta."

As the opening door chinked the bell, Barsky said, "Mister Peach —"

Dido turned. Barsky, smiling at him, said, "Don't overwork."

Cockeye knew that his granddad was in hospital but this did not suggest to him that his way of life was to be changed any more than the man in the street realises that the withdrawal of garrisons from far-off places is going to change his life.

He was not a pretty boy. Apart from the wild cast in his right eye he had a large ringworm scar that had never grown over on the back of his head, the rest of which sprouted clutches of dirty straw hair.

His name was Sammy Keogh. He was fifteen. His whole family of seven lived in one room in a corner of Jaggs Place. He had not worked since he had left school a year ago. It paid him better to prowl the streets as a snapper-up of neglected trifles from unwatched stalls and shopfronts. He was patient and watchful and never took unnecessary risks. He was swift to pounce and to run. So far he had never been caught. He followed his career of theft in a spirit of complete innocence and boyish pride of achievement. He measured himself against the great men of his clan. His only strong feeling was of loyalty to the name of Murchison. To grow so as to emulate the skill and ferocity of such men as his uncle Harry who had been a housebreaker was his only ambition. To be a Murchison was to be feared, to possess ruling privileges. He had found this out as a small child at school and to him it was still the natural order of things.

He was a self-sufficient little animal. No one ever cooked a meal for him. He lived on chips, saveloys and meat pies and in consequence his pinched dirty face was covered with boils and blotches. He smoked and when he could find his mother's gin he swigged it, to show his grown-up status, but his only real pleasures were in the smelly paradise of the fish-and-chip saloon, in spending his gains on such other luxuries of the belly as sausages and onions, roast chestnuts or hot potatoes bought at the street corners; at travelling fairs, picture palaces or card schools with other gamblers as small as himself.

Towards his own household his emotions were lethargic. Mother was a peevish creature best described by his father's favourite term — "fat cow" — who had been ill since the last baby was born and lived in a heap of blankets on the mattress in the corner of the room. She peered at him wearily through a fall of ropy hair and when she was not complaining she was drunk.

Towards his father he felt only a dull wariness. His father was a hulking ex-boxer who had only married mother because she was Ginger Murchison's daughter. Cockeye knew this because mother was always flinging it in father's face. He knew that his father had been a rotten boxer who had preferred the easy life of a bully to being battered several times a week; for this, too, was often stated forcibly to his father by Uncle Harry, who regarded him as an intruder. He knew that his father resented Uncle Harry being the boss, now that granddad was away, and thought that with his size and being handy with his fists he ought to be cock of the walk.

He set out this morning dressed in a ragged jacket down to his knees, a ripped and filthy pair of man's trousers cut crudely to size, and a pair of boots too large for him. He was as filthy as usual. He looked out for prey as innocently and naturally as a terrier trotting after rabbits in a wood.

His victim this morning was a small boy, neatly dressed, the son of a warehouseman. The boy was on his way to school with a packet of sandwiches and a halfpenny when Cockeye caught him in a side street. Cockeye took the sandwiches and money. Then, kneeling on the ten-year-old, he banged his head on the granite kerb until the child, with nose bleeding, was dazed and almost senseless. After that Cockeye, who was inarticulately enraged by the sight of decent clothes, rolled the child into a pile of garbage in the kerb and trod him and his neat suit into it.

He ate the sandwiches and bought a cup of coffee with the halfpenny. Breakfast over, he turned into Rabbit Marsh. He went into Blakers' shop.

He said to Blakers, "Gi's five Woods."

In his family's territory he neither snatched nor ran but swaggered in the knowledge of their power.

Blakers was a large man on the portly side, with brilliantined hair parted in the middle. He was usually to be seen in a full suit of striped blue serge with celluloid collar and knitted tie but just now he was standing on a stool to load cardboard boxes on to an upper shelf, his braces over a woollen undervest and an apron protecting his trousers. He went on with his work.

"'Ere," called Cockeye. "I said five Woods. You can make it ten now. And sharp about it."

Blakers said, "Clear off, you."

Cockeye, triumphantly. "I'll tell my ol' man."

Blakers looked at him. "What was it you arst for?"

"That's better."

"What was it you was askin' for?"

"Ten Woods. And you can give us a glass o' lemonade while you're over there."

Blakers wheezed down from the stool. He went to the end of the counter, reached beneath it with one hand, straightened up and, sighing again, lifted the flap of the counter. With his free hand he picked up a packet of Woodbines. "This what you want?"

"You 'eard."

"Come 'ere, then."

Cockeye stepped across to him. The hand clamped on Cockeye's shoulder. Cockeye started to yell as he was flung to the ground. Blakers brought out the concealed hand, in which was a plaited dogwhip. He began to lash at Cockeye, grunting at each stroke, using his boot to jam Cockeye down every time the boy tried to escape.

Cockeye's screams brought people to the doorway. More and more pushed in to watch, talking and laughing. Cockeye screamed threats. Blakers whipped steadily. He gasped, "I'm givin' you what you arst for. 'E been askin' for it a long time."

"You wait, you wait," Cockeye screamed. "I'll tell my ol' man."

"Yes?" Blakers gasped with the effort to speak and whip at the same time. "I'll tell you what to tell your old man. Tell 'im compliments of Dido Peach. Get that?"

Cockeye howled, as much with bewilderment as pain. Blakers panted, "Any time your old man wants a cracked noggin like your granddad, tell 'im come round 'ere. Plenty o' nice beds in the 'ospital. Dido Peach'll give 'im a ticket any time 'e asks."

He tossed the whip aside, grabbed Cockeye by the collar and the seat of his pants and threw him out. Cockeye scrambled to his feet. The neighbours crowded in, jostling each other for the chance to land a ritual blow on him. He wriggled and ducked out of their midst and bolted, pursued by their hoots.

When he trotted through the archway into Jaggs Place, his mind still baffled by the astounding upset of his universe, his back stinging with pain from shoulders to buttocks, he saw Harry Murchison in the doorway of his home. His father glared out over Uncle Harry's shoulder.

"I'm tellin' yer," Harry was saying quietly.

Cockeye approached as his father shouted back. "Nobody tells me."

Harry did not raise his voice. "I'm tellin' yer. Keep away from there. I won't tell you agen."

He walked away and went into his own door. Cockeye ducked indoors past his father. Indignantly, sure that he would be avenged, he began to tell his tale. He had not uttered a dozen words before a clenched fist swung, a dreadful blow caught the side of his head and hurled him across the room where he lay in a final extremity of astonishment. Half-stunned, he heard through the ringing in his head his father's shout, "You little bleeder! You keep out o' Rabbit Marsh!"

Everybody felt triumphant outside Blakers' shop. A month had gone by without action from the Murchisons. The punishment of Cockeye was a turning-point. When cautious old Blakers could cast off fear, everyone could.

In time they dispersed. One woman remained. Her name was Mrs Hackett. She was a scrubwoman, a faded little old woman with waxy skin who looked as if she had scrubbed most of herself away. "Well," Blakers said. "What is it this time?"

She crept into the shop and said, "If you could oblige, sir."

"Oblige." He sighed. "I'm not made of money, you know."

"I know, sir. Only seeing as 'ow I'm working."

"Working, are you?" She lived in the Bug Hole. Her husband, a labourer at the brewery in Brick Lane, had been off work since the spring, when a barrel had fallen and broken his foot. "Then you can start payin' off the last lot."

"I will, sir. As God is my witness, sir. Only I got nothing to go on with. I couldn' 'elp my bronchitis."

"It wasn't my fault, was it? I'm not made of money."

"No, sir. Only it's the bronchitis. 'Alf a sovereign 'd see me right, sir."

Blakers lent out small sums of money at exorbitant interest. "You already owe me two bob a week."

"I shall work 'ard, sir. I promise you, sir. Please." He sighed. "I could be living like a snob somewhere decent if I wasn't soft-'earted."

He took ten shillings from the drawer in the counter and gave it to her. "All right. Four bob a week. Friday nights."

"I won't fail you, sir."

"You'd better not. Just because Mr Murchison's gone."

"I'm sorry 'e was 'urt, sir."

"'E 'ad a short way with dishonest people, didn't 'e?"

"I'm not dishonest, sir."

"Well, there's someone nearer 'ome to keep an eye on things now. Mr Peach."

"Yes, sir." Even the poorest people in the street had felt the authority of Ginger Murchison, for he had rendered some return for Blakers' tribute, as his threatener. Mrs Hackett had already taken it for granted that Dido had assumed this responsibility together with his others.

"Thank you, sir and God bless you. I shan't trouble Mr Peach, sir. I promise you."

As usual in the afternoon, Dido sat in the teashop for an hour. He had noticed the place in Great Eastern Street, a main thoroughfare leading towards the City. Only fifty yards outside Bethnal Green in location, it was a hundred miles away in status, for it was one of a national chain catering for office workers and it was large, clean, and staffed by young ladies in waitresses' uniforms. Dido went there because he had a secret yearning for superior things; and because it was not a place where any other Rabbit Marsher would venture.

Passing the day was a problem. He could not bear to stay indoors. He would not loaf in the street. To spend too much time on his visits would appear over-sociable. He was without vainglory but unconsciously he was already dominated by the sense of his position. He dared not be seen slack and aimless in Rabbit Marsh. He did not wish to trudge all day about the East End or to sit with the old tramps in the public reading-rooms. He shunned the pubs and billiards halls. He had formed the habit of coming to this out-of-the-way teashop. For a penny cup of tea he could sit as long as he wanted to, stiff, silent but at least off his feet and in the warm.

He always sat at one of the tables in the row by the back staircase, and he was always served by the same waitress, a thin girl, prim and genteel, who walked with a light step.

It was because this girl served this group of tables that he always went to one of them. He had not yet acknowledged it but it was because of her that he now came to the teashop every afternoon. Apart from placing his order and saying, "Thank you," he had never spoken to her. He did not try to this afternoon.

Chapter 5

"Please, daddy, can I leave the table?"
"*May* I leave the table."
"May I leave the table. Please, daddy, may I leave the table?"

"No, you can't, Robert. Don't you like roly-poly pudding?"

"Yes, daddy."

"Mummy's going to serve it in a minute, aren't you, love?"

"Yes, dear. Lovely roly-poly pudding. And you can pour your own treacle on, Robert."

"But daddy said I couldn't have any roly-poly pudding."

"Not till you've eaten your greens."

"But I don't want my greens. So please may I leave the table?"

Mr Merry said, "Not till you've eaten your greens, old lad."

Robert, seven years old, subjected his father to a final momentary gaze, decided that the verdict was unshakeable and with no sign of ill-will started to shovel up his vegetables.

Jane, aged nine, said, "I've eaten my greens."

"I should think so too," Mrs Merry said, "big girl like you."

Mrs Merry matched her plump, smooth husband like the second of a pair of china ornaments. She was thirty, four years younger than him, a short, bustling little person with round, rosy cheeks, a mop of curly chestnut hair, a bosom that swelled her neat blouse and a general fleshy thickness of form that gave an impression of ceaseless energy. They lived off the Kingsland Road, not far from her husband's work, in De Beauvoir Town, an enclave of broad roads and classical villas in the midst of a poorer London, inhabited by well-paid artisans, small businessmen and minor members of the professional classes.

William Merry had married ten years ago. He was a young man for his rank; but he was keen and he had joined the Force at the minimum age of twenty-one. He had done so with the express ambition of becoming a detective; from an early age it had been in his mind as the natural thing to do. Seven years ago, when he had become a sergeant, he had been lucky enough to get this house on a long lease at a low rent. Its superior status suited him; he was a man with strong notions of getting on.

He had in his own phrase "made something" of the house. When he was not taking the family out he was forever painting, plastering, papering and repairing. The sight of the bright, white villa rejoiced him when he walked home down the street. He saw it as his own creation.

The maid came in with the pudding. Mrs Merry served out, and left a good portion on the tray. "Here's a nice bit for you, Sally," she said.

Sally's "Thank you, ma'am," was heartfelt as she went downstairs. Sally was fond of boasting to the tradesmen that she was treated almost as one of the family and had the best master and mistress in the world.

Mr Merry watched with pleasure while the children had second helpings and had some more himself, for he loved roly-poly pudding. He had his rules, which he enforced firmly but without harshness, the genial reminder of his authority being enough. But he did not insist on niminy-piminy table manners. He liked a good scoff himself and children were children. He let them play and gallop about the house more than most parents did, and sometimes joined in the horseplay that Robert loved.

Robert said, "Please may I leave the table now, daddy?"

Jane said, "Please may I leave the table?"

Mrs Merry said, "Run along, children."

The children got down from their chairs and chorused "Thank you, mummy. Thank you, daddy."

Mr Merry said, "Cut along. And work hard at school."

Mrs Merry said, "Get ready quietly, children. Daddy's on duty this afternoon. Let him have a pipe in peace."

Robert lingered at the door. He said, "Daddy, are the people near your police station very naughty when you're not there?"

Mr Merry puffed till he saw the glow in his pipe, then said, "No, son. Because there's other policemen there."

Robert said, "They must be a very bad lot. The people in this road don't do bad things."

"They are, son. Just that. They're a bad lot. Dirt, I call them."

"And you have to stop them from doing wrong."

"Well, son," Merry let smoke jet from between his pursed lips, and pondered. "It's like this. I don't think you can ever stop people from doing wrong."

"What about us?" Robert asked.

"I don't mean people like us. I mean —" He made a gesture with the pipe "— people. It's the way they're made, son. But those that do give trouble, it's my job to catch them and put them away."

Robert said, "You mean lock them up?"

"That's right, son."

"How long for?"

"As long as possible."

Mr Merry walked to Kingsland Road. It was October now. Shrivelled leaves scuttled away from him on the pavement. There was a pleasant nip in the air. He took a tram to Shoreditch and walked down Bethnal Green Road to the police station. He settled at his table and sent for Weldon. When the constable arrived, Merry asked, "Did you find when he was coming out?"

"Ginger Murchison —? Friday."

Mr. Merry took out a pocket diary and made a note in it.

Dido had been coming to the teashop for a couple of months. The waitress paused at the table and gave him a small, doubtful smile. "Tea and bun, Mr Peach?"

"That's right. Usual. Keepin' all right, Miss Matthews?"

"Mm. Thank you."

She went for his order. After a number of visits he had broken out of his silence with an "Afternoon, miss."

Then, familiarity growing by mere repetition, he had found ways to detain her with talk. The place was always empty. At first she seemed transparently loath to stay but without the strength to snub him. The first time he spoke he had to struggle to find words before she escaped. "Quiet today, miss."

"Afternoon always is."

"Glad of a bit of rest, I expect."

"Still on your feet."

"Won't they let you sit down?"

"Have to keep on your feet."

"Hard on the feet, eh?"

"It is a bit."

And the next time he noosed her with, "Been here long, miss?"

"I beg your pardon."

"Just wondering. Coming here every day. You been here long?"

"Two years. More."

"Good job?"

"They treat you very fair. Don't often get that."

"No. Not many treat you fair."

Until one day it was she who artlessly countered question with question and prolonged the talk. Curiosity overcame her instinctive recoil from his too intense look at her, for she and the other girls had speculated about the stranger in the navy serge suit who came every afternoon and sat stiffly among the empty tables. The other girls were always giggling, "He fancies you." So that one day she asked, "Do you work nights?"

"Nights?"

"You're in every afternoon."

He frowned at her, searching his wits for an answer.

She said, "I don't wish to be inquisitive. Every afternoon regular, I just wondered."

He said, "In business."

"Oh, I could see," she said. "I could see how you dress."

"Rags," he said. And quickly, fearing a bad impression. "Wholesale." His tongue went on. He had never heard it boasting before. "Fair way of business."

"I can see that."

"Got a depot. Other side o' the railway. Buy 'em in, sell 'em in bulk. It's a fair business."

"It must be."

When he first realised what drew him to this place he tried to keep away. A pain in his heart would not go away until he went back. It was just that; a sharp hurt as if a knife was cleaving something in the left side of his chest. She was thin. Her skin was sallow. Her face was plain. There was nothing to read in it. Sometimes he stared and stared and asked in vain what he saw in her.

Then one day he ventured, "Ah, fancied a nice hot cup, miss. Miss — 'ere, excuse me, Miss — er — what?"

"It's not Miss Watt." Her smile was more relaxed and truly touched with amusement than he had ever seen it; and he smiled genuinely.

"Don't mind me asking," he said. "Comin' here all this time. Doesn't seem polite not knowin'."

"Miss Matthews."

He said, "Miss Grace Matthews." He had heard the other girls address her.

"Yes." She seemed to be striving for a formula of rebuke; but in a moment she said rapidly, pleading, "You ought to hear them. Twelve o'clock, they're all in. Egg on toast, teas, coffees. One long rush. And it's "Gracie," "Here, Grace." All these men. "Gracie." Just because they heard my friends calling me. Strangers. No respect."

"Don't mean no harm, I reckon."

"No respect." Her face went stubborn.

"Yes," he said. He picked up his teacup. "Thank you, miss."

The quick tap-tap of her step as she went away sounded a thank-offering for release.

When he left, he called, "Day, miss."

She called back, "Good day, Mr ——" and his heart thumped because she had broken off interrogatively.

"Peach."

"Good day, Mr Peach."

Ginger Murchison had been fourteen weeks in hospital. When the ambulance had taken him away the family had been loud in its boastings that he would soon be back. They took it for granted that their patriarch, their grey old bull elephant who had suffered no worse than dents for fifty years, would come charging and bellowing back with hardly a scar to show. A jaw smashed by a hammer was nothing to them. They did not reckon with the effects on the brain of a fractured skull. He had lain in coma while doctors muttered about haemorrhages. Now that he was home, members of the clan came in to see him and thronged round him, and whispered to each other, crestfallen and puzzled at what they saw. But they had prepared a booze-up to welcome him, and they assured each other that there was nothing like a good old booze-up to put Ginger on his feet. He'd be his old self when he had a skinful inside him.

It was nearly midnight. The booze-up was in full swing. Jaggs Place was a courtyard entered by a deep, square arch in the front of a tenement. On each side of the paved yard were five doorways, and there was another doorway recessed into the irregular righthand corner, where the Keoghs lived.

Each of these doorways opened into a stone-floored scullery. The scullery led into a single room with a floor of bare, rotten planks. Each of these kennels housed a family; as many as ten people might live in one dark, small room on whose walls the naked plaster was soaked and evilly smelling of mould where it had not fallen away.

At the end of the yard was a wooden door, which always hung open and askew where a lower hinge had rusted away. This was the only toilet in Jaggs Place. It was always choked with muck. Its wooden seat had long vanished. A puddle always covered its floor and ran out into the yard. Its stench blended with the stench of blocked drains, foul rooms and unwashed bodies to assail anyone who came in through the arch. Another puddle spread beneath the only source of water in Jaggs Place, a single outdoor tap.

By slum standards the Murchisons were not poor. They lived here because they liked it. It was communal. It was their own, apart from the world. The stink and filth were those of an animal den, a comforting lair; and the crowding kept their bodies warm as it warmed their spirits in a hubbub of shared life.

A dreadful hullabaloo echoed between the walls of the tenement, which rose in black shafts to an oblong of night sky pallid with moonlight. No neighbour could sleep but no-one dared complain. Windows above still showed the glimmer of gas or candle light against which black heads looked down on the Murchisons' orgy.

Wild song, shrieks of laughter and shouts mingled. The archway was pitch dark and the yard unlit, but doors were open, and weak light filtered out into the court, in which, like clustered shadows, there writhed and leaped a horde of crazy figures.

Crates of beer and liquor were stacked against the walls. The din and shrieking was punctuated by the splintering crash of empty bottles hurled against walls or into the street. The Murchisons' idea of a celebration was purely liquid. No food had been prepared, although in one or two kitchens older women sat round tables like witches, in a flicker of shadows and yellow light, gossiping, drinking endless mugs of dark brown tea between their glasses of ale, and eating chips from sheets of newspaper. Children darted to and from the fish-and-chip shop with fresh supplies.

Mr Merry paused in the street outside. At his feet a man and woman wrestled, cursing and striking at each other. They rolled into the gutter and squirmed in a huddle of foul rags, the man heaving up, wrenching the woman's skirt up to the waist, her legs crooked apart, the two faces white and savage in the moonlight.

He stepped through the arch, between the panting and whispering and laughter of couples bundled black against the walls. A small boy scurried past him into a doorway leaving behind the oily smell of chips imposed upon the acid urine sharpness — the yard was puddled with it now, as people came out and relieved themselves against the walls. The bawled, discordant chorus of "Nellie Dean" smote him. Against it he heard shouts of derisive greeting to him, in tones of drunken bravado.

He looked in at the corner door. Keogh sat with his back to the door. His wife was on his knee, limp-drunk over him with her arms hanging down behind him. The other women were shrieking with laughter, doubling themselves up and smiting their bellies with enjoyment. Children sat on the mattresses or peeped from under blankets, eating chips. The table was covered with bottles and mugs.

"They was boozin' for two days," one of the women gasped. "Oh, it was a right booze-up when you was married, eh?"

Keogh's wife lifted her head up. "Yeh," she said, "an' 'e was dead drunk in kip after. No good to me for two days."

"No wonder," Keogh said, "I'd been shaggin' the welt orf your sister all that arternoon."

The women went off into fresh howls of laughter and the children on the floor laughed obediently. Mr Merry turned away. He moved on to another doorway. A woman said, "'Ere, 'Arry. Visitor."

Harry turned his head. "Mr Merry. Pleasure, Mr Merry. 'Ere —" With a free hand he poured whisky into a mug and held it out. Merry stepped forward and took it. He made no attempt to drink out of the filthy mug.

"Where's the old man?" Merry put the mug down on the window-ledge.

"Come to see the ol' man, 'ave yer?" Merry followed him out. They went to another door. Harry opened it. The gas-mantle in the scullery was broken and a tall flame fanned out blue and yellow with a throaty noise. On a wooden chair by the table sat Ginger Murchison. He was slumped down as if there was no longer a backbone to support his massive body. His large, grey-crowned head had sunk between his shoulders as if the neck had disappeared inside him. He looked dully towards the door. Beer dribbled from a corner of his mouth as he drank with a loud sucking noise.

"'Ere, guv'nor," Harry shouted. "Got a visitor."

The old man went on sucking his beer.

"It's Mr Merry," Harry said. No gleam of interest showed in his father's eyes.

"Copper?" Old Murchison's wife sat on the other side of the table. She was as skinny and fierce as a starved alley-cat. Her eyes were blazing. "Copper? Can't yer leave 'im alone, jus' come 'ome?"

"'E's all right," Harry said. "Friendly visit, that's all. Eh, Mr Merry?"

Merry said to the old man, "Came to have a look at you."

The old man mumbled, "Copper."

Merry said. "I see you'll give no trouble."

Harry said, "'E won't give you no trouble, Mr Merry."

"He'd better not," Merry said. "His brain's damaged. If he gets another knock, any excitement even, he could drop dead. Or paralysed for life."

Harry grinned. "'Ear that, guv? Drop dead any time, you could."

The old man lifted his head as if it was very heavy. He said, "Di'o Peach."

"Never mind Dido Peach," Harry said.

The slurred voice mumbled again, the lips working with the effort of speech, and the eyes now glaring with hatred. "Di'o Peach. Git Di'o Peach. Git that fucker, I will."

"Never you mind 'im," Harry said to Merry. "I'll keep 'im out of 'arm."

Ginger's voice struggled out of caverns, distorted. "Watch 'ow you talk, 'Arry."

The mother, shrill, "Don't you talk to your father like that!"

"Belt you yet," the old man managed.

"You? Belt me?" Harry showed his teeth in a sardonic grimace. "You couldn't git your own belt orf to do a crap."

The old man began to heave in his chair, trying to raise himself, "Show you oo's boss."

Harry's voice hardened. "Boss? Sit down, will yer?" He shoved his father back into the chair. "You, too —" He silenced a screech of protest from his mother. "You ain't the boss any more. Old tub o' guts, that's all you are. Finished. Sit there an' die, that's all you can do. Fuckin' die, do us a favour. Only one boss round 'ere. Me. Ask Mr Merry. Now you sup your ale, see? No more trouble. Enjoy yourself."

Merry went out with him. Harry walked at the detective's shoulder. Merry pushed through the cavorting throng, ignoring him. They reached the street. Harry said, "You leave it to me, Mr Merry. No more trouble."

Merry turned. The other man was very close to him. He spoke softly. "Harry —"

He moved his foot a little, so that the heel of his boot was on Harry's instep. He let all his weight bear down on the heel. He waited. Harry's breath reeked in his face. Harry stared perplexed, searching Mr Merry's face.

For a few long seconds Mr Merry waited, grinding pain into the other man's foot. Satisfied when his challenge was shirked, he said, still quietly, "Who did you say was boss, Harry?"

No answer.

"Who's the boss round here?"

Quietly, "You are, Mr Merry."

He shifted his foot. "That's right. Goodnight, Harry."

In the city of a million chimneys, fog was the rule rather than the exception in winter-time. At seven in the evening a yellow haze hung on a mist of rain to make a light fog which thickened dusk into premature night. High up the white globes of street lamps glimmered eerily, their posts invisible. Grace Matthews came out of the teashop, turned left along Great Eastern Street and almost at once knew that the dark-clad man who had hurried out of the gloom to her side was Mr Peach.

Dido said, "'Evenin', Miss Matthews."

She said, "Good evening," not turning her head, and walked rapidly on, frightened.

He remained at her elbow. "Which way you goin'?"

Her mind could not work fast enough to outwit him with an excuse or a deception. She was an orphan. She lived in a Working-Girls' Hostel in City Road. It was little more than ten minutes on foot from where she worked. She said, "City Road."

He kept his pace down to match her quick, short steps. "You don't mind?"

"No."

"No offence. Just passin'."

"Were you?"

"Always go this way. This time of an evenin'."

She was stung to say, "Funny I've never met you before. Been walking it every night for two years."

"Funny. You been workin' that place two years?"

"Yes. I remember telling you."

"Where were you before that?"

"Another branch. This one was nearer to the hostel."

"You in a hostel?"

"Yes."

"Not much of a life."

"It's a very nice place."

The hostel had long tiled corridors that echoed. It

smelled of kitchen grease and menstruation.

"Ah," he said. "That's a good thing anyway."

Her heart thumped faster than the tap of her feet. When he left nowadays, after holding her by his table in talk, the girls would make fun of her, and say, "See, he does fancy you."

Once she had said in answer to this, "He gives me the cold shudders."

Men came in all day, and crowded in at midday. Some of them joked with her. Some acted too familiarly. They were a herd, a species, she was able to think of them in the mass and so not be frightened of them. She was lonely and dreamed of someone nice, but she saw hundreds of men, and they were nearly all ugly or furtive or greedy. She would like to be taken out by a man, to go up West on the open top deck of a bus, not with girl friends but with a shadowy someone nice. Someone polite, gentle, handsome. She had never been out with a man. Sidney was not handsome. Sidney was the only one she had ever liked even a little. He came in every day at one o'clock, welsh rarebit, cup of tea, a book propped up in front of him. She knew his name because sometimes one of the other clerks from the railway was with him. It was a nice name, she sometimes said it to herself, Sidney. He was shorter than her, and he wore glasses. Not the one she was looking for. But she could feel sorry for him. She thought she would go out with him if he asked but he seemed the shy type. He looked at her as if he would like to ask her. Some hopes! Him take her out, on a railway clerk's pay? Besides, he was busy after work; classes at the Bishopsgate Evening College. They talked sometimes when no other chaps were with him. He was studying English Literature, poetry, all that kind of thing. He said it enriched the mind. She used to like poetry ever so much at school. Him ask her out, some hopes! And this Peach man was still walking next to her. What should she do? Every time he came into the teashop she was frightened but she couldn't get away from him. It wasn't just that she couldn't think of an excuse. Something gripped her. His eyes, the way they seemed to dwindle down and stare into her, they just kept her there. She had never known this thumping of the heart before, feeling breathless, scared, yet it made her feel alive, funny, did he attract her? She never thought anything like this would happen to her, not to her.

He was talking, talking, and she gave him answers. People thronged in the foggy dusk, hurrying bowed, in flight from the chill mist, jostling past, vanishing into it. Great shire horses loomed out of the fog, sparkles of moisture on their backs and manes, high-laden wagons from docks and rail depots rumbling behind them, carters huddled, grotesquely wrapped, on their perches. The clash of the great hooves on cobbles, the iron rims of wheels mingling their noise in a thunder, the wide road a jam of wagons, here and there the gawky, coloured upper deck of a bus among them, all in a pale yellow cavern of light that blurred away into fog. Her voice and his were small, senseless sounds among all the noise and movement. She was walking in a dream. Oh, she was frightened of him! Yes, she was. Why? He was a respectable man. In business, he was. It was funny the way some men, the more they seemed to want you, the more they frightened you. Not the joky ones. The serious ones. They put you off, that staring way they looked, looking at you, hardly talking. What was he talking about now?

Relief pierced her as, his words unheard sounding against her thoughts, she saw the steps, the wide, arched doorway, the lit hall inside with its black-and-white pavement and vaulted ceiling. She stopped. "I live here."

"Oh, this is where you live, is it?"

"Yes, well. Thank you. Good night."

"Miss —" His voice halted her. "Miss Matthews." He was going to ask her out. A man was going to offer to take her among the coloured lights, the crowds, perhaps into a dazzling restaurant with music, perhaps the Pop in Piccadilly where some of the girls had been. All he said was, "You didn't mind? Just as well in the fog, have someone with you."

"Yes," she said. "You never know in the fog."

"I often go this way of an evening," he said. "You never know. Perhaps another night. Just walkin' the same way."

"Yes," she said. "Good night."

Chapter 6

On Christmas Day, 1911, the people of Rabbit Marsh spent the greater part of the morning in bed, as was their custom. The street was deserted when the Peach family went to morning service; but here and there above the row of blank shutters a tousled head peered down from an upper window to watch them.

Their pace was slow, almost stately. Mrs Peach wore a high, old-fashioned bonnet and a black coat tight at the waist, its high collar lined with fur, falling to the toecaps over her black silk dress. Dido, her arm through his, wore a gent's black overcoat, a natty trilby narrow at the top and with rolled narrow brim, his best suit, a high winged collar, striped shirt and knitted silk tie. Chas and Shonny walked in step behind. Their shoes, like his were highly polished. They wore their best suits with bowler hats. It was not a new sight but this year Dido's position made it something of a procession of state.

At twelve o'clock they were back home and preparing to go out again. Chas stood in the hall doorway and said, "Oh, come on, mum."

Mrs Peach paused and put a hand uncertainly to her cheek. She murmured, "I was looking for something."

She stared at him beseechingly. "I can't remember."

"What's the use of wandering about if you can't remember."

But she was moving helplessly around the kitchen again, looking behind ornaments on the mantelpiece, opening the cupboard, trying to jog her memory. A shout came from Dido in the street. Chas shouted back, "It's mum."

Dido shouted, "Her glasses? Tell 'er they're in 'er bag."

The shout roused Mrs Peach. Like a sleeper awakened she snapped open the reticule bag that hung by a chain from her wrist. She peered in, and with a moue of annoyance as if someone else had hidden them there said, "Why didn't he say so?" Then, pettishly, "Shonny, what are you about now?"

Shonny had opened the canary's cage. He put in a slice of apple and a piece of sugar and closed the door. "That's 'im 'appy."

The canary was Shonny's responsibility and his passion. He made its care a life work. Twice a day he changed the water and cleaned the cage with scrupulous care. He was for ever putting fresh sand in, feeding the bird, coaxing it to sing or taking it out carefully in the palm of his hand to exchange kisses with the tip of its beak. He was small for a boy of fourteen and in spite of his long trousers and bowler looked like a school child with rosy cheeks and eyes bright with innocence and good nature.

They went out. Chas locked the street door. Dido was waiting with the pony and cart he had borrowed from Tommy Long. The boys helped their mother up on to the front seat next to Dido, then climbed into the back which was stacked with bags and parcels.

They were going to their older sister Ada for Christmas dinner. She was two years senior to Dido and lived four miles away in Walthamstow, on the marshes by the Lea. She had three children and a husband who made a good living growing vegetables.

Mrs Peach said, "Dido — you be careful with Herbert."

Ada had met Herbert at a revival meeting where they were both stewards. Every week for a year he had come to Rabbit Marsh to court her at solemn meals with the family, but he let his distaste for the background be seen. Then he married her and carried her off to Walthamstow. Mrs Peach was delighted at her daughter's escape. She approved of Herbert's dislike of Rabbit Marsh and hoped he realised that it was only through unfortunate circumstances that such a respectable family dwelt there. But after the marriage their visits became less and less frequent. When the children came they stopped. To see her daughter and grandchildren, Mrs Peach had to go to Walthamstow, for Herbert did not wish to recall that his wife came from Rabbit Marsh or let his children know of it. In this, as in every other aspect of life Ada ardently adopted her husband's views. Mrs Peach could not help feeling a little hurt. Her daughter might at least have come occasionally on her own.

Dido did not bother to answer his mother. From his first meeting with Herbert Fulcher he had known that he in particular was the object of Herbert's distaste. Herbert was a big, booming fellow who spoke in a tradesman's accent, genteel but Cockney at the edges, and Ada had soon learned to imitate him. To him Mrs Peach might just pass muster, but the boys seemed a rough lot, particularly Dido, a common labourer with a hard, dangerous look. Dido's ever-sensitive pride was inflamed in turn by the knowledge of this, and he had to keep a grip on himself in Herbert's presence.

The journey was pleasant, clop-clopping along Mare Street, across Clapton, down Lea Bridge Road and over the river in broad streets that were still sparsely peopled, cold air whipping their faces. They pulled up outside the neat little cottage of brick and slate in which the Fulchers lived. It had gardens in front and behind, a green wooden fence, a green trellis porch round the front door and a view across the flats to the river. Ada and her family came out with effusive welcomes as the Peaches climbed down, stiff with cold.

The boys carried the bags into the front parlour where a fire blazed in the grate. Ada at once began her annual presentation of gifts, which brought no surprises. She had sewn a handkerchief sachet for her mother and knitted for each of the boys a cumbersome pair of socks. In the past the Peaches had responded with trifling trinkets and cheap toys. But this time Dido took charge. He stood over the bags and parcels with an air of expectant calm that vaguely puzzled Ada. He reached into a bag and gave Ada the usual tin of mince pies baked by mother. Then, with no change of countenance, he brought out successively a huge candied cake that could only have come from a pastrycook's, a ham sewn in sacking, a flowered hat for Ada, a box of cigars for Herbert and (for although Herbert was chapel he did not despise the comforts of life) a bottle of port.

Ada crowed with gratitude but her eyes stared with astonishment and there was astonishment in Herbert's frown. Dido wore the expressionless face of triumph as he brought out the children's gifts, a huge and costly doll, a train set, a set of Chinese bricks and picture books, crackers and boxes of Russian bon-bons.

"Here, I say," Herbert broke out at last. "You're goin' it a bit."

"Christmas."

"You 'aven't been robbing the Post Office or something, have you?"

"No." Dido permitted himself a faint smile. "Have you?"

Herbert, his back warming at the fire, thought it best to let this go with a chuckle while Ada, half-joking, half-offended, cried, "The idea!"

Herbert asked, "Still workin' on the wharf, are you?"

Shonny was already on the floor, joining together the rails of the train set. He glanced up. "Our Dido's —"

"Be quiet," his mother said. "You speak when you're spoken to, Shonny. My Dido's doing very well."

"Looks like it," said Herbert. "On the wharf?"

Dido said, "Where else?"

Ada said, "What were you going to tell us, Shonny?"

Shonny's mouth fish-opened but his mother spoke with unusual promptitude. "He was going to say Dido's bettered himself. He's a kind of foreman now. Aren't you, Dido?"

"I'm doin' all right," Dido said.

"And the business is doing all right," Mrs Peach added, her voice eager with desperation.

"I can see that," said Herbert. "Very handsome, I must say. Money in rags, eh? Nice drop of port, this."

Mrs Peach's bosom subsided with relief. The critical moment of explanation was past; she had dreaded it for days past. The gifts or the money to buy them had all come from the tradesmen of Rabbit Marsh. They had not been solicited. In fact Dido forbore from his rounds of the shops during the week before Christmas. He could not bear to be thought of like some dustman or milkman calling for a Christmas box. But the gifts were brought to the door of Number Thirty-four. The street had enjoyed half a year of peace. And in contrast with the former innumerable exactions of an entire clan, there was only one man to placate, who pocketed in silence what he was offered but made no demands. Dido was a cheap protector.

They had roast goose with crackly roast potatoes and a splendid selection of vegetables grown by Herbert. There was soup before, and Christmas pudding to follow, flaming with brandy, with threepenny-bits in it to set the children squealing. Mince pies and tea finished off the meal. They pulled crackers and even Dido let the children put a paper hat on him. Everyone laughed, Shonny became as excited as the children and Chas refilled his glass so often with port that Ada at last said sharply, "That's enough, Chas."

She was fair and rawboned like Dido, and Chas had always been a little frightened of her.

Afterwards they sat in the firelight while darkness gathered. The parlour had a tablecloth and curtains of green plush, a harmonium, and mahogany furniture in whose polished panels the firelight gleamed. The little girl played with her doll, the women talked quietly and Shonny kept the two boys happy on the floor with the train set. Herbert, full of food and drink, half-slept in his armchair, the glow of his cigar rising and falling with his breath. On the other side of the fireplace sat Dido. He sat hunched forward, staring into the fire. The joviality seemed to have died out of him. He was deep in his own thoughts, unaware of the family around him, his eyes intent on the white cave of coals, as if finding there secret anxieties. Twice he took his watch out of his waistcoat pocket and looked at it.

They finished eating at half-past three. Two hours later the women busied themselves once more at the table and at six o'clock announced tea. The table was laid with a cold joint of roast pork, meat pies, the ham in pride of place, sardines, tinned salmon, plates piled with slices of buttered bread, two large cakes, the remaining mince pies, pots of home-made jams, a trifle and a moulded red jelly.

After tea Dido looked at his watch again and said, "Gettin' late. Have to be goin' soon."

Mrs Peach said, "I haven't heard the children yet." The little boy of four was lifted up on to a chair and at a gabble recited, "Little Bo-Peep." He was brought down and kissed by his grandmother and his sister stood up and recited, "The north wind doth blow, and we shall have snow." Her older brother rose to his feet and was applauded for his rendering of a new poem by Rudyard Kipling, "Our England is a garden —"

Dido sat tautly in his chair, one hand pulling at the hooked fingertips of the other. He made no pretence of interest now. His face was sombre, his eyes flickering with impatience. He said, "Gettin' late. Could come down foggy." Ada said, "We haven't heard from you yet." Herbert rumbled, "You can't get off so easy, old chap."

"Go on," his mother said. "You know what we like, Dido."

He looked from one to another of them, calculating whether it would be quicker to refuse at the risk of a long bicker or to agree. He stood up. "All right. Only we can't stay long."

Ada took her place at the harmonium and began the accompaniment. He sang Charles Wesley's hymns, "Jesu, Lover of My Soul", and "Hark, The Herald Angels Sing".

Each time, after the first couple of lines, all the family joined in. Dido was not a good singer but there was strength in his voice and he could keep in tune. Since he had been a child at school he had enjoyed singing. Shut off from other people by his nature, he needed them, and singing brought him together with them. He had forgotten his impatience. He lifted his head up and sang with conviction and with pleasure. He would only sing songs that had some dignity. He loathed the yowling and false camaraderie of the pub. For a little while he was at one with his family; until the last note was sung, and the last melodious groan of the harmonium had died away. Then he sighed, coming back into the world, and fumbled for his watch.

But suddenly the quiet was broken. Chas began to sing, "Sam, Sam, the dirty old man —"

Joyfully, Shonny joined in; and Ada's nine-year-old began to beat his drum and loudly bawl the words:

—Washed his face with a frying-pan,
Combed his hair with the leg of a chair,
Sam, Sam, the dirty old man.

The crack of a slap brought the ecstatic chant to an end. Ada's boy, his mother looming over him, began to cry, blubbering, "Uncle Chas was singing it —"

"More fool him," Ada cried.

Still somnolent and genial, Herbert said, "Christmas Day, Ada —"

"I don't care what day it is." She turned on Chas, who gaped at her, redfaced and stupid with port. "In front of the children. Don't you know any better?"

"No 'arm," Chas muttered.

"I'll be the judge of that. I expect better than that when I invite you here. You can leave that kind of thing where you come from."

Chas flushed darker. "And where you come from."

"All right," Dido said. "That's enough from you, Chas.

Boy's 'ad a glass too much. Time we were goin', Ada. Been a very nice day. Grateful to yer. Here, children —"

He laid three half-sovereign pieces in a row on the table in front of them. He said, "That's for bein' good. You be good all the time. Do what yer mum and dad tell yer."

The children stared at the gold pieces. Ada and Herbert looked at each other. Dido was master in the room.

When the goodbyes were over and the trap had driven away, Herbert closed the front door. He said to Ada, "How come your brother got that sort of money?"

"I don't know."

"Ade, I don't like it."

"You're not suggesting, I hope?"

"I'm not suggesting anything. Three half-sovereigns is very nice. Put it in their moneyboxes. Still, three half-sovereigns. Makes you think."

While the Peaches were on their way home the Murchison tribe were celebrating the birth of their Redeemer with another drunken orgy. This was a prosperous Christmas for them. Three nights before, Harry Murchison and his brother-in-law Keogh had broken into a Jew tailor's workshop in Hanbury Street and stolen two dozen bolts of finest worsted, with minimum risk and inconvenience for by previous arrangement they had sold it straight away to another tailor in the next street.

The transaction was a great comfort to Harry. The clan was barred from its old hunting ground in Rabbit Marsh by Mr Merry's edict, which Harry strictly enforced. A man who had done a five-stretch knew when to show respect to the police and keep on good terms with them. Mr Merry had said, "There's other places you can make a living. I won't tread on your heels," and to Harry a tip was as good as a wink. Where else was there? Every other street market was the territory of a tribe bigger and fiercer than the Murchisons. The only alternative for Harry was to go back to his old trade. He was after all a skilled craftsman. He took out his housebreaking tools and with the aid of his kinsmen brought off several jobs that were profitable but not (he prided himself on this perception) big enough to activate the police. With fifteen pounds in his pocket and the conviction that Mr Merry would honour their understanding Harry feasted his henchmen and their broods royally.

The game was easy enough. Among the howling revel in Jaggs Place sat a man known about the district as Albert. He was nearly seventy and he was enormously fat. Dewlaps of blubber and vast chins hung around his bloated face. His legs and arms were of elephantine thickness and his belly sagged like a huge sack in front of him. When he stood up he had to support himself with both hands on the top of a walking-stick. Albert sat quietly amid the din, emptying pint after pint of beer into himself as into a barrel. It was said that he could put twenty pints away without showing any the worse for it.

He was a retired burglar. Too old and too enormous for either work or felony he now lived by supplying information to those more young and active. He spent his days waddling from one pub to another. At each he sat for a long time putting away pints and listening. He was a marvellous listener. He learned from builders and decorators about houses they had worked in. He learned from servants and shopmen about their places of employ. Street hawkers told him what they had seen as they went from door to door. Some chatted innocently; some for money. Albert was the man who knew where the cashbox was hidden; and he regularly sold his knowledge.

Harry had an understanding with him. What with Mr Merry on one side and Albert on the other it paid to have understandings. Albert's jobs were always safe and easy and good days lay ahead. Harry had already paid him ten per cent of the proceeds, but tonight he gave him another half-sovereign and told him to drink up to his heart's content. "You play ball with me," Harry said, "'an' I'll play ball with you."

Grace Matthews lay on her bed, alone in the hostel room she shared with three other girls. She was having a rest. She did not like to stay out of things too long, or the others might think she was a wet blanket or stuck-up or something.

It was very nice at the hostel, Christmas time. There were paper chains and Chinese lanterns hung up in the dining-hall, and a Christmas tree. They had all gone to church in the morning and afterwards there was a very nice dinner. In the evening there was a concert. Some people called the Samaritan Players came and did turns. It was nice of them, coming out like that on Christmas night to cheer up the girls. There were quite a few gentlemen present. The vicar always came in with his wife. The chairman made a speech and gave out the presents from the Christmas tree. Last year Grace got a tiny book, small enough to keep in a handbag, though Grace did not. It was called Anthology of Christian Thoughts. He usually stayed about an hour, and other gentlemen and ladies from the Committee came.

It was very nice. But for some reason or other she was always down in the dumps on Christmas Day. There was no excuse for it. They made everything nice and cheerful and you only had to join in. But there was something about Christmas Day, it was too quiet. The streets were all quiet. It was much worse than a Sunday, it was deathly. Oh, it was lovely to rest, not being on your feet all day, not hearing the crockery clattering or taking back those trays of empties which were heavier than people thought; not breathing the hot, steamy gust from the kitchen, those food smells that turned your stomach. Just for the rest, any day off was lovely. Then why not Christmas? It was supposed to be the best day of all. Yet on Christmas evening she felt like having a cry, and the truth was, if she could have spent the whole day at work in the teashop, she would have jumped at it.

She had one nice thing, though. She took it from under her pillow. It was an envelope. In the envelope was a

Christmas card, her only one, apart from those she exchanged with her girl friends. Inside the Christmas card was a little lace handkerchief. That young man came in to the cafe yesterday, that railway clerk Sidney, and he didn't say a word till he went. Then all of a sudden he gave her the envelope and he said, "I hope you'll pardon the impertinence, miss. Merry Christmas," and he raised the brim of his hat and he went before she had finished answering, "Merry Christmas."

He was very shy. But how nice. She said the words to herself, "I hope you'll pardon the impertinence, miss." He could teach a few of those men in the shop a lesson in how to speak to a young lady. It was nice just to think the words to herself, dreamily, and it made her feel better, lying on her bed all alone.

From the dining-hall downstairs she could hear a piano, and the girls singing, "There Is A Tavern In The Town". That was how the concert started every year, a few songs to make the girls feel one happy family. It was no use staying up here and being miserable, not on Christmas Night.

She got up, put her Christmas card and present away in her locker, tidied herself at the mirror and went downstairs to where they were all singing.

The Merry children went up to bed at ten o'clock. Mr Merry stretched himself lazily and regretfully in front of the fire and said, "Well, my darling, all good things must come to an end."

"It's a shame," his wife said. "Even Christmas they won't leave you alone."

"A policeman's lot," he said. "Sally, my dear?"

The maid held out his heavy, dark-blue overcoat. He slipped into it, took his trilby from her and brushed the felt. Sally said, "Never mind, sir. It was lovely."

Mr Merry was touching his hat to the correct angle on his head, watching himself critically in the mantelpiece mirror. "It was that, my dear. I was lucky to have the day with you all. Off you go to bed now, Sal. I shall want a nice fire and plenty of hot water in the morning."

"Ooh, I shall be up, don't you worry, sir. Good night, sir. Good night, madam."

When Sally was gone he kissed his wife on the cheek. "I shall want a nice warm bed to get into, as well."

She touched her hair at the back and said coyly, "I shan't hurry to get up. Seeing tomorrow's Boxing Day."

"Ah," he said. "You're my favourite girl. Night now, my love."

It was a half-hour's smart walk to the police station. Weldon was waiting for him and they went on together to a house in Spital Square. Weldon knocked and a woman came to the door. She was well-dressed and governessy and although a dim gaslight burned in the hall she carried an oil lamp with the wick turned up bright. She held it up to inspect them. "Oh, it's Mr Merry," she said. "Come in, sir. Happy Christmas."

"Same to you, Bertha," Merry said. He led the way in. "All quiet this evening?"

"They're all home birds tonight," she said. They followed her upstairs.

"In the bosoms of their families," Merry said. He was well known at this house of assignation, not as a client, for he was the most faithful of husbands, but on his own business. It was known to the law as a disorderly house, although it was probably the most orderly house in Spitalfields. Unobtrusive with its grimed Georgian front and drawn curtains, it was conveniently near to the shops and offices of the City, and had a clientele of prosperous businessmen and tradesmen, some of whom dropped in for an hour before they caught their trains home to the suburbs from near-by Liverpool Street Station.

Merry would not have dreamed of interfering with its activities. This was not because of the probity and respectability with which Bertha ran it; for if the job ever came his way he would not hesitate to send her to prison; but because the job was not likely to come his way.

Bertha paid certain sums of money to certain of Merry's seniors in the Force with the regularity of wages; and she was not to be touched.

It happened that Merry had never taken a penny from anyone apart from his police pay, but he was quite unshocked by what he knew. He was not bitten by any puritan zeal to reform the Force. His own career was enough for him to worry about, and with his own career in mind he would certainly not question the ways of his superiors. "Dropsy" was an institution. Constables on the beat took their weekly half-dollars from bookies' runners as they took the pay from their packets. Inspectors took their banknotes from bookies, brothel-keepers and race-gang bosses in the same spirit; perquisites of office. The money, in fact, was a lubricant that prevented friction. Few if any of these officers would permit any serious breach of the law to escape unpunished at any price. They simply refrained from interfering as long as life went on quietly. Indeed, it was held by some of them (in their own minds, for no two men even though both were receiving "dropsy" would discuss the matter) that the institution was beneficial to law and order; for those who paid the money were so anxious to maintain peace and quiet that they frequently handed over offenders, and even sometimes arranged for their own underlings to be arrested for the sake of appearances and of certain officers' reputations; these underlings and their families being well looked after while they served their sentences. Merry had no illusions about life and therefore was immune from disillusionment. He was not envious for he had a serene and patient confidence in his own future.

The bedroom was clean and cosy, with bright floral wallpaper and a fire burning in the small grate. The double bed had a flowered cover which matched the curtains. On the wall was a coloured print in a gilt frame, of Roman lovers gazing into each other's eyes over a pedestalled urn. The washstand was of pink veined marble. Standing on it in front of the oval mirror were a large jug and bowl, of rippled china painted with pink buds and encrusted gold ivy-leaves. There was a chamberpot to match. Weldon said, "Very nice."

Merry said, "Psychological. Makes the customers feel respectable."

The door opened. Albert waddled in. He said, "Evenin', Mist' Merry."

Merry put out his umbrella and used the tip to stop Albert at a proper distance, "What's the form, Albert?"

Albert leaned on his walking-stick and wheezed, "Right ol' knees-up dahn the Murchisons."

"Well?"

"Never seen so much beer ahtside a brewery."

"Albert," Merry said in a gentle voice. "Do you think I came out on Christmas night for a social chat?"

"They done it, sir." Albert also had understandings on one side and the other. The sale of information to both police and criminals was an occupation that required a fine balance of calculations.

"Where did they sell it?"

"Tatchinsky. Princelet Street."

"One yiddle to another, eh? Did Harry see you right?"

"Lahsy 'alf-sovereign, sir."

"Albert!" Merry's voice was cautionary and he gave a gentle prod with the tip of the umbrella.

"On my sainted mother's knee, sir."

"Albert, do you see any green in my eye?"

"No, sir."

"What did he give you? Two quid?"

"Yes, sir."

"Don't make me cross again, Albert. I expect he's on the lookout for another gaff."

"Don't know, sir."

"You don't know?"

"What abaht me little consideration, sir? I done what you said, all fair an' square."

"Albert, you are making me cross." A harder jab with the umbrella. "Are you going to find him another bust?"

"Do you want me to, sir?"

"I do, Albert. I do want you to."

"I reckon I might put 'im on to something, sir."

"Right, Albert. You do that. No hurry. Tell him you're keeping your eyes open."

"Keepin' me eyes open. Yes, sir."

"Good. Now skedaddle."

"But, sir — Mr Merry —"

"You've had your money. From Harry."

"Now look 'ere, sir —"

"I'll tell you what, Albert. Seeing it's Christmas, buy yourself a drink." He spun a half-sovereign to the fat man.

"Much obliged, sir. You see me right, I'll see you right." Wheezing and chuckling as if at some private joke, he lumbered out.

When Albert had gone, Weldon said, "You're not going to take Harry in this time?"

Merry grinned. "For a few bolts of cloth? You're thick, Weldon. Let Harry work up an appetite. When I put him away it'll be for a long time."

When Dido came back from the stable his mother was alone in the kitchen, crocheting under the gaslight. She said, "You were a long time."

"Pony was 'ot after the run. Had to look after 'im." The kettle boiled on a low light. Two thick beef sandwiches were ready for him on the table. He took one and bit deep. "Where are the boys?"

"They had a bite and went out. Will that be enough, dear? I can hot you up some soup."

He shook his head, his cheeks bulging as he chewed. "What they gone out for?"

"Fresh air. That's what they said."

The street door banged and footsteps clattered past in the passage. "Well," he said, "they didn't go far. Reckon they 'ad enough fresh air coming back from Ada's."

He heard the boys go upstairs. The bedroom door

banged behind them. When he had washed the sandwiches down with a mug of sweet tea, he brought a bowl of water in from the yard and put it on the range to heat. He took off his jacket, collar and tie and rolled up his sleeves. His mother said, "Going to bed already?"

"Goin' out."

"Out?" The vague, puzzled look came into her eyes.

"Fresh air. Same as the boys. It's early yet."

He took the bowl off the fire and washed his face, neck and hands. His mother looked on indulgently over her crocheting. She had stood over him when he was a small boy and he had washed as if it were a fanatic ritual, both to please her and because cleanliness was his own passion. He was the same now at thirty, scrubbing as if he were trying to rub his skin away, twisting a corner of a towel in his ear, brushing his fingernails hard, then towelling himself fiercely. He glanced at his collar, "Clean one, mother?"

"In your drawer, upstairs. You're particular, just going for a walk."

"Just a walk, that's all."

"You haven't got a young lady hidden away by any chance?"

It was only a joke. But her heart suddenly thumped with shock at the look which Dido jerked at her, eyes wild for a moment under hunched eyebrows. He was himself again, mouth twisted in a grin. "You'll know when I 'ave."

"I'm sure I've prayed for it," she said. "A nice respectable young lady. She'd be made welcome."

The door closed behind him. He ran upstairs. On the landing he heard the window groaning open in the bedroom and two voices mumbling urgently. He threw open the door."

"'Allo."

In spite of the cold, the window was open. Shonny stood at it, waving his hands wildly until he saw Dido and froze into a statue of guilt. Chas was at the chest-of-drawers, hastily closing the drawer allotted to him. Dido said,

"Shut the window, Shonny. Come here, you two." He beckoned with his forefinger. "Come on, Chas."

His brothers stood in front of him. He opened Shonny's mouth with a horse-doctor's tug and sniffed. "Been smokin', son." To Chas. "All right. Come on. Open."

"I suppose I can smoke if I want to?" Chas exclaimed.

Dido sniffed. "Smoke yourself to death. It ain't smoke you reek of. Where is it?"

Chas, in indignant appeal. "It's Christmas."

Dido pointed at the chest of drawers. "Come on, son." Chas opened the drawer. A bottle of whisky lay on top of his clothes. Sullenly he gave it to Dido. Dido said to Shonny, "You been at this as well?"

Shonny went crimson. He mumbled, "It's Christmas, a'n' it?"

"I only give 'im a taste," Chas said.

"And some fags," Dido said.

"Five Woods. 'E's old enough."

"I'll say when 'e's old enough." Dido's tone was still benevolent. He held his hand out. Shonny surrendered the packet.

Shonny said, "I'm not a school kid. I work. They all smoke. Everyone but me."

"I'll tell you when, Shonny boy. You put on a few more inches first. Want you to be a big strong feller."

"I'm eighteen," Chas said. "You treat me like a bleed'n kid."

"Mind your language." Dido was no less gentle. "Not too old to 'ave your mouth washed out, boy. Got to bring you up decent."

"Dide, it's Christmas," Chas protested. "I only went down the pub for some smokes and a drink."

"Don't be greedy. You 'ad 'alf-a-dozen ports at Ada's. One more drink, you'll be sick as a pig."

Chas was flushed, swaying a little. He glared resentment as manfully as he could but his sudden outcry was a boy's.

"Oo's fault is that? Keep me in a bloody pinny, you do.

Never 'ave a drink, never lay a bet, never go in for a game of billiards. 'Ave a lark with a girl, there's ol Dido interferin'. I'm eighteen. You're not me dad."

"I am in a manner of speakin'. My job to keep you decent. The way mother brought us up."

"I'm not a bloody thief or anything," Chas cried. "I only want me rights."

"I know your rights, boy. All I want is keep you straight. We 'ave to live among riff-raff. We don't 'ave to be like them. Got to keep straight. All of us."

Chas kept a sullen silence. Dido said, "Tell you what, son. I reckon it's time you went back to work."

"'Ow can I?"

"'Ow can you? Simple. Just get up early, get your sandwiches from mother, nice healthy walk and you're back at the timber yard."

"You're away all day. Gawd only knows where. You gonna leave mother on 'er own with Shonny?"

"There won't be no more trouble."

"That's what you think. What about the Murchisons?"

"They've 'ad their bellyful."

"I wouldn't bet on it. Anyway, what about you?"

"What about me?"

"Why don't you go back to work?"

"Because I can't, that's why."

"Why? If it's so safe."

"Because I'm here. That's why it's safe." Dido fastened his clean collar and rapidly knotted his tie. He opened his drawer in the cabinet and took out a large, oblong parcel. He was frowning with thought. "All right. You'd better stay home for the time being. But behave yourself."

"Ta, Dide." Chas indicated the parcel. "What's that?"

"Ask no questions." Dido tossed the cigarette packet to him. "I'm trustin' you two. No more fags for Shonny. The whisky'll go in the cupboard downstairs for medicine. Into kip now, lads."

He went out. Chas said, "Christmas night. 'Alf-past nine. What a life!"

The parcel under Dido's arm concealed a two-pound box of chocolates. The box had a handsome pictorial top and a wide silk ribbon round it tied in a big bow. He walked rapidly, nervous as he never had been before. The business had been preying on his mind all day, while he tried to play his part in the family festivity. He had worried at the thought of her spending Christmas in a hostel. He had been savage with himself for not having approached her earlier. She might have spent a happy Christmas Day with the family. But that would have meant bringing her home. Bringing a girl home was a fateful act. It meant inexorably one thing, marriage. Did he want that? He didn't know what he wanted. He only knew that he was driven by strange energies that racked and burned his body; that pushed him always towards her.

As to this further step that now suggested itself, he was frightened of it. He had fought since childhood, faced brutes without knowing fear. But his heart shrank at the thought of taking a girl home. His mother said that she prayed for it. Yet he flinched from facing her with a girl at his side. He couldn't say why.

He walked up the steps of the hostel and pushed through the swing doors into the wide entrance hall. The porter's compartment was deserted.

He had not counted on this. He had meant to ask for her. She would come into the hall, and there would be words exchanged, the present given, she would flush with surprised gratitude, she would go and put her outdoor things on, they would walk in the streets, and then — And then? What to do and say would come to him, one thing at a time. He wanted to do the right thing. He was a respectable chap. He wanted to take her home. Yes, when it came to the push he would.

Of course he had realised that she might be out. Then he would leave the gift with the porter, with the Christmas card inside the parcel and his own name written in it. He wished he had given it to her before Christmas. He had meant to but he had kept putting it off. Well, all for the best. She would have time to think about him during the rest of the holiday. It would be a lovely surprise for a girl on her own to know that someone outside the hostel had been thinking of her. She would be grateful, he would feel it and speak easier. Then he would ask her to go out with him of an evening, and she would be his young lady.

For each eventuality he had forms of words ready. He had silently rehearsed them all day, sitting by the fire at Ada's. The exact words. He was a passionate man. His feelings were an enclosed violence. But he was not a readily articulate man. He thought and spoke deliberately; he had to get his words ready beforehand.

Here he was now, with his mind clinging to the alternative forms of words, fearful of losing or muddling them, and there was no porter.

He could hear the faint sound of a piano, a high-pitched voice singing. He walked towards it along a corridor. The white ceiling was vaulted. His footsteps echoed and made him feel alone. He stopped at swing doors through which he could see into a hall. The hall was decorated for Christmas. Girls sat in rows. A parson was in the front row. A big stout lady in a long spangly gown stood on the stage. She was singing something high-class accompanied by the piano. She kept putting out her arms in gestures. He couldn't see Grace.

Everyone started clapping. The woman went and consulted the pianist. Two girls from the back row took the chance to hurry out.

The doors swung back with a whoof. The girls came into the corridor and looked at Dido. He felt like stone. It all depended on them. If they would only ask him politely if they could be of help, he could ask if Grace was in there. One of them could go in and tell her.

For a long and wrenching moment the girls hesitated, staring at him then exchanging glances with each other. They walked away. One slipped her arm through the other's and leaned close and whispered and the other looked quickly back and there was a sudden explosion of laughter from both of them. He saw himself as they must have seen him, a man hanging about in the corridor with a big parcel, a foolish face with a trilby hat perched on top of it and a winged collar underneath.

They vanished round a corner but their laughter echoed in his ears and his pride suffered agonies. He could not go into the hall; not with all those women and the parson. Besides, the stout lady was singing again. If only those two girls had shown a little politeness.

He hurried out down the steps, and into City Road, walking towards Old Street. He walked faster and faster like a fugitive. He was running away from the thought of his own cowardice and he raged against it. He made excuses; he had been caught unprepared, he had not thought quickly enough. The rage still choked. Of course he was a coward, otherwise he would go back now. But he could not go back to stand in that corridor while a crowd of women swept round him. He could not risk the peeps and the whispers and the giggles. Suppose she came out arm-in-arm with her friends and they giggled to her about him? She would be ashamed or she would even laugh at him.

Rage became shame and shame became a greater rage, sometimes against the cause of it all, the girl. He was in Commercial Street and he turned left into the maze of dirty alleys that led to Brick Lane and Rabbit Marsh. Light and discordant song came from the pubs. Outside the doors clusters of children waited in silence for their parents; pallid, ragged creatures.

"'Ere." He stopped outside a pub. A boy of perhaps eleven, in a torn jacket without buttons, muffler, broken-peaked cap, long trousers tied at the ankles above black, bare feet, stared at him.

"'Ere." Dido tore off the wrapping and held out the box of chocolates. The boy just stared. Other children moved in closer. Dido pulled the lid off the box.

"'Ere, for God's sake, it's Christmas."

He put the box down on the pavement and hurried on. After a dozen rapid paces he heard yelping and he looked back. A scrum of shouting, struggling children surged where he had put the box.

Chapter 7

Mrs Peach was busy at the boiler in the yard when Shonny rapped at the kitchen window from inside to let her know he was home. He had gone out with his first barrow-load of deliveries at eight o'clock. It was ten now. She said to Chas, who was working the mangle, "I'll make some tea."

When she entered the kitchen Shonny had gone out again to load the barrow. As he came into the shop she called out that she was making tea, but he shouted back, "Won't wait, mum. They gimme tea at Dinsdale's." The shop bell jangled as the door closed and he was gone. She heard the barrow clattering away.

She turned back towards the cupboard to get down crockery for herself and Chas; and only then she saw the flowers, a penny bunch of snowdrops in a teacup on the table. She felt wetness in her eyes. The boys never saw her in tears. On her own, however, she often had thoughts that brought tears to her eyes. Bless him! (She was busy at the gas stove). Flowers in January!

Shonny was the only one of them who would think of such a thing. The others were good boys. They would do anything for her. Everything she had she owed to Dido. But he would never think of flowers. Only Shonny, her baby; would do that. He was so gentle and thoughtful and tender, although he was a sturdy boy, bless him, and he worked away all day long like a little hero. No wonder the headmaster gave him a lovely character last year when he left school and called him a manly little fellow.

She was proud of his character, which she kept in an envelope on the mantelpiece. "A smart, intelligent lad. Learns quickly. Honest, can be completely trusted. Comes from a good, religious home." The last bit gave her the most pride. It was a character for her as well.

But —

She called Chas in for his tea. After tea she went back to her work. In the yard Chas spoke to her and she answered but she could not have said what it was all about. She was thinking about Shonny. She dreamed, rather; for her attempts to think usually became dreams.

Like many timid people she lived withdrawn into a secret world of her own, which made her even more timid and vague. She was often absent-minded when people spoke to her because she was a long way away, in her imaginary life, which was more real to her than "real" life.

She lived this other life as if it were a "real" one, from day to day, dragged from it again and again by practical interruptions but always flitting back to it. She had no grand fantasies. In this imaginary life she lived in her present surroundings, much as she did now. It was beyond her even to envisage life outside Rabbit Marsh. She detested the street, but the effort of keeping herself and her family apart had given her a pride that she would not willingly lose. Only here could she feel above others. In a more genteel environment she would have felt inferior, crushed, afraid even to step out into the street for fear of her neighbours' scorn. Here it was she who could feel scornful. So in her wish-world she asked for nothing to be different — except that certain things in her family fell out otherwise than as they really were.

In this dream world Dido was married. One of the top-floor tenants had moved out and Dido occupied the room with his wife. This wife was very young, and had no clear face in the pictures in Mrs Peach's mind, but she was hardworking, obedient to her husband, and a nice respectful little thing to talk to. She stayed at home all day and was a real companion. Mrs Peach herself, in real life a tireless drudge, was not working and the two of them were always sitting in the kitchen having a good old chat. It was like being in service again and having a nice, well-brought-up under-maid for company and help.

Outside her dream, Mrs Peach did not admit that she was lonely. She had her three boys. Yet she had been lonely since the day of her marriage. Her girlhood in service was the last time she knew when life was happy. One by one the boys, when they had been small, had given her something that blotted out loneliness. That was when they were tiny, demanding creatures who depended entirely on her, warm little things she could press against her. But they had all grown big and separate and she dared not hug them. Shonny hadn't quite gone yet. He still had that lovely childhood bloom upon him.

Not that she believed in favourites. Chas was in her dreams, too. She dreamed that his employers saw what a bright boy he was, from a good home, and he did not have to unload the barges any more. In the dream he went to work every day in a suit with a collar and tie, a bowler on his head, and he stood apart from the common workmen with a board in his hand with sheets of paper clipped to it and a pencil stuck behind his ear. He could go into the warm office whenever he liked and in there he would one day meet a nice girl, one of those young ladies in neat blouses who worked typewriters and telephones and such things.

Shonny, though: snowdrops. In January. It was just like the dear, goodhearted boy. He was so cheerful, so eager to help, so keen to work like a man. Yet for all his energy and laughter she had a pang of anxiety every time he went out of her sight. He seemed so defenceless.

She had no high ambitions for him. But what use was that wonderful character to him as long as he was pushing his worker's barrow? She wanted him away from the rags. She could hire a boy to run the barrow.

It was Dido's idea that Shonny should help her. He knew she was fond of the boy, and he wanted to keep her happy, so he made the boy stay at home with her, with the rags. Dido thought he was doing what she wanted but he was doing the opposite. That was how people went on, never understanding each other.

Dido never thought about Shonny's interests, either. He was like a father who can only think, "What's good enough for me is good enough for my son." Dido thought no-one was better than he was, and so he never thought that Shonny deserved a chance to make more of himself. All he cared about was keeping the boys straight. That was quite right. But he never *thought* that anything more was needed. He kept on saying, "Keep 'em straight and they won't fear no man."

Dido's trouble was that he had no imagination. Mrs Peach knew her sons thought her silly, but she had eyes that saw a great deal. She saw Shonny's brightness fading, until he was just one more slum workman. She saw his eyes change and become wary, shifty, the eyes of a street boy.

She wished she could do something for him through the chapel. There were better-off people at the chapel, gentlemen with businesses, or who worked in offices, lady schoolteachers and so on. Surely one of them might find Shonny his chance. "Smart lad wanted" — that was the phrase that allured her. The trouble was, they only knew her as a face, all these people. She was a regular attender, she dressed decently, but they did not speak to her. The minister spoke to her sometimes and in the past had helped her, but she did not dare approach any of them. She might have plucked up courage if she had not gone in such fear of contradicting Dido's notions. She lapsed back into dreams. She saw herself getting Shonny ready for his first day as an office junior. She scrubbed him, inspected his nails, brushed his clothes down, gave him his spending-money and told him the respectful phrases to use to the older ladies and gentlemen. She made him up some lovely sandwiches, thick ham and plenty of mustard, and put them in a little fibre suitcase. No tin box when she could buy a nice case for sixpence and see him walking down the street with it like a little gentleman. She never got beyond the first morning in her dreams about Shonny. It was pleasure enough. She would never have been able to confide her thoughts or dreams to anyone; nor dared if she had been able. Least of all could she have opened her heart to Dido. It was not so much mother-love she now felt for him as a fearful reverence. She feared him in some way as she had feared his father. Behind his respect for her, behind his disciplined, impassive face, she sensed (without being able to define it) battened-down the same fury as that with which her husband had once terrorised her.

Not only did she fear Dido. She feared for him. Dido had tried to think out the implications of all that had happened to him, had found the effort too complex and had given up, accepting what the days brought. He imagined that his mother, once he had cut short her feeble questions, had bowed without further thought or question to the inevitable. He was wrong. She went about her business passive and silent as ever, but she lived in deep and constant alarm. She could not make out the situation clearly. On the surface of her thoughts she believed that Dido could do no wrong. She wished he hadn't fought that man but he had stood up for his mother's rights and he had done good for the street. Now he said he couldn't go back to work in case that rough lot came back. She didn't know what to make of him taking money and things. She had never thought he would take things. He just said it was only right.

But however much she stifled her thoughts she could not stifle her imagination, which was more far-reaching than her sons, and was secret. She dusted and made the beds and cooked and poked the paddle into the steaming boiler, and tried to fend off the fears that beset her. Dido was a mystery to her. She was a simple woman but she feared what he might become. She repeated like an incantation, "My Dido's a good boy. A good boy. A good boy."

The more she feared for Dido the more her thoughts went back to Shonny. In this dreadful street something was happening to Dido. Chas was in it, too. If only she could save Shonny from it.

She almost nerved herself to go to the chapel but fear of Dido prevailed. She settled instead on a more modest resolve. As soon as Chas had gone out she went upstairs to see Mr Valentine.

Mr and Mrs Valentine lived in the top floor front. The back room was occupied by an Irish navvy, his wife and two children. Mrs Peach slept in the back room beneath, and was kept awake at night by their footsteps and quarrelling and the crying of the children.

For the most part the Peaches had nothing to do with their fellow-tenants, whose presence only made itself known when boots tramped up and down the stairs. The Irish couple came in drunk sometimes and were occasionally glimpsed in a state of damage, since they both had the habit of getting into fights, the man with fists, the woman with fingernails or with the eight-inch hatpin which skewered her wide-brimmed hat with its fernery of dirty plumes. Sometimes they were sick on the stairs or fouled the yard lavatory, but they always cleaned up. The man had been warned by Dido and that was enough.

Mrs Peach was so repelled by them and by the stink from their room that she left even their gaunt children alone. Her pity for the little creatures was overcome by her disgust for their dirtiness. Unlike the boys, however, who also ignored the Valentines, she kept up a sneaking relationship with this couple.

They were childless, getting on for sixty, a pair of outcasts from the clerical middle class. The man was tall, with a big, bald cranium fringed with grey and thick glasses perched on an eagle's beak of a nose. He wore a black suit that was almost grey with dirt and dandruff, covered with lumpy patches of darning and frayed at collar, cuffs and ankles. The trousers were too short for him and he always walked with a stoop that made him look as if he had a hump between his shoulders. He was like a pathetic, anxious caricature of those gentlemen

Mrs Peach had glimpsed, like the minister and Shonny's headmaster, and she felt both sorry for him and respectful towards him, as she did towards his wife, a woman as waxen and frail as a lily, who always wore the same threadbare but ladylike grey gown and whose eyes always had the same haunted expression. Their past was a mystery and she would never offend them by asking, but she guessed at some chain of misfortunes that had brought them to this slum. They hardly ever went out; perhaps because they were terrified of Rabbit Marsh, perhaps because they earned so little addressing envelopes that they dared not leave off work for an hour.

Mr Valentine opened the door when she tapped. He peered at her so closely that it dawned on her for the first time that his sight must be failing. No wonder, sitting at that table day and night, more often than not in a weak gaslight, scribbling. Behind him she saw his wife at it now, all hunched up. How their shoulders and fingers must ache!

She explained her business shyly and came into the room at his invitation. She said to Mrs Valentine, who put down her pen dazedly, "Please don't let me interrupt you."

There was a row of perhaps two dozen books on the mantelpiece. Mr Valentine led her towards them. They were old and some of them were split at the back but they awed Mrs Peach. "Yes," Mr Valentine said, "you have the right idea, Mrs Peach. Books are what the little fellow needs."

She ventured, as timidly as if speaking up for her son to some great man, "He's a good little reader. He loved reading at school. He's always buried in his boys' papers."

"Something improving," Mr Valentine mused, echoing her phrase. He bent forward and put one eye so close to the backs of the books that her heart quite stopped with pity and fright. He pulled a book out. Without looking into the book, he recited:

Now sleeps the crimson petal, now the white;
Nor waves the cypress in the palace walk—

She murmured, "It's very nice —"

"The only thing that can lift our spirits out of these vile surroundings," he said. "Poetry."

"You see," she said faintly, "I thought of something more, well, practical. To help him find a good position."

"Ah!" Again he squinted along the row of titles. He took down another book. "This was a great inspiration to me when I was young. *Self-Help* by Samuel Smiles."

She took the book and looked at it helplessly. "Oh, yes, Mr Valentine. I'm sure this would be a benefit to him. It's just to give him the idea, you see."

She went downstairs and returned to her work in the yard. Chas went in. When she followed soon after she found him with the book in his hand. He said, "Where you get this, ma?"

"I borrowed it from Mr Valentine."

He read, "Self-'Elp." He uttered a hooting, prolonged laugh. "Fat lot o' good it done 'im."

Shonny was indeed a good and innocent boy; he was truly still a child. But innocent and good children live according to the modes of childhood, which are the modes of natural man and are incomprehensible to the conditioned adult. That is why they sometimes come into collision with the adult rules of "good" and bad. Shonny, moreover, was a child in whom the sap of adolescence seethed.

He liked going to Dinsdale's because (for one thing) they gave him hot sausages there with his mid-morning mug of tea.

Dinsdale's was a slop-shop in Cable Street next to an arched alley. The shop was crammed with a bizarre assortment of clothes, uniforms, dress-suits, blazers, composite suits whose separate articles were of different colour or in fashions thirty years apart. It was thronged by seamen from the nearby docks, and the locals had many a laugh when a black or chinaman or lascar came out, talked by the salesman into some fantastic rigout.

Behind the shop and fronting the alley was the workshop. A dozen women and girls worked here as alteration hands. Mrs Peach, like other rag merchants, sent them her most paying merchandise, anything that still bore the semblance of a garment. The women sewed, patched and ironed these relics until they were fit for the shop.

The women worked at benches and sewing machines. All through the year they kept a fire going with cloth scraps and waste wood, to heat the irons. The long, gloomy room was filled with the smell of scorched and steamed cloth, which Shonny liked, just as the sausages, cooked with forks over the fire, had an inimitable taste of charred cloth and wood.

He came in and dumped his sack and the women yelled their greetings. He was a favourite with them. The overseer started to empty the sack and one of the women grabbed him by the shoulders and pulled him close to her. She gave him a big kiss on the mouth. "Come on, love, give us a kiss."

He kissed her. He knew this game. It was regular when he came here. The other women were already shrieking with laughter as the woman cried, "Gawd, 'e's no good at 'e's bleet'n' lessons this one. A proper kiss, lovey."

She put her mouth on his and he kissed her with his own mouth open as the women had taught him, not liking the smell or the wetness of the big writhing mouth on his.

"Come 'ere, come 'ere —" This was a girl at the next machine, her arms open, and the woman pushed him so that he stumbled, exaggerating the stumble because this was a game, into the girl's arms. The girl clutched him tight, all down, against her, and when he felt funny she screamed.

"'E's 'ard, the little bugger's gittin' 'ard. Oo, you little bugger. I could put jam on it an' eat it."

Yells and comments from all round fell on Shonny's confused hearing. A woman near-by was shouting, "Greedy mare she is. Spends the 'ole night under 'er bloke an' she's after a bit more."

He span and lurched from woman to woman, from one hot cuddle and smoochy kiss to another. They stuffed his hands into their dresses and their own hands groped into the flies of his trousers. He yelled with anger and pushed and said, "Ah, pack up, leave us alone, go on, stop muckin' about," and though he was angry and at moments near to crying, he was also tickly and laughing and near to falling on the floor and shrieking with laughter. He liked coming to Dinsdale's.

At last they let him go, and he had his tea and sausages and a big bit of bread. The overseer came back from the shop and gave him twenty-two shillings in silver, which she put in an envelope for him. He buttoned it carefully away in his jacket.

Off he went, on the next stage of his daily adventure; for the streets were an adventure to him. He trotted among the looming dock wagons, a little chap in a cheeky cap and muffler and working trousers tied at the ankles; but wearing stout boots and a sporty jacket with leather buttons like little hot cross buns which mother had found for him among the stock; trotting behind an empty barrow, darting among the huge, laden wagons and beneath the muzzles of great horses.

In front of him he saw a small boy, no more than eight and dressed in such gaping rags that his bottom showed through the split seat of his trousers. The boy clung in a bunch of limbs, rolled up like a little money-spider, at the tailboard of a wagon. Shonny yelled, "Whip be'ind yer, mister!"

The carter reached without haste for the long whip in its sheath next to him, but by the time he flicked the thong at the tail of his wagon the little boy had dropped off and darted to the pavement, where he yelled obscenities at Shonny and threw a lump of horse dung which fell short.

There was no honour among boys in this matter. The children lived in the streets and their games were a continual gamble with death. And Shonny loved it. He had been happy at school, running in gangs with the other children and playing in the streets with them.

When he left school, proud to be a man, it had been a matter of accumulating grievance to him that mother and Dido no longer let him go out with his former playmates, who for some reason were now considered beneath him. Instead of achieving freedom he had lost it. He spent all his evenings at home, apart from the two or three times a week he went to the picture palace with Chas, and his only pastime before he went to bed at what he considered the ridiculous hour of ten o'clock was reading. He read penny "bloods" by the hundred. Sexton Blake and the boys of Greyfriars were his heroes.

He loved his work, because it gave him freedom to run the streets all day, to explore a huge and fascinating world, the whole eastern quarter of a great city. He plunged into all manner of adventures. He had no desire to do anything else, especially as he was proud to be helping mother.

He meant to go home by way of Vallance Road, but he had not yet reached Whitechapel when, "Oy — Shonny!"

He saw Cockeye on the pavement. He shouted back, "Wotcher!" and ran the barrow into the kerb.

At their age there was no time wasted on sociable enquiries. Cockeye said, "'Ave a fag," and Shonny, giving the matter no thought, took one. Two little old men stood there smoking.

It was not remarkable that they should be on speaking terms. Shonny had gone to school with Cockeye. There they had been enemies by tradition and had fought a hundred times. Shonny was not likely to forget the feud with the Murchisons. In fact he flamed with militant zeal in his big brother's cause. He was also aware that Cockeye was a predator and his first thought when he stopped was that he must be specially careful with his mother's twenty-two bob.

But there are no permanent barriers between children. In the intervals of fighting they assume truce as a matter of course. They talk amicably, join in common causes or against common enemies as a thing to be taken for granted. Also Shonny had a glimmer of admiration for Cockeye, whose dirtiness and lawlessness exemplified to extremes his own lost freedom. In the same way, although Shonny was always being adjured by his mother to feel thankful for the good boots he had always worn, he had never ceased to envy the barefoot boys who ran about in the most freezing or slushy of weather.

Cockeye said, "Bin up the Old Ford?" This was a picture palace.

"Yeh."

"Good a'n' it?"

"Yeh. Where 'e escapes over that waterfall. Did yer see that?"

"Yeh. An' that comic."

"The one that fell down the coal 'ole?"

"Yeh. See the other one walk on 'is bowler 'at just 'e was comin' up?"

"Yeh."

They stood and shook, heads back, mouths open with mirth, as if they were looking again at that rainy screen. While Shonny was still laughing Cockeye said, "J'ever go nickin'?"

Shonny did not answer. He was taken off guard and he was ashamed to confess that he no longer went nicking. At school he had gone along with the other children in a gang, and they all had to steal some trifle. Honesty did not come into it. It was a ritual, a tribal test which each had to pass.

"You gone windy, 'ave yer?"

"Not windy."

"Yes you are. You gone charlie."

The way to answer this was to hit Cockeye. Shonny had not fought for some time and he longed to; it was an itch in his muscles. But a fight would mean rolling, ripping, snarling on the pavement; and he had mum's money in his pocket, which he was afraid to endanger. He contented himself with, "Show you 'oo's charlie."

"All right. You ain't charlie?"

"Get a kick in the cobblers, you say that."

"All right." As if clouds had passed over, Cockeye was friendly again. He offered his cigarettes, they both lit up, and they started to walk together until they reached the corner of Whitechapel Road when he said, casually, "Come nickin'."

"What?"

"I'm goin' nickin'. Comin'?"

Shonny turned the barrow and walked with him down Whitechapel Road. This did not mean consent; it was a reflex ahead of his thoughts. His legs carried him along in the gutter while Cockeye walked on the pavement alongside. He was unable to start his thoughts going. He was an honest boy and he accepted without even inward dissent the eighth commandment. He *knew* stealing was wrong.

Yet as is the way of things each step prevented his mind from working and carried him towards the deed. He felt a great relief when Cockeye stopped opposite the entrance of a Penny Bazaar. His first thought now was: it's not real pinching, only nicking, a Penny Bazaar. In and out, that's all.

The thought was followed by a spasm of fear — for mum's twenty-two shillings; and even as he felt the spasm, it was transformed into an unbearable, irresistible thrill. His mind couldn't work any more; the inside of his head was a furnace of excitement. His heart was beating hard but steady. He went in after Cockeye and he was now not a thinking young man but a growing cub on the prowl; all necessary instincts and faculties working, nothing else.

He took his eyes off Cockeye. Mustn't watch Cockeye. Watch the counters, the girls, the shoppers who swirled into concealing clumps. He stopped at a counter and no face was looking his way. He picked up a pencil with an india-rubber in a little metal sheath on one end. No one was looking. It popped up his sleeve. At once he picked up another pencil and regarded it critically. As a shopgirl went past, her glance taking him in, he put it down and walked steadily out of the shop.

Cockeye was waiting by the barrow. They started off and turned into a side street. From inside his jacket Cockeye pulled out a large scrubbing brush. In the sport of nicking, it was less the value than the size of the trophy which counted.

Shonny produced his pencil. Cockeye, disgustedly, "Oh, fuck me, a bleed'n pencil!"

"I nicked it, didn' I?"

"Fuckin' kid."

"What I wanted. Nothin' else there I wanted."

"Bleed'n kid. Bleed'n windy like your brother Dido."

Shonny's knuckles hit Cockeye's teeth. In the second a return punch sent Shonny reeling back against the barrow. Blood trickled from a nostril. He squared up but Cockeye did not come on. Shonny did not go at him again. A spurt of recollection, fear for his mother's money, restrained him.

Cockeye jeered, "Teach you. You an' your bastard brothers."

He sauntered off, and Shonny yelled after him, as if a victor, "Show you."

Before the bleeding stopped his handkerchief was soaked and there was a stain on his muffler. His face hurt and so did his back where he had gone against the barrow. All the same, he went home without any sense of defeat, having performed once more his share of the initiations and tests which governed and sometimes destroyed the lives of the young.

His mother sighed when she saw him and asked him questions, and he only answered, "Nothing, mum. Fell over, mum."

She cleaned him up, sat him down to his meal, and put the book away for a more suitable time.

It was dark that evening when Dido crossed Brick Lane into Rabbit Marsh.

He was seething with rage against himself. He had not even seen the girl since Christmas. His nerve had failed after his flight from the hostel. Tonight he had stood in Great Eastern Street on the pavement opposite the teashop, as he had for several evenings, and had seen her come out and walk away.

His courage had never failed him before. Now he turned on himself with bitter anger as a coward.

He kept thinking over the scene in the hostel, each time seeing a different version of what he could have done. He could have approached her in the shop before Christmas. He could have taken her home for Christmas Day. He could have waited for her that night instead of running away. Why hadn't he stopped those two girls as they came out of the concert room and asked them to fetch her? His wits had failed him; and his courage. The humiliation rose inside him like pressure in a boiler.

He saw himself as they had seen him that night; the man the girls giggled at, stolid, dressed in clumsy navy serge, in shining but clumsy boots.

And tonight in desperation he had bought some new clothes. He was trying to erase that picture of himself from his mind. He had gone to a proper smart gents' shop in Houndsditch because he did not trust the shops round here to have any better taste than his own. He had bought for the first time in his life a pair of shoes; patent-leather, too. His mind flinched at the thought of walking down Rabbit Marsh in anything but big, solid boots, but the salesmen with their oiled hair and smooth, knowing talk had convinced him that gents wore shoes in the evening. He had also picked two new shirts, the first he had ever bought for himself; and some ties. Mrs Peach had always bought the boys' shirts. She kept her eyes open for cheap lines on the market stalls and always selected thick, serviceable shirts of striped flannel. It had never occurred to Dido to question this.

He had bought these things but now as he walked home he was prey to two conflicting shames; shame at the picture of his clumsy self when the girls had giggled at him; and shame that he was soft enough to ponce himself up against all his own tastes for a woman.

With the parcels under his arm he crossed the street and passed a policeman who was talking to two civilians. He took no notice. He was a few yards farther on when a voice from behind halted him. "Here! You!"

He turned. One of the two men in plain clothes was the detective, Mr Merry. He stood stupid with puzzlement but pierced by a needle-sharp intuition of trouble. The detective said sharply, "You! Come here!"

Chapter 8

"What have you got there?"

Dido did not answer. He had recovered from his surprise and knew what was coming next.

"Let me see."

Dido handed the parcels to Mr Merry. Dido knew the uniformed policeman, Gaffney, a man with a Navy beard. He and the second plain-clothes man stood unmoving and silent, watching Dido.

Dido knew better than to argue. It was common practice for anyone in these parts who was out after dark with any kind of package to be stopped by the police and asked to account for his burden.

Merry took his time, unfastening the knots of thin string carefully. He unwrapped the parcel and turned it towards the lamplight. "Where did you get these?"

"Bought 'em."

"Receipt?"

Dido was silent. They did not give receipts down Houndsditch, or for that matter anywhere that Dido ever went. Merry opened the shoe-box. He showed it to the other plain-clothes man. He was smiling. He looked up at Dido. This time with the faintest touch of mockery, "Buy these?"

"Yes."

"Gentleman of taste, our friend." This was addressed to the other detective. "No receipt, of course." Silence. "Perhaps you just found them? Someone left them on the pavement. Eh?"

"I bought 'em." Dido pointed at the names of the shops printed on the wrappers. "Go an' ask."

"We shall." He handed the two parcels to the other detective. "Weldon. See about these in the morning." He made a brief hand movement to the uniformed man. "All right, Gaffney. Take him in."

Dido said, "What's this?"

"Pending enquiries," Merry said. He and Dido stood looking at each other, the uniformed constable close to Dido's side.

"I done nothing," Dido said.

Merry said, "Pity you shopped in Houndsditch. No one on the premises at night. Have to hold you till the morning."

"I'm expected."

"Are you, indeed? Lady, I suppose."

Weldon laughed. Gaffney grinned. Merry's smile and his mockery were open. He said, "Patent leather shoes. Expected at Lady Londonderry's dance, are you?"

Merry knew Dido only as one of a large gallery of local faces; one of the small fry. But since small fry grow if not caught, one must know and have one's intentions concerning them all. He did not think of Dido as a workman. He had first noticed him on the night of Ginger's destruction, and marked him as a petty street rough. Since he did not work and did not to Merry's knowledge thieve, he must live by bullying. Merry despised bullies. If left too long unchecked this one might become another Ginger.

Dido remained silent and Merry said, "Perhaps Lady Londonderry would vouch for you."

Dido stayed dumb while the two other policemen laughed respectfully. At last he muttered, "Expected home."

"Ah," said Merry. "That was no lady, that was my mother."

The two policemen laughed again. The clenched muscles in Dido's cheeks were quivering. The lamplight showed to Merry the veins knotting on his temples, the rough skin of his face flushed — showing in the yellow light as a ghastly violet; and he saw the big, bunched fists being held back by all the man's strength. He said, "Is your mother married, Peach? Come on, must have particulars."

He wanted those fists to fly out at him. The other two policemen knew it and were ready. Dido knew it, simply because he was in the hands of the policemen. He did not know the colder reason in Merry's mind. Merry had no particular concern for Dido, but saw him as one of a large number of nasty little creatures who made life untidy. Mr Merry believed in tidiness and that his job was to tidy such people away. Dido, like Harry Murchison, was a fish to be played with patience. A conviction for violence tonight would add to Dido's record and mean a longer sentence on that future day when Dido would be up before the judges on a major charge. Mr Merry would have brushed aside any suggestion that he provoked trouble or that he was prepared, in modern idiom, to frame people. He looked upon his own endeavours as a scientist might regard his. The scientist knows that water boils at two hundred and twelve degrees Fahrenheit. If the scientist wants to show someone else that this proposition about water is true, he puts a thermometer in the water and lets it boil. In the same way, Merry, needing to demonstrate to the administrators of justice that a man was a bad lot who deserved to be put away for a long time, brought his subject to the correct boiling point. He could not see that he falsified or invented anything. He believed that he was merely by informed experiment demonstrating the properties of his subject.

It was Gaffney who saved Dido. The policeman cut in stolidly, "Widow, inspector. Respectable woman."

Merry gave him a sharp glance but said nothing more.

Dido's voice was thick and hardly audible. "I bought 'em."

"What with?"

A bible of contempt and hatred in one word, "Money."

"Where did you get it? Where do you work? How much do you earn?"

Silence.

"Take him down, Gaffney."

The two detectives walked away. Dido felt a surge of hatred for Merry as he had never known for anyone. The humiliation of this interview was only the climax to the gathering humiliation of the past days.

Gaffney said, "I'll take you down first. I'll tell her when I come back." They walked a few paces in silence. He said, "You'll be all right down the station. I'll see you get some supper if you're peckish."

"You mind you tell her," Dido said.

Chapter 9

At ten o'clock next morning when Weldon had come back from Houndsditch, Dido was set free with his parcels. He had suffered no worse than a night's enforced lodging, with bread and cocoa for breakfast; but he was in a state of intense misery. He had been treated like a thief and shown the door without apology, that was what flicked his pride. He had no means of protest or redress. That chap Merry was to blame. Dido's resentment focused on him. But Merry was protected by the law. Dido had had trouble enough and he could not touch Merry. His hatred became more intense for being helpless.

He reflected as he plodded home on Merry's behaviour last night. It almost seemed as if the detective had taken a personal dislike to him. He could not imagine why. Was the man in the pay of the Murchisons? Such things were taken for granted in the district. It was also a principle in the district that few worse misfortunes could befall one than to incur the particular dislike of a policeman.

It seemed to Dido that ever since he had done what he must do to Ginger Murchison life had been organising a conspiracy against him. He looked upon himself as a law-abiding man. He had a horror of even being known to the police. Things simply happened to him. He felt as helpless as in a dream. He was determined to keep a clean sheet but here he was for the second time coming out of a police station.

He thought, not for the first time, of going back to work. He liked heavy labour. It made his troubles go away. But as before arguments against it rose up: the argument of fear, for the Murchisons still waited outside the street: the argument of pride, which made him jib at the thought of walking down the street in working clothes once more, as drab and common and anonymous as any of those who witnessed his abdication. And now there was a new argument. His heart gave a knock of panic as he realised that if he went back to work he would not be able to go in the afternoons to see that girl. That damned girl! He wanted to forget her but he was not his own master any more.

He was tired and fed up to the teeth when he turned into Rabbit Marsh. He gave no greeting when he saw Blakers in the doorway of his shop and stopped reluctantly when Blakers called, "'Ere! Dido! Spare a minute?"

He did not speak and Blakers said, "Mind if I ask you something?"

He could read nothing in Dido's tired, heavy face. He went on, "Little favour, that's all. I 'aven't bothered you before, 'ave I?"

Dido muttered, "What is it?"

"Some o' them layabouts in the Bug-'Ole —" He expected immediate comprehension from Dido but there was none in the sombre eyes that looked at him. He said, "Gettin' be'ind with their payments. Owe me money. You know what them loafers are. It needs a firm 'and with that sort."

Dido said, "Well?"

"Needs someone they're feared of. Wake their ideas up a bit."

"Well?"

Blakers was not warned by the dull voice. "Ginger used to get round there. Ginger Murchison. Put the fear o' God into 'em. It's what they want."

"Ginger did your threatening. I know."

Surprise showed for a moment in Blakers' gaze. "I don't know about threatening. Not always. Question o' keepin' 'em up to the mark. Ginger obliged, that's all. I obliged 'im. 'E obliged me. Same as I oblige you. One good turn deserves another."

Dido said, "Do your own dirty work."

He strode away. Blakers lingered in his doorway. He

gazed thoughtfully after Dido, without visible surprise or indignation; then he disappeared into his shop.

Dido let himself into the house. He had no sooner closed the street door behind him when his mother came out of the kitchen. Pale and staring, she cried, "Oh, Dido —"

Chas was behind her. Dido stalked into the kitchen, and as they moved uncertainly into the room after him, both still staring anxiety, he said, "What's up with you?"

"Wondered where you was." Chas was still wide-eyed with wonderment.

His mother cried, "Oh, Dido! Wherever have you been?"

He looked from one to the other of them. "Didn't no-one —?" He broke off.

His mother stood with a hand pressed to her cheek. "You've never stayed out before. Not in your whole life."

Gaffney had not come, then. Dido felt no rancour against the policeman. The man might have been sent on some other duty; or, being a policeman, he might simply not have troubled; or at two o'clock in the morning he might have decided it was kinder not to knock up the widow. The feeling that dawned on Dido was of relief. It seemed to him that he was reprieved; that the worst blow for his mother would have been to know of trouble with the police, and that he could now spare her this. He said, "Nothing to worry about."

His mother began, "But where —?"

"Business." He turned on Chas. "Time you started work."

Chas said, "Mother was up all night."

She said, "I was so frightened."

"I'm sorry." Dido sighed, and put a hand on her arm for a moment. "You shouldn't worry though. I'm a grown man. Always liable to be out on business. Never know what hours."

"We thought it was them," Chas said.

"Them?"

"You know who."

"Them," Dido said. "Don't you worry about them. Time you got on with your work."

"What sort of business was it?" Chas asked. Dido lost patience. "Get out in the yard."

"Keep your 'air on," Chas muttered, edging towards the door in a daunted way.

His mother was busy at the range. Her voice was querulous, "You've never stayed out before."

"Then I bloody well should 'ave," he shouted. "I'm thirty, ain't I?" Remorse stopped him. He could not remember having ever shouted at her; but he was so tired and choked with bitterness. He said wearily, "Make me some breakfast, will you?"

"I am." She looked frightened again. Chas hung in the doorway for a moment, then went out without speaking. She said, "Nice pair of saveloys."

Nausea rose in Dido at the thought of food; some of his earlier breakfast came up sour into his mouth. "Just a cup of tea."

"You asked for breakfast."

He had to fight to keep his voice gentle. "Don't fuss, mother. Just a cup of tea."

He drank a mug of tea and went up to his room. He was dog-tired but he could not sleep. At least he could relax his aching body in the soft bed.

When he came down Shonny was in the kitchen, his nose buried in a mug of tea. A book lay on the table next to him.

Dido picked it up and looked at the title. "What's this?"

Mrs Peach was sewing. She said, "Just a book."

He was heavy with tiredness but the irritation that rose against his mother was as keen as it had been before. "I can see that."

"I got it for Shonny. It's about how to improve yourself."

"You want Shonny to improve 'imself?"

Shrinking already, she said, "Make something of himself, perhaps."

There was so much anger in him from so many sources that he could not keep quiet. "I 'aven't done enough for 'im, is that it?"

She lowered her sewing into her lap and said eagerly, "You've been wonderful."

"I brought these boys up. They need improving, you reckon."

She stood up and took an envelope from the mantelpiece.

She drew a piece of paper out of it. "I only want —" Her voice failed. Then a jag of desperation spurred her on again. "Look at his character. I only want him to get a good position. Not pushing a barrow."

Shonny was gazing at them over the mug held in both his hands. "I like pushing the barrow."

"Pushing the barrow like a street arab," Mrs Peach said with the courage of grief.

Dido was frowning: "Thought you wanted 'im."

"I can get a boy for half-a-crown a week. I did before Shonny left school. I shall miss him —" Again the pleading tone came into her voice. "But I want to see him well placed."

"Your daughter Ada's so stuck-up she don't want to know you. You want Shonny to go the same way?"

Mrs Peach said, "Ada's done well for herself."

Shonny repeated desperately, "I like pushing the barrow."

"What's wrong with *me?*" Dido demanded. "I never wanted for a job. Always brought you home wages. Always 'ad a good suit, money in me pocket. Reckon 'e can do better than me, do you?"

"It says here he was a good reader," she pleaded. "You know he's clever. He ought to be in an office."

Shonny said, "I don't want to be in an office."

"He won't have two farthings to rub together in an office," Dido said. "Stuck-up and stony broke. Is that what you want? I was a good reader too. Called me bright when I was at school they did. I left when I was twelve." He turned on Shonny. "You're lucky, you are, school till fourteen."

"I don't want to be in an office," Shonny said. "I want to be like you."

"Let him be a man," Dido said to his mother. "Like me. Don't you reckon I'm good enough?"

"You're the best son in the world."

He could not stop. "But I'm not good enough."

"I never said that," she cried. "He's not like you. You were always hard—"

Dido remembered himself at the age of twelve, small and puny, facing bigger boys with terror in his heart and his fists up to defend his right to a job. Misery tore him but he could not speak. "— you were always hard," she cried. "He can't look after himself like you. He's a child —"

Shonny shouted, "I'm not."

"Shut up!" Dido shouted at him. He turned back to his mother and the words stopped in his throat. A tear was crawling down from the corner of her left eye. She dashed it guiltily away with the back of her hand and met his stare with a look of distress and defiance.

He frowned in wonderment at this new revelation of her. He said, tired and resigned, "What do you want?"

"I want to ask the minister to look out for a place for Shonny."

Shonny said, "I don't want —"

"I told you to shut up," Dido snapped. He paused for a moment, then said to his mother, "All right. Do what you like." He saw Shonny's stare of consternation, picked up the book and thrust it at him. "And you, read this book."

"What for?"

"Because your mother says so. In this house you do what your mother says. And don't 'ang around 'ere all the morning. You're not workin' in an office yet."

He walked out without another word to either of them.

He strode hard in the cold morning, driven on by all his griefs, to which was added a new one, a childish smart of grievance against his mother. All these years his mother had not understood or valued him. She thought she had and he had thought so, but they had both been wrong. She thought he was hard, perhaps she even thought he was like his father. That was what created the deepest bitterness in him — the suspicion that his mother thought him to be his hated father's son, who had taken to fighting naturally instead of in terror and continual reluctance but also in dogged determination even as a puny little shrimp of twelve that he and his family would not be among those who starved.

Yet even if in ascribing such a thought to his mother he had been driven into misunderstanding her still more, there might have been truth in the thought that there was in him something of his father. Perhaps his anger against the thought concealed a fear of it. If he had taken to fighting reluctantly he had not been reluctant long. He had always wanted only to inherit his mother's gentility. Yet the fight to maintain it had promoted in him the growth of that savage element which exists at least as a seed in every man; and now it was always straining beneath the surface of his life, always to be sternly repressed. And the more he repressed it the more it became an inner violence that drove him on. Was this the paradox in him — that he was the son of a hated, violent father trying to be the son of a loved, gentle mother?

He was as his mother had brought him up. He was in truth superior in all his ways to those among whom he lived. He was proud, clean, chaste and honest. He despised meanness, greed and servility. He had a vague sense that he was fit for something better without having the faintest idea what it might be. And inside him although he denied it there existed a nature only too like that of his brutal father.

Opposing forces nullify each other. If Dido could fight, dominate and lead, yet not have the strength to resist circumstances, perhaps it was because his will and judgement were paralysed by the push of opposing inner tides, so that he was powerless to do anything but drift on the larger tide of events.

He did not think as he strode along Vallance Road. He was driven by a pressure of emotions which he discharged by expending energy. For those who have powerful emotions but locked tongues violence can be the simplest means of expression.

Yet self-absorbed though he was he came all alert in a second; shutters snapped down on his mood; he had stopped and his mind was clear, all his faculties turned outwards and as ready as the parts of a machine that only awaits the touch of a button. Standing on the edge of the opposite pavement a little ahead was Harry Murchison.

Harry was looking each way. It was impossible to say whether he had seen Dido or whether he was merely waiting for a break in the traffic to cross the road. Dido started forward in a slow relaxed stroll. Harry was crossing the road.

The coolness that always came upon Dido in danger precluded any heat of rage; yet he felt suddenly happy at danger, at the prospect of a fight. It was a release for the tumult of violent resentments in him. It seemed a solution.

Harry stepped on to the pavement in front of him and without looking his way walked straight into the door of a pub. Dido continued at his easy stroll. He wondered if Harry was waiting to spring out from behind the door.

Nearer to Dido was another entrance to the pub. He veered towards it and stepped quickly in. He was in the public bar and he could see across the counters to the saloon bar. Both bars were crowded and Dido easily remained unnoticeable; but he quickly picked out Harry in the saloon bar, sitting at a small table deep in talk with another man, an elderly man enormously fat known about the neighbourhood as Albert, who sat leaning forward on a walking stick.

Satisfied, Dido left the pub. Harry vanished from his mind at once as he resumed his walk.

A new suspicion had come to him. He walked like a machine and did not notice his surroundings but over the rooftops the riverside cranes and funnels came nearer. It dawned on him that he had not given way to his mother about Shonny simply for her sake. He recalled how in that moment when he had frowned at her a quick calculation had taken place in his mind. It had been unbidden, it was not the way he had ever thought before. In that moment he had thought how much better it would appear to that girl, that Grace Matthews, if his young brother had a respectable job in an office, how much nearer to the picture that he had given of himself as a man of business. It was ridiculous. It was like the new clothes he had bought. He was doing things, changing the life of his family, dressing himself up like a sissy, for a girl he didn't even have the courage to see. If he went on like this he might never see her again. He descended the cobbled slope of Tower Hill towards Thames Street more angry, despairing and perplexed than ever.

He was crossing Thames Street towards the strong smell of the Fish Market when he stopped again. For a moment he did not understand why he had stopped; until his mind took in what his eyes were looking at — a horse. It was as if he and the horse were looking at each other. The horse strained towards him, between the shafts of a cart which it could hardly move. The horse's eyes stood out like great glassy marbles and there was in these eyes such a wild glare of misery that he stared back, fascinated by this creature which displayed back to him what he felt.

A mound of black cinders of astonishing height filled the cart, like a slagheap on wheels. The cart creaked, the horse's hooves clashed and slipped on the cobbles, and the wheels barely moved. The carter was a cold-purpled face peering out of a long hood of sacking.

Dido stepped forward and seized the traces and the weary horse stopped at once, at the blessed, restraining tug. The carter's face came up. From the mouth came a surprised, protesting, "'Ere!"

He toiled down from his perch. Dido waited, fists clenched. Once again the happy clarity came upon him. He needed a fight as a man might need a woman. The carter puffed towards him. People were approaching from the pavement. The carter was a bent old man and there was a sag of disappointment inside Dido. He wanted to fight a giant, not a poor, asthmatic old man. Besides, there were people gathered round now, dockers, loafers, and their comments made a gruff clamour of indignation. He could not fight, even if he had a fit adversary, with a crowd on his side. He would rather have fought alone against an army.

The carter, answering the protests of the crowd, wheezed, "I ca'n' 'elp it. Can' 'elp it. 'E's a race-'orse."

Someone echoed, "Race-'orse?"

That was what had first clutched at Dido's attention; the fine legs of the creature, the graceful contours of neck and haunches that made the visible ridge of ribs all the more pitiful, the three long, raw wounds, bleeding under the harness.

The carter pulled the leathers away. The horse's withers were still twitching, "'E's a race-'orse. Never won a race. They grudged 'im 'is feed. No good for racing, not fit for this work neither. I ca'n' 'elp it if they put a race-'orse to me cart."

There was no fight to be had here. The sad, long muzzle of the horse, with its great nostrils pleading, was close to Dido's shoulder. He said, "At least you can walk him."

"Walk?"

"'E's got enough weight to pull without yours."

The carter looked at Dido and the hostile group. He said, "'E's a race-'orse. 'E's got a tender skin. Chafes easy. They ought ter give 'im a rest."

Dido said, "A bullet."

The carter said, in self-pity, "I dunno." He took the reins at the horse's head and, on foot, led his charge away.

The bystanders gathered round Dido, for the five minutes of self-righteous interchange that always follow such an incident. Dido ignored them, looking after the horse. He said, speaking to himself, "A bullet. That's what that poor nag wants. A bullet."

As if he could not see or hear the others he walked away.

Later he found himself on the platform of the District Underground Electric Railway at Liverpool Street. He was haunted by the horse. A racehorse. No good for the track. No good for pulling a cart. Didn't fit in anywhere. It needed a bullet to put it out of its misery.

It was not as if he liked the girl; that skinny thing with her pale, sad face, hardly a word to say for herself. He didn't want anything dirty out of her. That never came into his mind. He could do without that kind of thing. It was a mystery what dragged him — dragged him, that was the word, like a chain on a winch, to want to go after her.

He walked to the end of a platform and watched a train come in. A noise of doors, footsteps, porters shouting. He was not man enough to leave her alone. He was not man enough to face her. He was sick of himself.

If he could manage no better than this he deserved to do himself in. He watched the train pull out and the thought took shape: a man who wasn't a man might as well do himself in. Anyone could go on putting things off. If he had not done something about her by this time tomorrow it would serve him right to come back to this station and chuck himself under a train.

It was not the release of suicide that he considered. It was the punishment of a coward. He had no right to go on if he was a coward. He left the station.

The ultimatum was perhaps not a serious one for he was no coward and he had no intention of dying. In any case, he accosted Grace outside the teashop that evening and walked to the hostel with her.

A little before nine o'clock the same evening Harry Murchison was strolling in the neighbourhood of Victoria Park. Around the park are a number of broad roads lined by large houses. It was in one of these turnings that Harry was taking his evening walk. He liked this area. There was money in it. Some of the big houses were coming down in the world, already divided up into apartments, but there was still many a house occupied by a single family, with half a dozen servants all in neat white caps and black uniforms, and some of them with their own motor-cars.

It was not every boss who wanted to live out in the suburbs. Some still fancied living in the East End where they made their pile. They had their posh houses, real mansions some of them were, and their gardens, and the park across the road was as good as Hyde Park any day, and they didn't have to sit in a crowded train every night before they got to their own firesides. Sensible geezers. Harry approved of money; particularly if it was within reach.

He was respectably dressed. No one would turn round and look at him as an oddity in these parts. Nine o'clock was a good hour. It was dark. Most were indoors eating, but it wasn't like after midnight. Harry was not fool enough to make himself conspicuous when the streets were deserted and people peered out of windows at the step of a prowler, or suspicious policemen flashed their lamps in the faces of solitary walkers.

This was the street Albert had told him about, and here was the house. There were lights in the windows of other houses behind the thick drawn curtains but this one was dark. In the front windows glimmered the white of closed folding floor-to-ceiling shutters.

He did not loiter. He strolled on at a steady pace. There was a gravel drive in front of the house and a coach-house on one side of it. Motor-garage, now, most likely. On the other side, a wall with a door in it leading to the tradesman's entrance and back garden.

He went on to the end of the road and turned the corner. A long blank wall ran away from him. That was the length of the back gardens. Across a road was the park, which meant that there were no back windows from which neighbours might look down by chance and notice the slight noise or shadowy movement of intruders.

That was enough. Home now. People who walked up and down in a street were noticed. He had time in hand, and would walk this way again, a good many times.

Chapter 10

It was six o'clock the following evening; mother was up in her room sorting linen. Chas and Shonny were at the kitchen table finishing a meal of bacon, fried bread and tea. They heard Dido's rapid footsteps coming downstairs.

He came in. He was wearing his overcoat. In his hand he had his trilby and a brush. He went to the mirror and started to brush his collar, then the hat. The boys took no notice at first until Chas, glancing at the floor, said, "Bli!"

Dido put the brush down and was painstakingly setting the hat on his head. Chas said, "Patent leather. Since when you wear shoes?"

Without turning, Dido said, "Easy on the feet."

"I should cocoa. What about some for us?"

Dido turned towards them. "In good time."

"'Ere!" Chas rose, reached out and touched Dido's shirt-front with a fingertip. "Poplin."

"That's right."

"Proper knut."

Shonny said, "Where you goin', Dido?"

"Aren't you two off to the pictures?"

Chas, "Plenty o' time."

Dido dug into a side pocket, brought out silver coins and put them on the table. "All right. My treat. Off you go."

Shonny said, "Ta."

Chas, "Ta. No 'urry, Dide."

"Go on. Get off. Treat yourself to a drink on the way."

"Ta." Shonny contined to stare. "What y'all ponced up for, Dide?"

"Go on. Skedaddle. Don't hang round your mother all the evening."

Chas, again, "Bli!"

The boys went out, looking enquiry at each other. When the street door had banged behind them Dido took from the crockery cupboard a tea-mug and the bottle of whisky he had confiscated at Christmas. He poured until the mug was more than half full. He put the bottle away, then drank steadily until the mug was empty. He put it in the dirty-water bowl and went out.

At ten o'clock Grace and Dido came out of the Standard Music Hall. The Standard stood near the corner of Great Eastern Street and the evening before, when Dido had intercepted Grace as she came out of the teashop, it had not been difficult to steer her on a short detour past it, to stop as if by chance to look at the bill, and to suggest going there tomorrow. Grace had never been able to bring her mind to steady thought about this man. She waited for things to happen. Her blurted acceptance was part reflex, part a pang of pleasure at being asked out.

Both keyed up beforehand, they had both felt comfortingly relaxed during the show. The balconies, the gilt, the crowded audience, the lights, the warmth, the laughter, mellowed them. Grace had seldom been to the halls. Dido went sometimes, but never before with the pleasure he felt tonight. For both the enjoyment was heightened by its novelty. In the intermission he bought a port-and-lemon for her and a Guinness for himself.

It warmed his pride to have her with him. He had never seen her look so nice. She wore a little straw boater with a sprig of cherries on it, a nice fawn coat with a belt at the back and fur round the cuffs and collar, beneath which her pretty boots peeped, and her hands in a muff made her look dainty and ladylike. Laughter put life into her. For the first time he saw brightness in her eyes and a flush in her cheeks.

When the flow of the crowd carried them out to the street, both were tense once more. They had talked a good deal, awkwardly, Grace offering titbits about herself,

Dido unwilling to risk enlarging on the fictional account he had given of himself and sticking to generalities.

Now they fell silent, until Dido took her arm and with a curt, "This way," steered her in an unexpected direction.

She went meekly, stifled now with fright. Dido, too, was inwardly scared. He still had no intentions. His only thought on leaving the theatre was, "What now?" It was a challenge to himself, which was answered by a series of mindless actions.

"This way. Short cut." He steered her again, left from Shoreditch into the maze of back alleys which would take them across to Old Street. It was really a short cut, but Grace knew that it was not one which a gentleman ought to use with a lady. They walked in silence through narrow streets in which gaslamps flickered on ancient wall brackets. Blackened brick walls oozed gleaming moisture. Diamonds of pale light through the holes in barred shutters were the only signs of life from decrepit cottages. The mud underfoot was so bad that Grace had to walk with the hem of her skirt lifted. There were dustbins by the doors and a dense smell of garbage.

In the narrow ways Dido walked behind her. His mind was frozen stiff. He did not know what power guided his movements as he directed her from one alley to the next. All the time he could feel the thrust of a resolution but he would not permit himself to read it. He trudged behind her as dourly as a soldier under orders. Grace walked daintily, but she felt like a prisoner with rifle-muzzles behind her. It was beyond her why she had come meekly but she had had no power to do otherwise. She, too, refused to let her mind work; yet what she refused to read was a certainty of the outcome. And when, from behind, his hands clamped on her arms, turned her round and pushed her back into the dark doorway of a workshop, her muscles had been cringing in expectation for minutes.

He had been staring at her boots as he walked. The ankles fascinated him, so slender and pretty. In his head he was aware only of a packed blankness and he was taken more unaware than her when there was a wrench like a rupture of tissue inside his breast and he felt his fingers clamp on her arms.

They were close, feeling the steam of each other's breath in the cold. There was no fear in her gaze, only troubled enquiry. He leaned on her. He was only weight to her, but he felt her against him so pliant and springy that in a moment he was nuzzling at her mouth with his, groping and grabbing with his fingers.

There was no sound from either of them except for their breathing. She did not struggle. She had simply locked stiff with terror. Even her hands were still trapped in the muff. He fumbled her coat open and pawed in the lap of her skirt and with a grunt of exasperation jerked the waist so hard that the buttons burst. Only then did she utter a single mew of distress, let the muff drop and clutched at the skirt to stop it from falling.

He was jamming her harder and harder into the angle between brick wall and wooden door. Her back hurt. Utterly concentrated, as if not seeing her face close to his, he was clawing at the confusion of clothes his hands had found, pulling, tearing — he was panting now — until she felt fingers probing at her skin. He was doing something to his own clothes and then she felt it hot and hard, a blazing flesh heat and she went iron-rigid, not resisting but paralysed; his hand came up hard under her chin, she looked into his glittering eyes and in a flash she feared for her life.

She was limp now. It had been another of those seconds when the course of life is decided blindly; for the force in his hand had been enough to break her neck if she had not relaxed, yet he had not meant her harm, he had not even thought. She was limp, and he pressed on to her. She was not fainting, her eyes were open, clear and merely interested; it was an apathy of all her body; he sensed it, and it only stoked his rage of blind wanting.

He leaned right into her, and before he was inside it was finished. Absurd. In a second the wild blind flash of force had gone and he leaned on a woman, feeling weak and foolish.

He stood away from her. He did not look at her any more. He even turned away primly to button himself under his overcoat. He had always known there was nothing in it.

Grace stood wearily away from the door. She was too busy to speak. She was looking about herself for a safety-pin. She found one and fastened her skirt. Still loose, the skirt sagged. She began to stoop but he was before her and handed the muff to her. It was wet and spiky with mud. She looked at him at last and made a small, resigned grimace. She started to walk on and he followed.

Her straw hat was askew, she walked with a limp and her hands held her belly low down as if she were torn inside. Concern stirred in him, he said, "Here —" But she limped on.

It wasn't pain. She had expected pain but she was only a little bruised about the thighs. She walked awkwardly because her skirt still threatened to come down, and between her legs there was such a mess of creepy wetness, torn wool, bunched garments, dangling lace, that she didn't know where she was.

Dido at last found words. He said, "I'll wed yer."

She limped on. There was nothing in her mind but a woebegone wondering as to what she would look like when she got back to the hostel.

He said again, with a touch of impatience, "I'll wed yer." This time she took the words in. She had not wanted this man. She had no special feelings about him. Things had just happened to her one after another. She made no choice but her upbringing was such that she knew only one saving sequel to her situation and sulkily, without even thinking, she answered, "When?"

Chapter 11

Harry Murchison was in no haste to pull off the big job. He waited three weeks to get everything right. Albert had put him on to it. Albert was a wonder. If you went about it Albert's way, it was a walkover. Harry's confidence had grown. A cautious man, he had stepped cautiously and now he had enough trust in Albert to try something more ambitious.

How Albert had got on to the Dutchman's game he would not say but he had his sources. He was a bit of a genius, was old Albert. The Dutchman imported toys and he had a warehouse in Aldgate. But Albert knew that the Dutchman had another line. Free Trade was the thing as everyone knew, but for some reason the government had put a duty of seven-pence an ounce on saccharine. The Dutchman smuggled in saccharine. Sevenpence an ounce might not sound a lot but it meant over a thousand pounds profit per ton. The Dutchman brought it in by the ton, in bottoms of toy crates and the bellies of teddy-bears and rocking-horses. Albert also reckoned that he had another line in stolen diamonds from Antwerp, for he was stone rich.

The Dutchman lived in this big house near Victoria Park. He was not fool enough to put his money in the bank. Instead he had built up a fine collection of silver at home. But that was not the end of Albert's information. He also knew that the Dutchman had taken his wife and children to Bournemouth for a month of winter sunshine.

Down the broad roads each day came a succession of hawkers crying their wares. Two days after Harry's reconnaissance a young man of nineteen joined their ranks. He pushed a barrow laden with bins and he went from house to house, calling at the tradesmen's entrances offering to buy compo.

It was the custom for cooks to render down their waste cooking fats and sell them under this name as a perquisite. It was bought by itinerant tradesmen for resale to cheap cookshops and fried fish saloons.

The young man was stocky but muscular and light on his feet. He had a keen clean-cut face and a thick tumble of fair hair. A spot of laughter danced everlastingly in his eyes. He was of the lusty and merry type that is irresistible to many women. He went in through the side gate of the Dutchman's house and knocked at the side door. A maid answered and he was a long time talking to her.

He was the son of Harry Murchison's second brother-in-law Fred Gates and he was known in the family as Young Fred. He reported, "There's this maid an' a cook. The family's away but they got relatives stayin' there. Some other couple. They won't give no trouble. They go to bed round eleven every night an' sleep like pigs till nigh midday."

His listeners were his father Fred Gates, Harry and Harry's brother Jem. Keogh had been left out of the job. Of late he had been more and more of a nuisance. He wouldn't have it that Harry was the guv'nor. He knew nothing about the job. The cautious Harry had laid down that they must not let a word slip even to wives or mothers.

"I'm goin' back termorrer," Young Fred said. "Cook's knockin' up a couple o' pound o' compo for me."

"That's right," Harry said. "You get your feet under the table."

"Get your 'and under 'er skirt," Jem said. "The boy's a marvel with it. Nineteen an' 'e's 'ad more o' the other than I've 'ad 'ot dinners."

Not a flicker disturbed Harry's thoughtful melancholy. "You brought back nigh two stone o' fat today. That's good. Do a job you wanna do it proply."

"Do that maid prop'ly," Jem guffawed.

Harry said, "Can't you be serious? Don't take yer business serious you'll end up in chokey." To Young Fred. "You take yer time, boy. Cookin' fats bought an' sold. That's yer business. Take it serious."

Next day Young Fred went back to the house and was invited into the kitchen. The maid was a dark-haired little Welsh girl. She poured a cup of tea for him while the cook peeled potatoes and inspected him. The cook was a massive beefy woman of fifty well laced in. On his way out he made a whispered appointment for the evening with the maid. He was in the doorway when the cook called out, "Come again today a week. I'll 'ave another two pound o' fat for yer."

The maid kept the appointment. He took her to a picture palace and escorted her decorously back to the side door before eleven. She had told him that she had to be in by eleven o'clock because the boss's brother-in-law who was looking after the house went round at that hour. He was a very careful man. He bolted all the doors, made sure that the screwlocks on the windows were fastened and even tested the bars inside the shutters. Last of all he bolted the door of the servants' entrance and then went up to bed. Young Fred did not detain her at the door but let her go with a light goodnight kiss.

A week later he called and gave the cook a good price for her compo. She made him sit down to a hot meal. He and the maid exchanged secret smiles. They had an appointment for that evening.

Throughout the evening she was coyly insistent that he must take her home earlier than last week. When he asked why, she became giggly and mysterious. They were at the side door by ten-thirty. He followed one kiss with a second and became so venturesome that the girl, pressed against the wall, was panting. His fingers became busy with her clothing. She clasped her hand over his and whispered, "Not here. More comfortable inside."

He whispered, "What about this geezer that locks up?" She giggled, "Don't you worry about him." He followed her into the dark passage. Instead of taking him into the kitchen she led him down the corridor and opened a door. He went in. A match flared, a gas-mantel plopped and the room was vaguely lit. The cook was sitting up in bed, her hair down round the red pudding of her face, her breasts like two more enormous puddings beneath her nightgown.

He said, "What's this?"

"You can come in long as you be'ave yourself," the cook said.

Behind him the maid giggled. The cook said, "No point stayin' outside in the cold when there's a warm bed."

"You're a nice one," he muttered. The maid had slipped past him and was undressing quickly.

"Well," Young Fred said to the cook, "You're a good sort an' no mistake." He took off his cap and muffler, hung his jacket on a chair, sat down and slipped off his boots. "You gonna bring us a cup o' tea after?"

The Welsh girl giggled. The cook said, "You be a good boy, you'll be looked after. Man can't do 'is best in the cold."

Young Fred stood up to step out of his trousers. "Ca'n' even find it in the cold, lady."

In woollen vest, long pants and socks he padded towards the maid's bed. The cook threw back the blankets from over her and said, "Where you goin?"

He stopped. "What's that?"

The maid was a real giggler. He could hear her. The cook said, "Don't stand there gaping. It's cold. Don't you know your manners?"

He jerked a thumb over his shoulder at the maid. "What about 'er?"

"She'll wait," the cook said.

Next morning he sat with his partners. "It was 'orrible," he said indignantly. "She was murder that cook. Wen' at it like a beefy great ox." His father and Jem were shouting with laughter. He said, "You can laugh. I 'ad the girl to see to arter. Never know the like of it in me life. Disgustin' it was."

"Hoo-hoo!" His father was doubled up. "Boy 'ad to work for 'is livin'. That's a change."

"They do it regular." Young Fred's voice still rang with astonishment. "Only way the cook can get a bit at 'er age. Girl tol' me she's been up the spout twice, cook got rid of 'em. Never seen the like of it."

"Never mind." Harry's curt voice cut into the laughter. "What abaht this geezer lockin' up?"

"'E come round soon arter eleven. I 'eard the church clock. I was still in with the ol' mare. She tol' me to lay still all of a sudden. Then I 'eard 'is feet clumpin'. 'E shot the bolt an' turned a key an' went back through the kitchen into the 'ouse. I said to the ol' cook, "Ere, I'm bloody locked in.' I 'eard the maid, Olwen 'er name is, I 'eard 'er giggle. Life's one long joke for that cob. Then the cook said, 'Don't you worry, son, we 'ad another key made months since. An' the bolt is well oiled.' That's when I realised these two cows was doin' it regular."

Fred and Jem found the lad's account funny. Harry gave them a glance of contempt. "You can get a wax o' the key?"

"Look, 'Arry," Young Fred said. "I'm not in me nappies still. You leave that to me."

"Night we go in, you can get to the door an' unfasten. You can tell these two slags you're goin' to the bog."

"Do me a favour," Young Fred pleaded. "You don' 'ave to tell me everything."

"You listen. We don' take no chances. Where does this brother-in-law sleep?"

"First floor back. 'Im an' 'is missus."

"An' the silver?"

"In the parlour. Ground floor front. It's in cabinets. Maid was grumblin' about the polishin' she 'as to do."

"Open cabinets without no noise," Harry said. "No need to wake this pair upstairs. You said they sleep like pigs." He glanced at Jem. "Long as this clumsy ox don't balls everything up."

"'Ere!" Jem protested. "You leave orf!"

"You shut up," Harry growled at him. "I'm only takin' you 'cause I don't trust Keogh. All you know is the 'eavy stuff. We don' want no sandbags or coshes on this job. It's a scientific lay, see? And you," he turned to Young Fred. "We go in next week. Soon as you tip us the door key. Keep them two rotten 'ores well greased till then."

"Bli!" Young Fred groaned. "I 'ope I can last it."

It was just after midnight and there was no moon. Harry found the side door unbolted as Young Fred had promised. He and Jem slipped in. The police had Harry's fingerprints. He and Jem wore gloves and canvas beach shoes with rubber soles. He closed the door silently.

Light glimmered under a door down the passage. The two men stole towards it. They paused outside. They could hear the whispering of a girl and smothered giggles. She was a giggler all right. From elsewhere in the room the loud steady alternation of snore and sigh was audible.

Harry turned the doorknob cautiously and slowly opened the door. The first thing he saw, on a bed directly in front of him, was the rear end of Young Fred, a behind and a pair of crouched legs clothed in wool.

The two men came into the room. The snoring came from the other bed where the cook had turned away on her side in a great heap of blankets, from which her buttocks protruded like the white hindquarters of a brewery mare. The door made the faintest squeak as it opened and their shoes the faintest scuffle on the floor; and between Young Fred's parted legs Harry glimpsed a girl's face pinched and staring with terror. She uttered the start of a cry. Young Fred's hand clapped over her mouth. Using his hands and knees he held her down. In the instant the two other men had pounced on the cook. She heaved, showed a red startled face, uttered a few gurgles and moans; then she was trussed and gagged; and they went to tie up the girl.

Jem said to Young Fred, "I could fancy you meself. You look lovely in them John L's."

"You can laugh —" Young Fred rapidly slipped his clothes on. "I nigh done meself an injury gettin' the old one off ter sleep."

Harry had gone out and brought in their gear, which he was sorting. "Too much rabbit," he snapped. "Take them empty bags, Jem. Young Fred, cop 'old o' this."

He gave Young Fred a bull's eye lantern. The boy leading, they went along the corridor and through the kitchen into the house. Harry said, "Move. We got fifteen minutes."

He had the getaway all planned. It would be swift, in a cab driven by Fred Gates, which they had hired for the night from a not too scrupulous owner. But Harry was a cautious man. He would not have the cab waiting suspiciously outside. Fred would drive past in exactly fifteen minutes. They would slip out of the side door with no noise to rouse the people upstairs and watch for Fred from behind the wooden gate. He would drive on and do another circuit of the block unless he saw the flash of their lamp. Only when he saw their signal would he stop, take them up and whisk them away.

Weldon said, "A.C. Hayward. He scored three thousand, five hundred and thirteen runs in a season. Oh-six that was."

"I should have thought W.G. would have beaten that," Merry said. "In ninety-five he knocked up a thousand in a month."

Weldon said, "Hayward holds the record." A constable brought an enormous teapot of brown enamel. The two detectives pushed their mugs across the table for yet another fill of tea. Weldon sighed. "It's all waiting, this game."

Merry felt no suspense, only the complacent calm of a man who plays the winning cards out as planned. He had been Albert's source of information about the Dutchman. He was not concerned about the Dutchman's smuggling. It was none of his business; and, since the Dutchman appeared to enjoy immunity, he must be paying a decent cut to someone in the Force.

The house was already watched when Harry reconnoitred it. A discreet watch had been kept on Harry and his companions ever since and there were two men on duty tonight watching the house from a building opposite.

The telephone bell rang. One of the two detectives on watch reported that Jem and Harry had gone into the house. Merry said, "Right!"

He made a hand sign and Weldon led four uniformed men out. There was an old four-wheeler waiting outside. It would make less noise on arrival than a motor-taxi and would cover the short distance to their destination in a few minutes.

Left alone with the desk sergeant, Merry said, "You know what to do, John." The desk sergeant indicated his pocket-watch which was propped against a matchbox in front of him. He said, "On the dot."

"And then forget it. If the people in the house report it, we don't know anything."

"You're a dark one, Bill," the desk sergeant said. "I never know what you're up to."

Merry said, "What you don't know won't hurt you." He went out. The desk sergeant heard the cab drive away. He waited until the hands on the watch reached a certain position. He picked up the telephone and asked for a number. It occurred to him that the night operator would be able to say who made the call. But then, Bill Merry would see that no-one enquired. Bill was a dark one. The bell began to ring at the other end. When it had rung twelve times the desk sergeant hung up. That was what Bill had said. Even if anyone answered before he hung up, he was to cut off in silence. A long-sighted patiently waiting cunning man was Bill. The desk sergeant was shrewd enough to make his own surmises. Evidently Bill did not want a quiet, neat arrest. He wanted to stir things up before he got there.

This was exactly what Inspector Merry wanted. What followed was what he had planned. He meant to put Harry and his companions away for a very long time and the offence would be aggravated if to the charge of robbery could be added that of violence.

It turned out better than he had hoped; for when the Dutchman's brother-in-law was at last awakened by the jangling of the telephone bell and slipped out of bed, the first thing that he did after telling his mumbling wife to go back to sleep, was to don a dressing-gown, take a revolver from the bedside cabinet and put it in his pocket. His name was Moss de Groot and he belonged to a race-gang in Whitechapel. His brother-in-law had chosen a fitting custodian; Moss had no idea who might be telephoning at this hour but he would take no chances in the night. He was a predator more alert and dangerous than any of the Jaggs Place mob who, in fact, would never have attempted the job if they had known he was here; for in the hierarchy of slum crime the race-gangs were "flash", aristocrats not to be angered by lesser beings. Inspector Merry had known of his presence in the house; but he had not told Albert.

In the parlour a sack full of silverware lay by the door. Jem and Young Fred were holding a second sack open and Harry was quietly filling it when a telephone bell began to jangle somewhere at the back of the house. They all stood still and listened. Harry muttered, "It's in the back 'all. Young Fred, go an' stop it, quick."

Young Fred picked up the lantern, hurried to the door and went out into the hall.

Moss de Groot was half-way down the stairs when he saw the bob of a lantern come into the hall and the indistinct slim shape of a man holding it. He stopped. The man with the lamp stopped and stared back at him then flitted back into the parlour.

Moss was a man who had fought hand-to-hand with razors. He could hear muttering and hurried scuffling movements in the parlour. He uttered a buffalo grunt, went down the last few stairs and charged into the room.

The three men with the blackness of the shutters behind them saw him come in from the paler gloom of the hall. He had a revolver in his hand.

A shot deafened Harry. His head rang not only with the noise but with astonishment and rage because the shot had come from *next to* him. In the moment that furious understanding came to him the room was filled with the din of a fusillade, a war of red stabbing flashes and the bitter firework tang of powder.

The dark broad bulk of their adversary filled the doorway and the gun in his hand stabbed fire but Harry seized a silver coffee-pot, charged with no other weapon, smashed it down on the man's head and thrust past as the man fell. He heard Jem and Young Fred behind him. But as he pulled at the bolts of the front door his heart sank for through the small leaded panes of stained glass he saw dark figures waiting and he could hear footsteps behind him coming through from the kitchen entrance.

Resigned, he opened the door. Mr Merry stood in the porch. Mr Merry said, "You've dropped a bollock this time, Harry."

He came in followed by two uniformed constables. From the rear of the passage Weldon advanced with two more men. Mr Merry lit the gas light in the hall. The man on the floor was gathering himself up. Moss de Groot lurched to his feet. There was a patch of bloody matted hair on his head and a thread of blood crawled down his face. He pointed to Harry. "Hit me. That one. Spoiled a nice coffee-pot."

Mr Merry picked up a Webley revolver. "This yours?"

"No." De Groot glanced round and pointed to the floor. "There's mine."

"Well," Mr Merry said. "It's lucky you're all rotten shots Five rounds fired out of this one. Ah!"

The two detectives who had been on watch came in with Fred Gates between them. Mr Merry said, "Our amateur cabbie. Who fired the gun?"

De Groot pointed at Jem. "Him."

Harry was glaring hatred at Jem. He muttered, "You fool!"

Young Fred burst out, "We never knew 'e 'ad a barker, Mr Merry. Thinks 'e's Peter the Painter, 'e does!"

Harry spoke again to Jem, his voice low and intense. "I could fuckin' kill you for this."

Mr Merry said mildly, "I don't blame you, Harry. Carrying a gun! Dear, dear, I don't know what the Judge'll say."

Chapter 12

At midday on Saturday Dido came into the kitchen. He hesitated, then spoke roughly. "Mother — I'm bringin' a young lady home tomorrow. For tea."

Staring at him, his mother knew what an effort the words had cost him. She had to swallow spittle to speak. "Oh— Oh, that's very nice. That's very nice, Dido."

She busied herself putting his dinner out. He sat down. From now on he looked only at his plate. "Want everything look nice."

Her chest felt as if the breath in it had become a block of ice. "Well, of course."

"Extra nice." She saw his face clenching with another effort. "She's a good class young lady."

"No more than I would expect. I am pleased, dear."

"Put on a bit of a show." He was chewing food already. "No harm in that. Buy a few things." He fished a sovereign from his pocket and put it on the table. "This do? More if you want."

"It's too much —"

"Spend it."

"You won't be ashamed, dear. I promise. Oh — My best cloth. The lady of the house gave it to me when I wed your father. I've never had it out since. Oh dear —"

He ate as if he could no longer hear her. She said, "How did you meet your — your young lady?"

He ignored her. The sight of him sitting there looking grimly at his plate unnerved her. "I must look for it — it's upstairs —"

She was at the door to the passage when he said, "Get everything scrubbed. Not you. Get the boys. Tell 'em I said."

She fled.

Emma Peach had dreamed for years of this moment. Now she was stunned. She waited upstairs until she heard Dido go out. Then, to smother the whirl of confusion in her head she set to work like a madwoman. She raked out the fire, black-leaded the range and left it unlit until tomorrow, although the day was cold. She polished the brass fender and changed the back curtains.

Shonny came in at twelve o'clock. Mrs Peach had been to the chapel and the minister had promised that he would let her know when he heard of a suitable opening, but Shonny was still pushing the family barrow. His mother gave him his dinner, then set him to clearing up the yard and sprinkling the mounds of rags in the shop with carbolic. Chas would hang new curtains at the back for her when he came in. In the meantime she laid fresh coloured paper with scalloped edges on the shelves and set out her best crockery.

The afternoon passed and Chas did not come in. She hung the curtains with Shonny's help, covered the windows of the shop door with a bright flowered curtain so that a visitor could not see into the shop, moved the furniture back and — she must work, she was unable to think — began scrubbing the floor.

Chas had a secret hoard. He kept it in a knotted handkerchief in the bottom drawer, which was his, of the bedrooom chest-of-drawers. He had taken it out and gloated over it dozens of times when he was alone in the room. He had watched the little pile of gold coins grow steadily higher. Today he could no longer contain himself.

He was walking in the Mile End Road, which is in layout the grandest thoroughfare in London. It is treelined and as wide as any Paris boulevard. Each pavement alone is as wide as a fair-sized street. On Saturday afternoons it became the great promenade and fair of the East End of London.

Chas had set out meaning to do no more than carry the

money in his pocket. All he wanted to do was to chink the coins in his trouser pocket, to permit himself to enjoy the weight of his wealth, perhaps to spend just a little of it.

But somehow the joy, the madness had taken entire possession of him and he had found himself as in a dream inside a gent's outfitters' shop. Sleek and swarthy young men had taken hold of him and advised him volubly, and there had been no escape. But in the warm smell of cloth his intoxication had grown and there had been no wish to escape. When he came out he had left his old clothes inside and he was wearing a chocolate-brown suit with a white pin-stripe. The waisted jacket came almost down to his knees, fastened high with four buttons and piped all round with brown braid. With a braided lapelled waistcoat, drainpipe trousers, yellow pin-stripe shirt, large red and white polka-dot tie, new check cloth cap and black boots with elastic sides, he felt splendid and defiant; splendid because he at last wore the uniform of a man; defiant of Dido.

Like Shonny he revered Dido but chafed at Dido's iron rule. He, too, wanted to be himself. His ideals were not those of his elder brother but of an East End boy of eighteen. He saw himself in the shop windows, and felt the extreme of bliss. He was at last his own ideal realised, a proper knut.

He had money in his pocket and this marvellous day would not end for an infinity of hours. At last he had broken free and become a man. Playing the part, man of the world, he passed an hour knocking the balls about in a billiard saloon. He strolled along the boulevard within a dense human tide, amid the warring music of steam organs. There was a street fair on the broad pavement at Mile End Waste. A travelling roundabout whirled its cargo of screaming children. Swing boats soared and fell. Boys bought penny ticklers from hawkers and darted among the crowd puffing the rolled tubes which they shot out to strike happy shrieks from the faces of girls. A strong man performed amid a ring of onlookers.

Within another circle girls skipped with hired ropes while the proprietor shouted, "Skip as long as yer like for a penny."

Chas had a go at the shooting-booth and tried his strength with a mighty hammer. He bought hot sarsaparilla, jellied eels, a dish of pigs' trotters, and plates of vinegary whelks. Outside a public house in a side street a row of shawled women and men in caps and chokers leaned against the wall drinking pints while a barrel-organ jangled. Onlookers blocked the road, and in the space around the barrel-organ a dozen girls danced like furies, whooping to and from each other with skirts uplifted, whirling each other tight-clasped, joining and breaking to prance in lines and rings.

Dusk closed in. Lights pricked the deepening gloom. A whole population poured from thousands of narrow streets to drown their troubles and forget the cold everlasting fear of destitution. They bought joy by the pennyworth — drink, a sideshow, a song, a dance, a plate of winkles; and it cost nothing to walk in the noise and the pageant of stalls whose naphtha flares hung in mile-long carnival festoons in the dusk.

It grew colder. Snowflakes began to whirl. The sting of the cold on his face and the friendly heat and jostle of the crowd added to Chas's exultation.

There was a good bill at the Paragon Music Hall and he went in. He treated himself to a couple of whiskies — blow Dido! — and he left after an hour. He could have stayed all the evening, but a man of the world just popped in and out of the halls. The odd bob meant nothing to him.

In the same dandiacal spirit he dropped in at the Wonderland where there was boxing on Saturday night. Inside the great hall he was jammed in a dense mob of men, most of them in their working-clothes. Lifting on his toes he could just see, beyond a sea of heads, the fighters prowling and darting to and fro like white mannikins beneath the lights, and hear the thud of punches.

He looked around him. All the faces were lifted, were

staring in one direction; all grim, ruthless, hypnotised. Every hard case in the East End seemed to be here. They were men who fought to survive. This was their cathedral.

His glance, taking in the faces, passed a face and came suddenly back to it. Fear shrivelled his stomach. It was Keogh.

A few days ago the news had gone round that Harry Murchison and three of his lot were in chokey. They had been committed for trial at the Old Bailey but everyone was already sure that on a charge of armed robbery they would all go down for a good few years. That left Keogh the guvnor in Jaggs Place. He was the nearest relation left apart from youngsters. He was a bad one. Chas might swagger and boast that Dido was cock of the walk. He might brag truly that he was afraid of no-one his own size. But he had always been secretly frightened — ever since that night when Dido smashed old Ginger Murchison — that one day on his own he might come face to face with one of the grown ones, the bad ones. And Keogh was a bad one, pure trampling bully.

Keogh's eyes were fixed on the ring. He watched the boxers as if only they existed; as if he were a beast of prey waiting in the dark outside the clearing to pounce when one of them had fallen. Chas told himself that he was safe. He forced himself to look at the ring again. His heart went on beating hard. He could not keep his eyes on the ring. The thud of gloves made twinges of sickness inside him. He glanced to his right again. Keogh was pushing towards him. For a moment he could not believe that he had really been detected; until his eyes met Keogh's; flaming yellow at him like a tiger's.

He thrust towards the exit. He was in an anguish of terror. Men resisted him and shouted at him. He risked glances back and each time it seemed that Keogh was gaining.

He was at a door and out into the street. Blue night had descended, filled with a whirl of snowflakes that vanished before they reached the pavement. Not looking back he raced through the crowd and across the wide road, grateful for the pell-mell of buses and wagons that came charging at him out of the snow-whirl, hooting and clanging bells at him as he ducked among them at risk of his life.

He was on the far pavement, past the line of stalls, past the endless chain of naphtha lamps, and into a crowd more dense than ever. He hurried on, towards Whitechapel. After five minutes he slowed down to a walk. He was out of breath, but he was sure that Keogh could not have kept after him among this multitude, even in the unlikely event that he had wanted to.

It was late evening. The snow was a white confetti but the crowds did not diminish. As long as they surged up and down these pavements the traders would remain, trying for the last penny of livelihood; some shouting gaily at their stalls some standing silent and dejected behind wretched little displays of junk set out on the flagstones, or wearing trays of matches, bootlaces and other trifles. There were stalls hung with clusters of poultry, stalls hung with immense cleft carcasses and decorated with pigs' heads that stared as if alive between joints of beef. Other stalls were carpeted with the glitter of cheap trinkets, piled with second-hand boots or a theatrical variety of hats. Others were hung with dense racks of clothing which customers were trying on in the snowstorm.

Every kind of hot food and drink was on sale. There were cripples, entertainers, beggars, the "Guess-Your-Weight" man with his shining brass jockey scales; and in the crowds, people in workclothes, people in their best, families clustered round perambulators, Jews and their women togged up to the nines, women in black bonnets; soldiers in grand red uniforms strutting with their girls, Chinamen in funny clothes, lascar seamen, and drunks — more and more drunks as the evening went on, reeling among the mob, singing or muttering in their private worlds of misery or alcoholic happiness, or offering fight to those around them.

Chas felt happy again. The snow whirled in curtains through which the endless faces came. It darted and disappeared around the wild naphtha flares like millions of white insects speckling the night. The flakes flew into Chas's face, lightly stinging before they melted, reviving his exhilaration.

Yet in a little while depression settled upon him. It was not because of Keogh. He had forgotten Keogh. It was a restless sense of something missing. He was troubled by all the young couples walking out. They seemed to be everywhere, hugging each other tightly round the waist or hanging round each other's necks, all so happy.

Chas was eighteen. All the boys he had known at school had girls. Some of them were married, perhaps with children. Some walked out in a respectable way and were proud of their young ladies. Rougher boys boasted of more sordid-satisfactions, which they talked of as commonplace. Dido said they might as well be rats in the sewers the way they carried on. The less the boys had to do with them the better. The trouble was, Chas felt, that he had never been allowed to have much to do with anyone. He hadn't got a single pal of his own. He looked at the girls, they were so nice, brazen as brass, kissing their boys, but nice girls, he could see. What chance did he have of meeting one? He'd stuck out for his rights this last couple of years — at least, when Dido wasn't there to see. He could have a smoke, a drink, a game of billiards; he'd stroll down Whitechapel to look at the girls. To look at them, that was about the size of it. Here he was, as smart as anyone, money in his pocket, and he still didn't know a soul outside his family. It made him feel lonely and miserable.

He was in Aldgate. He came often here of an evening when he was alone. He came because of the women in the doorways. They were all shapes and sizes, foreign mostly, and some of them were lovely. He walked slowly and one by one they leaned forward in the doorways and spoke to him.

"Fancy a short time, darling?"

"Want a bit, love?"

"Baby boy, baby boy —" This was a big blackie; so he called her, though she was the colour of milky coffee. She had wonderful teeth and flashing eyes, big feathers on her hat and a peacock-blue coat. "— you come with me, I'll eat you right up."

One stepped right out in front of him. She was fat, with dyed fair hair showing under a wide hat piled with flowers, and he saw gold teeth when she smiled. "Looking for a naughty girl, mister?"

His feet hurried until he was almost running. He turned into Commercial Street, crossed the road, and in no time was away from the crowds, in streets that were dark, dirty and deserted. It made him feel funny inside each time he walked past those women in Aldgate. Sometimes he felt he was going daft. There was no feeling like it. He went back as often as he could. But he only went to look. He hardly even dared to look. His neck always felt stiff. He stared straight in front of him. He only saw them out of the corner of his eye and he heard them whispering like pigeons to him. He never did anything more. He always hurried home, feeling breathless like he did now.

He turned into a deserted Rabbit Marsh. A few flakes still danced and vanished around him but the snow-storm was over. The air, however, had become more chill, damp and penetrating. He walked down the pavement opposite his home, as empty of thought as a young animal trotting towards warmth and shelter.

"Lovey —" It was a hoarse whisper from an entry.

He slowed down. He recognised the whisper. Usually when he heard it he hurried faster, as he always hurried away from the women in Aldgate.

"Have a cuddle. Keep the cold out." His back was still to the doorway but he had stopped. No thought, no recognisable intention or emotion had stopped him. His legs had stopped on their own and his heart was racing.

"Come on."

He turned to stare. The entry was a cave of darkness. She was a bundle in the darkness, glimmers of colour like a pile of his mother's old rags. On top of the bundle a face was painted on the darkness, as clear as a phosphorescent death's-head in a darkened fun-fair booth; a face as gaunt as a death's-head, the hollow cheeks violet with powder plastered as coarse as a topsoil, slit by a lipless mouth which grinned to show a few teeth in brown clumps askew on pale, naked gums. A broken, big straw hat, filthy, a lady's garden-party hat resurrected from some dustbin, was jammed on top of this scarecrow.

He could not move away. He could not breathe properly. His mind had stopped. He had walked away from the women. He did not know what had happened to him now but he could not walk away. She croaked, "I ain't made a copper all night. I'll take anything you give. Come on. 'Ave a 'eart."

Helpless, all his body throbbing now with fear, he took one step nearer. Dirty Aggie. He knew her. Everyone knew Dirty Aggie, the old brass for the old down-and-outs who only had a few coppers to spare. In doorways and in yards among the dustbins. The entry breathed its close night tenement smell at him and in it were mingled woman odours, sweat, dirt, he did not know what, and the cloy of cheap powder through it all, sweet as sewer stink. Ill, repelled, he swayed towards it, wanting to cry. He had run away from handsome women and something was pushing him towards the horror of Dirty Aggie.

The nightmare ended in the second that the hand came down on his shoulder, hard and cruel. It was dispelled by a new nightmare, fear riving through him as all in one second he waited for the impact — oh, he had forgotten Keogh! Here in the silent street he had walked careless and let himself be trapped — the impact of boot, fist or club. All in a second, flesh cringing —

"All right. Get on home." A hard, low voice. Not Keogh's. It was Dido. A new shock pierced him. The shocks paralysed him. "Get on home. Go on."

He took a few steps. His legs were weak. He heard Dido, "Clear out, you."

The woman's querulous croak, "You leave us alone."

Weak with relief that it was not Keogh, weak with relief that he had been saved from the woman, Chas watched, a few yards off.

"Go on or you'll get my boot."

She was out of the doorway, a shuffling bundle, a pallid violet face pocked and scarred in the lamplight. "Talk to a woman like that?"

"Woman, Bag o' worms. Muck. I don't want you here. Go on. God 'elp you if I see you here again."

She began to move off but she croaked, "'Oo are you givin' orders?"

"You know who I am. I've warned you. You take notice."

"You ain't the law."

"Ain't I? I catch you in my street again, you'll find out."

Stubborn with misery, but sidling away, she moaned, "Not a bleed'n' copper. All night on me feet. I'm freezin'. Give us a copper at least. 'Ave pity."

"Pity for you? My boot's all you'll get. I could see you burned an' sleep easy."

She went away muttering her griefs. Chas walked home and he heard Dido walking in silence behind him.

They stopped outside Number 34. While Dido reached for his key Chas waited for the onslaught about Dirty Aggie. Instead Dido eyed him and said, "Where'd you get them togs?"

"Bought 'em."

Dido stood there, as if considering. Then, "That old bag. I tried to keep you a decent boy. Find you with that old bag."

Chas kept silence. Dido's voice belaboured him. "Rotten. Didn't you know that? Everyone knows. She's rotten. Know what you're askin' for, goin' with that ol' brass?"

The words battered upon Chas's mind but they only increased his confusion. He felt more reliant upon Dido than ever, utterly grateful for having been saved from that dreadful, mystifying nightmare. At the same time he wanted to cry out that he was not a kid any more, that his life was his own. Without seeing anything clearly he felt a lump of accusation at the core of his mind, that Dido was to blame. Meanwhile he said nothing.

Dido was saying, "They're no good. I told you. Women. Not till you find the right one."

He wanted to ask how that could ever come about while he was kept away from them, but all he could murmur was, "The right one?"

Dido was studying him again. "Bought 'em, did you? What with?"

For a moment Chas did not follow. At last, "Money."

"Don't come the old acid. Where'd you get money?"

Chas was dumb; but he could never lie to Dido. At last "Where you got it."

"What are you talking about?" Dido sounded genuinely puzzled.

Chas indicated the row of shuttered shops. "Off them."

"Off the shops?"

"Same as you."

"Are you mad?"

Chas was silent. Dido said, "You been round the shop gettin' money because I got it?"

"That's right." A touch of defiance now in Chas's voice.

"What d'you reckon I get it for?"

"Lookin' after 'em."

"That's right."

Defiance asserted itself more. "Same as I do."

"You?" Dido opened his mouth wide in a derisive "Ha!"

"That's what you keep me off work for, ain' it?" Dido was peering at him, busy with thoughts. "You been at this all the time?"

"That's right."

"Since last June?"

"Since you coshed Ginger. What else you keep me off work for? We're the guv'nors in this street, ain't we?"

Dido pondered. "You reckon you're a guv'nor, do you?"

"You an' me. We showed the Murchisons off, didn't we?"

"Well," Dido said. "I'll tell you what, guv'nor. You did all this 'cause I kept you off work, you'll go back to work, Monday."

The last words took Chas completely by surprise. He echoed, "Work?"

"Monday morning. Straight back to the timber yard. An' no talkin' yourself out of it this time."

Chas managed to say, "What for?"

"Devil finds mischief. That's what for. Back to work Monday."

"'Ow will you manage?"

"Better without you under me feet. The trouble's over an' done anyway."

The memory of Keogh came back to Chas. He was still trying to steady his mind to tell Dido when Dido said, "Where's the rest of it? The money?"

Chas gave Dido three sovereigns and a handful of silver. Dido gave him back the silver and dropped the sovereigns into his own pocket. "I won't ask you how much you've spent, from now on you'll give mother your wages and get your pocket money like a respectable boy. And another thing. I want you dressed respectable tomorrow. Not like a corner boy."

"This is what they all wear —"

"Not in this house. And not tomorrow."

"What's special about tomorrow?"

"You didn't flog your Sunday suit in that shop?"

Chas was indignant, "What you take me for?"

"You'll wear your Sunday suit tomorrow. Look a gentleman."

"What for?"

Dido ignored him and went in. Chas followed into the kitchen. Mother was there, sewing under the gas. The canary was covered up. The fireplace shone black and empty. Chas said, "Bli! What's up, ma? It's freezin'."

She said, "Dido is bringing a young lady home tomorrow."

Chas could not speak. He looked from one to another of them. Dido's mouth was clamped and mother was at her sewing again as if neither of them wanted another word. He managed to breathe another "Bli!"

Dido said, "Get to bed. Up early tomorrow. You'll 'ave a good hot wash, all the way down." He turned to Mrs Peach."

"'E's goin' back to work Monday."

She turned her vague look on Chas for a moment, then said, "I'm glad of that." She peered at a stitch. When she had pulled the needle through, she faltered. "Are you thinking —?"

Dido said, "Thinkin' of what?"

Her voice became like her unfocused eyes. "I was — I don't know. Back to work? I —"

Dido said, "You can get a lad in to work the mangle instead o' Chas. 'E'll do to push the barrow as well when Shonny finds a post." He noticed Chas was still gaping. "You go to bed."

It was not till Chas was between the sheets, next to the sleeping Shonny, that among the whirl of his thoughts he again remembered Keogh and wondered if he should have told Dido about him.

"Glass of port?"

"Only a tiny drop, please." Dido poured and Grace, sitting upright with her bottom perched on the edge of the sofa, took the glass daintily. He poured for Chas and himself, and filled a thumbnail glass as a privilege for Shonny. He said, with a touch of pride, "Mother's T.T."

"Forty-three years ago I took the pledge," Mrs Peach said. "I've never regretted it." She sat on a bentwood chair by the table. She wore a shiny black dress with a bib of frills sewn on the front and a snowy white lace collar. With her hair pinned up neat and shining and her hands in her lap she looked a real lady. So did Grace in her beige costume. They looked a pair of ladies, both sitting upright. The best cloth was on the table, decorated with needlework, and there was a fine show set out, the best cups and plates, a big plate of buttered bread, three jars of jam richly shining red, green and orange, some of mother's fairy cakes smelling oven-hot, a hock of bacon, milk in a little flowered jug and sugar in a bowl, the way mother used to lay for her lady's tea when she was in service, a cake studded with candied fruits and the port which Dido had brought home. Mother had spent most of the sovereign on dainty crockery. Dido's mood had been changing all the afternoon but at the moment he felt gratified. This scene was what he wanted life to be.

"My auntie was very strict," Grace said. Her voice was as careful as if she was reading. "She brought me up very strictly."

"Your auntie brought you up?" After the first stunning shock had worn off, Mrs Peach was all anxiety for Dido. She still did not know her own feelings; except that she had not yet experienced the joy she had expected; but she was so anxious it made her want to scream. She looked at the girl all the time. She tried not to look too hard. The girl avoided her eyes but kept looking at her, and each time Mrs Peach made a little smile so as not to be caught looking.

"My auntie in the country. Sittingbourne in Kent."

"Kent is very pretty," Dido's mother said.

"Yes, it is very pretty. My auntie had a pension from the Government. Her late husband was in the post office."

"Your auntie?" The woman's eyes were grey like Dido's. They rested on Grace, vague yet speculative. "Did she bring you up?"

Grace knew what she was getting at. She looked straight back. She had nothing to be frightened of; she could deliver her credentials. "Mother's sister. She was two years older than mother. Mother and father died when I was little. They died of the typhoid. They were married at Sittingbourne though father went to work in Chatham." So there! Who did this woman think she was? Wouldn't be surprised if she wanted to see mother's marriage lines. Grace heard herself rattling on, "Auntie was very good to me. She always went to church till her rheumatism got bad. C. of E. we were. I never missed a week Sunday School."

"All the boys went to Sunday School. We are Wesleyan of course."

"I know. The vicar says there are many mansions in God's house. The vicar at our hostel. That's because we have different denominations there. The parson at Sittingbourne found me a post in London. It was him got me into the hostel. He said he wouldn't let a young lady go to London else. That was after auntie died. I looked after her till I was eighteen After I left school she was a cripple with her rheumatism. I was all pretty in the country and peaceful and we didn't know anyone. I hate people, they make me frightened, that was my happiest time, when I was a little girl with auntie. My auntie was like a mother to me."

"I'm sure she's happy with God," Mrs Peach said. "And your dear parents. You *will* see them." She sighed. "I don't think there's any happiness on earth."

"You see," Grace said, "my employers engaged me on the parson's recommendation. They only take young ladies of approved background."

Grace vaguely heard herself. She was astonished at her own assurance. She couldn't remember ever having had so much to say for herself. And she was speaking up as if she wasn't going to let anybody come between her and this chap. That was the strange thing. After all, what was she *doing* in this room? In a few weeks an extraordinary change had come over her life. She had not wished for it. She had not wished for this chap. It was all just happening to her. Yet she had been as frightened before coming here as if her life depended on it. Walking down the street with him she had felt so heartsick, so disappointed, because it really was a slum, there was no getting away from it. But here she was telling herself that appearances weren't everything, he was in business, he was his own master, and it paid to live on top of your work. Mrs Dowll the manageress had said, "Where there's muck, there's money." The room smelt of carbolic.

They had cold bacon and pickled onions for tea, and a bread pudding hot from the oven. Offering the butter dish, Mrs Peach said, "I've always given the boys real butter. I've always managed."

"I can see they've been well brought up. When Mr Peach first came to the teashop I thought to myself, he does seem a gentleman. We didn't speak to each other for ever such a long time and then only out of politeness. You can always tell when there's a good home."

The girl spoke nicely and ate daintily enough. Mrs Peach felt a certain relief. She still could not make up her mind.

Grace, too, felt easier. The mother spoke quite nicely. Dido spoke a bit roughly, but not as bad as the real Cockneys. It must be the mother's influence. Really if he tried he could make something of himself. The two boys sat and stared at her. They were ever so stiff but they looked nice boys, with those shining red, clean faces, and they were neat enough for church in their dark suits and spotless stiff collars. She rather wanted to go to the lav but there wasn't an earthly of whispering to the mother.

Mrs Peach was wondering about the same thing. She was no longer terrified that some unscrupulous harpy had got hold of her boy. She was glad she had made a good show for Dido. But what would the girl think of them if she had to go to that freezing brick shed outside that was smelly in spite of all the disinfectant they poured down it?

Dido let the women's talk go past him. Something about it vaguely disconcerted him. There was something different about his mother. Then he realised what it was. The vagueness had gone from her face. She spoke in the same weak voice as ever but she was rattling away as if she had just found out what words were for; and her eyes darted at Grace as bright and alert as those of a sparrow. Grace was talking nineteen to the dozen as well. It was queer, here were these two women who'd always seemed to him too frightened or something to say much, and now they were together they were chatting away like billyoh.

He was glad they talked. He felt detached from it. He was bored by the whole affair. After that astonishing episode in a dark doorway all the madness had suddenly gone. The girl did not interest him any more. He could have happily forgotten her. The trouble was, he was a man of his word. A chap had to be straight, to do the right thing. And there was another side to it. He had walked arm-in-arm down Rabbit Marsh with her and though there had been hardly anyone in the street he knew that the news would be all over by tomorrow: Dido Peach with a young lady. He didn't care. More, he felt like chuckling over it. He despised the people round here. Let them talk. He could hear the old hags telling each other how la-di-da she looked, a stuck-up piece, a proper lady, and pleasure swelled in him. That was what he wanted. To be respectable. To be looked up to. A respectable fellow settled down, didn't he? A man had to settle down some time.

Grace's voice came to him. "I think you've made it lovely. You'd never dream outside it was so nice inside. I mean, you've got to live where the business is, haven't you?"

"Oh, did Dido tell you about the business?" Mrs Peach was surprised that Dido had talked about the rag shop; she had thought he might be a little shamefaced about it. She knew how proud he was. But she saw now that he must have been telling Grace of his mother's struggles and achievements in bringing up her boys. "I don't mind telling you it's been very hard work."

"I can imagine," Grace said. "Still, now that Mr Peach has employees to do the work —."

Dido came awake at these words. Having lied to Grace

out of pride, he had been too proud to warn his mother. The two boys were gaping. He cut in, "We don't make a bad thing out of it. Do we, mother?"

He looked a warning at Mrs Peach. She said, "Oh, no. My boy looks after me wonderfully."

"I can see that," Grace said. "You have the best of every thing here. It doesn't matter what the street's like, does it, if you have a good home."

Dido spoke curtly, still looking at his mother. "We live where our trade is. The people round here are nothing to us. Scum."

Mrs Peach said, "I've never let the boys have anything to do with them."

"I should think not," Grace said. "It's bad enough having to live here."

Dido stood up. "Go for a little walk, eh? Before I see you back."

Grace said, "Oh, I must help wash up."

Mrs Peach said, "Don't you worry, my dear. I've nothing else to do."

"Oh, please. Where's the scullery?"

Shonny blurted, "Scullery —?"

Angry eyes, his mother's and Dido's, cut him short; and Chas nudged him under the table.

"At least I can carry the plates out for you. It's less bother once they're in the sink."

Mrs Peach was still brooding upon "It's bad enough having to live here." If the girl found out that there was not even a sink in the house.

"Mother frets when she's idle," Dido said. "She'll potter about all evening. Best thing, leave her get on with it"

Grace did not resist; she was dying to get to a lavatory; and with a prolonged exchange of farewells, the ceremony ended. The ordeal was over for all of them. Mrs Peach was glad to be left alone in the kitchen. The boys were glad to escape upstairs to their bedroom, where since their reaction to the new turn in their lives had not yet gone beyond simple wonderment, they talked about

Chas's adventures of the previous day.

Dido and Grace walked for an hour, arm-in-arm, up East Road to Islington, and down from the Angel to the hostel door. Dido uttered only a few commonplaces, and Grace spoke even less, mainly because her bladder was full to agony.

On the hostel steps she hastily agreed to his appointment for tomorrow; then waited. Seeing her upturned face, Dido realised that he was now accorded the right to kiss her. He dabbed a kiss on her cheek and she ran in.

He walked away with sinking heart. He was in for it now. There was still a faint hope that it might peter out somehow; but he could not see that it was likely now that the women had got together. He was in the cart all right. Then the thought of the women together called up a picture that changed his mood. He saw again the two women sitting upright and dressed like ladies, on each side of a splendidly laden table with a snowy cloth. Wasn't that what he wanted life to be?

Chapter 13

They were married four weeks later, in mid-March.

It came upon them as unexpectedly as a railway accident. Once more they obeyed fatality.

After the rape in the doorway, Grace had already missed her first period when Dido took her home to meet his mother. She had been late before and she knew that it was possible to miss a period in cold weather. She tried not to think about it. But there was a core of fear inside her all the time as impossible to ignore as a pain, and it was perhaps this unacknowledged but growing desperation that emboldened her to claim with such spirit in Mrs Peach's kitchen her status as Dido's young lady.

By the end of February she was so demented with fright that she was able to blurt out the news to Dido. She was neither ignorant nor innocent about life. She lived in a world of young women. They were all poor and over-worked. Some were led into sexual adventure by the hunger for a little fun. Some even found it a way to augment their pitiful wages. Grace in her distant way remained on friendly terms with everyone. In the teashop and at the hostel she and the other respectable girls tut-tutted among themselves and would not become too intimate with the fast ones but listened eagerly to their tales. She knew about their good times. She also knew about abortion and disease. Behind her prim face she was not easily shocked.

She knew enough after missing her first period to buy camomile tea and brew it in the hostel kitchen. It was a furtive business for she dreaded being found out by the other girls; the respectable ones always showed a certain vindictive relish when one of their number fell. The camomile tea did not work; nor did the pennyroyal pills which she nerved herself to buy at the chemist's when she missed her second period. She did not even consider an abortion. She had heard of girls dying after they had been to those horrible old women and she knew some who had never been the same again. In any case only one course leapt to her mind. She would have married the devil to stay respectable. The man had made a promise to her. When she told him her news — incoherently, for she was frightened of him — she had his promise in mind though she did not dare to remind him of it. She did not have to. After some moments of silence Dido said, "I told you I'd wed you, didn't I?"

From now on she was as passive as a match in the current of a river. Her courage was spent in the effort of telling him. Dido, as cold and curt as he had been to her ever since the rape, made a rapid decision. There was no time to lose if they wanted to pass the baby off as legitimate but premature. He went to the chapel and fixed the date.

He had a series of disagreeable tasks to perform. The first was to break the news to his mother. Ever since his father's death Dido had felt himself master in the house and had spoken to her with a quiet authority that permitted no questions. Now he discovered that he was as timid as a little boy. He dreaded the look in her eyes when she knew what he had done.

One day when they were alone in the kitchen he told her, gruffly and briefly, when the marriage was to be. He gave no reason.

He was sitting at the table. She was stooped over the dirty-water bowl, washing up, her back to him. She did not speak or turn round but continued to rinse a plate. Finally she said, "Where will you live?"

"Here."

She scrubbed at the rim of a saucepan. "When is she expecting?"

"October."

She kept her back to him. He knew just what she was thinking. Grace had made a good impression. Now it was all gone. He knew the blow his words had been. Most other women regarded what had happened as a natural part of courtship. It was the way many a marriage date was decided, and people made good-humoured jokes about it. Not so his mother. She would blame him for having acted the beast like his father. The thought of it upset him. Or else she would choke with bitterness against the girl who for all her good manners and demure face had lured a good boy to behave like an animal; had trapped him, taken him from his mother. He said, "It was my fault."

She did not answer. He repeated, "It was my fault."

She said, "It takes two."

He felt pity for the poor girl. He wanted to defend her but he could not bring himself to confess what had happened. He said, "Wedding's on a Monday."

"That's a mercy," she said. There were less people in the street on a working day.

"All the girls'd be comin' otherwise. Girls from 'er hostel."

"There'll be others to talk."

"Talk!" His voice was contemptuous. "Let them talk."

He stood up and took his cap. He nerved himself once more. "Mother — it's not her fault. Give the girl a chance."

Her mouth stayed tight. All her attention was on the pan as she held it to her chest, burnishing it fiercely, while he went out.

Dido was a man with decent feelings but he had to crush them to perform his second task. He needed a room for himself and his wife. He would have to take one of the two rooms on the top floor. To do so he would have to turn out either the Irish labourer and his family or the Valentines. It was hard to choose between the two because although the Irishman was a rough his family was in a pitiful state. However, the front rooms in the house were larger than the back rooms. Dido was determined to have the front room, and this was occupied by the Valentines.

They were broken creatures, old and ailing. They had found a refuge here and if they were ejected from it, there was no knowing what a pit of misery they might fall into. Dido was ruthless to the strong but he had never bullied the weak. He had scarcely noticed the Valentines in the past but when they had come to his attention he had felt a vague pity for them as he did for all those who were too weak to fight.

Well, they were in his way now. He had to have the room. His wife must have the best he could provide. He went upstairs raging with misery and he turned the rage against the old couple. A man must look after his own, he told himself. He was sorry for the old couple but it only showed that the weak went under. He'd given all his strength since he was a boy to look after his family and if he had been weak they would all have gone under. He couldn't spare any pity. No one had ever pitied Dido's mother. No one had ever pitied Dido. He had to go on and not look down to see who was under his feet. And now his burden was to be increased. First a wife, then a child. Damn that old couple. He wasn't a charity. He couldn't worry about their troubles or anyone else's. Life was one long, dirty trick. He only wanted to live quietly with his wife and it had brought him to this rotten job. It did not occur to Dido that he might live elsewhere than in his mother's house.

He showed a grim face to the Valentines and told them at once, curtly, that they must get out within a week. He needed the remaining time to redecorate the room. They did not say a word. All their questions were in their terrified eyes. Where were they to go? Where were they to find another room at half a crown a week unless it was some wet verminous den that would kill them both? What was to become of them?

He faced their pleading eyes and said, "I'm sorry. I'll tell the collector."

The rent collector called every Friday. He came from "the office". No one in the street knew whose office it was.

Dido put five pounds on the table. It was all the money he had, and he told himself it would make them better off than they had been for years.

They trudged off at the end of the week, pushing a hired barrow piled with their sticks and parcels. Mrs Peach hovered in the hall as they went past and followed them as far as the doorstep. She looked stunned. Dido had done no more than tell her that they were going and when she had gone upstairs to them they had only looked at each other and murmured fragmentary and unfinished sentences that conveyed nothing. Suspicions which she could not believe moved in her mind. She gave Mrs Valentine a large parcel into which she had put food and some warm clothing; and received in return a pallid smile and mutter of thanks. She called goodbye to them when they moved off. They looked round, Mr Valentine raised his old-fashioned square bowler hat and they trudged away behind the barrow with heads bent.

Dido had gone out that morning. He would not let Mrs Peach lend them the family barrow and he would not let Shonny help them to their new abode; for he did not want to know where they were going.

His third task was easier to face but in some ways rankled even more deeply. He needed money, all the more since he had emptied his pocket for the Valentines.

So far he had not asked the shopkeepers for tribute. He had merely accepted it. His wants were modest, and the half-sovereigns, the gifts in kind offered by the tradesmen had sufficed. The discovery of Chas's petty exactions had angered him. They had been a stain on the family's pride.

Now he himself had to inflict a greater blow on his pride. He had to ask, and since he proposed to tell the street nothing about his forthcoming marriage, to ask without apparent reason.

He reckoned that it would take all of twenty-five pounds to furnish the bedroom. It was more than he had ever had in one sum. He had no strong feeling for the girl yet he was determined — it was like a brazier in his breast — to give her better than she dreamed of. On that first Sunday when he had walked her down the street he had not been insensitive to her thoughts nor careless of them. He knew that she had been bitterly disillusioned. She asked him nothing about his supposed business as a rag merchant but she must be wondering how much of his boasting had been true. He felt her expectations keenly. To be found out by her would be a cruel humiliation. Besides, he felt responsible to her. He could not help seeing that she was his victim. Her situation was all his doing.

He would not take her to a room furnished with second-hand sticks. Theirs would be a room such as Rabbit Marsh had never seen. He had looked out a bright new wallpaper and best quality lino. He had his eye on a bit of nice carpet to go by the bed, a mahogany suite of dressing-table with three swivel mirrors (he would buy all the slap-up brushes and whatnots to go on it), chest of drawers and double wash-stand. He would get the best chinaware, a couple of comfortable armchairs, the finest brass bedstead he could buy, as well as a brass fender and irons for the fireplace, a new wall mirror and ornaments for the mantelpiece, and Grace could pick out pretty curtains and bed covers and all the rest, and he would buy her a new outfit of clothes, money be hanged. He wanted to console her for what had happened to her. Yes, he wanted her to be happy. He also wanted to so surround her with comforts that she would never quite realise what lies he had told her. He needed the respect of people and most of all the respect of his wife.

To satisfy these new needs he began to levy taxes. Each subject paid as Dido judged his means. When a shopkeeper protested that it was taking the bread from his mouth, Dido showed him a threatening face. It was enough for Dido to look at them. They paid.

He kept away these days from Barsky's shop. He had not asked the man in the past and he could not do so now. There were in fact only half a dozen shopkeepers in the street who could afford half a sovereign and Dido spared the others since he could not bring himself to accept less. He always felt that Barsky's black-button eyes could see through him; and he was afraid that if he went in the wife would come with a basin of eggs for his mother. He knew that he would take them, and say, "Thank you," and not be able to say a word more. He did not go in.

As for his regulars, he had devised a formula that inflicted the least hurt on his pride. When the customary half-sovereign was put down on the counter, he said, both parties recognising the fiction, "Make it a pair. I'll give you a hand in the shop."

He was faintly surprised by his own weakness in offering this excuse. Of course he did not make good his word. On the contrary he never stayed on the neighbours' premises even for a chat these days. He was embarrassed by the demands he made upon them and wanted to see as little of them as possible. Also he did not want any news of his coming marriage to reach them and to further insure against this he made all his family shun the neighbours even more than usual.

One day he went in to Blakers' shop. Ever since Dido had refused to be Blakers' threatener, the tobacconist had shown his coolness by paying Dido his half-sovereign and going about his business in silence. This time he greeted Dido with a "Mornin'," and after a moment's pause added, "Quite the toff these days, I see."

Dido answered with a questioning grunt. Blakers said, "Nice young lady I see you with. Takin' 'er 'ome, are you?"

Dido said, "I mind my own business."

"Do you?" Blakers was a head taller than Dido. The habitual lack of expression in his pudding face and the deliberateness of his speech gave him a certain air of power. He tossed a half-sovereign on the counter. "This what you call mindin' your own business?"

Dido did not offer the customary excuse. He said, "I'll have another o' them."

"Will you now? What for?"

Dido looked straight at him, grinning slightly. "Token of your esteem."

"Ah!" Blakers pursed his lips at the sight of Dido's eyes deadly above the grin. "You know, I'm not so green as I'm cabbage-lookin'."

"Dare say."

"One good turn deserves another, I say. I used to do Ginger a good turn, 'e used to do me one."

"Dare say he did."

"I'd look after you well if you did."

"I can look after meself."

Blakers hesitated. He was a man who weighed the odds carefully before making enemies. He put down another half-sovereign. Dido pocketed it and turned away in silence. Blakers said, "You wanna go easy."

Dido paused and looked round interrogatively. Blakers said, "Pride goes before a fall, you know. You're not the only chap in these parts as can 'andle 'imself. I'm tellin' you." He saw the compression of Dido's lips and he added, "As a friend, mind you. Only as a friend."

There had been a good deal of speculation in the street about Dido's young lady but the departure of the whole family in a carriage one Monday afternoon, all in their best clothes, settled the matter. The knots of chattering women on the pavements all agreed that it could only be a wedding.

The carriage vanished from the street and Rabbit Marsh for the time being knew no more, for the chapel was a far-off and unknown place.

Fifteen people sat down to tea, strictly temperance, in the chapel hall after the wedding ceremony. The minister and his wife were there. Ada and her family had come by train. Mrs Dowll, the teashop manageress, had taken the afternoon off to bring an electroplate cakestand that the girls had collected for. The hostel girls had also subscribed, for a pair of hand-painted vases. The gift was brought by the hostel matron, who always liked to see her girls off.

Mrs Peach had given the young couple her treasured best tablecloth and two sets of bed-linen. Shonny and Chas had bought a clock with Westminster chimes. Ada had demonstrated her goodwill and her prosperity with a canteen of cutlery.

The minister made a short speech and the rest of the meal passed in a muted, uncomfortable chatter. In spite of her gift Ada looked on the hasty marriage as a disgrace to the family and the girl as its cause. Mrs Peach sat looking at her lap and wondering if the child was really Dido's. Such girls were capable of anything.

Soon after four, Dido and Grace set off in a cab for London Bridge Station. They were going to spend two days at Brighton. Grace, to Dido's astonishment, had awakened from her sleepwalking passivity a week before the wedding to demand this. She had done so because she had boasted of a honeymoon to the girls and because she could not bear to go straight to that awful slum house.

Dido was glad to give way. He wanted to please her; and he, too, wanted to defer the ordeal of coming home with her to Rabbit Marsh.

Before they got into the cab, Mrs Peach kissed her son and then did her duty by quickly pecking the bride's cheek.

The landlady had lit a fire. Their room was small. They had taken lodgings in a cottage near Brighton Station. Between the bed and the fireplace there was not much room, and they had to exercise great care in moving from place to place while they prepared for bed, so as not to bump into each other or look at each other. In fact anyone seeing them making their moves, waiting for the right moment, frowning to themselves as if each of them was deep in private thoughts, might have thought they were playing some comic game of chess with their bodies as pieces.

Dido held himself close to the fire, warming his front, hands outstretched. He always slept in his underclothes and he was dressed from neck to ankle in two tight, thick woollen garments. Behind him, he heard her get into bed. Now he could do the same.

She was sitting up. She wore a flannelette nightdress with long sleeves, some embroidery on it, and frills standing up at the neck and wrists. She had let her hair down and Dido was surprised how long it was. He turned down the gas. She looked pretty in the firelight. He felt for the first time a stir of tenderness for her, and a faint pride of possession.

If at this moment she had only smiled at him, the whole nature of the man might have been changed like magic; or some part of his nature hitherto denied and buried might have begun to free itself. But she went on braiding her hair, gazing placidly in front of her, at nothing. She was no frightened, shrinking bride. She was a practical girl and she knew what to expect from marriage. She waited as she might wait for a bus.

She lay back and lifted the honeycomb quilt for him. He climbed into bed. He stayed sitting up, frowning down at her. She lay and looked up at him with empty, tranquil eyes.

Seconds passed. Dido felt the time crawling on his skin and the perplexity growing in his head.

She had only to part her lips in the faintest smile, or even to reach up and lay a hand on his shoulder, and he might have grinned in response, leaned down to touch her hair back from her forehead, or said a friendly word; and it would all have turned out differently.

But all she saw was a man looking down at her with a sombre frown which puzzled her. She wondered what was bothering him and, afraid to do the wrong thing even by a gleam of expression, she waited impassively.

And as he felt the seconds taunting him he nerved himself for the only answer he knew to a taunt. He flung back the covers and with a suddenness that knocked the breath out of her was upon her.

She had been ready for him; but not for this attack. Her wits were scattered. In reflex, a scared animal, she arched herself hard in resistance. The flexed resistance of a body, thrusting back against him in the room's heat, touched off all the sensuality in Dido that had been disciplined since boyhood and disappointed by that brief rape on a freezing night. A heat indistinguishable from anger possessed him. The more closely he felt the softness and hard springiness of a pliant female body wrestling his own, the more he was mastered by the will to take what was his.

The nightgown was long and clinging, and demented by his clumsy failure to pull it up he seized the neck and tugged with both hands until it ripped. For the first time in the firelight he saw a woman naked and he fell upon her insensate, pulling and writhing at his own garments until he had thrown them away and he, too, was naked. The heat and soft slither of skin upon skin was a torment and a pleasure beyond all his imagining. He was mindless and his emotions were without name so that even now one whisper or bodily flicker of response might have slowed him to tenderness, changed him, changed her, altered their future.

After all, she had not come averse to the notion of pleasure. She had heard from different women accounts both delightful and awful. She had been prepared to discover that there was "something in it". It was the remoteness of this body fighting upon her, the anger in the clenched face, his impersonality, not his roughness that daunted her. She could feel only that she was something used, and she responded no more than something used.

He rested and in a neutral voice he told her that he had ordered hot water for eight in the morning. As neutrally she said that it was the right time for her, too. Then he was at her again; and later, again, till he had used up his strength.

In between they held their quiet, calm conversations, like an old married couple. She was not the sort to weep, broken, on her pillow. The roughness inside her was expected and easily borne. Rather as if she had to endure the buffetings of an energetic child, she lay in his grasp busy with thoughts that were far away from him.

She thought about her mother-in-law. She had visited the house twice in the fortnight before the marriage. She and Mrs Peach had kept up a brisk, pleasant chatter, but each was aware of secret thoughts behind the other's placid face.

She thought about the house. She had no idea whether he was a rag merchant in a large way or a small; and she understood about living where the business was. But surely he could afford something better than what she had seen, those bare wooden stairs all rotten in places, not a sink in the house, only a tap outside in the smelly yard. One nasty outside lavatory, and worst of all, that dreadful Irish family upstairs to share it with.

She was bewildered, between two moods. Whenever she thought of the house she felt a slump of wretchedness. She was with child and she was trapped in this place. Yet whenever she saw the room that Dido was preparing, the nice paper and lino, the fresh paint, the beautiful shining pieces of furniture as they were brought in, she felt a real lady. She felt such a lady when she went round the shops buying the new clothes Dido had given her and watching him pay out in gold sovereigns. He had the money all right. He must be in a substantial way and this thought made her feel that for the first time in her life she, too, was someone of substance. It was only natural for a bachelor not to care how he lived. A frumpy old mother wouldn't know any different either. It needed a wife to teach him how to live according to his station.

And then again, the pleasant mood died and she felt sick at the stomach remembering that time she had gone up to their room and on the landing outside had seen a horrible bucket, which the Irish people used so as not to have to go all the way downstairs to the lavatory. Again and again the smell of stale urine rose in her memory to revolt her, and she remembered how she had gone into the bedroom and there alone as she listened to the Irish couple trampling and shouting in the next room she had cried. It was the only time she had cried since all this business started and she had soon dried her eyes.

Afterwards she had plucked up courage to say very casually to Dido that it would be nice if they found a place of their own. He peered at her incredulously. He said, "Don't be silly. Can't leave the business. Can't leave mother. Isn't the room nice enough? You say so, I'll chuck everything out, start again."

She said, "No, it's lovely," and then she managed to tell him about the bucket.

He said, "Oh, I'll stop that. Promise you that."

There was something hard and intense about him that made her believe him. But the smell of the bucket would not leave her memory. She would still have to live in that house next to that drunken couple. And with that mother-in-law.

Thank goodness, he was asleep at last, turned on his side away from her. What couldn't be cured had to be endured and made the best of. At least she was married, and to not a bad fellow. That was something a girl should be thankful for. Her nightgown was ruined. Heaven only knew where it had got to. Marriage was all very well but who ever heard of people in bed without a stitch of clothes on? The fireplace was black and dead and the room was getting cold. She pulled the covers up to her chin and drifted towards sleep, wondering meanwhile how much a yard of flannelette cost down here and whether she could pick up any other bargains for the house.

Chapter 14

They came home on Wednesday evening. Dido treated Grace to a cab from the station, a last luxury before the hard truth of daily life was broken to her.

It was dusk, the lamps already glimmering, when they came down the street, and it was not till the cabbie slowed his horse that Grace saw the man outside Number 34.

He was huge. In a shapeless jacket and baggy, concertinaed trousers of grey, he appeared in the twilight like a two-legged elephant on the pavement. He was banging continuously at the knocker, and he paused only to sway back, stare upward and shout.

Dido knocked on the ceiling and the cab stopped some yards from the house. Grace peered out of the window and, looking up, saw a curtain in a first-floor window lifted slightly, and Mrs Peach's face, with Chas visible behind her.

Dido put a hand on her arm and said, "You stay here."

He opened the door and stepped down. She could hear the big man shouting now. "Fuckin' Peach! Fuckin' Dido Peach! Come out an' fight, Dido Peach! I'll fuckin' kill yer!" He was swaying all the time. The crumpled trousers made his legs seem as if they were giving way under the weight of his massive body. His uplifted face was twisted and red with rage. His heavy square head wore a mat of cropped grey hair.

Dido said something quietly. The man turned and saw him. He came lumbering towards Dido. His weight thumped down on one step after another, as if each was an effort. Grace had come home in a mood of slumbrous calm. Suddenly the sight of the man had awakened her to a cold fright. Now he seemed all the more frightening, like a figure in a dream, some giant raised from the dead to lurch and sway along by a magic that might let him fall at any second. His arms were out wide like those of a baby trying to balance and as he came closer to Dido, shouting obscenities in words that became more and more slurred, he raised a great bunched fist in threat. By the sound of his voice and the way he swayed, he must be very drunk.

She sat in the cab frozen. A lump choked in her throat. Dido stood there silent, hands down at his sides. The giant took step after step towards him; then paused; stood there rumbling in fury, the words now a bass gabble that ran together unintelligibly; and suddenly pitched forward. He fell all in a length, like a tree, and the awful thump was another sickening blow in Grace's stomach.

She hardly knew what happened after that. There was a crowd, all chattering. There was Dido helping her down, and Chas taking the bags, and Mrs Peach helping her into the kitchen. She was sitting on the edge of the sofa, her teeth chattering as she tried to sip hot tea. Dido was saying, "It's all right. All right. Only some ol' boozer."

But later when she came down from her bedroom she paused outside the kitchen door and caught snatches of their talk. She heard Chas say, "Ginger —" and, in Dido's deeper voice, the word, "dying —" All her acceptant calm had vanished. She was terrified by her homecoming. She had a chill dread that things were being kept from her. She suppressed her fright and went in to join the family for supper, but she had no stomach to eat.

Ginger Murchison had sat at home for six months, just able to dress himself, waddle about the courtyard of Jaggs Place and sometimes appear for a little while in the street. He had lived in an intermittent fog of forgetfulness. His family did not keep him from the drink, and he was little trouble to them.

But always the name of Dido Peach throbbed in his

injured brain. He sat for hours muttering vengeance to himself, seized sometimes by fits of rage that empurpled him and brought on fearful headaches. The vague muddle of his thoughts was sometimes interrupted by a sharp reminder from Harry that he was no longer the guv'nor; more lately from Keogh; or he was made aware of his own downfall by the jeering of children. He brooded on the time when he was held in awe. His anger against those who taunted him fused into anger against Dido. He slumped in his chair drinking, deep in fantasies of strength and power regained, and the starting-point of all these dreams was a triumphant public annihilation of Dido.

For some reason he did not understand Harry shut him up every time he mumbled threats against Dido. Harry would not even let him totter towards the corner of Rabbit Marsh. Now Harry was in jail. Keogh was the guv'nor but he let the old man roam about without check. One evening Ginger heaved himself out of his kitchen chair, managed to walk the few hundred yards to the house of his enemy; and there, in the grip of a climactic anger, suffered a brain haemorrhage. He lay for two weeks in a death coma.

Grace had been brought up as one of the genteel poor who lived in frugal neatness and to whom the slums were what hell had been to their ancestors: a pit of horror all the more feared because anyone might fall into it. Now she lived in a slum.

On her first night she heard the Irishman's family in the next room; children crying, a man cursing, breaking of wind. For one night that dreadful bucket was on the landing. After that Dido spoke to the Irishman and Grace did not see the bucket any more. But she heard them using it in their room at nights, and Dido did not seem to think anything of it.

She had to wash in her bedroom and carry the dirty water down to the yard. She had to go outside in all weathers if she wanted to use the lavatory. It was dark. It had a massive box seat built from wall to wall. Dido kept scrubbing it white but after the Irish had been there it was filthy with muck round the edges or there were puddles on the floor, and the smell was awful. Dido was ready enough when she asked him to go out and see if it was clean but his rag business seemed to keep him away from home a lot, and what was she to do when he was out?

She did not like to go out. The street was always crowded and noisy. Dido told her that she was not to lower herself by talking to any of the people and she was only too glad to obey. There were drunks at all hours outside the pubs. It would have been nice to go, even on her own, for a bus ride to look at the smart shops in the West End or the flower beds in a park; but she was not prepared to run the gauntlet of these dirty, frightening streets. For the time being she was content to stay indoors.

She was quickly relieved to find that her mother-in-law gave no trouble. They did not fall into each other's arms; but there was no bad feeling. Grace just could not think of much to say and she could see that the same was true of Mrs Peach.

When she came down the first morning she wanted to help in the kitchen, but Mrs Peach said, quite nicely, "You rest your feet, my dear. There's no room for two in one kitchen." And since Dido did not want Grace to go out in the locality, Mrs Peach did all the shopping.

After the teashop Grace was only too happy to rest her feet. It was lovely to be idle like a lady. It was easiest to let her mother-in-law get on with it if she was so keen on it, and keep out of the way. She would not talk to Dido again about moving, not for a while. She had decided that in married life one needed tact. It was best to learn to get on with him and show appreciation of all he did for her. Later, when they were more man and wife, would be the time to open his eyes to things.

Meanwhile she fell into the habit of passing her days in her bedroom. She was no sloven. She made the bed and saw that the room was spotless. It was a pleasure to stay in it then, with lovely furniture around her, lying on the pretty blue quilt and admiring the curtains she had chosen. At least she had something to get on with. She bought dozens of twopenny romances and read them all day long. A pleasant fire crackled in the grate and she could have imagined herself a lady in her boudoir if it had not been for the noise of trains going past every few minutes, goods trains that rattled slowly on and on as if for ever, and the noise of great horse-drawn carts, the carters' shouts and the crack of whips, the shrieking of children, the voices of women yelling from window to window; and the air full of smuts that made all her nice room dirty. But Grace got used to it.

Vaguely, in fleeting glimpses of a lost and distant childhood, the neat room at auntie's was a princess's little bower. Illusory memory made even the hostel seem a pleasant and superior place. Most people, however, are not crushed by worsening circumstances. They become used to them. The new life is the normal. This is what happened quite rapidly to Grace.

She never expected much from life. As much as to any other of the poor the future had always been a darkness to be feared. Only pleasant things were to be thought of, and warm visions dreamed, the kind of visions supplied by her twopenny romances. Since she was, however, a practical girl, she did not let the visions intrude too much. On her level of life the one unalterable dream, the one haven for which everyone prayed, was to have and keep "a good place". This marriage was to Grace "a good place". And if it was in the kind of surroundings she had always dreaded, she consoled herself with the standard formulas of the unfortunate. "It could be worse." "Might as well make the best of it."

So she adapted; and so, rapidly, became outwardly and with no awareness of change, a different person from the prim, scared, hardworking hostel girl. She became adept at making the best of it. She could stay in bed till nine o'clock. Dido seemed to be pleased rather than put out when she did so. Once she let herself do it, she realised what a blissful, positively aching luxury it was. She could read her books to her heart's content. She bought boxes of lovely soft-centre chocolates, for Dido left her plenty of money. One had to be sociable, so sometimes she went downstairs, made a pot of tea and exchanged a few words with Mrs Peach. She even began to eat more and Dido said her face was filling out. All the ill-effects of her pregnancy had gone. She had never felt better than now.

She was also quite used to Dido at nights. Not that there was anything wonderful about it, the way some of the girls had said. But Dido was quieter now. She felt rather nice holding this man like a big baby while he did it. He was so hard and frightening by day and during those interludes in bed she felt that it was her turn to have the upper hand; for he was never again mad and fierce like on that first night — he was quick and quiet and never said a word, and soon turned over with his back to her and fell asleep.

This was a terrible place to live in if she stopped to think of it. But it never did to think too much. She could be a lot worse off. And after all, she *was* a married woman.

Dido was also contented with life. He looked back on that frenzy of his wedding night with no deep scrutiny but all the same he felt a certain mild puzzlement. Pulling all his clothes off like that! What a way for a man to behave!

He would never think of doing it again, yet half-consciously he savoured the memory of skin upon skin. Those moments were the only time in his life since he was a babe in arms when he had achieved something of which he was starved and for which his unsuspected self craved — closeness to another human being. Not that he was aware of this. The contact had been only half-achieved.

Each time as he spent himself there had been a sag of bitterness in him, as he acknowledged once more that "there was nothing in it."

Yet there was pleasure in having her next to him in bed every night. He did not want her all that often now, but she settled comfortably up against him when he did, and she put her arms round him. He slept well afterwards; and he had a satisfied feeling as if here was something he securely owned.

They never spoke at these times. But then, they didn't speak much during the daytime. He didn't want her asking questions about his life. It was not a secret, but the more she got used to him, the more naturally she would accept things as she found them out. They had quite nice chats about things to buy for their room.

She was bored at home all day. He asked mother how she got on with Grace and she said, "All right." He asked Grace how she got on with mother and she answered, "All right." He did not know what women got up to. They must pass the time somehow, but Grace never went out. She could not very well hobnob with the other women on the pavement or in the shops and she said she was frightened to walk up to the main road where the buses ran. He could understand a sensitive girl like her being frightened.

He made it up to her by taking her out in the evenings and he, too, found these evenings enjoyable. He had never enjoyed company like this before. They went to music-halls and picture palaces, for walks in the City, bus rides; and they looked forward to the warmer weather when they could enjoy some fresh air in the parks. He did not mind going up the street with her on his arm; on the contrary it stung him with pride at the fine clothes he had bought her, and with contempt for the people on the doorsteps who would start jabbering as soon as he had gone past. Grace was more than ever an assurance that he was not their sort.

The traders were paying up like lambs these days — those with the money. Well, they could afford it. Thanks to him they had never lived so peaceful and quiet. Perhaps they thought they owed him nothing just because things were always quiet now. That was silly. As soon say there was no need for the army because it was not fighting, or that the police should not be paid because the streets were quiet. Those shopkeepers would soon find someone robbing and squeezing them if he wasn't here.

There was no doubt life was treating him better. He had never had this easy enjoying feeling before. A man certainly needed a wife. He gave Grace credit for her part and he sometimes wanted to say nice things to her. In bed sometimes he only wanted to pat her on the shoulder and say, "You're a good girl." It was strange, he could not get himself to say anything of this sort. A man could not be expected to talk sloppy. He could not think of a set of words that would say what he felt without sounding sloppy. During their evening out they could walk for quite a while without talking but not feeling embarrassed. They both had their own thoughts. She seemed to have no curiosity at all about what he did during the day. He was grateful for that, too. He showed his gratitude by encouraging her to go out. She could not stay indoors all the time. It was like being in prison. She admitted so herself.

He gave her a couple of sovereigns and told her to go for a ride up West and buy something. That gave her the courage. She went out and bought a hat and a lot of ribbons and some material to make a dress at home. She showed him these things and it gave them something to talk about in a nice and friendly way.

After that she went out on her own more often and he gave her more money to spend. It was better than words.

The daytime when he was on his own was difficult to pass. There were no more sociable spells with the neighbours. He could not go and sit in the teashop any more. He took to riding out with Tommy Long, the rag-and-bone man. Usually Dido took the reins and left Tommy to his street cries and his chaffering for wares. Dido loved the sturdy pony, and his pleasure was to turn into a long, broad street and set the alert beast to a trot so brisk that Tommy complained he had no chance to do business. "What do you think this is?" Tommy said as they rattled home one evening, "A bleed'n' Roman chariot?"

Dido slowed down as they approached Rabbit Marsh. Soon the pony was stabled and rubbed down. Tommy said, "Goin' up the brick?"

"My place to."

"Come with yer."

"No. Go on my own."

Dido walked away; down the street, past his own house and across the road to "The Railway".

As he drew near he heard a caterwauling female voice sing the chorus of "Lily of Laguna", accompanied by an out-of-tune piano. Other voices joined in discordantly and over them all sounded the piano, a din as if the player crashed bunches of knuckles into the approximate neighbourhood of the notes he wanted.

The tune ended as Dido pushed the door open. The clamour of applause and talk died to a hush. Everyone looked at him.

At the far end of the room a table stood in front of the partition. Behind this sat Meek, the publican. He was dressed in his best suit. On the table in front of him was a plate full of silver and copper coins.

Chairs were set in front of the bar to one side, all occupied by men in their best and women in draggled finery. Facing them, on the benches against the wall, sat the Murchisons: all who were old enough to be admitted and were not in jail. This was the brick — the traditional collection and tribute to the dead.

Dido walked steadily between the two subdued rows. As the greatest enemy of the deceased, it was his duty to make the largest contribution. Dido did not look to right or left, but he saw a man start from his seat as he went by. It was Keogh. He heard the mutter of anger and glimpsed two other men holding Keogh back by the shoulders.

He stopped in front of the chairman's table. He said, "'Evenin', Sam."

"'Evenin', Dido."

Dido put a sovereign in the plate. He turned, and at that moment Keogh pulled free from the restraining hands, stood up, shivered the base of a bottle against the wall and stood in Dido's path, the jagged end of the bottle towards him.

From all parts of the room came reproachful murmurs. "Respec'."

"Respec'."

Dido walked towards the door.

"Respec'."

"Sit down."

"Respec' the dead."

Men moved forward and seized Keogh by both arms. He strained, glaring with rage, but he made no sound. Dido walked past without looking at him.

Keogh did not turn his head to look after Dido. He sighed and went slack, and let himself be disarmed. He sat down again even before the door had closed behind Dido.

A crowd gathered in Brick Lane to see Ginger Murchison off. There were three carriages and a hearse drawn by two glossy black horses with huge black plumes, paid for by the brick.

Two men stood apart from the crowd, on a corner near Jaggs Place. They were Mr Merry and Weldon. They were talking and laughing to each other, and they did not stop when the hearse went past; but they both took off their hats.

Chapter 15

At the beginning of May Shonny started in his new post. The minister had got him into a surveyor's office in Bishopsgate. Mrs Peach had taken Shonny for the interview. She had been awed by the stiff gentleman who sat behind the table but exalted by the fact that this great personage had approved of her neat, shining and respectful boy.

Shonny felt very frightened on the morning that he set out to begin a new life. It had its consolations, though. There were three other boys in the office. They were all bigger than him though none of them looked much older. At first their unfriendly stares had intimidated him but the one who showed him in for the interview had winked at him. Perhaps he would have fun with them like in the boys' books he read. They were all smart-looking fellows and he saw himself strolling round the City with them, publicly smoking Woodbines. Then the gentleman had explained that part of his job would be to carry documents to and from other offices. This, too, was a relief, even a promise of excitements. He would still have the freedom of the streets. And he would from now on really be a man; for he would bring home five shillings a week.

He set off just as his mother had imagined him. He wore a dark-grey gent's suit, stiff collar and straight black tie, bowler hat and polished new boots; and he carried his sandwiches in a tiny fibre attache-case. The suit made him feel especially grand and grown-up; for, an incredible experience, he had gone to a tailor's with Dido and been measured for it.

His mother stooped to kiss him. Her eyes were wet and her voice broke as she murmured, "Be a good boy."

Grace gave him a kiss and said, "You look a real gentleman."

Chas was already at work; but he had slipped a packet of five fags into Shonny's new jacket before he left; and now Dido looked down at him, with a stern smile. "You be a credit to mother," Dido said. "I want you to get on. Here —" Dido gave him a half-crown. "Money in your pocket you're beholden to nobody."

Shonny walked away down the sunny street like a little man, feeling frightened and proud.

Later, when Dido had left the house, Grace went upstairs. She smiled at the picture of Shonny as a stiff, solemn and (she was woman enough to sense it) scared little man, walking away down the street. She loved him. She always wanted to hug him. No one else ever made her feel like that. She could not say that she felt loving about Dido. She liked him. He did his best for her. But there was nothing in him to make a woman go soft and warm like there was in Shonny. Shonny was a little red apple that she could eat. She went into her new drawing-room; the back room on the top floor, next to her bedroom, and she opened the window wide. The sun touched her face benignly and a light breeze made the air as sweet as a cool drink, free from its usual taste of sulphur and soot. The house-backs that faced her across the back yards were stamped black and sharp against a blue sky dappled with puffs of white cloud. It was good to be alive; even here.

She heard the rumble of the mangle in the yard below. A little figure stood turning the handle, a ragamuffin hired at half a crown a week. Today he would take Shonny's place with the barrow. The sight of him made her smile at another memory of Shonny, this time in his old street garb. She thought she preferred Shonny in his ragamuffin guise. It made him look such a cheerful and cheeky little tinker.

Of course (the memory of Shonny at the barrow made her thoughts run again) she had known almost all along that the business only employed one small boy. She had sized the situation up quickly enough. She knew that Dido had spun her a yarn before their marriage. She ought to know by now. She had been in this house two months and indoors most of the time. She had never seen any other employee but Shonny or the street arab down there now. It was obviously a very small business. Dido was a proud sort of chap. It was like him to feel ashamed of having such a small shabby business. All the same, it paid. She could see that, too. He was never short of money and he never kept her short. His mother always kept a good table. It was silly of him, there was no need to be ashamed of a business that paid.

She certainly would not shame him by letting him know that she had seen through him. A still tongue meant a wise head, especially for a wife. The first thing a wife had to learn was to act as if she knew who wore the trousers. The more the husband felt that, the more she would learn to manage him, as long as she took her time.

Then, in the end, she would get her way about moving to a nice home. After he had brushed aside her first suggestion she had not raised it again. It didn't do to nag. She must let time do its work. And then she would also open his eyes about the business. She was sure it could be built up. It only needed ambition and push. Dido needed someone behind him, otherwise he would have got out of this house long ago. Why, in the end he might have just the kind of flourishing business he had romanced about that time (ages ago, it seemed) in the teashop. And he would have his wife to thank for it.

In the meantime she could not complain. He did anything she asked. Think of what led up to this new drawing-room. It began one night when the Irish were making a noise in the next room. She sat on the edge of the bed and told him that she couldn't stand it any more. She was not hysterical. She simply told him that she had stuck it as long as she could and she couldn't bear any more of it.

"I'll tell 'em to be quiet," he said.

"You're always telling them to be quiet. You can't stop children crying. It's no use telling them. I just can't stand them. They're awful. They're a danger to health. How can you keep bugs down with them living in there in dirt?"

Dido pondered. "Only get someone else if they go."

And the flash of inspiration had come to her. "Why?"

"Why?"

"Haven't you got *any* ideas?" she cried. "Do we always have to live in one room? It's not right living in one room."

"We don't live in one room."

"You mean sharing the kitchen with your family? One room. And it's not right for people in business. We might have friends to entertain."

"Who would we entertain?"

"One day we shall want to bring children home to play with our little one. Children of a nice class. Perhaps their parents will come. And are we going to bring a child up in one room?"

Dido brooded again. At last he said, simply, "Right."

He certainly was a terror when he started. The next morning she heard Dido talking to the Irishman on the landing. Their voices rose. She heard the man swearing. Then she heard a blow and a tumbling noise. She was afraid to open the door but Dido came in and she said, "What happened?"

"Raised 'is hand to me. Knocked 'im down the stairs."

Her Dido was a strange chap. She couldn't say why but there were moments when he frightened her. It was the hard, narrow way he looked at a person sometimes. Anyway, the Irish went, and now here she was with a drawing-room of her own.

Everything was rich, the dark floral wallpaper, the thick, flowered carpet that she loved to walk on in her stockinged feet, the sofa and heavy curtains in dark green velvet, the china cabinet, table and chairs of rich, red mahogany. She spent hours polishing the mahogany; and hours on the sofa, sleeping, daydreaming with books and thinking no more than a cat with a good place on the hearth. One day she would get a piano. It would be nice to learn the piano.

Not many girls had two fine rooms — a flat as you might say — two months after they were married. She had no cause to grumble. She stretched out on the sofa and took up a romance and was lost for a long time. She paid no attention when the Westminster chime of the mantelpiece clock sounded the quarter hours; but she answered to the stroke of eleven. She put her book away and went into the bedroom to prepare for her visit.

She put on her latest costume; a plum-coloured coat of corduroy velvet with deep revers. Rich was the word for this, too. It was a beautiful rich colour and the hat matched. The coat set off her figure. She admired herself in the mirror. She really was filling out. She wasn't big yet — goodness she was hardly four months gone, but her cheeks had a good colour. She had a lovely oval line and she had a bosom at last. She used to be depressed by her thin sallow face and flat chest. Marriage had certainly done her good. It wasn't only the baby. For the first time since her childhood with auntie she was eating good meals with plenty of meat, milk and butter; and when she lay on her new sofa she was popping chocolates into her mouth all the time. Yes, a full figure suited her. It made her look womanly; and what was more, prosperous.

She walked lightly in the street, ignoring the slatterns who stared with folded arms from their doorways as she passed. She was no longer nervous in these streets. She knew no-one in the street, even to nod to. She never set foot in a local shop. Why should she know them? She was not going to spend her life here. She did not want them to know anything about her and she did not wish to know anything about them.

In the main road a large shop-window showed her again to herself; a lady with a nice figure walking with her head up in a rich velvet coat and good shoes, and she thought, "Wait till I walk in there."

At the back of the teashop Grace sat upright, with teacup poised, a lady visitor. Across the table sat Mrs Dowll, as much a lady.

"I must come and see you one of these days," said Mrs Dowll. Grace had just concluded a description of her drawing-room.

"I wouldn't dream of it," Grace said. "Not that my friends aren't welcome. But it's a dreadful street. We shouldn't live there a minute if it wasn't for the business."

"If that's where your husband wishes to live, my dear —"

"You said yourself once, where there's muck there's money."

"As long as the money's there."

"Oh, it is. Believe me, Mrs Dowll. The money's there all right. My husband has a wonderful business there."

"Well, dear, that's the main thing, isn't it? As long as you're happy."

"I'm very happy. He's a wonderful husband. He gives me just everything."

"I can see that, my dear. And a lovely home from what you tell me."

"It's a beautiful home. I wish I could ask you to see it. I will soon. Really. When I can ask you somewhere nice."

"I expect you're looking out for something."

"Oh —" Grace launched into the flow of happy untruth. "I am. You see, we wouldn't have stayed this long only we're saving up. We don't *have* to live over the business. But we're saving up. My husband wants to expand the business first. Capital, you know."

"I can see he's a sensible man."

"Oh, he is. Mind you —" Grace remembered how Dido had appeared to the women in the teashop; and their derisive comments "— he is a bit of a rough diamond. But he has a heart of gold."

"I admire a self-made man. It's nothing to be ashamed of."

"That's what I say. And he does appreciate being married to — well, someone like me."

"He's very lucky to have a wife like you. You can teach him, can't you?"

"Oh, I can assure you," Grace said, "he's not ashamed to learn."

At the far end of the restaurant a young man entered. He wore glasses. He sat at a table by the window. He had not seen Grace but she recognised him. It was that young railway clerk, Sidney. Once noticed he was forgotten. Grace said, "You see, what my husband says is, what we sow now, we shall reap later."

"I call that very sensible."

"The more we put back into the business the more we shall have later on and that means a bigger house. I think it's worth waiting for."

"So do I, my dear."

Grace had reached the point at which she was so inspired by the picture conjured up by her words that she had to go on, not so much lying to Mrs Dowll as creating a fantasy for herself, acting a delightful part. "We don't want to go too far from his business, of course, but there are plenty of nice districts quite handy."

"There are houses fit for lords," Mrs Dowll said. "And not ten minutes' ride away."

"Oh," Grace cried. "You don't have to tell me. I'm keeping my eyes open. We shall want a nice class of neighbours, of course, and a garden."

"A coach-house is nice," Mrs Dowll said. "I wouldn't be surprised if one day you came in and told me you were keeping your carriage. Or your motor-car."

"That's what my husband says. Oh, if you knew the ideas that man has."

"That's the sort who gets on."

"When I go out — because I do go out looking, you know, I go all round keeping my eye open for a nice property — when I go, he always says, mind there's servants' quarters. There's got to be plenty of room for servants, he says. Of course, I don't have to do any housework now, but my husband says — well, the day we married he said he knew he'd married a lady and one day I would live as a lady should, waited on hand and foot."

A waitress with a tray of empty crockery had paused at their table and Mrs Dowll cocked an eye up at her, saying, "Well, what do you think of that?"

The waitress said, "Hallo, Grace. How's married life?"

Grace spoke coolly. "Very well, thank you."

"You look well on it." She leaned forward and said slyly, "Nice having it regular, isn't it?"

"That's enough, Maud," Mrs Dowll said. "Never dawdle with empties."

Maud went through to the kitchen. Grace said, "The cheek of some. It's not as if I was ever thick with her."

"Common as dirt," Mrs Dowll said. "Knickers down before they've raised their hats."

"If she wears them."

"Not that I like to speak of such things." Grace stood up. "I must run now. I have so many appointments."

Mrs Dowll rose and followed her out. "I'm glad there are some that remember old friends."

"I can't abide snobs," Grace said. She came upon Sidney from behind and as she passed she could not resist stopping. She turned and bestowed a small, patronising smile upon him. He stumbled to his feet, thrown awkwardly forward by the chair against his legs. Grace said, in just the tone the lady patrons used when they inspected her room at the hostel, "You come in early these days, I see."

He took her fine appearance in with a vague, startled gaze. "Yes, miss."

She was delighted at the effect. She uttered a gracious laugh. "I see you remember me. I'm not 'miss' any more, you know."

"No. No, I —"

In the same patronising tone. "Are you still with the railway?"

"Yes. Yes." He spoke with difficulty, looking at her doggedly.

"Prospects, I expect."

"It's, it's very slow, but —"

"It's steady I'm sure. You still go to your poetry classes?"

"Oh, you remember? — Yes, I —"

Smiling with small pursed lips she gave him a gracious, dismissive nod and passed on. Mrs Dowll at her elbow sailed past the table. Maud, who was serving another customer, called, "Ta-ta, Grace."

With the same minimal smile Grace nodded to her and went out. Maud came to join Mrs Dowll. Together they watched through the plate-glass window.

Maud said, "Stuck-up thing. And that lump she married! D'you remember him?"

Mrs Dowll said, "He's got money by the look of it. And she's four months gone, I'd say. So next time you're in the pudden club, make sure you're as clever as she is."

"'Ere," Blakers put a sovereign down for Dido and spoke in the voice of a man too wise to bear malice. "'Ow you gettin' on these days?"

Dido flicked a suspicious, questioning look. "All right."

"Keep busy, do you?"

"So-so. Why?"

"If you were lookin' round to pass the time I thought you might like to pick up a few more sovereigns."

"You still lookin' for a dogsbody?"

"I wish you'd forget that. Stanley collects my debts now, don't you, son?"

Stanley, his eldest son, was leaning against the doorpost of the back kitchen, listening with a folded newspaper in his hand. He was a pudgy, pasty youth of eighteen. He had a good job in the borough treasurer's department. He said, "It's quite simple really."

"I do wish you wouldn't bear a grudge, ol' man," Blakers said to Dido. "It was only a suggestion. You only 'ad to say yes or no. No 'ard feelings. You see, what I found is, they're more frightened of an educated man than they are of a fist. Stanley talks to 'em quite nice but they all pay up. No, it's fags I was thinkin' about."

"What do you mean, fags?"

Blakers treated him to a lowered, you-know-what-I-mean grin. "If you kept your eyes open. While you was goin' round. You might be able to put me in the way of some fags. Well —" For Dido was silent. "You're a man o' the world. Stock's runnin' low. It's 'ard enough to make a living without paying the manufacturer's price. I'm always in the market for a few thousand fags on the cheap."

"Where from?"

"Now do I ask? Can a man in my position afford to ask? You bring me ten thousand fags I won't ask questions. You'll be safe with me. Pay you any fair price I will as long as it's under the manufacturer's. You could make a quid or two."

Dido kept the long, hard look on him, then broke into a low, pitying chuckle. "Do I look like a tealeaf? Some business man you are. You'll be askin' Mr Merry next."

He went out. Blakers said to Stanley, "Dead loss that feller."

"Why d'you keep giving him money then?"

"I don't like trouble."

"Trouble with him or with the Murchisons?"

"'E 'as kept 'em away."

"Do me a favour, dad." Stanley came forward and unfolded the newspaper on the counter, indicating an item. "I read you the report. Harry, Jem and the two Gateses got twenty-eight years between them at the Old Bailey. The Murchisons are finished."

"Not while Keogh's on 'is two feet. You 'eard what 'appened at the brick."

"That was two months ago."

"'E's the guv'nor now. 'E's not a quiet one like 'Arry was. 'E's a terror. 'E's after Dido."

"He's taking his time about it. He hasn't let out a dickybird for two months. And as to Dido, you're not frightened of him, are you?"

"What if I am? 'E's got a nasty bunch o' knuckles."

"You can soon settle him."

"How?"

"Put the law on him. You could never put the law on Ginger or Harry because whoever got put away you still had the gang after you. Dido's got no gang behind him."

"I still don't like that Keogh."

"He'll get Dido. He's bound to. He's got men to back him up. You might as well get in with him now. He will do you a favour, you know. Ginger did, didn't he? You go and talk to Keogh about a crate of fags. You'll see."

Blakers sucked his lower lip and nodded slowly. He did not look upon the purchase of stolen cigarettes as wrong. He was a law-abiding man. The traders in Rabbit Marsh sold their groceries by the pennorth and cigarettes in ones and twos. Stolen goods were a godsend to eke out their small profits. One reason why they did not call in the police to protect them from the gangs was their fear of cutting off their supplies; not to mention the danger that their own transactions with the gangs might be exposed. Blakers was in a bigger way than most and for him the question of supplies was decisive. At last he said, "That's true."

He lumbered to the shop window and gazed out, deep in thought. "That's true," he repeated. "I told 'im that. They did oblige. Which 'e never will. They did give value for money. 'Ere —" This was a sudden bark of indignation. "Come 'ere. Look. Look down there."

Stanley joined his father. Grace Peach was coming down the street. She wore a smart hat and costume. "Look at 'er," Blakers fumed as she went past. "That's what I'm payin' for. I paid for the clothes on 'er back. 'E comes in 'ere, asks for more. It's only since he married that stuck-up bitch. Furniture I seen goin' in their place. Finest me'ogany."

Stanley said, "Well, then?"

His father nodded, and said, "Ah!" And a moment later.

"Can you mind the shop for me, Stanley?"

He was slipping his jacket on. Stanley said, "Keogh'll be in the pub in Brick Lane. Don't go in there. Go in the cookshop, in the back room, and send a boy for him."

Dido had just come in freshly scrubbed from the yard when Grace tripped into the kitchen from the street. His midday meal awaited him on the table, half a crusty loaf cut into thickly buttered slices, a plate of cold mutton, a jar of pickled onions and a big "father's mug" ready for tea.

His mother, sitting opposite him in the narrow space between table and dresser, composed herself in anxious piety to watch her son's performance.

Grace put down her packets and gave him a gay "Hallo, dear," and as he smiled in answer she pulled off her hat and started to unbutton her coat. "Run upstairs with these, will you, Didy?"

He waited placidly for the garments and went out with them while his mother looked on, hands in her lap, Grace went past Mrs Peach and took two dinner plates from the dresser. She put them down, opened one of her paper bags and emptied out shrimps, which she divided into a portion on each plate. She began to hum a tune. She took a lettuce from the other bag, glanced at the bowl which always stood on a chair in a far corner, saw clean water in it and washed the lettuce. Still humming, she shredded the lettuce on to the two plates.

She was aware that Mrs Peach's eyes were following her. It was out of sheer thoughtlessness, in her high spirits, that she had failed to greet her mother-in-law when she came in but now she felt glad of it, though she told herself that the woman was not a bad old stick. Live and let live was her policy; but something, her own good spirits, drove her on today. She smiled at Mrs Peach and put the pickled onions back on a shelf. Mrs Peach said in a faintly protesting voice, "He likes his pickled onions."

Grace turned on her mother-in-law the most friendly, woman-to-woman of smiles. "You don't have to live with him." She spoke playfully. "Well, you know what I mean."

She took a bright, flowered apron from a hook on the door and tied it deftly on. She touched her hair up at the mirror. She saw her mother in the mirror, and her odd, vindictive mood grew. Dido came in. She turned and said, "Brought you a treat, Didy. You can take your pick."

He looked at the two plates on the table. "Cold mutton? Not likely."

He drew the plate of shrimps towards him and Grace could not resist the quickest sidelong glance at Mrs Peach. She stood with her head on one side watching him fondly. He ate with concentration, rolling big mouthfuls inside his cheeks. Grace darted forward, took away the mug and brought from the dresser a dainty cup and saucer. She said, "I don't mind you having the big one for breakfast, Didy. It's what they call a breakfast mug, it's manly. Only not in the day."

Dido said through his food, "All the same to me."

Grace took another cup, poured tea for herself and sat down. Between ladylike sips she said, "Had a lovely morning."

"Good."

"I went to look at a house. Oh, it was so nice. It wasn't very far either."

He went on eating for a moment with his head down. He swallowed the mouthful and raised his head. His grey eyes scrutinised her mildly. "What you do that for?"

"No harm looking. It had two bedrooms and a garden and the people next door have had a bath put in their house. It didn't cost much. I spoke to the lady."

Sidelong she took in Mrs Peach's eyes upon her, filled with a stricken wonderment. She had not meant to bring the subject up again just yet; certainly not to discuss it in front of her mother-in-law. But she was still all breathless with her triumph at the teashop. The need to pour it all out was irresistible. The thought itched in her that it might work out like her honeymoon. She had boasted about a honeymoon to Mrs Dowll. Then the need to make good her boast had given her the courage to speak to Dido about it. Now she had told Mrs Dowll all about the house she dreamed of. And this breathless excitement was making her tell Dido. Perhaps once again it would work.

"You just went lookin'?" Dido said.

"That's all. It had a lovely garden." But what had made her take the plunge in front of the old lady? Oh, why not? The old lady didn't say much to her but silence could speak more than words. She just sat with her hands in her lap and followed Grace with those mournful fishy eyes. Grace felt that she had been under scrutiny ever since she came to this house and the object of forbearance. Without warning she felt that her own patience had snapped. She felt immensely gay and cheeky, determined to assert her status, to remind the old woman that a wife came before a mother. If she ever wanted to get her way about the house she would have to make Dido see that, too. It was only his attachment to his mother that kept him here now. The old woman was like a big stone in their way. "It wasn't dear either. I've got the particulars."

"I thought you were only lookin'," he said.

"It's as well to be informed," she said. "We have to think of the future."

"You're never satisfied, are you?" But his voice was good-humoured and he was smiling.

"Oh, Dido —" Grace was very indulgent and gentle. "Satisfied with this?"

She thought her mother-in-law would speak up at this but the old woman's face shrank smaller and her eyes went away from Grace, hard and small. It was Dido who spoke. "Ah, mother's always kept a good home. Looks after us both."

"Oh! —" Grace's cry was heartfelt. She reached out, dropped a hand on the clasped hands in her mother-in-law's lap and gave Mrs Peach the tenderest smile. "Bless her, she's a treasure."

"Got two nice rooms." Dido still spoke in good-humoured reproach. "What more do you want?"

"There's no end to what you want if you're ambitious," Grace said. She turned to her mother-in-law. "Don't you think Didy ought to be more ambitious?"

Mrs Peach seemed barely able to whisper, "He's a good, hard-working boy."

"You don't have to tell me, mother. I'm his wife. I am grateful, Dido. You've made us a lovely home."

"Might as well enjoy it, then," Dido said. "We're all right here. Anything you want, just say."

"What do I want?" Grace said. "You give me everything." She crossed the room with her cup and saucer and put them in the bowl. "There is one thing. We could bring water into the house."

Dido said mildly, "Why spend money for the landlord? It's 'is place, not ours."

"It would be nice. It's not as if we're short of money. For that matter we could have some lino on the stairs."

Dido finished his shrimps before he spoke again. "All right. Consider it done. Happy?"

Grace said, "Oh, you are a love."

Mrs Peach sat through it numb. She stared bitterly down at her hands. The girl had never had an affectionate word for her since she came. She spoke friendly enough but it was cold and uncaring. She was no daughter. She put an apron on for Dido and tidied her hair and sat in front of Dido, quite the little housewife, but she never did a hand's turn. Just this minute she had put her cup and saucer in the bowl, not a thought of washing them up herself. And sending Dido upstairs like that to fetch and carry; to Mrs Peach it was like an offence against the Holy Ghost. She was a Christian woman. She only wanted to see her son settled but all of a sudden her denied grievances overflowed and every moment brought another blow to the heart. The way the girl patronised! "Bless her, she's a treasure!" Once, in service, Emma Peach had heard the lady of the house speak of a scrubwoman like that. She had tried not to think before of the wicked waste of money but it was like a hot coal in her bosom every time she saw the girl come home with another dress or hat. The money that girl must be spending! And those two rooms upstairs — what must they have cost? She spent Dido's money instead of being thrifty as a wife should. She put ideas into his head. She ordered him about. She had turned him against his mother. He wasn't a son any more. He had always liked cold mutton and onions. Shrimps, indeed! This creature had changed Dido and made him a fool who could be led by the nose. She took away his breakfast mug that was his right as the master of the house. It was one slap in the face after another. It was plain she had lured him on (buried night after night it all erupted into thought again) before they were married. A good, clean-living boy led into sin and a forced marriage. It was madness, a sink in the house! Lino on the stairs! For thirty-four years it had been good enough for his mother; but what was good enough for his mother wasn't to be thought of for his wife. On the surface of her mind she told herself that she must turn the other cheek. Dido had made his choice. As long as he was happy — She told herself that she was a Christian woman. She must turn the other cheek. But beneath these thoughts ran the anger. He had no time for his mother now. Easter had come and gone and he had not gone to church with her as in past years. At last, at a pause in their conversation, words forced themselves out of her. She made herself say the words in her ordinary, timid voice. "Dido — I was thinking. On Sunday morning — it's a long time since you came to chapel. Would you like to come?"

He frowned. Anyone would think he had never been before, instead of having taken her every year, dressed up in his best. "What for?"

"I thought — you might like to."

He still looked puzzled. "I'm takin' Shonny up Sclater Street. Promised to buy him a cock canary."

"I'm sure Shonny could wait."

It was the girl's turn to watch, her face peaceful, all

smug and silent. Dido said, "I promised 'im. For startin' work. Mustn't let the boy down."

Mrs Peach was silent. He had no time for his mother anymore. Hot bitterness poured through her against the girl who had lured her son to sin and made him like this.

Every Sunday morning for decades past the Bethnal Green area of London has turned into a vast maze of street markets. There are markets for foodstuffs and cheap clothes, a market for bicycles where every other variety of decrepit vehicle is also to be seen on sale, streets in which nothing is to be seen but piles of mechanical spare parts of every kind. It is the great mart of London's poorest, and till two in the afternoon the narrow streets are choked.

Dido and Shonny started out for the bird fair in Sclater Street before nine o'clock, to get there before the crowds thickened.

Dido asked, "How d'you feel after a week's work?"

"All right." Seven days had worked a change in Shonny. Dido had remarked that he seemed a more serious boy and mother had said it only showed that they were making a little gentleman of him, thank heaven.

"Like bringin' home wages, do you?"

"Yes."

"My treat this morning. You can keep your pocket money."

"Ta."

"Boss treat you all right at the office?"

"Yes."

"What about the other boys, they treat you all right?"

"Yes."

"Made any friends yet?"

The boy's eyes roamed over a gaily painted sarsaparilla stall. He shrugged his shoulders. "You know."

Dido smiled and left the boy alone. He reminded himself that he had been at work three years when he was Shonny's present age; not quite as small as Shonny but a shrimp for all that, yet thinking himself a man. No doubt Shonny thought himself a man, too, now that he gave wages to his mother. He still looked a child with his chubby red cheeks, but he had stopped dashing about and yelping all over everyone like an eager puppy. He looked as if he had private thoughts now. He came home and sat down and buried his nose in books.

When he looked up at anyone his face revealed nothing and he only spoke in brief snatches. It was best to leave the boy alone. He would find his feet.

Outside the shops in Sclater Street another wall had been built, of cages and hutches piled six feet high, broken only where the shop entrances were. Another pile was springing up in the gutter. Shonny and Dido walked the narrow strip of pavement in between. The smell of birds clung in their nostrils. The street echoed with the din of singing birds, crowing poultry and screaming parrots.

Shonny's face brightened. He stopped every few moments to inspect a canary, a crate of proud pigeons, or a tiny, vivid tropical bird. Poultry clamoured at him from their chicken-wire coops and tethered ducks strutted in his path. He darted into the roadway where lone vendors wandered, to inspect the birds in the cages which they held up, and ran back to look at rabbits in their hutches.

He was in no hurry. They would go all the way up and down the street to look at everything before they picked their canary. His big brother Dido was eyeing the line of cages with intent and expert eyes. Dido knew all about everything and would not let him pick the wrong bird.

More and more often he stopped at a window or in front of a cage and called, "Hey, Dide! Didy!" — and Dido grinned, for each time Shonny's voice was more high and boyish. With every step they took he became more his old eager self.

Dido stopped indulgently as Shonny scurried away once more into a side alley. It resounded with the barking of hundreds of dogs. They were nearly all little dogs, every kind of mongrel and common breed. Here and there a grim, muzzled yard-dog stood as if on guard above the sea of puppy bodies that squirmed and frisked on the pavement. Some looked up from barred boxes with appealing eyes. Some peeped out of the lapels of kerb vendors. Some leaped at the end of their leashes with eager barks as if they wanted to pick their future owners.

One terrier puppy was jumping and yelping around Shonny's legs. He stooped to stroke it. He laughed and teased the puppy with his fingers. The office and all that had happened there was forgotten. He was a boy of the streets again, free. He and the puppy played and yelped in the same excitement.

He was squatting in front of the puppy, holding it in both hands and nuzzling it against his cheek, when a sound shrilled in his ears. It failed to catch his attention. He turned to show Dido the dog and he saw Dido pushing away from him through the crowd with an odd, urgent violence. The shrill sounded again and again. He dropped the dog and rushed after Dido. He knew what police whistles sounded like. The police whistles were blowing in Rabbit Marsh.

He ran after Dido into Rabbit Marsh and he saw the helmets of policemen bobbing among the crowd. The crowd poured past him, thinning out as the police pushed them back. A policeman was in front of him. He ducked past and caught up with Dido. From the pavement as the crowd was cleared, he saw what had happened. From the top of the street almost down to Blakers' shop every stall, a half-dozen on each side, had been overturned. Their contents were spilled across the cobblestones. Heads clustered in every window. There was a hubbub of voices. The crowd in the street thickened with newcomers who tried to surge forward to see what had happened but more and more policemen appeared to hold them back and prevent looting.

Dido looked terribly angry. Two policemen had started asking questions from door to door but Shonny turned his back on them and followed Dido. Dido ignored him and strode on, only stopping when he encountered Tommy Long in the arch that led to the stable yard. Tommy started telling what had happened but Dido looked very angry as if he knew already what had happened.

Some men had rushed into the street, turned the stalls over and run off. Everyone had got out of their way. People knew better than to interfere. The intruders had vanished among the crowds in Brick Lane by the time the police whistles started to sound along the street.

"Look at 'em —" Tommy indicated the policemen. "Askin' questions. Why don' they save their breath? They know it's a waste of time. No one's fool enough to split."

"No," Dido said. "They stand there an' let their stalls get smashed up in front o' them."

"If they split they'll 'ave every bone in their body smashed," Tommy said. "Course they reckonised 'em. Everyone round about reckonised 'em. I see 'im in front as plain as I see you."

Shonny had already guessed before Dido grimly said, "Keogh."

Chapter 16

Dido lifted a corner of the curtain and from the bedroom window watched the street. Keogh was coming down the pavement, his three bravos crowding around him, gesticulating, letting the street hear their loud, confident laughter. They were all of Keogh's age, in the late thirties; men hardened and matured by lifelong street fighting. One of them who darted on the edges of the group was small and thin; the others were big and muscular like Keogh, all of them as scarred, dangerous and crafty as warrior tomcats of the slums.

They were not Murchisons. Of that tribe, besides Keogh, only children and youths remained at large. They were hangers-on of the clan, Jaggs Place bullies who had drunk the booze of their chiefs for years and had now come forward for mercenary service.

The group stopped outside Arkell's. Keogh went in alone. He came out and the four of them went in to Barsky's, where the same thing happened. They continued along the street and disappeared into "The Railway".

A week had gone by. This was the second time they had come to the shops to collect their money. No tradesman failed to pay. From time to time they went down the street unchallenged. Sometimes they entered "The Railway" for a drink. The old masters of the street were back and there was no-one to challenge them; for Dido Peach kept out of their way.

Their rule was harsher than his. On Sunday morning they roamed the market and helped themselves from the stalls. The shopkeepers had to supply them with food, clothing, cigarettes — anything from the shelves that the restored dynasty might fancy in the first flush of greedy delight. The poorer people, too, felt their presence. They beat up a coster in the Bug Hole who was too bronchitic to work and had borrowed money from Blakers. Dido, from his window, saw them stop old Mrs Hackett in the street and take her purse from her. He reflected that one person in Rabbit Marsh seemed not to be the worse off for their return.

The shopkeepers did not have to appease two masters. From the moment that the Jaggs Place men had reappeared Dido kept out of the way. He did not go into the shops for money. He did not go into the pub. He only went out in daytime, and walked cautiously, close to the wall and alert to every door, archway and street corner ahead of him. Between forays Keogh and his men, with sovereigns in their pockets, held court in their own pub in Brick Lane. From here Keogh broadcast that Dido Peach was finished. He asked the neighbours who crowded around him each evening to go and tell Dido to come out and fight if he was a man. Dido did not respond. He walked the streets carefully by day, ignoring everybody, enclosed in his thoughts; and by night he was not to be seen. So, with little fuss, it was accepted that he had abdicated. The new order was accepted like a change in the weather.

All the week he thought about his predicament. He was alone against four men. Overnight in the street he had become a man unfeared and despised. He mattered no more than a forgotten politician. His predicament was urgent for his money would not last long. During his time of power he had been lulled by the deceptive peace and had not saved greatly. He had lavished money on Grace. He did not know how he could confront Grace if he had no money. He could think of no other lies with which to conceal his true position. His pride made exposure unthinkable.

He was tight with anger as he watched from the window; but he knew that he must contain himself. He could not hope for fair fight with Keogh alone and one man against those four would be murdered.

Thoughts of retreat had crossed his mind but retreat was impossible. He could not go back to work. A man with such a demon of pride inside him could not go back to the wharf, where he had enjoyed status and respect, and beg to be allowed back in whatever inferior job might be going, humbled among men who knew him. Such a man would not seek elsewhere, jostling among the servile crowds of unemployed. He could not bring himself to walk down Rabbit Marsh every morning in working-clothes, and trudge back each night, parading his downfall in front of everybody. Above all he could not stand in front of Grace self-confessed in a cap and choker and shabby clothing as a wretched, common workman.

Even to swallow humiliation would not save him. Keogh would not spare the vanquished. His adversary's submission would only feed his lust for revenge. He was a bully who needed to trample and smash. He would want to destroy Dido to consolidate his rule over the Murchisons, to appear as the avenger of the dead patriarch. Fifty new hangers-on, made brave by the smell of an easy kill, would join him to scour the streets for Dido.

Accepting defeat, Dido could be sure that sooner or later he would be smashed almost to death. He must fight them, or be destroyed. But time was short and he was alone against four.

A week later Keogh and his men came for their money again. They went from shop to shop like a patrol of occupying troops, and all the street heard the clatter of their steelshod boots.

It was a sunny Monday morning. Loud and confident in themselves, the four men came out from Blakers' shop and started for home.

Behind them, Tommy Long's pony and cart emerged from the stable yard. Dido was up on the seat, alone. Barsky, arrested by the passage of the cart, glanced idly, then glanced again, for something out of the ordinary had caught his eye. Dido held in his right hand a whip that was monstrously at odds with the little cart — a six-foot waggoner's whip, with a thong even longer and a butt two inches thick. Barsky hurried back to his shop.

Dido swung the cart sharply out of the entry, so that the inside wheels mounted the kerb. He flicked the pony to a trot, and — it happened in seconds — pony and barrow were on the pavement, faster and faster, while women at the windows gaped.

There were only a few people out of doors. The four men leaving the street heard only their own laughter and the conqueror's clatter of their boots. They ignored the familiar sounds of a street, the rapid clop of hooves, the headlong rattle of a cart; and not one voice was raised in a warning shout, perhaps because it was all so quick, perhaps because the few onlookers knew better.

It was only at the last moment when the noise and rush of the cart was upon them that they turned, one looking round and shouting, then all four scattered in amazement; scattering too late, for one of them, crushed to the wall by a swerve of the cart, fell to the pavement and did not rise. The others ran down the street and Dido, standing up with the reins like a charioteer, steered back into the road alongside them, lashing with the whip, herding them in towards the far wall. Keogh and his two underlings ran with heads down, arms raised protectively, and the long whip lashed rapidly one-two one-two from right and left, driving them in upon each other.

They gained a few yards at the corner, where Dido had to slow to turn, but he caught them up in Brick Lane and lashed them towards their own street.

There was one more corner before they could escape to Jaggs Place. Dido slowed again and turned into the side street. Two of the men, their faces welted red, were bolting into Jaggs Place; but one sprang forward, head down — Keogh with a knife, going for the pony's hamstrings.

Dido swerved the nimble beast and the knife slashed wide in a flash of sunlight. Dido reversed the whip and brought the solid butt down on Keogh's arm. Keogh howled and dropped the knife. Dido struck again, at his head and missed. Keogh was running again. Dido raced alongside, lashing, until Keogh stumbled through the archway of Jaggs Place, out of range.

Dido slowed the pony down and went on. He completed the round of the block at a walk, to cool the beast. In Rabbit Marsh, he saw people stooping over the injured man. He ignored them and drove into the stable yard.

"Come on, you must have seen something," Mr Merry said. "Speak up. I'll look after you."

Blakers stood with his hands on the counter. His glance moved from one to another of the two policemen. Weldon saw the deep interior calculation and thought that the man was going to talk. But— "I never saw nothing. Heard a bit o' shouting. You get that round 'ere. Never even bothered to look."

"Marvellous," Merry said. He looked keenly at Blakers. "One chap's in hospital, broken ribs and a perforated lung, Keogh's laid up with a bad arm, neither one of them remembers how it happened."

"You want to ask them that was out of doors," Blakers said.

Merry laughed softly. "Oh, everyone's blind down here. Aren't they, Weldon?"

"Never see a thing," Weldon said.

"Nobody saw when the stalls were overturned. Nobody saw this time. Marvellous. Marvellous." He lapsed into silence and stood leaning on his tightly rolled umbrella, shifting his gaze over the shelves laden with stock. He broke silence. "Been buying any cheap lines lately?"

"Cheap lines, Mr Merry? I try an' get a bit o' discount. It ain' often. You know what it is for the little man."

"Yes —" Merry was still looking over the stock. "That's hard lines. Few thousand fags on the cheap's a big help. No luck that way? Ever?"

"All legitimate stock 'ere, Mr Merry."

Merry swivelled on his umbrella to look directly at

Blakers. "You want to think twice about annoying me, you know."

Blakers only sighed and returned his gaze. Merry said, "I'll look after you."

Blakers said, "I live 'ere all the time. You don't."

The two policemen went out. In the street Weldon said, "That's it, then."

Merry said, "I think we'll have a word with Peach before we go."

Weldon started off alongside. "Peach? He's laughing."

"He who laughs last — You know what they say."

Weldon said, "I don't see it's worth all the boot-leather. Let 'em smash each other up. You ever lived in the country? Country born I am. The vermin in the fields keep each other down."

Merry stopped and lifted the tip of his umbrella like a teacher's pointer. "Let me tell you something. If we want these people to respect us there's only got to be one God Almighty round here." He jabbed the point of his umbrella towards the sky. "And not that one."

They walked on. Merry said, "And another thing. We both know what happened. It's only evidence we lack. From now on Peach'll start getting too big for his boots. If he gets away with this. Which he looks like doing."

"At least he's no thief," Weldon said.

"He's a street bully. You mark this if you want to get on. Nothing worse than a street bully. He lives idle, he reckons the world owes him a living. Sooner or later he'll thieve. Like Harry Murchison." He paused outside Number 34. "In the meantime, the more convictions on his sheet, the better. Come on. Might get something out of the womenfolk."

A bell jangled as Merry opened the shop door. In the shuttered, gaslight gloom a small woman with grey hair was stooping over a mound of rags. She rose to face them. Merry had never spoken to her before but he could see that she recognised him. He said gently, "Mrs Peach?"

She stared for a second, then before he could stop her

she darted to the door of the kitchen and opened it. She called, "Dido! Dido!"

Merry grimaced wryly to Weldon. The two men heard heavy footsteps.

Dido came into the shop. He looked them over as if unaware why they might be here. "Afternoon."

"Afternoon. Taking it easy?"

"Doin' a bit in the yard. For 'er." He indicated his mother who stood with hands clasped looking at the mound of rags.

"Thought you might be resting after this morning."

"Why? What happened this morning?"

Merry chuckled. "Ah! I'm not going to waste my breath. Just wanted to take a look at you."

Mr Merry saw the mother staring at him. There was fear in her eyes. He shot, "Where were you at ten o'clock this morning, madam?"

Her lips moved. He heard only the faintest frightened sound. Dido said, "She was shopping."

"Let her speak for herself."

She said faintly, "I was shopping."

"Till nigh twelve o'clock," Dido said. "Then she made dinner."

A glance at her decided Merry to cut his losses in that quarter. He said to Dido, "And you?"

"I was out as well."

Through the open door to the kitchen Merry saw the side door of the kitchen open. A girl entered the room as Dido spoke. She was in a dressing-gown and she walked as if recently asleep. She glanced into the shop at the sound of Dido's voice but she did not appear curious about the two well-dressed strangers talking to her husband. She went towards the stove but Merry called to her, "Mrs Peach."

She came to the shop doorway, her look questioning but still dull with sleep. He said, "I am a police officer —" The question in her eyes became astonishment. She looked at Dido. She started, "What —?"

Dido said, "Go back in the kitchen."

Merry had not seen the wife before. She looked a nice girl. It was odd the way these brutes got hold of nice girls. He began to feel a more intense and personal dislike for Dido out of pity for her. He said, "Mrs Peach, I wonder if I might have a word with you alone."

Dido said, "No, you can't."

She said, "What is it, Didy? What do they want?"

Dido said to Merry, "Any special reason why she should?"

Merry said, "Mrs Peach, there was an affray in this street, at ten o'clock this morning. Where were you?"

She said, still wonderingly, "In bed."

"Didn't you hear anything?"

"I was asleep. I only just woke up."

She was obviously speaking the truth. Merry said, "Do you know where your husband was?"

Her lips parted in bewilderment. "He goes out on business. Why are they here, Didy?"

Dido said, "It's routine enquiries. They're calling all down the street. Isn't that right, Mr Merry?"

Merry said. "Then your husband was outside the house?"

She said, "Well, of course. Didy, why is he asking me?"

Dido said, "Mother, take her in the kitchen."

Mrs Peach came out of her frightened trance. She put her arm behind Grace and led her into the kitchen. Merry did not intervene. Dido shut the door. He said, "Anything else, Mr Merry?"

Merry said, "No. You were out on business. Your wife said."

"That's right. Anyone say different?"

Merry went to the door, and turned back. "Dido — do you know? This is a bad day for you."

"Is it, Mr Merry."

"Yes, Dido. Today I've decided that you're not a nice man."

"I'm very sorry about that."

"Not as sorry as you will be, Dido. There's going to be law and order round here."

"I believe in law an' order, Mr Merry."

"Do you? It all depends whose, doesn't it?" He went out, with Weldon.

In the street, Merry said, "We shall deal with that fellow now. He's had his run."

Chapter 17

Dido made a round of the shops to collect his toll. All paid and none made any comment on what had happened. Keogh was laid up in bed with a bad arm and they would submit to whoever was in power. Nevertheless all the street was speculating about how Keogh would decide to strike back when he was up. Dido expected him to. Mrs Peach knew well from the talk in the shops what had taken place and went about the house without a word, hunted by her own fears. Only Grace remained in innocence. She had seen the police calling at other doors. There was no reason for her to doubt Dido's assurance that the visit of the detectives to their shop was only one of many.

After a week the news went round that Keogh was out of bed. Dido walked warily again. But unexpectedly another and longer reprieve came.

One night the people of Rabbit Marsh were brought to their doors by the sound of shouting and the clatter of tins beaten like drums. They swarmed to the comer, to see the whole tribe of Jaggs Place streaming along Brick Lane, men, women and children. The howling troop brandished iron bars, hatchets, eight-inch hatpins, nailed slats torn from packing-cases — any object that would serve as a weapon. Keogh marched at their head.

The first to witness this procession were struck with panic. But the band straggled past without a glance at Rabbit Marsh. It was no vengeful invasion. It was (the word quickly travelled) one of those legendary events, a slum war party. A boy of eight, marauding through a window incautiously left open in an alley off Brick Lane, had been fallen upon by a mob of all ages. He was in hospital with an eye knocked out. The Jaggs Placers did not often grieve over the knocks and bruises of their prowling young, but this was too much.

After a drunken corroboree in the Brick Lane pub they had marched forth in a frenzy.

Some venturesome spectators followed at a safe distance and were rewarded by the sight of a battle that would long be remembered in the pubs. The inmates of the alley were as drunken and ferocious as Keogh's army; and they came out to meet the attackers.

It took forty policemen to put an end to the riot. Sixty-seven people were taken to hospital. These included three women whose pregnancy had not kept them from the battle, an old man of eighty-one whose broken bones were never to heal, and a dozen children. Cockeye escaped injury but was among the thirty-two arrested. He was sentenced to twelve strokes of the birch.

One of Keogh's three henchmen was injured. The other two and Keogh went to jail for making an affray. Keogh received a sentence of four months' hard labour.

Supper was over. Grace had gone up to bed. Dido was sitting under the gaslight with a newspaper. The boys were out. Mrs Peach was in the shop adding up her takings in a halfpenny exercise-book. Rather, she tried to add them up; every time the figures came out differently. She returned to the kitchen. She put the exercise-book on the table next to Dido. "Dido —" There was more than the usual fatigue in her voice. "Do you mind?"

He folded his paper, put it aside and applied himself to the column of figures. She tried to look upon him with pride. He was a smart boy. He always had been good at his figures. If he'd had his chance goodness only knew what he could have been. But the pressure of terror remained. It had stopped her from adding up properly, made her dizzy in her head. She had been confused and dizzy in her head all the week, choked with the need to speak to him but struck silent by terror.

"There you are." He pushed the book back to her.

"You are a help," she said, her voice almost failing.

His eyes flicked up at her. "You're tired. Why don't you pack up? Go to bed?"

"I will." But as she turned and started to shuffle away the fear struck her again and brought her to a halt. She stood with her back to him, her heart thumping to make her sick.

She heard him speak. "What is it, mother?"

She turned. "Dido —"

He was frowning at her, anxious. "What's up? You out of sorts?"

Ever since those detectives had stood in the shop her tongue had been paralysed by terror. Today the news of Keogh's sentence had struck her with a new shock, the shock of reprieve. But it had been no relief. She was flooded with new fears, of the future — the future when Keogh came back. She was driven by the fear that she had one more chance to save Dido and that she might not have the nerve to take it.

"Well, come on —" His voice was sharp with disquiet. "Speak up."

"Dido, I do wish —"

"Mother," he said. "I won't eat you."

She could not manage more than a mutter. "Those two in the shop. Those police."

Relieved, he smiled. "That's all over. I told you."

Still in a mutter, "We've never had the police."

"Oh go on, it was routine. They went everywhere."

She made a hopeless grimace, not looking at him. "I don't know why you want to get mixed up." He did not answer. She cried, "There were four of them. You could have got hurt."

He pondered, then sighed. "It was them or me."

She looked at him now, appealing, and her voice was a cry again. "It won't end."

He picked up the folded newspaper as evidence. "'E's been put away."

"And then what?"

He put down the newspaper. It was his turn to look away and to murmur, "Time enough."

She wrestled with her fingers in despair, wrestling for words. "Dido, I don't want you to."

"Don't want me to what?"

"All this money."

"What about it?"

"You've always worked for your money."

"I've always been straight. Anyone say I'm not?"

"You're a good boy. I know you are. Only —"

He shook his head wearily. "Oh, mother, give over, will you?"

She cried, "You shouldn't take it." His gaze at her was perplexed now. She said, "I don't want you to take their money." He was silent and her terror of him made the words pour out. "It's wrong. It's not like you." The next words jerked out before she could stop them. "It's like your father."

He smiled sadly to himself and shook his head as if in pity. She had gone too far to stop. She was carried on by a kind of ecstasy at hearing herself speak up. "Promise me. Dido, promise me."

Numbed once more into silence she waited for his anger. All he did was to sit there, elbows on the table, brooding. He said at last, "Got to live."

Freed and eager again at the evidence that he had at least listened, she said, "You've always worked. I don't know what's been happening all these months. It's not like you. I want you to stop. There's nothing to fear. That man's away."

"He'll come back."

"You can be gone by then." She heard her own words with astonishment. Then happiness filled her. She saw herself as the mother sacrificing all. "You can find a nice place and move. He'll never know where you are."

His lower lip fell in bewilderment. "Move? Away from here?"

There was no limit to what she could say. It was really

ecstasy now. "Why don't you listen to your wife? She knows. It's not right for you and her to stay here. You should move somewhere nice. Make something of yourself."

His frown narrowed as he tried to take it in. "What about you?"

"Oh, I'm all right. I've got the boys. I've got the business."

"He might take it out on you."

"On an old woman? Don't be silly."

"Suppose he did?"

He was arguing — he was taking her seriously. She was incredulous that she could stand up to her son and be listened to. "You've got a wife and a child to think of. You must think of them first. Your child, Dido."

"I can't leave you like that."

"Then take us later. Help us too. When you're settled you can look round for a little premises and a couple of rooms, that's all we want. But you move first. Before that man comes back." There was no difficulty in finding the words now. "If it's me you're thinking of, then do what I'm asking. I can't stand it any more, the disgrace. Taking money from people. You were never like that before. You must go away."

He leaned his head in his hand and seemed to forget her for moments. He said, "It'll take time."

Near to crying with happiness, she said, "You've got four months."

"Don't think I'll get my ol' job back. That's filled long since."

"You'll get another. There must be plenty of places for a smart man."

He sat back and looked at her. "I don't want her told."

"Grace? Why not?"

"Not till I've got a decent place. I kep' tally at the wharf. I ought to get a managin' job somewhere. Wait till I got a place, then I'll tell her."

"Oh," she understood, she understood her proud son. "Of course."

He said suddenly, "Do you two 'it it off?"

"Grace and me? The idea, of course we do."

"I wondered sometimes," he said. "Treat the girl nice, mother. Give her a chance."

"Oh," she cried in her ecstasy. "Don't you worry. I'll be good to her. Dido — you do promise? You're not going to take any more money?"

It was his turn to say, "Don't worry. Don't worry. I won't."

Chapter 18

Chas came home from work in good spirits and determined to have it out with Dido. He washed and changed into his good clothes before he sat down to supper; and when Dido, who had already eaten, cocked an interrogative eye at his appearance, he said, "Goin' out after. Come with? Buy you a drink."

Dido said, "Don't know about a drink. Could do with a walk."

Impatience made Chas eat sparingly and quickly. They set out and walked in a silence broken only by a few commonplaces, till they came to a churchyard. Dido liked to come here on a fine evening and often sat alone for an hour. They went in through the gate and Chas said, "Sit down if you like."

Dido threw him a quick, amused glance. "Want something eh?"

They sat down. Dido said, "Well?"

Chas said, "I earn good money."

"Twenty-one bob. What about it?"

"It's good money for my age. I give it all to ma, nearly."

"Get your pocket-money."

"'Alf a crown a week. Not much for a feller my age."

"You're all found. You got the price of a pint an' a packet o' Woods. You never go out. What more do you want?"

"That's the trouble."

"What is?"

"I never go out."

"No-one's stoppin' you?"

"Not a brass farden in me pocket? 'Ow can I?"

"What you in need of? A new suit? Get you anything you want."

"You took three sovereign off me."

Dido gave him a hard look and a warning silence. Then, "Tell me what you want. I'll get it."

"I'm nineteen. You don't buy things for a feller my age. Dide — it's in me pocket I want it. Money in me pocket."

"I seen what you do with money. That night."

"Don't keep on. An' it was my money. Well it wasn't yours, was it? You took it off me. You never give it back to no-one."

"Rotten ol' slag. I nigh pulled you off her."

"No you never. I wasn't gonna do nothing. It was my money. Dide — there's this feller at work. 'E's a nice respectable chap. 'E's like my mate. 'E's always askin' why we don' go out of an evening together. 'E's engaged. 'E's a very respectable chap. An' 'e's got a corkin' sister. She'd come out for the foursome. 'E says 'e wants 'er to meet a nice feller."

The disdain in Dido's look made Chas's heart sink. Dido said, "All these years. All these years I've told you. In one ear out the other. Nothin' between to stop it."

Chas pleaded, "'E's a nice feller."

"You 'ave to work with them. Don't 'ave nothing to do with 'em. I've told you. Never lowered meself. All the time I worked."

"But this Bert is a very respectable chap."

"Wharf labourer."

"So am I."

"You're a cut above *them*."

"You always said meet a nice girl. Where am I gonna meet a nice girl? You won't let me."

"Go up the chapel. There's a young men's club."

"What?" Chas yelped it. He was dumbfounded. That pen-pushing lot of cocoa-drinkers with their celluloid collars handing round the prayer-books? Dido had never had time for them. He had never made a suggestion like this to his brothers. What had got into Dido?

"Nice class o' people. You wanna think o' your sister-in-law. My wife's a lady you know. You wanna think who you bring 'ome."

Yes, that was it! Grief and anger fumed up together in Chas. He would never have a chance, never. He would spend his days going to and from work, toiling with no more hope than the horses who pulled the canal barges. He could hardly ever afford to go for a drink with the fellows in the dinner break. He couldn't have a mate. A nice girl wasn't good enough for Dido, didn't suit his brother's new ideas. Oh, it was no good. He was done for. Dished. Anything he tried he could expect the kibosh on it. He might as well tie a stone round his neck and jump in the canal.

He had no more spirit to argue. He sighed, stood up and they walked home in silence.

Grace was already in bed. Dido unfastened his tie at the mirror. He felt pleased with himself. That boy would have gone down the pan years ago without a brother to look after him. Chas and Shonny the pair of them should thank their stars they had a brother. He would have to see that Chas started minding his ways. Put a good suit on Chas and he could look any of that chapel lot in the eyes. There was none that had a better home. Time enough for him to think of girls. He hadn't wiped the mother's milk off his mouth yet. When he did he could bring home the proper type of young lady. It was a nice thought, a young lady like that and Grace. They would be company for each other. It all went with the thought of the new home, a decent flat in a decent district. Chas could bring his young lady there, all in good time. Dido went to bed stirred by his good secrets.

He had not lit the gas. It was a clear white night of early summer and even with the curtains closed there was enough light in the room for every object in it to be visible. He could see Grace lying on her back, looking at the ceiling with mild and empty eyes. He settled his limbs and closed his eyes for sleep. He heard her voice. "Didy— "

He opened his eyes. She had turned his way and was looking down at him, supported on an elbow. He grunted a question but she only repeated, "Didy," and waited.

Then she sighed as if tired and settled down and she uttered a long, private, going-to-sleep noise; and sank down; but she did so still turned his way, so that her weight was half upon him. Her hair was in his face.

He pushed an arm underneath her and levered her weight and she came on top of him. He felt the brush of her lashes as her eyes closed and her breathing was regular as if she was trying to sleep but she was wide awake all right. In fact because her belly was starting to swell she supported herself on her forearms; but she started to press the lower part of her body upon his under the blankets, unobtrusively but regularly, yet as if she had no idea what was happening. He felt himself get hard. She puzzled him and although he was getting hard he lay still, to find out. Then she began to wriggle, just the lower part of her raised up and her hands moving under the blankets. He let one of his hands move cautiously and the side of it touched her bare warm flank. She had wriggled up her nightdress. For some reason he made himself lie inert and wait. She waited, too. When he did not move her hand brushed lightly over the top of his thighs and now his wild suspicion began to find confirmation. Her fingers pried, in the most absent-minded way, and took him, yes, guided him. It was incredible, somehow it was a laugh; all the time the sly little piece was breathing as if she was asleep with her eyes closed. This beat the band.

He had never felt so strange all over doing this, tickled until it was enough to drive a fellow mad; and they had never before gone on so long and slow. Usually it was over before you could say "Harry Tate". And her breathing got deeper and longer, until her chest was heaving up and down, and there under the blankets where something was happening on its own that they both pretended they didn't know about, she gripped him harder and harder, rose up and down more fiercely. She began to turn her face quickly to one side and the other as if she was having hysterics in her sleep. Her cheek came down against his chin. She was blazing hot and damp. She was breathing like sobs and she started to make noises. He finished but it didn't stop her. She was making these shuddery breathing noises and then all of a sudden she slumped on his chest. She was soft and loose as a sack now and so still she might have been a corpse, except that she was breathing long and slow, and warm.

They lay for a long time like that, she apparently asleep, he in a mingled state of astonishment and satisfaction. After all she was his wife. It was a rum business, being married, but he liked to feel he had a wife and he couldn't say why but at this moment he really felt he had a wife.

She muttered, "Oh, well," in the most ordinary way and slipped away from him. She lay next to him. She raised herself up on her elbow and once again she looked down at him. He could see her eyes gleaming in the faint white light. She said once more, "Didy —"

He didn't know what to say. He felt so married, that was it, married at this moment, that he wanted to tell her everything, all about his real life that she didn't know about, and his plans. A wife should share his plans. But a shutter of caution came down. It didn't do. It didn't do at all. All in good time. He was doing things so as to keep her respect. Her eyes gleamed down at him and he couldn't think of anything to say except, "Restless?" He touched her cheek. The damp had gone cold.

"No. I can always sleep. You know me."
"Me too."
"Good night."
"Good night."

He stuck to his new plan. He had promised his mother and he was a man of his word. She must have been astonished at the ease with which he had given in to her for he had been master in the house since boyhood. He left the shopkeepers alone and looked for work.

Partly he was moved by genuine filial piety. Overbearing he had always been, stern as a father in the house, but he had always longed for his mother's approval. Inside he wasn't much different from the little boy who had stood up to his father. Then he had hated his father and had wanted only to show his mother that he was the opposite of that beast, her good dependable boy. And this was what he still wanted, always. Her everlasting praises were meat and drink to him. Her cry, "It's not like you. It's like your father," her appeal, her talk of feeling disgraced by him, the implied withdrawal of her admiration — these had been enough to make him promise.

Yet he had only promised so readily because his own thoughts, far cooler calculations, were already moving in the same direction. On that Sunday morning in the shop he had faced Mr Merry calmly enough — mockingly, almost. But the interview had left him appalled. Dido was a law-abiding man. Until twelve months ago he had, like his mother, held as an article of faith that one's existence should not even be noticed by the police. The fight with Ginger had been fated. He still could not question its rightness. But since then his life had not been his own. He could see from the outside, as it were, all that was happening, and the self that stood outside was incredulous.

Behind his calm he feared a conflict with the law. He did not want this duel with Mr Merry to go on. He only wanted the man to forget him. Until Keogh had been sent away Dido had been conscious only of the need to fight, to survive. As in all his previous life it looked as if he must fight and fight until it was his turn to go down. And then the reprieve — he had already felt the shock of it when his mother spoke to him. She had spoken his own longing back to him, given shape to his thoughts. He was not held back by pride. He had no compunction about clearing out before Keogh returned. Let those who wished call it running away. He wouldn't be here to listen.

It was no easy matter to find work. He was determined to take only a responsible position that would show him in a good light to Grace. Luckily he had a few pounds in hand. He had obtained from the manager at the wharf a reference which stated that Dido Peach could read, write, keep tally, manage men and be trusted with money.

He had imagined that his smart presence, his good suit and the testimonial would be easy passports to a good job — foreman, checker, overseer, something of that sort — but everywhere he went there was an ante-room full of competitors, most of them men who looked as if they had come down from an even higher station in life. He tramped London for one week after another, dog-tired, swallowing snubs, often kept waiting uselessly for hours, fighting off discouragement, his carelessly saved funds dwindling.

After a month, when he was at the end of his tether, he saw an advertisement in the *East London Advertiser*. A dairy in Clapton wanted roundsmen. The phrase that drew his eye was "promotion for smart men".

The dairy looked a goodish size. A wide entrance — on the high wooden gates now opened could be read the two halves of the inscription: *D. Owen. Cowkeeper.* — opened into a large yard around which were cowhouses, stables and a glass cubby of an office. Mr Owen was small, with a bald, fringed head. There was still a faint Welsh lilt in his voice. He greeted Dido civilly; that was a change from most of the others; and asked about previous experience. Dido said, "No, sir. But I can 'andle a horse. I'm good with figures an' I can turn my hand to anything."

"You look a smart man —" Mr Owen eyed Dido in his good suit. "The ladies like that. We'll try you in the yard. No use wasting your time if you can't take a float out. Is it, man?"

As they walked out, Owen said, "It's four rounds a day. In between you look after your horse, clean your churn out and wash your cans. It's not a job for idlers, you know."

Dido began, "It says in the advert about promotion —"

"One thing at a time, man," Mr Owen said cheerfully. "Take this float round the yard."

Dido did so. When he stepped down, Mr Owen said, "I can see you can be trusted with horseflesh. You can start Monday. You'll draw a straw hat and two aprons, five shillings deposit, returnable when you leave. Not for a long time we hope. I pay ten shillings a week and sixpence in the pound commission. You can count on twenty-five shillings if you work hard."

Dido said, "My young brother gets twenty-one bob carrying timber. He's only nineteen."

"Ah, well," Owen said equably, "If you think you can better yourself, I mustn't stop you. Only it's the prospects we offer, see?"

"That's what I wanted to ask about," Dido said. "In the advert. It says, promotion."

"Ah, yes, well," Owen said, "you see, I've been in this game since I was a boy. Started from the bottom I did. I've worked up a nice business, you can see that. Forty-two years I've been at it, and shall I tell you? This whole place depends on me. From dawn till dark I have to be here if I want to see things right. I'm getting a little tired, Mr Peach. You can understand that."

"Lookin' for a manager, are you, sir?"

"In a manner of speaking, exactly. Not that I want to pack up, mind. Too young for my grave I am. What I want is a man I can trust so I can take it easy a bit more. You got it exactly, a manager."

"That's the post I want, sir. You'll not be disappointed."

"I've been disappointed in others, Mr Peach."

"You try me, Mr Owen."

"Steady, steady." Owen made a little song of the two words. "I'm not one for buying pigs in pokes. You must show what you're made of on the milk round, Mr Peach."

"I'll do that providing it's understood."

"Probation, Mr Peach. Show what you're made of."

"What would you pay a manager?"

"Oh, depends what the man is worth. Talk about that later."

"I'd like to know."

"Oh, two pound ten, for a good man. Of course if he put up business he wouldn't be unrewarded."

"A bonus you mean?"

"The men have commission. I would certainly encourage the manager, Mr Peach. Monday, then? Terms as agreed. Tips at Christmas, of course."

"I won't be on the round till Christmas, Mr Owen. If you can't sum me up in a few weeks you never will. It's manager I'm after."

"I like an ambitious man," sang Mr Owen.

Chapter 19

For the next eight weeks Dido worked as a milk roundsman. He rose at half-past three every morning and walked to work. He was able to return by train at the end of his thirteen-and-a-half-hour day but he was never home before seven in the evening.

He wore his good suit every day. He wore it to preserve face in front of those people in the street who saw him come home each evening. (No one saw him set out in the darkness.) He wore it to remind Mr Owen that he was a manager-designate. Above all he wore it to impress Grace; for he had told her that he had put a bit of money into another small business over Dalston way, rags it was like the shop here, and he went across every day to keep an eye on the other chap. He did not talk to her much, for he had little more than eight hours of his own in the twenty-four and he slumped into bed dog-tired each night; but although he did not want te tell her lies, he had started the story and he had to keep it going. He had also told her that they must economise now with a baby coming. This did not seem to put her out. She was getting on in her time and did not go out much. Besides, she was a good wife. Ever since that night he felt more that she was a good wife. He did not know what to make of the episode, and with him dog-tired every night she had been considerate enough to leave him alone since then, but the memory set up a complacent feeling in him.

He was getting on famously at the job. In a good suit, striped apron and straw boater hat he was popular among the women on his round, in the little streets of pretty cottages and redbrick terraced houses that ran toward the River Lea. Whether tweenies or housewives, they liked his smartness and civility, although some preferred a cheerier type of milkman. He was punctual, attentive and rapid. He was able to pick up extra trade and push up his commission until now he was taking home sometimes well over thirty shillings a week. Some weeks he was able to put away a half-sovereign towards his savings. He enjoyed riding on the step of his float, reins in hand and he enjoyed working up trade. He kept busy between rounds polishing the brass on his float and churns and horse's harness till it sparkled. Mr Owen often stopped to nod approval or pass a civil word, but he had not yet said anything about the managership. Dido decided he must give the man a nudge soon. He was keeping an eye open in the neat streets of Clapton for a pair of respectable rooms. With a fiver in hand he could move but he had not much time. Keogh would be out by the end of the month.

Once he had the managership he wouldn't look back. With a wife like Grace behind him he would earn well over that two pounds ten. He had already looked round the yard and thought of a number of ideas for improvements, which of course he kept to himself until the job was his. Not that he would stay long at the dairy. It would only be the first step on the road to better things.

Merry and Weldon came out of Blakers' shop. Once again the tobacconist had refused to speak. Merry knew well enough that Dido had been taking money for months from the shopkeepers. Now that he had lost patience with Dido he wanted to collect enough evidence to arrest Dido on a charge of demanding money with menaces. But he was faced with a phalanx of closed mouths. The tradesmen all reasoned, as Blakers had just done openly to him, that it was a case of Dido or Keogh, and if they squealed to the police they would incur such odium that whoever survived to oppress them would treat them badly, even if they had secured his rival's downfall. To Mr Merry's assurances that the police would protect them they replied with open laughter.

"The funny thing is," Merry said, "they all swear blind they're not paying anyone now."

"They would."

"I believe them. Truth or lie, I can always smell it."

"What do you make of it then?"

"Don't see him about these days."

"See him of an evening. Comes home dressed like a bloody poxdoctor's clerk."

"Where is he all day? Up to some mischief, eh?"

"He could be."

"He must be. They haven't paid him for weeks down here. Yet they're all still frightened of him. This street isn't big enough for him. Seeking bigger game. Pastures new. Shall I tell you what you're going to find out for me?"

"You want me to find out where he goes."

"And what he's up to."

At six in the evening Grace's drawing-room was still gilded by sunlight. A cloth was laid on the small mahogany table and two places were laid, each with a plate of sliced ham and a precise array of cutlery. There were plates of washed lettuce and tomatoes, a piece of cheddar, a loaf on a board, a butter-dish and a teapot in a cosy. A kettle hummed on the gas-ring in the grate.

Grace and Mrs Peach sat on plush-upholstered chairs by the window, knitting. Mrs Peach was in her housekeepery best. Grace wore a tea-gown and slippers. She was not hugely swollen in her seventh month but she was big enough to look clumsy, and she felt burdened. Her legs were troubling her and the doctor had said something about blood pressure. She was supposed to take it easy. She did not miss the shops as she had lost all interest in new clothes. She had lost interest in most things and was quite happy to obey the doctor, lying down in a doze for hours or making baby clothes or reading. She ate chocolates all day and Mrs Peach brought her a succession of cups of sweet tea. She had become good friends with Mrs Peach.

"Ham was nice," Grace said. "Nice and lean."

Over her twinkling fingers Mrs Peach said, "Dido likes a bit of fat."

"Oh," Grace said. "I know what my Dido likes."

It was all of the friendliest. She had no wish to needle her mother-in-law and she never felt nowadays that her mother-in-law was needling her. But now that her status in the house was, as it seemed, recognised, she was always prompt to maintain it with the necessary turn of phrase. "He does work hard these days," she said. "I worry sometimes."

"No need to worry about Dido. He's a good boy."

"You don't need to tell me that. Who knows better? But he does work hard."

"He's always been good."

"My word, do you think I would have married him else? He does work hard in this other business. I hope it's worth it."

"I'm sure you can trust Dido."

"I do trust Dido. Do you think Dalston's a good part?"

"Dalston?"

"For a rag business. I mean competition and all that. It's where you were in service, isn't it?"

"I'm sure I don't know. Dido could tell you."

"Oh, Dido tells me precious little. I thought perhaps he told you."

"He doesn't tell me. He used to of course. But then he's a married man now."

"He is a close one."

"He always was one for few words. Still you can trust Dido. I can tell you it's all for the best whatever he's doing. Dido's a hard worker. He's as honest as the day, my boy. He would cut off his two hands before he thieved."

"Thieved!" There was an indignant touch in Grace's fervour. "Who said anything about thieved? My Dido?"

"I was only saying." Mrs Peach was a little worried that she might have blurted out too much. She took a conscious pride in her newfound ability to speak up but Grace's questions about Dido had taken her off balance. A few more questions and she might give everything away. Dido had warned her that she must not tell Grace nor the boys either, for they might blab, and it was a strain all the time to watch her tongue. She felt quite reconciled to Grace. Knowing that Dido was her own boy again and true to his promise, she was determined to keep her promise to be nice to Grace. Also she was full of joy and excitement at the prospect of once again having a little baby to hold. She couldn't help noticing that Grace had turned nice, too. Perhaps it was the baby coming. Grace had invited her up to the sitting-room and that had started a new life for her. Now that she could sit in the room every day in her best black dress and white collar she no longer detested it. She was proud of it and of herself in it. Oh, it had been an awful year, but now Dido was on the right road, she could not deny credit to this girl. Grace had to rest. She needed her mother-in-law. It was a privilege to Mrs Peach to be permitted to take over the dusting of the sitting-room; and she looked after Grace with the patient care that a herdsman might devote to a gravid cow. She had always wanted a daughter-in-law who was real company. Now, sitting up here, knitting, daintily holding her teacup, prattling away with a tongue set free, she had one. She said, "I think you've done wonders, dear. I do."

Grace said, "I only hope Dido appreciates."

"He does, I'm sure. He wants to do everything. You'll have everything sooner than you think. A new home even, I wouldn't be surprised."

"Oh, that." Grace spoke listlessly. For the moment she had lost interest in moving. "— That must be Chas."

Footsteps clumped up the stairs. Chas entered in his working-clothes. "'Lo ma, 'allo Grace. What's up? Shonny sent me up."

"Is he reading in the kitchen like a good boy?" Mrs Peach asked.

"Yeah. 'E said to come up."

"He's had his supper and we've had ours. There's yours on the table. Grace has invited you."

He looked in amazement from one of them to the other. "What's up?"

"Grace has made supper for you. She's invited us to spend the evening with her. In her sitting-room."

"I —" He was still turning an open-mouthed stare from one woman to the other. "I'm goin' out tonight."

"You can go out another night. Go and wash and change."

"I told the fellers."

"Grace has made supper specially. I never heard such a thing, other fellows. Do you want me to tell Dido? You might say thank you to Grace."

He muttered, "Ta."

"Now come back in your decent suit," his mother said. "I'll pour your tea soon as you come."

He lingered, sulky, then went out. He sat down to his supper when he returned and ate in silence. Mrs Peach rattled on and Grace listened to her without much attention. Nobody had much impact on her these days. She experienced no keen emotions about the child. She felt too lethargic to be eager (what with her legs and her blood pressure) but the burden and movement within herself was the centre of her life. Dido came and went. She did not bother her head anymore about what he was doing. Her questions to Mrs Peach had only been for the sake of talking. She did not even wake up when he got out of bed to go to work in the middle of the night. Of course he had stopped doing anything to her when they were in bed. She should think so, in her state! Not that he had ever troubled her much. It was strange, when they first married he was at her like a terrier. Men! Then he lost interest and it happened less and less often. It amused her that she could feel annoyed because he left her alone. She ought to be only too glad. It was a fact, though, she did get annoyed. That night — oh, she remembered that night.

She was still surprised at herself. That must have been what those girls at the hostel told her about, the ones that frankly said they couldn't have enough of it. Well, he hadn't shown what he thought about it; "Good night" and off to sleep. He must have thought her very forward. Certainly if he couldn't be bothered she wouldn't, not when she was her own self again. Losing his respect for all she knew. It was the man's place not hers. Without hostility she thought, blow him! She said, "How much did you lay out, mother? For the shopping."

"It doesn't matter, dear, really."

"No, no." Grace heaved up and went to the sideboard. She opened the top drawer and took out a tin. "Must keep it fair."

"Two and thrappence, dear."

Grace emptied coins on to the table, scrabbled out Mrs Peach's money with her fingertips, returned the rest to the tin and put the tin away. They heard Dido on the stairs. He came in, heavy with fatigue, wearing his good suit. He said, "Do with me supper. You can pour. I've washed."

He sat down to his meal. The women at once returned to their prattle. He champed stolidly, ignoring them, as he felt himself ignored. They had turned into a real pair of jaw-me-deads, his mother and Grace. These days he didn't get so much as a look sometimes. He was amused and pleased and a little put out. He said to Chas, "What's up wi' you?"

"Me?"

"You look as if you lost a quid and found a farden. What you got the 'ump about?"

"Nothing."

Chas was seething. Every second he felt nearer to going off bang like a balloon. Tonight was the limit. His pocket-money was a joke but he had saved up for weeks and he had won a couple of bob in the dinner-hours at cards and he was supposed to meet some of the fellows from work tonight for a friendly drink. He finished supper in silence.

Dido said to Mrs Peach, "Take you for a walk, mother. Up the churchyard."

She gave him one of her grateful smiles. He was his old attentive self these days. "I could do with it, dear." Grace said, "I'm going to bed."

They all got up and Chas got up. At last he could get away. Dido turned to him. "Take the crocks down, Chas." Chas expostulated, "I'm goin' out."

Dido spoke patiently. "Chas, you don't want to leave it all to Grace, do you? Make yourself useful for a change. Take the crocks downstairs and wash up."

Chas did not say a word. Intimidated as ever by his brother he started to stack crockery; and his fury choked inside him. When they were all gone he worked on, rattling the crockery. He felt finally and utterly hopeless. They would go on keeping him in and shutting him up and treating him like a child for ever if he let them. It was no use, he could never stand up to Dido. If he didn't show them once and for all he would stick in this house without friends and without a girl for years and years like a bloody old maid. No one had time for him in this house. He couldn't stand it for a second more and that was flat. He left the pile of crockery, sat down and sank his head down on the table upon his arms. He was there for a while without moving, while he heard Grace get into bed in the next room. He sat up. All his resentments had focused to one resolve. He opened the sideboard drawer and took out the tin. He opened it. There they were, five sovereigns, besides the silver. A little while before Grace had emptied the golden coins on to the table in front of him and he had thought, that's my money, that's what Dido took away from me. He took it away from me and he kept it. So much for him being honest.

Chas would never dream of stealing. But he was driven inside by something near hysteria. He raged against Dido and his mother and Grace. He needed to strike back at Dido and he felt all the more savage because he could only do it when Dido's back was turned. He felt like weeping, like a little boy, as he looked at the coins and thought, that's my money, that's mine.

He took three sovereigns and put the box away. He was only taking what was his. He went out in a child's unreasoning rage, to give the boys the treat of their lives, to make an irreparable gesture of defiance to Dido.

He met the boys and treated them. He got drunk and went up to the West End in a cab. He had some more drinks and looked in at the Empire Music Hall where a perfumed and beautiful young foreign lady spoke to him and took him home. Next morning he found himself in the street. His head ached. He was penniless. He dared not go home for he was filled with an anguished terror of Dido. He went to St George's Barracks, near St Martin-in-the-Fields, and joined the Army.

Chapter 20

Dido came in from his round, unharnessed and fed the horse, unloaded the float and went to cash in. Two other milkmen were in the office with Mr Owen. Dido did not go in. He wanted to talk to Mr Owen alone. He was in no hurry to wash his cans. He went into the cowshed.

In the cool gloom he sat on a milking-stool and watched the cowmen at work. They were carrying feed to the dozen cows chained against the rear wall. Working in the dairy brought back his childhood. As a small boy he had always run out in excitement when a herd of cows wandered down Rabbit Marsh, on their way to or from a spell at pasture; and he had always been eager to go on errands to the cow-keepers. He still liked to breathe the heavy odour of the beasts, of warm milk and rotten straw. He could relax here. The big, patient eyes of the cows, unlike those of humans, were unjudging.

Mother was still upset about Chas. She huddled in the corner chair by the dresser, her old, bewildered self, muttering her fears for the boy and bemoaning the disgrace that he had gone for a soldier. Dido was upset, too, but he told himself that Chas had made his own bed. The boy had jibbed at a little family discipline. He had gone to the right place to learn what discipline meant. The loss of money had hit Dido harder. Three sovereigns was the greater part of what he had saved. Time was running out before Keogh's return and he would have to start again. He could not hang about any more for that promotion.

They had waited for a day after Chas's disappearance. Then Dido had had a word with Gaffney, the bearded constable. Gaffney had smiled a little. He was a man who had heard such stories before. That night he had called to tell them where Chas was.

Mother had insisted on going with Dido to the barracks. "Lord love us," the brisk Colour Sergeant had said. "Take him home? Lad's over eighteen, isn't he? Have you brought a certificate to say different? Then it's all legal and proper. Lord love us, ma'am, we get mothers and fathers coming here all day. Proper wailers some of 'em are. But it's no use if the lad's over eighteen. You can see the young feller if you like. In barracks. Oh, we don't let 'em out. Not once they've attested. Don't you worry, we'll make a man of him. Well looked after he'll be. Smart as new paint when you see him in his red and blue. We'll make you proud of him, ma'am. Infantry of the line. We'll have him away in the next draft... Can't say. Wherever the next draft goes. Dorsets like as not. A very fine regiment. Yes, sir. If you'll wait. You can see the Attesting Officer."

The Attesting Officer, a very tall thin mournful gentleman, had explained that it was all in order. He had shown them a bundle of forms with Chas's name filled in sixty-two times. And the officer's signature twenty-nine times. Chas had only signed once but that was enough. And they had seen a sullen and silent Chas; and not long after he had sent them a postcard from Dorchester Barracks. Well, that was that.

Dido went out to the yard. The men were still with Mr Owen. He strolled into the disused stable opposite the office to have a look at Mr Owen's motor-car. It was inside against the wall, under the boards of an old hayloft. It was a nice piece of work, shining with new green-and-gold paint and polished brass. Dido knew nothing about the mechanism but he had a good eye for workmanship.

The two men came out of the office and he went in. He said, "Mornin', Mr Owen" and emptied the contents of his leather moneybag on to the table.

Mr Owen, without looking up, busied himself with the money. "Good morning, Mr Peach."

He began to stack the coins in piles. Dido said, "Two more customers in Newick Road. I'm doin' eight gallons a day down there now."

Mr Owen was intent on the coins. He only made a "mmhh" of approval. Dido said, "Mr Owen — I think I've shown what I can do."

Eyes on the money, Mr Owen said, "Very good. Very good, Mr Peach."

"About that job?"

"Job?"

"Managing."

Mr Owen said, "Managing?" as if the word puzzled him. He still didn't look up.

Dido began to feel uneasy. "Eight weeks, Mr Owen. On trial for the managing job. It was understood."

"Oh —" Mr Owen uttered the word lengthily. His lips moved in silence as he counted a pile of shillings and he leaned intently across to make a note in a book. "Managing job? Yes —"

Dido said firmly, trying to draw the man's attention. "It was understood."

Owen murmured, "Let me get this booked, there's a good chap."

Dido obeyed for a moment; but the feeling grew that there was something amiss. "Ave I given satisfaction?"

"Satisfaction?" Owen was still murmuring as if to himself. He looked up in an odd, quick way. "No fault to find, Mr Peach. But managing? I wasn't thinking so soon —"

A hardness came into Dido's voice. "You said I was on trial."

"I never had a date in mind, man. I don't know yet if I want anyone."

Dido said fiercely, "It was understood."

Owen said, "I've had men with me twenty years if I was in a hurry to find one. Stands to reason, doesn't it?"

"You said."

"I said I'd give you a chance. I give every man his chance." He sighed, shovelled up the coins and let them cascade into the compartments of a drawer. "This is very difficult, Mr Peach."

Gathering anger made Dido silent. Owen said, "You see, Mr Peach — this very day I — Well, I have to reduce my staff."

"What is this? Eh, Mr Owen?"

Owen's eyes were on the table again. "Last in first out. I'm sorry. It's only fair."

"Are you —? Are you givin' me the boot?"

"No, Mr Peach. I have to reduce staff, you see. Things aren't so good."

"You're sellin' your whole yield. Only Monday you was looking where you could put in more cows. What is this?"

Owen looked to his front, at Dido's midriff, in unhappy silence. Dido repeated, "What is this?"

Owen picked up a small packet. "I've got your money here. I'm paying you for a full week, on last week's commission."

Dido almost shouted, "Ave you gone mad? Don' I even finish the week?"

"I'm sorry, Mr Peach."

"What you turnin' me off for?"

"I'm paying you a full week, Mr Peach. I'm sorry. You have to do things you don't like in business."

"What for?" Dido was shouting now, grasping the front of the table. "Why?"

Owen pleaded, "Be reasonable, man. It's business. I can't explain any more."

"You can explain why you turn me off mid-week. Not even wait for a man in my place."

"Leave me alone —" Owen was starting to shout. "I can't sit talking. I'm busy. Take your money, man, and leave me alone."

Dido was breathing deeply. He had been a man at peace for a long time but he felt an old, dangerous self stirring in him. "I won't go till you tell me what's wrong."

"Nothing's wrong. I can't keep you on, that's all." Dido

shoved the table, pinning him in his chair, shouting, "Tell me!"

Owen was panting now with fright. He raised his voice and shouted, "Vaisey! Colston! Come here, quick!"

"Tell me!" Dido shouted, his fists up and clenched. "I'll kill you!"

He glanced round as the two cowmen came in from the yard. Owen panted, "Wait here, both of you." To Dido. "Go on, get out. Quickly."

Dido stood paralysed, glaring in anger and entreaty. Owen said, "They told me you were violent."

A pause; then Dido, in a thick, stunned voice, "Who did?"

"It's none of my business, man. The police were here. Not half an hour. I've got my clients to think of. I've nothing against you, man."

"Who told you?"

"The inspector."

"Ah," Dido said. "Him."

"I can't have the police coming round about my men? Not with a previous conviction. Can I now? Be fair."

"Five quid fine. More than twelve month ago. You don't call that a conviction."

Owen shook his head in despair. He said to the two cowmen, "I'm giving him a week's money. I can't do better than that, can I?" To Dido, "Go home, Peach. You don't want more trouble with the police. Do you now?"

Dido said, "I've got one apron in the wash."

"You can send it. I've paid back your deposit. I'm sorry, Mr Peach. Very sorry."

"What did I tell you?" Merry said to Weldon in the train home. "Housebreaking. That's his next lay. Oldest dodge in the world. Get a nice little job that takes you round the houses, size up a few gaffs, then break in one after the other. Do 'em all in one night and you're off." He chuckled. "Trotting round behind a milk float, innocent as a babe. You see he went outside the borough. Wanted to shake us off, I don't doubt. Well, he'd have to get up early to do that. The cheek of the fellow. Why, someone else might have nicked him. We can't have that, can we? Not with our little pigeon."

Chapter 21

Dido walked straight down Rabbit Marsh with the step of a man who had a purpose. He went past his own front door and continued until he turned into Blakers' shop.

He went into the shop with his first words ready; and was taken aback to find it empty except for Blakers' ten-year-old boy who sat on the counter, legs swinging. The boy looked at Dido and said, "'Lo, Mr Peach."

"Where's your dad?" The boy called, "Dad!"

Through the curtain of coarse lace that covered the panes of the kitchen door Dido saw Blakers get up. His wife sat at the table, a shrivelled little woman of the same stamp as Mrs Peach. Blakers opened the door and said, "Ah! Return of the prodigal."

"I want to talk to you."

"Fire away," Blakers said. "Stranger lately."

Dido said, "Go to your mother, Roley. I want to talk to your Dad."

The boy dropped from the counter but as he went to the door Blakers put a hand on his shoulder. "You can stay 'ere, son. Learn the business, eh?" He spoke to Dido. "Bin 'elpin' me in the shop all the school 'olidays, 'e 'as. Likes to do a bit in the shop. Don't you, Roley?"

"I don't want 'im 'ere."

"You don't? Do you pay the rent?"

Dido said, "I don't want trouble." Anger had sped his steps all the way from the dairy; against Owen; against Merry who had caused him to lose his job; and against all Rabbit Marsh which had brought him to his plight. Anger made him want to drive a fist into Blakers' fat, complacent face; but he restrained himself. He had only a few pounds, of which some would go on housekeeping. Keogh would be out in four weeks at the most. Dido had no means of knowing. His dismissal had taken him by surprise. He had not yet found a new home. It would have to be a decent place or Grace just would not move. He needed money quickly. From the half-a-dozen shops that had paid in the past he could get three, perhaps four pounds in a week. Blakers was foremost among the shopkeepers. He must be made to pay up.

"I fancy that means you do." Blakers took his hand from his son's shoulder. "Go in the kitchen, Roland."

"What's 'e gonna do, dad?"

"'E thinks I'm 'idin' be'ind a kid. 'E reckons I'm afraid of 'im. Go to your mother."

The boy said, "You leave my dad alone."

"Good boy," Blakers said. "Your dad can look arter 'isself, though. Leave the door open. Don't mind 'im watchin', Dido, do yer? Educational. Maria, we got a visitor. Stay where you are. Do as I tell yer, woman. You can see from where you are. Well, Dido?"

Dido moved closer and spoke low. "I don't want trouble. You know the arrangement."

"Arrangement? It's a long time since we 'ad an arrangement."

"All right, let's 'ave it."

"Dido, you're a funny feller. I don't see yer face two month or more. All of a sudden you walk in and 'let's 'ave it.' Where you bin?"

"Never you mind. Just let's 'ave it."

"Don't be unsociable. You 'aven't bin in the nick. I'd 'a known about that. Where you bin this two month?"

"Look," Dido said. "Don't rely on them two to stop me. If you want trouble you can 'ave it. Outside in the street."

"Where everyone can see? 'Ave sense, Dido. My name's Blakers, not Joe 'Unt. What I wanna know is, what for?"

"What for what?"

"No trouble from the Murchisons since Keogh went away. Can't say you bin lookin' arter us, can you? You didn't come for yer money, fair enough I thought. Dido's actin' like a gentleman. All of a sudden you turn up, talk about trouble. 'Ere, Maria, you 'ear 'im?"

His wife started to get up. "Ought ter be ashamed of 'isself."

"Sit down, Maria," Blakers said. "I told you once. Now look, Dido, you don't give me the wind up. You talk too much to be a real 'ard nut. If you was a real 'ard nut you'd 'ave 'ad me on the floor be now kickin' me cobblers in. Missus an' kid wouldn' 'a worried you. You'd 'a clocked them too if they come the acid."

"You've 'ad it too easy," Dido said. "A sovereign. Quick. Before I ask for two."

"Well, then —" Blakers' jowls sagged in a mild grin. "Suppose I say, 'it me. Go on, then, 'it me."

Dido's right fist clenched like a brick but he did not raise it. Blakers turned to his wife.

"'E'd like to be a 'ard nut," he said. "But 'e can't do it. Brought up in a good 'ome. I'm not surprised."

Mrs Blakers quavered, "It's not right, 'im comin' in like that. Call the police you ought."

"Do keep quiet, Maria," Blakers said. "Don't make me keep telling you. Look 'ere, Dido, I'm interested. There's the cash drawer. Go on, be'ind the counter. Take. Go on, take yer sov'reign. Take more while yer at it. One thing they always said about Dido Peach, 'e never thieved. Be worth a sovereign to see you thieve."

Dido seized him by the shirtfront and muttered, "Right!"

"All right, Dido," Blakers said. "Only jokin'. Known you long enough for a little joke, ain' I? You'll get your sov'reign. I don't want me face bashed in."

Mrs Blakers was in the kitchen doorway, dragging her son by the hand. "Don't you give 'im," she shrilled. "It's a disgrace. I'll fetch a copper. I'll go myself, I will."

"You'll get the back of my 'and," Blakers shouted. To Dido, "Don' understand, do they? Maria, you seen 'im grab me by the neck. You seen 'im offer violence, didn't yer? 'E meant it. You seen it. I'm no mug to ask for a bashin'. 'Ere, 'ere's your sov'reign, Dido. All right?"

Dido said, "All right."

He picked the coin up from the counter, put it in his pocket and went out.

"It's a disgrace," Mrs Blakers said. "'Er walkin' about with 'er Bible like a bleedin' duchess, an' 'er boy robbin' us blind. Tell the p'lice and be done with it."

"Look, Maria," her husband said pityingly, "Leave the brains to the men. I'll tell the p'lice when it suits me. I got somethin' to tell 'em now, 'aven' I? Demandin' money with menaces. You seen it. 'E's never threatened before. This time 'e dished 'isself. Used threats in front o' witnesses. Remember that, Maria. You're a witness if it comes to it. An' you, too, Roley. You're not too young you can't stand in the box."

"All the same," Mrs Blakers said. "I'm goin' ter tell 'is mother. Give 'er a piece of what for I will. Do me good to let that 'oly mary know what I think of 'er. Come on, Roley."

As she lugged the boy towards the street, Blakers said, "Young Stan ain't the only brains in this family. Yer ol' man knows what 'e's doin'. I can shop Mr Peach any time I please."

Perhaps it was because he felt more angry than ever and somehow defeated in his encounter with Blakers that he walked down to "The Railway". He went in and ordered a whisky. Sam Meek, as he served him, said, "Not your usual, Dido."

Dido drank it in silence and ordered another; and several more. Each tot of liquor burned in him like a concentration of his anger; and his anger grew; but his mind remained clear and he was quite steady when he stood up.

A few other men in the bar had kept their distance and Meek, talking to them with his elbow on the counter, had come from time to time to serve Dido in silence. When he saw Dido about to leave he said something to the other drinkers as if inviting their attention, then came along the counter to Dido. "Off already?"

Dido nodded, and took in with a glance the men all looking his way.

"'Ave to keep your eyes open, now on," Meek said.

"Why?"

"Aven't you 'eard?" He turned a quick, barely-detectable grin from the men to Dido. "Keogh's comin' out Tuesday. Full remission. 'Is missus is ailin' again."

He came into the house. No-one was in the kitchen. He called, "Ma — Grace — Mother." There was silence. He went upstairs.

Grace was sitting up in bed. One of her books rested on the counterpane in front of her. She gave him a bright smile and said, "You're home early."

"You're early to bed. Where's mother?"

"The doctor said. She's downstairs."

"Never seen her."

"I heard her. Only a minute ago. Proper carry-on in the shop there was. Some woman was in there screeching and screaming like an old cat."

Dido looked at her closely. "What was she screamin' about?"

"How do I know? Can't hear from my bed, can I? In the shop it sounded. My word, she was carrying on." Dido started for the door and she said, "Don't run away, Didy. The doctor was here. I want to tell you."

He closed the door and went downstairs. The anger was still in his chest, a dark pain which seemed to stretch and tear increasingly as the consequences of the day's disaster — the abrupt end of his hopes and the return of his peril — became more and more plain. He went into the kitchen and opened the door to the shop. There was no gaslight in the shop and in the faint daylight glimmer that seeped through the shutters his mother sat on a stool, wiping her eyes. He said, "I called. Why didn't you answer?"

She sniffed in her handkerchief and rubbed round her eyes again. He said, "What you sittin' in the dark for like this?" She looked at him, bitter eyes in a pinched face. He said, "She upset you?"

She spoke low. "You promised me." He did not answer. She said, "You gave me a promise." He stood glumly in the doorway. She said, "You've given up your job I see. Home this early."

He said wearily, "Leave us alone, mother."

Mrs Peach said, "She shouted at me. Dreadful language. And a child with her."

He said, "Mother, I got to move. Keogh's comin' back."

He turned his back on her and started towards the staircase. She rose and followed. She walked upstairs at his heels. "Why aren't you at your job any more?"

Without turning round. "Because I got the sack, that's why."

She walked like his shadow. "You said you wouldn't take any more money. You promised."

He stopped on the landing. "Will you stop whining after me? Didn't you 'ear what I told you? Don't you think about me at all?"

He started up the next flight. She said, "It's against all I taught you. Taking money. There's no excuse."

"Isn't there? You want worse trouble?"

"You've been drinking. I smelled your breath in the shop. You never came in drunk before."

He stopped again and turned to laugh at her. "Drunk!"

"Bullying people. Threatening. Fighting. Having that woman in the shop telling me all about it!"

He said with desperation, "I must 'ave money. Do you know what could 'appen to me if I don't clear out?"

"More fighting," she said bitterly. "You should never have started it."

"*I* started it?"

"I told you not to. Drinking, fighting, every day you're more like him."

"Him?"

So far she had roused him to no more than exasperation but the next words were a blow in his face. "Your father."

He could not speak for a moment. Then, incredulously, "My father?"

"All these years I feared it would come out."

"All these years? After all I done?"

"I was always frightened."

"For you. Everything I done was for you."

"I've been shamed. That's what you've done."

"Don't you care about anything? Don't you want me to make a new start? Free of all this?"

"It's wrong what you've done. No good comes from evil."

"Keogh —"

"Those that take to the sword."

"Don't give me the bloomin' Bible, mother. I've lived by it since I can remember. Like a bloody parson, for your sake. I kep' the boys straight —"

"You drove Chas away."

"*What?*"

"You drove Chas to the devil with your bullying. To the army, it's as bad."

"Well," he said. "This beats the band."

From the next landing came Grace's voice, "Didy! Didy! What are you talking about down there?"

He went up to the bedroom. His mother followed and closed the door behind her. Grace said, "What were you on about? Hammer and tongs it sounded." He said, "Grace — how'd you like to move?"

"Oh," she said gaily. "That's a silly question. Is that what you were on about?"

"We're goin' to move."

"Well of course we are one day."

"No. Now."

Her laughter was innocent. "I think you've gone potty. Has it escaped your notice I'm three weeks from my time?"

"No. I can arrange things."

"Didy, if you hadn't run out before I was trying to tell you. The doctor was here this morning."

"I'll find a room. Something to get on with —"

"You mean you haven't even found a place? Didy, why do you think I'm in bed in my nightie at three in the afternoon? It's my blood pressure. The doctor made me go straight to bed and he says there I must stay till baby is born."

He absorbed this for a moment. "That'll be three weeks!"

"Oh, and a couple of weeks after. I can't get up and do the valeta, you know, the minute after the stork's been."

He cried, "We can't wait."

"Why ever not? I've lived here this long. I can live here a bit longer. Do you think I shall want to move house with a newborn babe? There'll be plenty of time after Christmas. I don't know, all this time you wouldn't listen, all of a sudden you go mad. It's just like you. And you haven't even found a place. Didy, you are daft!"

He stood there in despair. "Never mind the doctor. I'll look after you. Carry you downstairs. Put you in a cab."

She said jovially, "Oh no you won't! Let me tell you, when you find a place I shall have to inspect it first, and then we shall decorate before we move in. We're not going to rush anything. Meanwhile I've got swollen legs and I'm not getting on my feet for anyone."

"You will if I tell you."

"I won't," she cried, as merrily as in a children's game. "You won't get me out of this bed in a hurry."

He cried, "You stupid—" He checked himself, his fist clenched and uplifted in a gesture of frustration and distress.

His mother's thin voice from behind went through him like a fretsaw blade. "Raise your hand to her! Your father hit me when I was carrying you."

He looked at his fist in astonishment. Then he turned and shouted, "Get *bloody* out!"

She stared in a moment of utter shock at the first angry

words he had ever spoken to her. She went out. He turned to attempt explanations but Grace only giggled. "Oh it's about time you told her." She laughed aloud. "Her *face!* It was better than a plate of okey-pokey." She held out her hand. He came close and let her take his hand. She said, "Why were you in such a hurry to move?"

He could not answer. The truth was more than he dared. She said, "You are potty, going mad over it all of a sudden like that. Was she getting on your nerves?" He stood with his hand imprisoned. She said, "I could hear her on the stairs. She's a dear but I'll tell you now she does get on my nerves sometimes." He nodded. She said, "Mind you, I wouldn't be without her for a mint of money when baby comes. It was silly all that about moving, but you're a dear. Six months' time we shall be out of here, don't you worry."

He left her in despair and to be alone went down to the lavatory. He bolted himself into the dark shed, sat down and put his head in his hands. He was trapped. He was in despair and anger growing all the time. He wanted to pay them all out — Keogh, Blakers, and that copper. That bastard plain-clothes creeper Merry who had lost him his job for nothing and brought all this upon him.

He could not stay at home for fear that Grace would ask questions about the supposed business in Dalston. He took to going out with Tommy Long once more but he did not take the reins. He sat at Tommy's side in a brooding and withdrawn silence, vainly searching his mind for a plan to meet the new situation.

They were coming home on Tuesday evening when Tommy roused him with an "Oy!" Tommy flicked the loop of the rein towards the corner of Brick Lane. On the pavement was a group of men. None of them looked round but as the cart rattled past Dido saw that one of them was Keogh.

Chapter 22

It was fight or go under now. Dido no longer had even Chas. Alone he could scarcely hope to scatter his enemies again. He would be hunted down. His only chance was to defeat Keogh before the other had a chance to rally a fresh group of followers; to seek a fair meeting, man to man. Keogh was longer in the arm than Dido and three stone heavier but Dido was prepared to face him. It was the least perilous course.

Days went by without a move from Keogh. He was said to spend a lot of time in the Brick Lane pub, washing down the taste of prison with ale. He was apparently kept busy fetching and carrying for his wife who was laid up in bed. He had never been a bad chap to her by Jaggs Place standards. He did not appear in Rabbit Marsh. From the perch of Tommy's cart Dido sometimes glimpsed him in the street but the enemies never came face to face.

Dido began to frequent "The Railway" of an evening. On his first visit he leaned up against the bar, choosing contrary to his custom a place next to a large group of drinkers. He called Tommy Long and ordered two pints. When they had sunk their first long draughts he asked Tommy in a voice that rose above the chatter, "What's Keogh doin' these days?"

"Boozin'," Tommy said. "In Brick Lane."

"'E ever say anything about me?"

There were listeners now. Tommy said, "'E keeps sayin' 'e wouldn'' like to be in your shoes, not when 'e's done with you."

"Well," said Dido, "I got something to say to Keogh." He turned to take in the listening group. "What I say to Keogh is, let 'im come and fight it out man to man."

There were murmurs of approval. Dido said, "Strip to

the waist. Bare fists. Make a ring to see fair play. If 'e gets me down 'e can kick me to mincemeat. No one'll nark on 'im." He looked around him. "Anyone sees Keogh or any of 'is pals, pass the word on. Fair fight, that's my challenge."

He knew that the news would spread fast. Nothing happened. Each night Dido repeated his challenge and broadcast taunts, which he knew would reach Keogh. "Let Keogh show he's a man. Come without 'is mates. 'E'll get fair play. If 'e don't come he's no man. 'E'll be shown up for a charlie."

But Keogh did not appear.

At dusk one Friday night he lingered at the stables. Tommy Long was still rubbing down the pony. Dido said, "Tommy, I got to get him out. It's me only chance."

"'E won't be such a fool," Tommy said. "'E'll wait for you to make the first move."

"Do something for me, Tommy," Dido said. "Go an' give Keogh a message."

Tommy said, "What? Up that pub? They'd murder me."

Dido said quietly, "If you don't, Tommy, I will."

"I thought you was my mate."

"I thought you were mine." Tommy went on wiping the pony's back. "I never arst for trouble. Makin' a crust, that's my only business. You got your troubles, I got mine."

"You live in this street," Dido said. "What I say goes. Now listen. Never mind the pony. I'll put 'im away. You go to that pub. Now. This is what you're gonna say. Say, 'Dido Peach'll meet you half-way'."

"'Alf-way?"

"That's right." Dido led the pony into the stable. When he came out he said, "Keogh won't come to me. I'm not fool enough to go to 'im. Tell Keogh I'll meet 'im half-way. On the corner of Brick Lane. No one at the back of either of us. We can both see if anyone else is comin'. 'E comes alone. I come alone. Tell 'im."

Tommy said, "They'll murder me."

Dido ignored him. "Now listen carefully to this. Say it in front of the others. I want all 'is lot to know. Say, 'Dido's game. 'E wants to know if you are.' Say, if you don't come, Dido'll put it all round Bethnal Green that Keogh is a charlie."

Tommy said, "Oh, Gawd!"

Dido gave him a half-sovereign. "'Ere, I'm not askin' you to risk your neck. Use your loaf. Go in there and say 'allo to Keogh. Tell 'im you don't wanna be bad friends with no-one. Buy a round o' drinks. Pick your moment, wait till they're matey, then say you got this message. Tell 'em, no offence. This is just what Dido Peach said, it's none o' your business, you're just passin' it on. Then give Keogh the message."

"An' all I get," Tommy said, 'is the change out of 'alf a sovereign."

"There's another 'alf-sovereign when you come back."

"Gawd 'elp me," Tommy said. "Why wasn' I born somewhere else?"

"That's what the Boers said in the Boer War. Go on, skedaddle."

Tommy went off. Dido sat on a trestle by the sheds at the back of the yard. The housebacks of Rabbit Marsh loomed high in front of him. The rows of oblong windows glimmered with darkness or pale gaslight. Inside the rooms figures flitted to and fro and voices came to him. A train rattled by on the embankment behind him and its smoke rolled over the yard in a thick, choking cloud. The smoke dispersed. From a top floor he heard a baby crying, then from another house a burst of voices in raucous quarrel.

His gaze wandered back along the windows, then paused, on the nearest ground-floor window. It was the Barskys' kitchen. Ornate lace curtains hung on either side, but in the space between them he glimpsed a scene that fascinated him.

The table, up against the window, was laid with a dazzling white cloth. In the centre of the table stood two brass candlesticks, polished to a high gleam. In them two tall candles burned with pure flames. Four places were set at the table, each place laid out with plates, patterns of cutlery and rolled napkins, like in films about rich people Dido had seen at the picture palace. There was a platter of fried fish and other dishes of food; and on a board in front of Barsky, an enormous plaited loaf of shining deep brown, fit for the centrepiece of a pastrycook's window. Red wine in a tall bottle caught the candlelight in a ruby gleam and a full wineglass stood by each plate.

He was no less fascinated by the transformed appearance of the people who sat at table. Barsky's wife wore a handsome dress of shiny black with a locket hanging by a fine gold chain round her neck. Her hair was done up in a pile of glossy curls like the Queen of England's, and she sat upright like a queen. Barsky and the boys wore black serge suits, spotless shirts and ties, and small black skull-caps on their heads. The wife stood up, put her hands over her face and bowed a little to the candles, two or three times, as if she was praying; and then it looked as if Barsky was praying.

The sight aroused no train of thought in Dido. He was too sunk in his own dilemma. But he was held by vague wonderment. They were all raising their wine-glasses. Barsky was cutting the loaf, Dido knew these people but they looked like strangers; a tableau around the pure flames of candles.

"'Ere! — 'Ere, for Gawd's sake!"

The voice broke into his reverie. Tommy was standing in front of him, arms out, flapping his hands helplessly. His hair was plastered in wet spikes, he was soaked from head to foot and his clothes were covered with horse dung. "Well," Tommy said, "Well, are yer satisfied?"

Dido said, "They didn't break any bones."

"Not your fault they didn't. They poured beer over me. Rolled me in the road. 'Cause you used my pony that time. I told 'em I didn't know. Keogh said I'd a broke my neck if 'e thought I 'ad. This is what they call lettin' me off light."

Dido gave him a coin. "I'll make it a sovereign. You never earned one so easy. Did you give 'im my message?"

"Yes I did."

"Did 'e say anything?"

"Yes 'e bleet'n" well did."

"What you waitin' for? Another sovereign?"

"'E said there was no green in 'is eye. If you wanna fight 'im you can go up there. Up 'is pub. 'E'll give you fair play. 'E says 'e'll wait for you there. Then everyone can see 'oo's charlie."

Dido did not speak. Tommy said, "You goin'?"

"There's no green in my eye, either," Dido said.

Tommy limped away. Dido went to the mouth of the entry, made a precautionary survey of the pavement and of all the dark doorways, then walked rapidly home. He had offered fair play in good faith. He knew he would not receive it if he went to Keogh's pub. The whole pack would set on him.

His only move had failed. He must live in peril. Yet when he lay in bed next to his sleeping wife, it was not his danger that occupied his mind. Unaccountably he kept seeing that tableau in candlelight framed by a window. It was like a vision of unknown people. It disturbed him. It awakened in him drifts of longing which he could not follow. It made him feel lost and sad, something that drew him but was infinitely out of reach behind the panes of glass. Then his mood changed and he went off to sleep half-wishing he had thrown a brick through the Barskys' window.

October came. While Dido watched and waited he did not know that he was being watched. Inspector Merry had anticipated trouble from the day that Keogh returned to Jaggs Place. He could not keep a round-the-clock watch on the vicinity; that would be too much attention to give to a slum feud. The constables on the beat had instructions to keep their eyes open and each evening there was a plain clothes man strolling in the area until the two antagonists were safely in bed.

Merry kept on at the shopkeepers, to get evidence for his charge. It was clear to him that none of them would open his mouth without a lead from Blakers; and Blakers remained adamantly silent.

"Look arter me?" he had said at the close of Merry's latest visit. "You'll look arter me? It's Number One you look arter, Mr Merry. With all due respect. And it's Number One I look arter. Oh, I know what I know. And I know what you want. You'll 'ear me soon enough if I need the law. Till then —" And he had closed an eye in a solemn wink.

Dido glimpsed Merry on the opposite pavement. He walked on in one direction and the detective in the other. Neither looked round. From the passage as Dido entered the house he heard his mother's voice in a low grumbling monotone. He went into the kitchen. She was huddled on her chair by the dresser, hands in her lap. "I'm left with nothing," she was saying. "It's all gone to pieces. Everything I hoped for. Every one of my boys."

She raised her eyes to see Dido but did not break off. He was looking at Shonny who sat miserably on the sofa. The boy held a handkerchief brown with dried blood to his nose. His hair was rumpled, his face flushed and dirty. Dried blood discoloured his shirt and his suit was rumpled, dirty and blotched with ink stains.

"It's not my fate to be happy," Mrs Peach was muttering. "All my children fail me."

Dido said to Shonny, "What is it, son?"

Mrs Peach said, "He's got the sack. Fighting."

Dido stood over Shonny. Thunderclouds gathered in his expression. "Is this true?"

"He was fighting in the office," Mrs Peach said. "Things got broken. The firm's property. He's been sent home without a reference."

Shonny sat with his face closed in a sulk but with a light of desperate appeal in his eyes. "All right," Dido said to him grimly. "What 'appened?"

Shonny muttered, "They called me Beffnal Green." He cried out, a child's squeak in his husky, breaking voice. "I don't say Beffnal Green. I say Bethnal Green."

Mrs Peach said bitterly, "They were nice boys there. What did he go fighting for?"

"Ever since I started they were on at me," Shonny said. "Soon as I said I come from Bethnal Green. They never called me anything but Beffnal Green."

They were nice boys," Mrs Peach said. "From nice districts. Good families. He fights them."

Shonny's spirit rose. "What else you expect me to do? Every day since I been there. Callin' me names. Beffnal Green. I never 'ad a proper name far as they were concerned. Jus' Beffnal Green. They locked me in the bog. Put ink in me san'wiches. Every day. I 'ad just about enough."

Mrs Peach said, "What about that boy who was nice to you when I went up with you?"

"That's Dennis. 'E talked to me the first day. After that 'e went in with the others. Didn't want to know me, none o' them."

Dido's silence over him was like a gathering storm. He said fearfully, "I couldn' stick it any more. I wrote out all these envelopes. This morning. I put my 'and in the drawer to get 'em out, it was all full o' glue."

His mother's voice was thin and accusing. "He attacked them with a ruler. The manager sent him home without a reference. I don't know what I'll tell the minister. He'll never do anything for the boy again."

Dido was looking down at Shonny. His hand moved and Shonny flinched. But the hand dropped on Shonny's shoulder. Dido said, "Poor little bugger."

Shonny was wide-eyed. Once in a blue moon he heard Dido use a swear word. Dido said, "You stuck it all that time?"

Tears were nearly breaking out in Shonny's cracked voice. "I wanted to get on. I did. I did try, Dide."

"You never told me? Why didn't you tell me? I'd 'a gone up there."

"Didn't want you to. I can mind myself."

From Mrs Peach, venomously, "Yes! Fighting!"

Dido said to her, "Make 'im some tea, mother. Shonny, you go up an' get changed. If we can't get that suit cleaned I'll buy you another. Tailor-made as well."

"That's right," Mrs Peach said, "let him think he's a hero. After he's thrown away his chance."

Dido turned to her and said resignedly, "I suppose this is my fault, too?"

"Fighting?" She said it on a hopeless sigh, looking away. "It wasn't me that set the example."

"Go on, son," Dido said to Shonny. "I know what you fancy. Bread an' scrape. Dripping an inch thick and plenty of salt, eh? Go on, mother'll get it ready."

Shonny said, "I don't wanna go back there, Dide. She wants to take me back there an' ask pardon."

"How will he get another job without a reference?" Mrs Peach cried. "He's let the minister down. There'll be no help there."

"They can stick their jobs," Dido said. "Now on you stay at 'ome, Shon. The other lad can run the barrow. You give your mother a hand. I want someone at 'ome anyway. Keep an eye open."

Shonny said eagerly, "Keogh?"

"Go and get them dirty things off. When you've washed yourself you can 'ave your tea."

Shonny went out and ran upstairs like a child. Mrs Peach shuffled about for the tea things, sighing to herself. Dido said, "It's all right, mother. Boy's no worse off."

She did not answer. He said, "I'll see 'e don't lack money in his pocket. Enough of that an' you're a gentleman."

A last flash of spirit broke out of her misery. "Gentleman!"

"That's right." He looked at her steadily. "Money. Never you mind where it comes from. Long as 'e's got it, nobody'll call 'im Beffnal Green."

"Dide! Dide!" They heard Shonny's voice, juvenile again when raised, from the first-floor landing.

Dido opened the door. Shonny was calling, "Dide! Mum! Grace wants you."

Behind the boy's voice they could hear Grace's faint, distressed cries from the top bedroom. Dido went up the stairs in bounds. His mother and Shonny hurried after him. He went into the bedroom. Grace was grimacing and clutching the sheets and gasping his name. She said, "I think it's starting."

His mother came in. She went straight to Grace. The men and their misdoings forgotten she stooped over the girl and said, "There, there, dear! I know. I know."

Chapter 23

Grace was listening to Mrs Peach. Her left hand lay on the coverlet and Dido, on the other side of the bed, put his hand on it. She ignored him and he drew away, feeling unwanted. He said, "Adn' I better go down the doctor's shop?"

Mrs Peach said, "What do we want him for? She's a healthy girl. Send Shonny for Mrs Trewitt. We shall be wanting her in an hour or two."

Mrs Trewitt was the midwife, an elderly, scrubbed, church-going woman who looked after the doctor's shop round the corner and did most of his deliveries for him.

"You go and make a nice pot of tea," Mrs Peach said to Dido. "I'm sure we could all do with it."

Dido went downstairs, feeling as if he was being dismissed like a little boy who is given a task to keep him out of the way. Afterwards he took Shonny out. He treated him to a fish-and-chip supper and a music-hall. It was not out of indifference that he spent the evening away from home but for the boy's sake, and because he did not want to hang about uselessly.

When they came home Mrs Trewitt was there. Grace lay with her eyes closed grimacing now and again as a spasm came. She opened her eyes, looked at Dido and said, "You go to bed."

Dido shared Shonny's bed for the night, in Chas's old place. He listened for a little while to feminine voices and tramping on the stairs; then he fell into a sound sleep.

He woke up at six in the morning. For a moment in the October gloom he had no recollection of what was afoot; only a puzzlement at the unfamiliar surroundings. Then remembering, he listened and heard only a low tranquil murmur of women's voices above. He got up, slipped into trousers and shirt and sluiced his hands and face at the wash-stand. He left the room quietly, not to awaken Shonny, and went upstairs.

He tapped at the bedroom door; something he had never done before. His mother opened it. She bewildered him; for the first time since his childhood she put her arms round his neck and he had to stoop to be kissed. She said, "Oh, Dido! Come and see."

The midwife had gone. Grace was awake, covered to the chin, one arm round a bundle wrapped in a shawl. A tiny face peeped up at him out of the bundle. He had thought that newborn babies were red but this little face was of a lifeless white. Its eyes were closed and it had an aggrieved, discontented expression. It was so puckered, so like the face of a tiny old man, that he was astonished to hear his mother's reverent murmur, "Isn't she a darling, bless her?"

All this time Grace was gazing at him, not with any expectation or readable meaning, but with eyes calm and neutral as mirrors. She turned her head and looked at the baby, and smiled a little, privately.

Dido felt nothing but awkwardness. He wanted to make some gesture but all he could do was put his hand on Grace's shoulder and say, "All right, gel?"

She turned the faint smile up at him. Then she looked past him, at his mother, and said, "Give him his breakfast."

As she followed him downstairs his mother said, "It was an easy birth. She was lucky, the first is usually the hardest. Mine was. You took a long time coming. I was in agony." She spoke fondly. All her griefs against him seemed forgotten. "She's a lovely healthy baby. Seven pounds. The doctor's looking in later, just to see. I'll fry you some sausages."

She disappeared into the kitchen. He went out to the yard for he would not eat until he had shaved. When he came in the sausages sizzled appetisingly. He sat down. His mother said, "I haven't fried any onions with them. I can cut some up in a minute."

"It's all right."

"A man must be fed. The baby came very quick. Grace was lucky. Mrs Trewitt said she'd never seen such beautiful clean linen." She put Dido's sausages and fried bread before him. "Of course I'd had it all ready for weeks — Oh, Dido —"

His mouth full already, he looked up at the sudden thickening of her voice and saw her eyes brimming with tears. In a moment she was weeping freely. She cried, "A beautiful little girl. Seven pounds. Like a little doll. My own grandchild."

Dido ate stolidly. His mother found a handkerchief and mopped her face, radiant while the tears brimmed out. "Are you glad it's a little girl? Did you want a boy?"

"All the same to me." Dido's words implied a surliness that he did not intend. He had no feelings yet. He added, "A nipper's a nipper, ain' it?"

Mrs Peach made the first effort to check her tears. When she had blown her nose, she said, "She's a good girl, Grace. She bore it wonderful. I shall look after her. I shall, Dido. She'll always have a good mother in me. I think this has brought us all together, don't you?"

He looked up, his grey eyes clear. She said, "I was silly. I shouldn't have carried on at you. You should have gone away before now."

"I couldn't. Could I?"

"You must now. As soon as you can. For baby's sake."

He looked directly at her and said, to test her, "Lucky I got a bit o' money, isn' it?"

Her eyes were innocent. "I couldn't feel more for Grace if she was my own flesh and blood. That lovely baby. It seems a miracle having another little one to hug." She laughed. "I don't know. The time does go. It doesn't seem no time since I held Shonny in a shawl. And you —" Suddenly she burst into fresh weeping, still smiling but with gasps of anguish in her throat. "It all comes back. I can see you as little as that one upstairs. Oh, why can't they stay little?"

He made himself look at her, warily. She said, "You must go away. You must think of your baby. I shouldn't have gone on at you. I don't understand, really I don't. All that money, I can't understand such things. As long as you do the right thing. I wish you'd, I wish you'd pray to do right. You used to pray when you were a little boy. Next to your bed kneeling down. I'm only thinking of the baby. Dido, all I want is for you to be a good man."

He drank his mug of tea in a long draught. All her courage left her. She stood in front of him, a small creature mopping the last tears from her lowered face. He looked down at her with a long, worried frown. He sighed and went out of the room.

Grace opened her eyes when he came in. He returned her smile and went to glance down into the cradle which stood between the bed and the wall. He said, "Asleep. You feelin' better?"

"A bit tired. I've forgotten it, really. Funny." Her voice was normal but weak. "I'm afraid I shall be in bed a few weeks."

"I don't want you gettin' up till you're fit. Understand?"

"What did mother give you?"

"Pork sausages."

"Did she fry you up some onions?"

"I told 'er not to."

"But you like onions."

"She must 'a' been tired after last night."

"She could have got some sleep. The midwife was here."

"She reckoned she ought to stay by you."

"Yes. She means well. But she does fuss so."

"It's a new life for mother. 'Avin' the baby."

Grace smiled. "It, was me that had the baby, not her."

He sat down at the bedside. "Well, she's been through a lot in 'er time. The baby'll do 'er good. You rest now."

She reached out and took his hand. "Stay with me."

"Shut your eyes, then."

She obeyed. He said, "That's right. You rest. I'm here."

When her hand relaxed, he took his away gently, got up

and went round to the cradle. It was a little nest of frilled muslin in blue and pink dots. It stood on a low stand of polished walnut. He gazed down at the baby.

"She's got your hair." It was Grace, her eyes open.

"You rest," he said. She shut her eyes contentedly. The baby's eyelashes were long and dark but there was a floss of fair hair on the front of its head, just visible within the shawl. He was fascinated by the face, it seemed so tired, he saw so much human grief and experience in it; all his own sufferings in this tiny offshoot of himself. He could not formulate this idea, he could only stare, while a strange sensation went through his veins, the recognition of this scrappet of life as a small *himself*. Vague feelings drifted in him, of identity with it, of pity for it.

He heard Grace say, "I suppose you've been thinking what to call her?"

He did not answer. In the instant that Grace spoke the child opened its eyes. They transfixed him. They seemed to see everything and to see nothing. They looked directly up at him and held him without acknowledging that they saw him. They were like two tiny blue flowers, nothing in them but beauty; pure Me, unspoiled by experience.

"You must have been thinking about it," Grace said. "I'm sure other people talk about it all the time. Names for boys. And for girls. I often wondered if you were thinking about it. Only you're so wrapped up in your business."

He barely heard her. The baby's eyes held him in the same spell as the white cavern of a coal fire in which one discerns all one's own visions.

"Dido," Grace protested. "You must have thought about it."

It required an effort of the attention to turn away from the baby and sit on the edge of the bed once more with Grace. Among all his recent troubles Grace had only been a shadow; at night a silent bulk next to him in the bed. Another and fearful world outside had filled his mind and now he did not want to think about it. He said at random, "Emma."

"After your mother."

"Please the old lady."

Grace assumed a stubborn, slightly sulky expression. "I'm not saying anything against Emma. It is very ordinary, though, I thought of Lydia Evelina."

He was remote from her. He made himself talk. "Is that after your auntie?"

"No, I made them up. Well, from books and things."

"A bit la-di-da, isnt it?"

"I'm only thinking of the future." She made of this remark a manifesto, looking at him directly. He sat in thoughts of his own and she said, "Didy, talk to me." She reached for his hand and he let her take it.

He said, "Doctor ought to be comin' soon."

"Oh, bother him. When are we going to move, Didy?"

"Soon."

"How soon?"

"Soon as you're well."

"I'll be up in a few weeks. Can I come with you and look, Didy? I have looked already. I did tell you. I know all the nice districts."

"You get well."

"Mother can mind baby. We shall want two rooms at least. And our own kitchen. If we had another room we could make a nursery."

"Whatever you say."

"And if there's a garden — well there must be, and we must have use of it."

"Put the pram out on a nice day."

"Yes. I believe in fresh air."

"Best if we're near a park. Victoria Park. Or Hackney Downs. Take her for walks." He was smiling and truly interested now. His hand in Grace's warm clasp, he felt unwontedly close to her. He had no overt consciousness of their greater intimacy but it was for him a new degree of marriedness. Talking like this made him feel secure. It excluded other, unpleasant realities from his mind.

"Didy," she said. "You know what I want you to do as soon as I'm up. I want you to take me out."

"Take you out again. Course I will."

"No. Not just for a bus ride. Get some nice clothes. Go to a restaurant for supper. Well you ought to get used to it, Dido. It's how people in business live."

"We got no money to burn, Gracey. Not if we want to move."

"We could go to the Pop in Piccadilly. It doesn't cost much. I used to hear all about it from girls. There's a balcony and a band. Dancing. It's ever so smart and it doesn't cost much. I wouldn't waste your money, Didy. I'm not extravagant." She paused and said, "How is the business?"

His throat went dry. "The business?"

"I do save. I'm very good at economies. But we're not hard up for a penny, are we? You don't tell me anything about the business really. Is it going all right? With this man and all that, in Dalston?"

"Yes," he said. "Goin' all right. Only a bit slow at the start. Always is."

"Well of course. I'm no fool. You have to put the money back in a business."

"That's right."

"I'm not so green as I'm cabbage-looking," she said. "I know all about you."

"About me?" He was taken by surprise. She looked so calm. He hardened himself for the attack.

She let go his hand. "You open that."

She was pointing at the drawer in the base of their wardrobe. He went and opened it. She said, "Take out the parcel. You open it."

He took out a large brown paper parcel tied with coarse string. He was looking at her all the time, a keen, trapped expression in his eyes. She said, "I know what's in it. Well I am your wife, aren't I? I don't think I was being nosey. I just like to know if there's things to keep clean and all that."

The parcel lay open at the foot of the bed. In it were folded his old working-clothes, stained and patched; and on top of them a pair of big boots, clean but creased, scarred and scuffed by much scraping. He had not worn them since his last day on the wharf. Grace said, "You used to go out to work, didn't you?"

"Anythin' wrong in it?"

"Well it wasn't very nice work. I can see from the clothes."

"On the wharves."

"I thought something like that. You are a silly."

"What for?"

"You never told me, did you? Were you ashamed?"

"You've never been short of a sovereign."

"I didn't say I had. It was silly to be ashamed of your past. Same as you exaggerated. Well, when you met me. All about the business. Anyone would have thought you had dozens working for you. I didn't mind when I found out."

"Found out what?"

"That you were just working for mother. You've certainly made it pay. You're right, my goodness we've never been short. And now you branching out. Didy, I'm not ashamed of your past. I'm proud of you. A man should be proud of bettering himself."

He was doing up the parcel. He turned to put it back in the drawer. She said, "What on earth do you want to keep it for?"

He paused. "I don' know."

Then she laughed, "Oh well they'll do for gardening or something. I shan't be satisfied till we have our own garden. I know you're going to get on, Didy. You have got me behind you. And baby now. She *is* going to be a lady — Didy, I know what. Lydia Emmelina. That's what we'll call her. Emmelina. After your mother, that should please her. Lydia Emmelina for the christening. And we shall call her Lydia."

He closed the drawer and straightened up. "You rest,"

he said. "Sooner you get well, sooner we can move."

"Oh I can save," she said. "Don't you worry about me, I mean look at the cradle."

He said, "I did give you money. I told you to get everything you wanted."

"I did," she said. "But look how I saved. I bought it for a penny. A banana crate, all round, just the right shape to rock. It's all padded out and covered with lovely muslin and I bought the little mattress. Baby couldn't have had better if I'd bought her a Moses basket."

"What's a Moses basket?"

"Oh, it's what people with money have."

"I gave you money."

"I wanted to save. I'm not extravagant, Didy."

"You didn't 'ave to put our baby in a banana crate."

"It's lovely. You didn't know. How would you ever know?"

"I gave you the money. You didn't 'ave to."

"Oh you are potty."

He stood at the foot of the cradle looking down at the baby's infinite eyes. "Didn' 'ave to put 'er in a banana crate."

"Everyone does."

"I'm not everyone. You ought to know that by now. Nor is she. What did you call it? What you said just now."

"A Moses basket. Why?"

"You get some rest. I want you up as soon as you can."

"Where are you going?"

"To get one. Where d'you think?"

Grace said, "Give him another glass."

Dido left his chair by the fire and poured another glass of fizzy kola for Shonny. He said, "You'll bust if you 'ave any more."

The boy loved drinking pop. Grace liked to have him by her now that she was up. She lay on the sofa propped by velvet cushions and sometimes while she talked to him she touched his cheek affectionately as if he was another child of hers. Baby was asleep in the bedroom. Mother was downstairs ironing napkins.

It was late evening. Two weeks had passed. Grace was still officially an invalid but she dressed in the evenings and was brought into the parlour by Dido to have her supper on a tray. Against the window the yellow gloom lay thick as a blanket, shutting them in cosily. It was a sign of approaching winter; even when there was no fog, the season's fog hung dispersed to darken and chill the air. The gaslight thrummed palely in its small, flowered globe and the mahogany table gleamed with the greater, purer light of a handsome oil-lamp. The coal fire in the grate was cheerful. Dido sat close to its warmth, warmed too by his thoughts while the voices of the other two murmured outside his attention.

Day by day, imperceptibly to himself yet bringing him to a state of which he could not help being aware, the last two weeks had changed him. The train of his thoughts, the subterranean flow of his feelings, had undergone a kind of chemical change.

Even on that first day when he had gone to the baby outfitters' for the new cradle, new impulses had governed him. He had walked briskly to the Kingsland Road, his steps jaunty with a new elation. The shop, crowded with baby carriages, cots, toys and displays of pretty linen, had intoxicated him, redolent with the warm cosy smell of fabrics and teddy-bears' fur. Although until this day he had been hoarding the money that he needed to get away, he bought a wicker cradle on rockers, a toilet basket, a parcel of rattles and toys and a tiny quilt of pink sateen sprigged with forget-me-nots. He had been fascinated by the big, stately perambulators. He had imagined his baby riding in one of them. His feelings for the child only a few hours after its birth were still unformulated but its coming into the world had provided a tangible shape to his own egoism. There it was in the cot, his own possession and future. It was himself that he saw enhanced, his own pride fortified, his own future bodying forth in a series of pictures that became ambitions; the first clear ambitions he had recognised. His pleasure on that first day was all in himself. Lydia Emmelina. It was the right sort of name for his child. Grace who could think of such a name was the right wife for him. He saw her in nice clothes pushing a high, splendid baby carriage, with its springs and silvery fittings and gleaming panels and lining of softest white leather. But he could not take such a carriage back to Rabbit Marsh. It belonged to another setting. And he saw a quiet road lined with leafy plane trees and neat houses fronted by scrubbed steps and new painted railings. At Grace's side he walked; a different himself.

As day followed day he spent more and more of his time indoors. At first it was because he preferred not to think of the menace outside; but in time the menace became unreal. When he was with Grace and the child he could pretend that he was a man like others, a man unthreatened; and then he did not have to pretend for indoors he was able to forget that there was an outside. Perhaps it was this that drew him all the more quickly to his child: its power to give healing forgetfulness.

He could sit and watch the baby for hours. At first he felt no positive emotion; only a stirring of his senses, dulled by the years and now breathed upon by the presence of fresh life. Sometimes Grace put the baby into his arms. Secretly he was afraid to handle her. Grace had told him that the baby's head was soft and he was obsessed by the idea of the tiny creature's fragility.

Her face seemed to smooth out with each feed. Within a week all the creases and the pallor had gone. Her cheeks, which he sometimes touched gently with the back of a finger, were of an incredible softness like the surface of warm milk and they bloomed with the subtle rosy flush of a petal. He was fascinated by the wondering wide gaze of her eyes which saw him now, and by their ineffable pure blue irises. With her down of golden hair she was like a little living doll.

And each day the strange, undirected stir of emotion changed into something more positive. At first he only knew that when he came in and shut the door behind him and sat down near the cot, he felt peaceful at last. Then, sitting there, his peace was disturbed by vibrations of tenderness that did not even translate themselves into thought; until the time came when Grace, wanting to prepare a napkin, gave him the baby to hold, and at the first feel of the tiny warmth and weight cradled against him he was swept by a wild flame of attachment. It was blind, still untranslated, but the most profound emotion he had ever known. It was in fact the first time that passion had ever swept over him; something far different from anything he had ever felt with his mother or with Grace, whatever he had unconsciously sought from them; and because it was the first time it was all the more fierce and consuming.

What pierced his heart was the helplessness of this little scrappet. The anguished tenderness that as a small boy he had felt for his suffering mother was far surpassed by his need for this tiny creature which needed him. It could do nothing for itself but wail if it was hungry or uncomfortable. It had to be picked up and put down. Nourishment had to be put into its mouth. It had to be most gently washed and wiped. It would die if its mother did not care for it and he was responsible for mother and child. It was the most vulnerable to hurt of all human creatures and he alone could protect it.

And in time thoughts smote him with astonishment. It will know me. It will love me. It will call me "daddy". A strange yearning came to him for his own lost childhood. He saw himself small and innocent before all the awful unwanted things had begun; and the child was himself reborn, a new start for him, a clean blank page. Oh, he would protect it. He would look after them both.

For in this strange dream of contentment in which he dwelt, a world in a small bedroom and nothing beyond, Grace had her part. He liked to sit in silence and watch while she fed the baby. She always turned away modestly but he was fascinated in the shadowy room by the outline of her lowered face, by the baby's face pressed in a scowl of effort against the breast which was hidden by her hand and by the fold of her opened blouse. He found her beautiful at these times. He was amazed at the natural expertness, absorption and patience with which she fed and handled the child. He felt closer to her; a sharer with her.

He talked to her more. It was beyond him to tell her the truth. But he told her of his plans, which were a simple extension of the lie he had told her. His ambition now was simple. It was to make a reality of his lie. Then she would never know that he had lied. His trips with Tommy Long had given him a taste for the totting game. A few pounds behind him and he could set up with his own pony and cart. For a few shillings a week he could rent a shed up Dalston way and his business would be a reality.

Thus with a good conscience he now went on telling his tale to Grace; but now he believed it. He need not merely scrape a wretched living like Tommy Long. It took an expert eye to know the value of the innumerable articles that were collectively called "rags" and after living with mother all these years he had that eye. He would comb all the boroughs of north-east London for old rags, he would go into partnership with his mother, cutting out the profits of the dealers who sold to her and himself selling on an ever-growing scale through the outlets which she already had.

He did not mind starting in a small way. He liked handling a pony, he liked being his own master and he liked being out on his own all day. As Grace became eager at his stories he grew eager, too, for the future he would carve out in one of those nice districts beyond Dalston, with their little girl going to a school where clean and well-dressed children went and growing up to be happy, prosperous, educated and respected.

All this life in his mind had become, as he sat staring into the fire's glow with Shonny and Grace murmuring in the background, his real life. He had almost persuaded himself that the menace no longer existed. It is the human way; under a persisting threat fear dulls and dies away. After all, Keogh had been back for nearly a month and he had done no more than brag in his pub. It wouldn't be surprising if a spell in jail had cooled him off.

Shonny didn't want to wake up but three glasses of pop before bedtime was asking for trouble. He kept his eyes shut for a long time. He stuck it out while the distant clocks of the City struck two quarters. In the end his bladder hurt so much that he had to get up. He did a long jimmy riddle in the chamber and he felt better.

The trouble was, now he felt hungry. He always did when he woke up in the night. He was sleepy and wanted to crawl back into bed; but just as the pain had tormented him before so now he was tormented by an exquisite taste in his mouth, the taste of his favourite delicacy, a thick slice of fresh bread heavily smeared with beef dripping and sprinkled with salt. The longer he held out the more his mouth watered. The more his mouth watered at the beloved taste, the more famished he felt.

There was nothing for it, he'd have to go down. He often did. Mother didn't mind. Nor did Dido. Dido was strict. (Only to be expected from a hard man like that.) But Dido and mother always said, there was plenty of food in the house, thank goodness, and the boys were always welcome to it. As long as they didn't make a noise. Funny Chas being away. Shonny had got used to it but sometimes in the middle of the night when he woke up it seemed strange that Chas was not there.

He opened the door cautiously, stole out of the room and crept downstairs. He was coming down to the half-landing when a faint noise made him pause. The noise came from the kitchen. His heart skipped with fright. He called himself a charlie for being frightened of the dark but he started down the last flight of stairs even more quietly, and stopped once more; this time with terror.

The back door to the yard was open. He thought he

could hear faint scuffling sounds from the kitchen — or were they from the shop? He clung to the banisters, dizzy, the throb of terror rapid in his chest. He was afraid to go down. He was afraid to wake Dido, perhaps for nothing.

The door from the kitchen to the passage opened. In the same moment that a faint acrid smell came to Shonny's nostrils he saw a human figure in the slot of lesser light made by the open door. The figure flitted out like a shadow. It was small and slight and as it came into the area below the stairs where the light was even paler because of the open yard door, Shonny recognised Cockeye. But already behind Cockeye had appeared another, massive bulk; his father, Keogh.

Intent on escape neither of them looked up. Shonny was paralysed and could not utter a sound; until there escaped from his throat a terrified, croaking, "Ah — ah —" and the two in the hall below glanced up, and in a sudden burst of running steps that thudded in the hall and scuttered outside, bolted.

Shonny stood hanging on to the banister, gasping, managing to force a shout out of himself, "Dido! Dido!"

He ran down to the kitchen door and there, through two open doors, he looked into the shop and saw a glimmer that as he stared in terror became a ragged red line running along the shop floor. Shonny could only scream, pouring out the one word again and again pell-mell like a child awakened from a nightmare, "Dido! Dido! Dido! Dido! Dido!"

Chapter 24

White smoke rolled along the floor and the stench of charred rags rose up the stairs. Shonny was in the doorway to the shop, coughing, yelping, "Dido! Dido!" In an attempt at action he emptied the washing-up bowl over the fire. The line of tiny flames three feet long at the base of a pile of sacks vanished in a hiss and a new choking white billow, then reappeared defiantly as a thread of embers out of which burst once more small tongues of fire. Coughing — "Dide! Dido!"

He was thrown aside. He glimpsed Dido, dishevelled, in shirt-tails, plunging past him into the shop, heard his shout, "Buckets, you ninny" — then to his astonishment the shop door slammed in his face.

In the darkness of the shop Dido choked, his lungs racked by the thick, stinking smoke. With the door shut to stop the draught, he pulled down sacks and flung them on to the nibbling line of flames. He threw one upon another, stifling the fire, and pressed his own weight down on them. He sprawled on the sacks, trying to hold his breath against the smoke.

He staggered to his feet, opened the door and lurched into the kitchen, drinking air. He focused on Shonny's staring face, seized a bucket which Shonny held out and shouted, "More!"

He pulled away the sacks. The ragged line of fire at the base of the stack had been stifled but the black line of ashes was quivering with heat and would burst into flames once more if he could not douse it in time. The indoor tap which thanks to Grace they now had was in the passage only a few steps away and Shonny appeared at once with a full bucket which Dido emptied along the ashes. Shonny ran back and forth and Dido poured water continuously over the lower sacks. Kitchen and shop were filled by the strong sharp smell.

He put down the bucket and stepped into the kitchen to ease his lungs in the draught which came through a broken windowpane. It was only then as he stood tired and breathing slowly, that he heard his mother's faint cries from the landing. He went out to her. She whimpered, "Come upstairs, Dido. Quick."

He followed her upstairs. On the top flight Grace sat doubled up. He stooped and raised her head. Her eyes stared dark and unfathomable into his. She whispered, "What was it? What was it, Didy?"

He helped her up to the top landing then gathered her up in his two arms and took her to their bed. Behind him he heard his mother's plaint, "She must have fainted. She shouldn't have got up. She's not strong enough yet." He put Grace into bed and over her agitated whispering he said, "Nothing, love. All over now. Go to sleep."

He turned away. His mother was fretting, "What was it? Dido — was it —?"

He said, "Stay with her," and went downstairs. The baby slept.

The intruders had with professional quietness broken a pane and opened the back window of the kitchen. Cockeye had crawled in and opened the yard door from the inside. Keogh had joined him, they had gone into the shop, poured paraffin (Dido found the empty can) at the base of a pile of sacks and set light to it.

The gas was lit in the kitchen. Dido made tea. The charred stench still hung in the air. The shop floor was sodden. Dido checked Shonny's chatter and prowled about, silent, looking around him as if making some mental tally.

Doors, stairs, floorboards, the house was a shell of dry wood more than two hundred years old. If Dido had not killed the fire at birth, if he had come a few minutes later or if he had done the wrong thing, the whole ground floor would have been ablaze, flames roaring up as from the bottom of a furnace to engulf the family upstairs.

Shonny cried, "Dide, we'd all 'a' been burned in our beds." Dido did not answer. He walked to and fro on noiseless bare feet, silent as a cat, the glitter of his eyes harbouring secrets.

Shonny thought that he would never sleep for his mind was seething, but as soon as he climbed back into bed he dropped into oblivion; and then Dido was shaking him. It was an hour before his normal getting-up time but Dido told him to dress.

He followed Dido downstairs. Without explanation Dido set him to work helping to remove all traces of the attempt. All the ashes and those sacks which were in the least charred were taken out to the yard. Dido even sniffed at sacks to make sure that none remained which smelled of smoke. All the charred rags were stuffed into the boiler to be burned just as rags were burned every morning. The sacks which were merely soaked were dumped near the mangle; just like any other wet rags.

They had to hurry because Dido wanted to finish before the hired boy came in. Dido lit the boiler. They went indoors. Dido scrubbed the shop floor so that the soaked patch was no longer conspicuous. Windows were opened to let in fresh air and Shonny sprinkled carbolic all over the house to cover the ashy tang. Dido took the empty paraffin can under his coat to Tommy Long's dump and came back with a pane of glass which before breakfast he had puttied into the window.

Then he and Shonny had their usual vigorous morning wash and Dido, without waiting for mother, prepared a handsome breakfast of fried bread and bacon for Shonny.

The boy was mystified. He had not imagined that Dido would go to the police but he could not see any reason for his brother's clear determination to arrange things as if the incident had not happened. Dido moved about like an animal following a scent, hardly aware when Shonny ventured to speak.

The hired boy came and Dido sent him out at once with the barrow. Mrs Peach came down. She was struck dumb, bowed and shrivelled so that her size appeared diminished.

She sat down and took in silence the cup of tea that Dido gave her. He sat at the table between the two of them. He said, "Now listen. Nothing happened." Shonny said, "But why —?"

Mrs Peach only stared, haunted. Dido said, "Nothing happened — Shonny, you 'ad a bad dream. Like when you were a little boy. Neighbours'll know nothing. Might 'ave 'eard you shouting. Or seen the kitchen light on. Nothing else. You 'ad a bad dream. Anyone asks you what, you can't remember. Understand?"

Shonny could not speak. He nodded. Dido said, "Brought you down to the kitchen, give you a cup of tea. That's all. Don't say nothing else. Anything else, just say, you don't know."

Shonny managed, "But who? — tell who?"

"Anyone asks. That's all. Mother — you understand? Nothing else. Nothing else at all."

Her eyes stared at him in terror. She nodded.

Dido took a tray upstairs with some breakfast for Grace. She was sitting up. He put the tray in front of her and said, "All right?"

She nodded. He felt her brow. "Still hot. Brought the fever back a bit."

She spoke as if her lips were slightly swollen. "I'll be all right."

"Keep to your bed day or two."

Her stare was searching. "What happened?"

"Nothing. Shonny had a bad dream. Made him yell. Used to be like that when 'e was a kid. I went down, give 'im a cup of tea. Put 'im back to bed."

Her stare did not waver. "Someone ran away. I heard them."

He said slowly, patiently as to a child. "Nothing happened."

Some expression — fear perhaps — passed across her eyes. "Then you're not going to call the police?"

He put both his hands on hers and moved closer. He looked into her eyes and spoke again. He was deliberate, backing the words with an unspoken message, an appeal. "Nothing happened. Shonny had a bad dream. Nothing else. Do you understand, Grace? Nothing else."

She was silent. He stood up. "Eat your breakfast. Go back to sleep."

He went out. She stared after him. Her mind was alive with fears and questions long suppressed. Someone had been in the yard last night. Dido was afraid to call the police. He was mixed up in something. As on that first frightening day when she had returned from her honeymoon and that terrible man had fallen down on the pavement in front of her eyes, she was seized by a dread of things kept from her.

Mrs Peach had nerved herself for speech by the time Dido came down. She said, "Dido, what are you going to do?"

He turned to Shonny. "Get out in the yard, son. You're on the boiler today. See all that stuff is well burned. Give the ashes a good poke. You forget last night. Bad dream, that's all." Shonny went out. Dido said, "Any more tea in the pot?"

His mother poured. "Dido — you can't stay. Not another minute."

He looked up at her and his eyes struck her silent. For the rest of the day she shuffled about bowed in fearful quiet. Grace stayed in bed. Dido went up to the bedroom and sat down by the cot. His back was to Grace and they did not speak to each other. The baby woke and slept; she was lifted from her cot, fed, cleaned, dressed, laid down. Dido did not lean over her or touch her or take her or react to her sounds and smiles. He sat stiffly on a chair at the foot of her cot. His eyes followed her; that was all. His hands in his lap were laced together as if each were striving to crush the other. He looked at his child for hours but no softness came into his expression. His face was hard, muscles lumped behind the mouth, his eyes set close with points of light in them as if they were intent upon an adversary in a deadly arena. He sat for hours looking at his child, whose life had been threatened.

He went out after breakfast to tell Tommy Long not to wait for him. He lingered for a while in the stables before coming back to the house. All day he pottered about the house. He was calm but he seemed so far away in his own thoughts that neither Grace nor his mother spoke to him except to utter commonplaces.

At ten in the evening he went up to bed. Grace watched sleepily as he poured for her the nightly glass of port which the doctor had prescribed to restore blood. He gave it to her. "Tired?"

She nodded. "The more I sleep the more I want to."

He moved quietly about the room, folding his clothes with care. By the time he was undressed Grace was fast asleep. He went to the window, pulled the curtain aside and looked out at the yellow haze thickening as it now did almost every night into brown fog. He nodded. He padded back to the bed, looked down at the sleeping Grace and nodded again with a slight smile. He climbed into bed and fell asleep.

At the time which he had set inside his mind he woke up. He slipped out of bed and stood for a moment watching Grace. She was fast asleep. He went to the window and looked out once more. The fog had thickened. He had been pretty sure of the fog but if it had thinned out he would have gone back to bed; for tonight, at least.

In the fog-darkened room he moved like a cat with movements mentally rehearsed. He found the door, turned the knob with the slowness of infinite patience, slipped out and as carefully closed the door behind him.

He moved downstairs as stealthily as if he were a thief

in a stranger's house. On the lower landing he paused for long seconds before he dared move on. Down to the passage, into the kitchen and into the shop where he dressed swiftly, in old garments he had sorted from the mounds of his mother's stock; a jacket, trousers, a pair of rope-soled shoes and a pair of woollen gloves.

The bolts of the yard door which he had oiled during the day slipped back without a sound. He left the back door unfastened and moved to the front door, which for the same reason opened as quietly. He peered out. Fog filled the street, whose length was marked only by the blurred haze of spaced gaslamps. He stepped out, closed the door with care and flitted along close to the housefronts, watchful for a lit window, keyed to hear any approaching footstep. Neither disturbed him.

He slipped into the stable entry and a minute later came out again. Silent on rope soles across the road, hurrying now along the opposite wall, alert, unseen, he turned into Brick Lane, continued to the next corner, turned into the thicker gloom of the next side street and soon stopped. He moved into the deeper darkness of a doorway. He was a little way from Jaggs Place, on the opposite pavement.

He stood absolutely still as does the animal or the soldier using darkness and he let his eyes become accustomed to the fog. Nothing stirred across the road. He slipped into the next doorway and watched again. Nothing. Then to the doorway directly opposite the arch. This time his watch was longer for the archway was itself a sheltering darkness. Only when he was sure that no shadow moved in it did he flit across the road and stop once more to peer round the angle of wall into the entry. He meant to take no chances. His enemies might be alert for a reprisal.

He edged slowly into the archway. The courtyard inside was still. Not a light showed in the unshuttered windows. The tenement walls above vanished like black cliffs into the fog. He was at the inner edge of the arch. There was no sentry. During the day, putting himself in his enemy's shoes, he had thought that he would have bought a dog and chained it outside his door. There was nothing. Secure in his den, with all his tribe sleeping around him, it was beyond Keogh to imagine anything that one man alone could do to him. Well, he would soon learn.

Keogh's hovel was in the angle to the right of the archway. A foot from Dido's face as he slid along the wall was the window, beaded with moisture over its coat of grime. He stood in the utter stillness of a city halted and muffled by fog.

Dido fumbled in a pocket. He lifted the object that he had brought from the stables, a glass vinegar jar, gallon size. It was full of paraffin and its neck was stuffed with paraffin-soaked flannel, a tongue of which hung out to make a fuse.

Dido brought the hand out of his pocket and scratched a vesta against the wall. It sputtered. He put it to the flannel and there was a flare of smoky flame.

He brought back his arm level with his shoulder; then with all his force like a discus-thrower he swung it in a flat arc at the window, let go and as the crash of glass sounded, ran. He was into the archway, the night's foggy silence shattered by a chaos of noises fast as the echo of a shot; tinkling of glass, behind it an odd roar like the roar of air up a chimney, and bursting into this a sudden dreadful commotion of human voices, child wails, woman's screams, a man's deep bellowing — all a wall's breadth away from him in the moment that he flitted out of the arch.

He ran along the walls and the medley of noises increased in Jaggs Place as doors opened, new voices shouted; but more and more faintly as he ran in the fog.

His luck held. He was back in Rabbit Marsh and he padded rapidly across into the stable yard. Now, with the swift sureness of a man who had throughout the day rehearsed in his mind every moment of this night, who had sat at a back window memorising every yard, dustbin and hencoop, he climbed a wall and ran along the high rear wall like a cat, confident that the choking stench of the fog would loll his scent in the nostrils of the yard dogs. None barked. He dropped into his own back yard.

In by the unbolted back door. Into the kitchen. He was out of the clothes and out into the yard again with the clothes, the gloves and the sandshoes rolled into a bundle. The telltale garments, torn and marked with grime and dust and whitewash from a dozen walls, were stuffed into the boiler. They had been well splashed with paraffin beforehand. Into the house, back and front doors bolted, hands and face sluiced in the dirty-water bowl in the kitchen, and silently up to bed.

It was a couple of hundred yards in a straight line over the opposite block to Jaggs Place and as he moved with caution from stair to stair he thought he heard a faint babble of voices from that direction; but the fog played all sorts of tricks. However, there was no doubt about the noise he heard a little later; the clangour of fire-engines going along Brick Lane.

He began carefully to open the door of his bedroom; then he saw the glimmer of light within. It was too late to stop. He opened. Grace was sitting on the edge of the bed, a candle alight on the table next to her. She was rocking the baby in her arms. He started to make a hushing noise but in the same moment she whispered, "Sh! I've just got her off to sleep."

He crept into the room and climbed into bed. She put the baby down in the cot and returned to bed, and whispered. "Have you been?"

She meant, to the toilet in the yard. Neither he nor she would use any indoor vessels to empty their bowels at night. He nodded, and said, "Sh!"

She whispered, "I can hear fire-engines."

"Sh! Go to sleep."

He woke up before his brother, went downstairs, wiped the oil from the bolts, stuffed the oily rag in the boiler and lit it. When the clothes within were well ablaze he rammed the charring fragments into yesterday's ashes, pushed in more rags, cabinet-makers' chips and shovelfuls of sawdust. The fire roared in the boiler: the start of a normal day.

He took a tray up to Grace with tea, bread and a boiled egg. While she ate he looked out of the window. It was a drear winter morning, wet dark pavements at the foot of the grimy walls, clouds low above them like a gathering of grey factory smoke, from which fell a fine sleet that would chill the ill-clad poor to the marrow of their bones.

He went into the front room to look out of the window. In spite of the weather there were clusters at all the doors busy in talk, and at the corner of Brick Lane the tip of a black crush overflowed, thick as the tail of a swarm of bees. People hurried towards the crowd, whose density at this point meant that Brick Lane must be packed for at least two blocks.

Grace got out of bed. Instead of going to the cot she walked to the chest of drawers and started to comb her hair at the mirror. She said, "I feel a lot better."

"You're just as well in bed this weather."

"The doctor said I should start to take exercise."

"You 'ad one bad turn."

"That was the fright." She could talk of it now casually, without looking round. Her spirits had returned because Dido appeared in good spirits, his old self again. She was always quick to forget fears. She peered at herself, arranging her hair. "I think I shall come downstairs for a bit."

"What about your backaches?"

"I shall rest on the sofa. I can feed baby and put her down, and mother can bring her down to me later."

"Don't want baby catching cold."

"She can't stay in the bedroom for ever. Look at her red cheeks and her chubby little legs." Grace laughed. She was already slipping into a long woollen dressing-gown. "There's nothing ails her. You go down and see the kitchen's warm."

His mother was in the kitchen preparing Shonny's breakfast. She was her old busy self. For her, too, yesterday's fears seemed to have receded. Dido started to build up the fire with wood blocks and coal. Shonny came running in. He cried, "Dide, there's all people in the street. I could see from the window —"

Dido said, "Get washed. Mother's waiting with your breakfast."

"Can' I go out an' see?"

"Get your breakfast. You can see after."

Mrs Peach said, "I thought I heard fire-engines last night.

"I expect that's it," Dido said. "See after breakfast."

Shonny was at the door when the hired boy came running in. Out of breath, he panted, "Mister — missus —"

"You're fifteen minutes late," Dido said. "Bed too warm?"

"There's been a fire," the boy gasped. "I been lookin'. Everyone's up Brick Lane —"

Dido cut in, "Don't pay you stand gawpin' at fires. You get on the mangle."

"There's been a fire," the boy cried. "Jaggs Place. They say all been burned. Burned to a cinder."

"'Expec' someone's chimney caught fire," Dido said. "Lot of ol' women. If you drown a cat they say Southend Pier's gone down with all hands. Get out to your work, lad. Won't earn your livin' gossipin'."

The boy went out reluctantly; but before he had closed the door Shonny cried, "I'm goin' to see," and darted out.

Dido went upstairs. Grace was ready and he helped her down. She lay on the old sofa. Mrs Peach said, idly, "There's been a fire. Down Brick Lane somewhere."

As indifferently Grace said, "Oh?" She was sipping tea, warming her hands on the mug. Footsteps thundered in the hall. Shonny appeared in the doorway. His face was white. "Dide — Dide — It's them. Keoghs. All of 'em. They're all in 'ospital."

Grace said vaguely, "Who are the Keoghs?"

Mrs Peach was staring at Dido, clutching her apron as if she might faint. Dido said, "Go on. Keoghs, eh?"

"But, Dide —" Shonny gasped. "You —"

Dido stepped forward and grasped his shoulder. "Shut up! I don' wanna know about the Keoghs. None of my business."

"But he was — he was —" Shonny was almost in tears. Dido stood over the boy. He looked down at him with fierce eyes. "I don' know what's 'appened to the Keoghs. I don't want to know. Nothing to do with me. Whatever 'appens to them it's nothing to do with us here. Understand?"

"Don't carry on at the boy," Grace said mildly. "He was only telling you. Who are these Keoghs anyway?"

Shonny stood staring up into Dido's eyes paralysed with fright. Dido said gently, "You understand, boy."

Shonny said, "Yes."

"All right. Get off with the barrow now. You know your calls?"

"Mother told me." On mornings when there was a good deal of money to collect Shonny did the round with the barrow. He went out. But as he vanished into the passage the echoing bang of the street-door knocker sounded; once, then again.

Shonny's voice could be heard, a piping of alarm, a deeper voice, the scuttle of Shonny's footsteps and the trampling approach of heavier footsteps.

Inspector Merry came into the room and said, "Right, Peach. I want you."

In the doorway stood the other plainclothes man with two uniformed policemen behind. A blanched and gaping Shonny slipped past them into the room. Dido faced Merry with a calm, enquiring gaze. "What's this about?"

Merry turned. "Gaffney, you take the yard. Weldon, the shop."

The two men went about their tasks. The remaining policeman moved into the doorway. Dido said, "What's all this about? What you want me for?"

Merry said, "You'll swing for this one."

Mrs Peach clapped her hand to her mouth and moaned, "Oh, dear God!"

Grace cried, "Didy, what is it?" She stared at Merry in a dawning of recognition and reawakened fear. "What's he doing here? What's he want to come here again for?" She threw a glance of petty anger at Merry. "Banging the door down. If you've frightened my baby —"

Merry lowered his face, his lips puckering in a savage travesty of amusement. He spoke low, as if to himself in wonderment. "Frightened your baby, eh? A baby was burned to a crisp at three o'clock this morning. Seven people fast asleep in a roomful of rotten old wood, rags, boxes, mattresses. All packed together for warmth with every rag they had on top of them."

Dido said, "What is this?"

"They got warmth all right," Merry said. "Room went up like a blowtorch. You'd think a bomb went off in there. Seven people." He turned to look at Dido and said matter-of-factly, "Little girl of ten got out with a few burns. She's in hospital. The woman's dead. She was ailing. Burned in her bed, she was. Do you know that lad Cockeye? He did very well. He brought out the two little boys, five years old and three. Then he went back in for the baby. It was like a furnace by then. People tried to stop him but he darted away like a goldfish. Good lad was Cockeye in the end. Still, he might have saved himself the trouble. Baby was in an orange box packed with newspaper. Burned to a crisp already. And so was young Cockeye."

Weldon came in from the shop. He said, "There's some scorched floorboards."

"Ah!" Merry pondered, eyeing Dido. "I think I see, said the blind man. You did a better job than they did. Three dead, four in hospital."

Grace was looking at Dido without alarm or entreaty; simply with a long, vacant yet surmising stare. Dido said, "So you pick on me."

Merry's grin was bitter. "I have news, my friend. Keogh's

alive. There's a constable by his bed. As soon as he comes round I only want one word from him. One word. Your name."

Dido remained silent. Merry turned on Grace. With sudden savagery, "I suppose you'll swear blind for him again."

Her eyes opened a little wider but she said nothing.

Dido said, "She's not well. Leave 'er alone."

She said vaguely, "Swear blind?" She looked from one of them to the other. "Swear blind what?"

Dido said to her, "He wants to know —"

"Quiet!" It was a snarl, as Merry with the flat of his hand sent Dido reeling into the shop. "You don't work that one twice. Gaffney —" He called to the other constable. "And you out there, take him down." To Dido. "You won't be laughing sixty minutes from now."

"I'm not laughing," Dido said quietly. He let the two policemen lead him to the door. He paused when he heard Grace's voice.

She had raised herself on one arm. She looked at Merry with wide, frightened eyes. She spoke as if fearful of the consequence. "What did you want to know?"

Merry went back to the kitchen. He stood looking down at her. He saw a frightened, puzzled face. He said, "I'll talk to you afterwards."

She faltered, "What you said. All that. Was he supposed to —? Do you think he —?" She stopped as if it was too terrifying even to ask the question.

Merry said, "Three o'clock in the morning. You were asleep of course. Don't know a thing."

In the same faltering voice. "No. I was up. I was up for a half-hour feeding baby. She wouldn't go off."

They were all looking at her; the detective, the policemen, Dido, Shonny, Mrs Peach. She lay there propped on her arm staring at Mr Merry. He said, "Well?"

She stared at him, her breath quick and short as if she was about to cry. Then she said, "Well of course he was with me. Where else should he be?"

"All right," Merry said to the policemen. "Get him down there."

Dido was taken to the police station on foot. A small crowd followed all the way. He turned his head once after he left the house and beyond the swirling mob he glimpsed his mother standing on the doorstep.

Chapter 25

Merry had arrived on duty at the police-station at eight o'clock in the morning. As soon as he heard of the fire, the name of Jaggs Place set an alarm ringing in his mind and he hurried there. When he arrived the firemen were dismantling their apparatus and poking about the room, which was a black charred cave with a litter of burned remnants on the flooded floor. It was clear from the fire chief's answers to his questions that although no cause of the disaster had yet been discovered no-one had even thought of possible foul play.

Inspector Merry drifted among the onlookers and spoke quietly with a few of his acquaintances. Then he sent for a taxi-cab and went with a constable to the hospital. Keogh, in a swathe of bandages, was still unconscious. Merry left the constable at the bedside with instructions and returned to Brick Lane.

What had sent him so swiftly to the hospital was the information from one or two old cronies of Keogh that in the pub the previous evening Keogh had hinted that he had nearly done for Peach once and for all; and had boasted that next time he would bring it off. Merry could only cull hints, and these were not precise. One man reported Keogh's saying that Dido would not sleep safe of a night from now on.

It was these hints which had sped Merry to arrest Dido for questioning. He thought he saw the whole thing now. He was sure that he had his man at last. It was only a matter of holding him until Keogh regained consciousness and talked.

After two days the police had extracted nothing from Dido and were still unable to bring a charge. The matter was out of Merry's hands now. He was only a junior in what had become an important affair. The station bustled with the comings and goings and conferences of senior officers from the Division and from Scotland Yard. Merry found himself no more than their errand-boy, passing on orders and tramping the streets at their bidding.

Police called at every dwelling in Rabbit Marsh and Jaggs Place. Hundreds of people were questioned. There were no more sealed lips; not, that is, about the feud between Dido and Keogh. The police were swamped with statements. Reams of paper were closely studied at the station. But not a word could be found which would stand as evidence. Everyone was ready enough to talk. People talked out of malice, for beneath the servility accorded to a master there is always malice. They talked because the sheer atrocity of the crime had overcome their normal reluctance to help the police. They talked because a crime so lurid and melodramatic excited them, and because their own closeness to it made them feel self-important. They vied in their attempts to provide information which would secure them the glory of a mention in future newspaper reports. All that they offered, however, proved on careful sifting to be no more than rumour, hearsay, exaggeration.

On the night of the crime no-one in either Rabbit Marsh or Jaggs Place had seen or heard anything. There was not even the bark of a dog to report. A few people in Jaggs Place claimed that before the shrieks they had heard the great whoof, as one of them put it, "Like a 'uge gas oven being lit," and others spoke of the noise of breaking glass. The police were fairly sure that an inflammable missile had been hurled through the window; but they could not prove anything. Repeated and minute searches of the gutted room produced nothing but spats of melted glass clinging to charred timbers.

As to Keogh's earlier raid upon Dido, all that could be gleaned was the testimony of a few neighbours that on the previous night they had heard shouts from Number 34 in the small hours, and one man had seen a light in the kitchen. Even the rescued children had slept through the night and could not say whether Keogh had been away from his bed.

Dido, as impassive as a lump of wood, blocked this line of attack with the simple statement about Shonny's bad dream. He never elaborated and he never varied his wording. He was questioned day and night to the extreme of strain and sleeplessness. He only sat patiently and in a quiet voice gave the same brief answers in the same precise words.

He had an answer for everything. He was asked why the floorboards in the shop were scorched.

"I was in there night before. Turned over an oil lamp."

What was he doing in there?

"Lookin' for a bit o' cardboard to block the window I'd broke."

(This before they could confront him with the broken window.) Why did he use an oil lamp when there was gaslight in the shop?

"Not near the floor there isn't. You try lookin' for a bit o' cardboard under all them piles by that gas-light."

They came back to the window. How did he break it?

"How?" Dido said, as if bored by silly questions. "I was 'alf asleep. Middle o' the night. The table's by the window. You saw. I swung round not thinkin' with that big enamel teapot an' I broke a pane in the window."

Why did he repair it so early the next morning?

"Because," Dido said with the patience of one explaining the alphabet to small children, "my missus wanted to come downstairs. On the sofa. I couldn't let a draught blow in."

They produced remnants of burned clothes raked out of the boiler.

"That's right. We burn rags all the year round in that boiler. Rags an' carpenters' chips. We pay a lad 'alf a crown a week to stoke it. You ask 'im."

They confronted him with statements about the bad blood between himself and Keogh.

"Bad blood between 'im an' a lot o' people, far as I know."

"You challenged Keogh to a fight. We have witnesses who heard Tommy Long deliver your challenge."

"That's right. To a fair fight. He never took it up."

"You burned him out because he tried to burn you out the night before."

"That's what you say."

"Save yourself trouble, Peach. We know."

"Then I reckon you'll charge me, won't you?" But they could not charge him. There was a stone wall at the end of every path. Among Merry and his superiors a mood of bitter anger grew hour by hour. It was not only the man's impassive stolidity which mocked them more than any show of defiance; it was not only their sense of frustration and of their authority flouted. Children had died; it was one of those few crimes which arouse the loathing and fury of policemen. A dozen times a day Merry asked the same question, and he knew that his superiors were asking it, too. It was becoming his last hope. "Has Keogh talked yet?"

"You'll have to do better than this," the Chief said, pushing aside a report of Merry's. "We can't hold him much longer without a charge."

"The man's committed murder."

"He may have. But he hasn't been charged. And if he knows his rights he can leave or stop answering or call a solicitor any time he likes."

"And you'd let him? Why don't you let me get down there for an hour with him?"

"Listen," the Chief said. "You ought to know better. You'd be wasting sweat. You could thump that man 'till Kingdom Come and he wouldn't feel it. Merry, this case is too big for rough handling. If you've got a drunk in the cells or a petty larceny you can laugh in his face if he asks for a lawyer, you can let the lads go down and give him a leathering he won't forget. But not when you want to put him in the dock at the Bailey. Not when the newspapers are on the doorstep. Not when you've got the D.P.P. sending down swell civvies in cabs from Whitehall every day. This man is protected by the enormity of what he's done. You're a smart man, Merry, but if you're not too smart to learn, mark this. When you've got a big one you have to wear kid gloves. You give us another charge — a holding charge — anything — or we'll have to let him go."

'He horsewhipped Keogh in the street last May. There's witnesses' statements in front of you. Hold him for that."

"I will if Keogh comes round and testifies. But if he comes round, we won't need a holding charge, will we? It was five months ago, Bill. An affray. Hardly anyone in the street. You haven't got a single reliable witness here." He put his hand on the papers. "This one glimpsed him. That one saw the cart go round the corner. Others are hearsay. Damn it, a holding charge is no use if you can't hold a man."

"Thank you for telling me."

"Keep your shirt on, Bill. What about Keogh's mates? They're the only real witnesses. They felt the whip."

"They're the ones that won't talk. They were guilty of a much worse affray the week before. They won't put themselves in the manure."

"All right, Bill. No evidence from the principals. None from the police. We couldn't do it. I'll tell you what will hold him, though. Money with menaces."

"I'm working on it."

"He's been taking money off these shopkeepers for how long —?"

"Sixteen months."

"And you're still working on it."

Merry said, "I understand others have tried."

He spoke with no more than a touch of asperity but he was stirred deeply by anger, not only against Dido but against all the higher-ups who were trampling over his patch. He regarded those streets as his own province. Now Superintendents and Chief Inspectors were going down there and even talking to people, presumably to show a mere underling how the job should be done. Well, so far they had gone in vain. He knew that the Chief was getting at him. If the Chief ever had to make a remark on Merry's work or send in a report on him he would never use any but the highest commendation; yet, though there was no overt dislike, the Chief was an old stager, a rough old East End bobby at heart, and although a considerable freedom was permitted in the matter of plain clothes he must secretly consider that Merry as a supernumerary, an inspector on sufferance as it were, was coming the gent a bit too much in his rakish trilby and smart overcoat. So that it touched raw flesh when the Chief said, "I thought you were the guv'nor down there."

"Did you?"

"You get back there. Money with menaces is what we want. Give us one statement from one tradesman and we'll hold him on it."

Merry said to Blakers, "There's half a dozen at least been giving money to Peach. I know why they won't talk."

"Ah," Blakers said. His son Stanley was in the kitchen, with the door open. "What you're after is a 'oldin' charge. I sympathise, Mr Merry."

"Do you want him to come out again? You're not paying money to anyone now."

"Payin' money?" Blakers echoed.

"Come off it. If he swings you're done with him. There's no gang behind him. Only a kid brother of fifteen. Is that who you're frightened of?"

"Me frightened, Mr Merry? Why should I be frightened?"

"It's very funny, everyone's falling over themselves to talk. Only they've got nothing to tell us. But you and your mates have. And you keep mum. I wonder why."

"Why would you say, Mr Merry?"

"Could it be anything to do with stolen goods?"

"Stolen goods down 'ere? All honest tradesmen we are, Mr Merry."

"When do you think I was born, Blakers? There isn't a shop or a stall that doesn't rely on stolen goods for a living. And who's got the contacts down here? Who's the one that can tell 'em all where they can pick up a cheap lot? You've put the gag on 'em, Blakers. You're the boss and they're keeping their mouths shut on your sayso. Why?"

"You're bein' very unfair, Mr Merry. I'm just an' ol' chap that minds 'is own business."

"Listen," Merry said. "Don't think you can play me up. I can put one on you for receiving."

"Stanley," Blakers called. "Do you think that's right? Did you 'ear what the gentleman said? I'm sure my conscience is clear. 'Ave you any proof, Mr Merry?"

"I won't forget this," Merry said, and went out.

What enraged Merry even more behind the steady gaze with which he faced the world was the fact that he had not been able to get anything out of the family; neither he, nor his superiors, in many interrogations. A lad, an old woman and a sick girl; and he could not get the better of them.

Shonny sat every time like a limp, scared child. Provided by Dido with the simplest of stories he stuck to it. Repetitions, catch questions, shock questions, threats even, could produce nothing but the same answers in the same monotone, or scared silences, or a mumbled, "I don't know."

Mrs Peach's strength was the fact that she knew nothing of Dido's raid on Keogh and firmly believed that he had been in his bed all that night. And she knew so little of what had happened on the previous night that by a trick of the will she had forgotten all but Dido's story about the bad dream, which she believed as firmly. Yet it was not in her persistence that her strength lay. The detectives could never catch her out because she had retreated for protection into her old private world of absentmindedness. Her answers were whimpering and pointless, she drifted into irrelevances that drove her questioners to distraction, she broke off into long, helpless silences, directing her frightened gaze everywhere but at her interlocutors. She seemed to just sit there and daydream; and all the ears that strained to catch her private mumbling learned nothing of value.

Grace, too, had found a refuge. She had taken to her bed and insisted that she was too unwell to move. After a few questions her eyes went bright with fever and her cheeks burned, and the doctor warned that she must not be bullied. Merry had to sit by her bed and hear the same dull answers to his questions; and after a little while she would sigh and close her eyes and pull the sheets up to her chin; and he would leave, defeated. After he had visited her on the third day of Dido's detention he went back to the station and all he could find to say to the Chief was, "Anything about Keogh yet?"

"Yes. He died this morning. Never regained consciousness."

"All right, dad," Stanley Blakers said. "He's snuffed it. Keogh has pegged out. He died this morning."

His father let him continue with an interrogative, "Ah?"

"I don't know what you're waiting for," Stanley said. "They can't keep Dido there without a holding charge. Do you want him to be let out? — Well you're not sorry for him, are you?"

"It's 'ard enough lookin' arter Number One in this world," his father said. "Every man for 'isself."

"All right then," Stanley said. "I dunno why you wouldn't help Mr Merry when he was here but it's in your interest to help him now."

"And why is that?"

"Because," Stanley said, trying to be patient, "you won't be bothered with anyone then. No Keogh, no Dido."

"No others?"

"What others?"

"There's always others, son. Now you listen to me. You may be educated and you may 'ave a job with the council, but your ol' dad can still teach you a thing or two. Why should I 'elp Merry?"

"You want to keep in with him, don't you? He's the only one you've got to fear now."

"Son," Blakers' voice was pitying, "you're a young man an' you 'aven' got long sight. That's your trouble. Dido is laughin' at 'em over the murder charge. Right?"

"Now that Keogh's dead, yes. But they can get him for money with menaces."

"For which if you don't know the top price is five years. Not that 'e'd get anythin' like that for takin' a few mingy sov'reigns off a few traders. Why, 'e never threatened anyone but me, an' that was only once."

"You can say different."

"Can I? Thank you. Year or two in the nick, less I dare say, Dido comes 'ome. D'yer wonder they was all afraid to shop him to Merry? 'E's a good conduct man if there ever was one. Not very long is it? Long enough for 'im to sit there chewin' 'is grudge, though. An' what 'appens to me then?"

"Merry'll look after you."

"Be your age, lad. Merry don't care a fiddler's fuck for me. 'E'd split 'is guts laughin' if I got done. Why, 'e'd pray for it so as 'e could git Dido inside again. Fat lot of good it would be to me. Let Merry fry 'is own fish. What you can't see yet, son, is, where the profit is."

"What profit?"

"For your ol' dad, Stanley. That's 'oo. Look. Let Dido come 'ome. It suits me. You shut your gob for a change and pay attention. First — I can put 'im inside for money with menaces. I'm the only one 'e threatened an' I've got witnesses. I tell him that. Right? No, no, you listen. I know an' you know that it wouldn' pay me to do it. But Dido Peach is dead scared of the nick. I know my Dido. Once they've let 'im go 'e'll cut 'is throat sooner than go back in the nick. Because all 'e wants is to be respectable. You can laugh. Respectable. And that's why I can put the 'alf-nelson on 'im. All right, let 'im keep the roughs out. There's plenty waitin' to move in if there ain't someone like Dido to keep 'em off. Let 'im take 'is 'alf-sov'reigns off the other shops. Long as I get my whack. An' what's more, if I want a crate o' nicked fags 'e won' be so 'igh an' mighty any more. 'E won' turn up 'is nose at collecting my debts neither. Long as Dido knows I can put the screws on 'im, 'e'll do as I say. Your dad's king o' the castle. 'Bout time there was a respectable tradesman in charge of things, 'stead of all these roughs. I tell you, Stanley, with my brains I ought to be on the Borough Council I ought."

The side door at Number 34 was open. Merry walked in without knocking and went straight past the scared old woman who bobbed out of the kitchen at the sound of his steps. He went upstairs. He walked into Grace's bedroom without knocking. He didn't care if he caught her naked.

She was in bed. He came to the bedside. "All right. You're going to talk now."

She said, "You'll wake baby."

"I've come to tell you something, my lady. It's about your baby. You're going to lose your baby. Did you know that?"

She didn't lie down and start her exhausted act. She gazed up at him in apprehension. He said, "You didn't know that, did you? You cross me any more, I can have your baby taken away."

It was not true. He was going beyond his powers. He was ready to go farther. The Chief had told him that unless they turned up some evidence they'd have to let Dido go. The man had been kept for four days without a charge. The Yard was scared stiff and they said the Home Office was, too. Merry had persuaded the Chief to hold Dido for a few more hours; two hours, that was all; and he had come here. He was a cautious man and not one to risk his career but it would be his word against hers afterwards. There were no witnesses inside these four walls. Complaints against the police were ten a penny; the police officer's word was always taken. This was his last chance. He said, "And you'll go to prison. D'you know that? He's going on trial. Don't worry, we've got evidence. He'll swing. You're not doing him any good. But you'll go to prison for telling me lies. Well? Now tell me. What happened that night?"

She lay there moistening her lips. He said, "I'll ruin you. I swear on the Book. You'll go to prison and your baby'll go to a home with bastards. Do you want that? Do you want your kid to grow up a murderer's git and a mother in prison?"

She lay quite still, her hair on the pillow, her eyes on him. He changed his tone. "You don't want that. I can tell a decent girl. You couldn't help getting mixed up with him. It's no use being loyal any more. Be loyal to your child." He walked round the foot of the bed and looked down into the cradle. "Lovely. Little doll, she is. I've got two. Best time when they're babies. Never the same after." He returned to the other side of the bed, drew up a chair, sat down and leaned forward. He put his hand on hers. She did not take her hand away. "Grace. I know a decent girl when I see one. I want to help you. For heaven's sake, we're not monsters. Helping decent people is what we're for. I often wondered why you married him. I expect he told you a tale."

She looked away from him and the faintest private smile came into her eyes; a scarcely-discernible flicker of reminiscence but enough to encourage him. He said, "I've seen it time and again. Sweet nice girl meets a chap tells her a tale. Before you know where you are she's married to a bad lot. Don't know sometimes. Don't know right up to the last. When the truth comes out they won't believe a word of it. Did you know?"

He waited and she looked at him again, interest now in her eyes. He said, "I wonder what he told you when he went off every day? He was out all day, wasn't he? I know. I know all about him. Did you know he was taking money off people by threats? I wonder. Did you know he was planning a burglary when I stopped his game a little while ago? What did you think he was up to? Where did the money come from? Did you ask? Or did you think he was getting it on the Stock Exchange? All right, I'm not making fun of you, Grace. Many a woman I've known thought her husband was running a respectable business somewhere when he was up to every kind of villainy. That was it. Wasn't it? You couldn't have known. I can see the kind of person you are. I'm willing to let the whole world know you're a decent respectable girl and you had nothing to do with all this. Nothing. Only you must let me help you." He paused a little. "You must help me. You don't have to get feverish or frightened or anything. Just tell me quietly. Tell me the truth. Look, he wasn't with you that night. You were up feeding the baby. You told me so. But he wasn't there, was he? You don't have to say anything. Just nod. I'll write it down, that's all. You just put your name. Nothing else. You won't be bothered after."

She licked her lips and opened them and he thought he saw the effort to speak in her face. He leaned forward and said, "Yes?"

She only sighed and closed her eyes. He said, "I'll look after you. He won't hurt you, I'll see to that. I'll give you money. How much do you want? Eh? How much do you think you'll need for a fresh start?"

She turned her head. Her eyes roamed about the room as if she were seeking something. He said, "It's the disgrace, isn't it? That's what you're frightened of. Do you think I don't understand — the wife of a hanged man? I can get you away from that, too. You can go away. I'll get the money for you. Make a fresh start. Change your name. You'll be free to marry again. Think what it'll mean — for your baby."

She lay with her eyes closed, and in her harsh quick breathing, the woebegone fall of her lashes he saw the breaking-point he sought. He waited. He took out a pad and scribbled in it. He put his mouth close to her ear and murmured, "I've written it down, Grace. Be a good girl. Give me your hand. I'll help you write your name. A few seconds, it'll be over. Nothing to fear. Nothing to fear."

Her mouth opened in an extremity of distress as if about to cry in pain. Then she shook her head, her eyes still closed. "Grace. D'you hear me?"

She shook her head violently in a tumble of hair. He lost all restraint. He seized her shoulder and shook her cruelly. "Don't come that lark." His voice was low and harsh. "Don't come the old faint on me. Wake up you bitch. Come on you little cow. You murderer's whore. I know you. Two of a kind, you and him. I'll fix the pair of you. Listen. You didn't know. You didn't know, did you? —" He tried his final lie. "He talked. Keogh talked this morning. We're going to break Dido's neck and by God if you don't —"

She opened her eyes. "He didn't," she whispered. "He didn't talk. Someone showed mother the midday paper."

She shut her eyes again and Merry let his hand fall to his side.

Dido was released an hour later. He walked out of the police station with an expressionless face and his head up. He did not look round and he did not see Merry and Weldon in the doorway of a back room.

Weldon said, "He's still laughing."

"The Chief says watch him." Merry's voice was calm. "I'll watch him. If I can't get him by the book I'll do it my own way."

Chapter 26

Dido walked down the street as steadily as if he had just been out for five minutes to buy a box of matches. He ignored the bystanders who turned to look and the faces that suddenly crowded in doors and windows, so many carnival masks gaping with black apertures.

The family had been given no warning of his release. He looked into the kitchen. It was empty. He went upstairs, heard voices from the sitting-room and went in.

As he opened the door his mother and Grace froze into a tableau, his mother standing behind the table with hands upflung and no sound but a gasp in her throat; Grace lying on the couch in her dressing-gown, the baby in her arms.

His mother pressed a hand on the flat top of her chest and murmured, on a long, shaky breath, "Dido!"

She was on him in two unsteady paces, her hands out groping, relief melting her face, and he let her stand slumped against his chest, her arms tight round him while he looked at Grace on the couch, who looked back at him vaguely as she rocked the baby.

He ventured a signal to Grace, the glint of a smile in his eyes as he nodded towards the baby while his mother pressed her head on his chest and moaned, "Oh, Dido, thank God. Oh, I prayed, I prayed all the time!"

He patted his mother's back. "It's all right, mother," and to Grace, "Baby asleep?"

His mother's voice wept, "I knew you'd come home. All those wicked things they said." She lifted up her face. He was still looking at Grace. His mother's voice rose. "You asleep in your bed that night. Wicked, it was wicked."

He freed himself gently. "All over now, mother." To

Grace. "Glad to see you up again."

His mother said, "I thought it would cheer her up. Sit in here with a nice fire. After that man upset her."

"What man?"

"The detective. You know the one. He was here this morning. He kept coming every day. Made life a misery. You must be hungry. I'll make you something."

He said, "After," and to Grace, who had risen quietly with the child, "Where you goin'?"

Walking to the door, "Put baby down."

"I'll take her." He was at her side and she let him take the baby.

"You must eat," his mother said. "Oh, I'm that glad to set eyes on you."

He said, "After."

Grace passed out of the room while he paused to speak. He followed her into the bedroom. He put the baby down into the cradle. To Grace, "Sorry I surprised you."

She lowered herself on to the bed and put her feet up. She turned her head towards him but her expression denoted no more than attention. He came to the foot of the bed, leaning upon the rail. "I give you a surprise, didn' I? Comin' in all of a sudden."

She had the air of a wife listening vaguely while she reckoned what she needed from the shops. He said, "Did 'e bother you a lot?" She did not appear to comprehend. He added, "Merry?"

A little grimace of her lower lip was his answer. He said, "'E's 'ard man. You're a good girl."

He paused, a little nonplussed. He did not want to forfeit any of the closer relation they had attained before his arrest; but he did not know what effect his crime had had on her. For him, what was done was done. Nothing laid on his conscience. He looked to the cot and smiled. "She knows me." He moved. "I'll take her up."

Grace put her feet to the floor, stooped before he could and lifted the baby. There was nothing hasty or ostentatious in the action. Her attention was only for the baby now, her fingers busy. She murmured, "It's time for her feed."

Dido eyed the tableau of mother and child. He had made himself hard and insentient as a block of corned beef for the last three days. It had brought him through. What he saw now touched him with the first softening warmth. He said, "You've 'ad it bad. I bet 'e shook you, that swine. You take it easy. Soon be all right."

Her head was bent over the child. He said, "She cry at night?"

"No. She's good as gold."

Her tone was neutral, her eyes vague, not noticeably averted yet always restlessly taking stock about the room. She talked, but each conversation came to a dead end. Silences lay between them which did not bother her but which stirred uneasiness in Dido. He put it down to shock. There grew in him the notion of how great a blow the events of the past days must have been to a girl like her and he decided that he must give her time. He took off his boots and jacket and stretched out on the bed, "Ah! Nothin' like your own bed. Precious little sleep they give me."

Grace said, "Have a sleep."

He shut his eyes and lay for an hour; not sleeping but dazed, far away, relaxed. He heard her return to the sitting-room at some time during the hour. When he opened his eyes he was alone in the bedroom with the sleeping child. He went to the washstand, sluiced, and went downstairs to the kitchen.

There was no vagueness or puzzling quiet about his mother. During his walk home he had felt more forebodings about her than about Grace. She had already turned on him in bitterness. He had disappointed her, he had betrayed her years of toil and Christian teaching, he had broken his final promise to her; and she had cried out that he was no better than his father. His arrest must have been the final shock to bring down her life's hopes in ruins.

On the contrary. She was in a transport of love. Somehow the whole dreadful train of events had not only convinced her of Dido's innocence; but that she herself had been unduly harsh to him and must make up for it. Her reasoning was simple. She had been fast asleep in her bed that night. All her household had been fast asleep in their beds. This was an unshakeable conviction. Therefore Dido was innocent, cruelly treated, misjudged — as she herself had misjudged him. She flamed with eagerness to show once more her faith in him, and with indignation against those who, as she cried, had it in for him.

Nor was she deeply affected by the crime. It was terrible. But to her it was one more tale in that dreadful slum world in which she and her family had been compelled to live although they were people apart. Such things went on. Every day there were accounts in the newspapers — the father of five who cut the throats of his wife and children and hanged himself, the old woman discovered in a garret five weeks dead, the baby bitten to death by rats, the prostitute found strangled, the jealous wife who threw acid in the face of her rival, the rough who trod his enemy to death. Such things happened all round them. All her life she had shut them out; her house a little Christian fort among the hosts of misery and vice. These things had nothing to do with her or her family. And now that something had happened quite near, they were trying to involve her family, they had picked on her boy. For he was her boy again; and her joy that he was restored to her heart only added to her ardour. When he entered the kitchen she cried, "I've made your favourite. From when you were a little boy."

She drew from the oven a heaped, steaming plate. "Toad in the hole. With bubble and squeak."

He looked at the four fat sausages that peeped from a mass of batter, surrounded by a greasy mess of cabbage and sliced potatoes. He was suddenly sickened; not at the food but at the gush of affection. She said, "You used to beg me for it when you were little. Eat it up. Be a good boy."

He put his head down and attacked it doggedly, forcing himself to chew and swallow each mouthful, to cut and stack his fork deliberately. She hovered by him, hands clasped, eyes bright with happy tears. He ate through it, feeling a prisoner, and when he finished she clapped her hands together. "Oh, good boy! You haven't left a mouthful. And now look what I've made for afters. A treacle pudding."

He went up to bed early. He undressed and turned off the gaslight. Grace was a silent mound under the covers. He eased himself into bed next to her. "You asleep?"

"No."

"Glad to be in me own bed at last."

"You must be," She turned on to her back and he saw the glimmer of her open eyes gazing at the ceiling.

He said, "You'll get over it." She closed her eyes. He said, "I'll make it up to you." He lay for a few moments, then, "Lot to think about. Arrangements to make for the christenin'. Then there's Christmas soon. It'll be all right. You'll see." Her face was relaxed for sleep. He said, "Good night."

Her mutter was sleepy, "Good night."

He would have liked to get close to her warmth for a little while. There was comfort in the thought on this first night back. Not to do anything to her. He wouldn't think of it only a couple of weeks after her time; and he didn't feel like it himself. Just for the warmth of it. He listened to her steady breathing, turned his back on her and made the effort to sleep.

Troubles had never before kept him from sleep but tonight he slept badly. In the darkness he could see farther than in daylight. Something in Grace's vague, sleepy remoteness disquieted him. He had to hold himself back from waking the girl who lay next to him in a sleep so profound that he could no longer hear her breathing. Once he was awakened by candlelight from snatches of disturbing dream to see her sitting on the far edge of the bed. She was feeding the baby. He could not come out of the cavern of sleep enough to speak to her. She seemed unaware of him; he accepted this for she had the ability to rise like a somnambulist, attend to the baby without herself really waking up and sink back into sleep almost as she blew out the candle.

He was awake when the late gloomy daylight of winter infused the room. He crept downstairs without waking her, washed and made his own breakfast. He did not take any tea up to her; he thought it better to let her sleep.

In the bedroom once more he cautiously opened the bottom drawer of the wardrobe, took out the brown paper parcel, opened it and slipped into his working trousers. Grace opened her eyes and muttered fretfully, "It's cold. You haven't lit the fire." He sat still and she said, "I want to change baby."

He busied himself with sticks and paper at the fireplace. When the flames sprang up he squatted in front of them, warming his hands. She got up and put on her dressing-gown. As she stooped over the cot he said, "'Ave a good night's sleep? Feel better?"

"I feel all right."

"Get over it. Soon be all right."

She was busy with safety-pins, turned away from him. He said, "You needn't worry."

Not looking round, one word scarcely audible, "No?"

"I'll do what I said."

Still low, "What was that?"

"Get you out of here."

"Good." She bit the word off like an end of cotton.

Her brief, low words increased his unease. "Don't you believe me?"

"Why not?"

"Something to look forward to, ain' it?"

No answer.

"Grace, I'm talkin' to you."

"I'm changing baby."

"I'm talkin' to you."

"I can hear you."

He rose and went to stand over her. "What's up?"

She did not look at him. "What do you mean?"

"What's got into you?"

"Nothing."

"Look at me, will you?" — She turned an expression up to him that gave nothing away. He stopped himself from shouting. "You can talk, can't you? — It's no use broodin' on things. Get you nowhere. What's done is done."

"Oh, yes?" The slight, distinct, derisive change of note between the words was a statement.

"It's over and done."

"Oh, yes?" She might almost have thought him funny.

"Look! —" He grasped her arm and she muttered irritably, "Mind baby."

He brought it out at last. "I done it for you."

"What?"

"It was for you. For you two."

"What was?"

He could not think what to say next. She said, "There's a fresh tin of powder on the washstand," and he went to get it for her.

She powdered, folded the napkin, pinned it. She lifted the baby and put its face gently against hers. He said, "You can talk to me. I am your husband."

She held the baby at arm's length and her eyes bathed it in fondness.

He said, "She's mine as well."

Lightly, turning away from him, putting the baby down, she said, "Oh, yes?"

Doggedly, "Grace, we got to talk. We got to make plans."

"Plans?"

"We 'ad plans, didn't we?"

"Did we?"

"Well then —"

She turned quickly, and cried, "Well then?"

She was trembling, staring at him with an incredulity he could not fathom. He shouted, "They would 'a' done for you an' the baby. I 'ad to do it!"

"Did you?"

"It was them or me."

"And what about me?"

"I'm tellin' you —"

"What about me? There's something to be proud of. My husband taken away by the police. For everyone to see."

"They let me go."

"Hooray."

"Grace, you got to put it out of your mind. People get killed in fires every day."

"Fires! A fat lot I'm bothered about that. Good riddance to bad rubbish I say."

He was dumbfounded. He was still stunned by the intensity with which she had lashed out; but shocked even more, truly shocked, as the truth dawned on him. He had dreaded that she would loathe him for the crime; but she hadn't given it a thought. "Lot of savages," she cried. "I've no tears for that sort. You never thought of me, did you? The disgrace you've brought. You had to? Thank you very much."

"All right," he said. "I tell you I'll get you out of here."

"You'll tell me. You'll tell me anything. You told me a few old stories, didn't you? You and that old cow downstairs. You and your business in Dalston."

"That's what I'm gonna do," he shouted. "I'll have that business. Just wait."

"And the band played believe it if you like." Her glance fell on the parcel; then quickly at him. "What's that getup for?"

He started to pull on the big boots. "I'm goin' out."

"To start a business? In that rigout? Some business!"

"Lookin' for work."

"What sort of work?"

"What does it look like?"

"I know what it looks like." She stooped and lifted the

baby. Its clear blue eyes gazed in hurtful innocence at Dido. Grace said, "Look at your father."

"Shut up," Dido shouted. "It's 'ard enough."

"Why? Don't you want your baby to see you?"

"I got to make a start. I must earn something. I'm goin' down the docks."

"Look at your daddy. A common workman in dirty boots and a cap and choker. He'll come home stinking with ale like the rest of them. Clay pipe in his mouth. Spit on the floor."

"What do you want me to do? I've got to make a start. Save something."

"Oh, sing me another one, do. We'll be here ten years while you're saving. A dirty common labourer. And I'll turn into a shabby drudge. And my child a ragamuffin."

"Shut up!" He heard his own thick shout and his fist flew up.

"Ha! That's the second time you've raised your hand to me. You don't know anything else."

He let his hand drop. "What do you want? What do you want of me?"

"I want to get out of here."

"I've told you —"

"Now."

"Be reasonable."

"I'm reasonable. You've done enough to me and my child. I'm telling you now. I won't wait."

"You'll 'ave to."

"There's no have to. If I don't go with you I shall go without you."

"You'll what? You'll —? With her?" He pointed at the child.

"You don't think I'd leave her."

"I'd kill you first."

"Oh no you wouldn't." She faced him in a silence that seemed to read him. "What good would that do baby?"

After a moment he said, "Where would you go?"

"Back to the hostel. Matron would help me. So would

the reverend. They'd find a good home to take me in. — I do mean it."

"What can I do?" His voice was weary. "They say there's fifty thousand out of work in the East End this month. If you won't wait what can I do?"

"Don't ask me. You're the man."

"Look, I'm standin' 'ere, Grace. Say what you want an' I'll do it."

"You're the man. You haven't lacked ideas in the past. Some fine tales you spun me. Use your brains. Do something. Or are you all blow and no show? You've got a wife and child and if you want to keep them you'd better do something. Don't stand there. Go and do something. Go on."

Blakers called from his doorway, "Hey! Dido! Come 'ere a minute."

Dido paused. Blakers said, "Come in 'ere."

Dido followed him into the shop. "'Aven't seen you in them togs for a long time," Blakers said. "You're not goin' out labourin' agen?"

"Work's work."

"Wicked shame, smart feller like you go labourin'".

Dido had no strong purpose to look for work. Numbed by Grace's attack he had continued to dress automatically in the clothes at hand; and he had wandered out into the street without aim. "My friend all of a sudden, are you?"

"Don't like to see a smart feller wasted. Sooner use a smart feller meself. Well, in my own interest, ain' it?"

"I know your sort of jobs," Dido said.

"Well," Blakers said mildly, "they do say beggars can't be choosers. After all I done you a good turn already. Keepin' quiet."

"About what?"

"Merry's arter puttin' you away on a charge of money with menaces. I only 'ave to tell 'im 'ow you threatened me that time for a sov'reign in front of witnesses, an' you're inside. Well —" He spoke hastily at the glitter in

Dido's eyes. "I'm only sayin'. Shows I'm your friend, don' it?"

"You reckon you got the drop on me," Dido said. "What d'you want?"

"Nothin', Dido. I'm just sayin' it pays you to play ball with me. Might pay us both, come to that. What you want now is a job. They'll be watchin' you, you know. You wanna box clever long as they're watchin'. Git down to a reasonable job. They see you workin' steady, they'll get tired in the end."

"Easier said than done."

"Well I tell you, Dido, I been thinkin'. You're 'andy feller. I got a lot to do in this shop. New shelves. Cab'nets. Cost less to take you on than a shopfitter. Why don't you come in, 'ave a go at it? You can 'elp stocktakin' as well. My Stanley's busy with exams, young 'un's workin' for a scholarship too. I could do with an honest man on the premises. Not all that common, honest man in these parts."

Dido, after a moment, said, "All right."

"Start termorrer then. 'Ow are yer fixed for the oof?"

"Couple o' sov'reigns left, I reckon."

"Yer know where to come if yer short. Always oblige a chap like you."

As he passed the kitchen his mother called, "I've got a nice plate of ham for you, dear," and he hated her.

He found Grace in the sitting-room. He said, "I've got work. With Blakers."

"What will you earn?" Her voice was neutral.

"It's not what I'll earn. 'E lends money. Soon as I've done his job I'll borrow enough to move."

"Dido," she said conversationally. "Where do you think of moving to?"

"I don' know. Anywhere. You said you knew some nice parts round Dalston an' Islington."

"Dido," she went on patiently. "Do you realise the police have got their eye on you?"

"Merry?"

"Not just him. There's thousands and thousands of police, and they'll all have their eye on you. They won't forget."

"What can I do?"

Her sigh was quite maternal. "I've been thinking. Someone's got to think for us and I can see it won't be you. Do you really want to make a fresh start?"

"Don' ask silly questions."

"Well see who's silly. Because if you do, there's only one way. Emigrate."

"Emigrate?"

"He thought I was silly, too. That Mr Merry. Promising me a fresh start. He stood there and he said I could just move away and change my name and no-one would know I'd had a husband hanged. He said himself my baby would be a murderer's git and then he expected me to tell him. As if I didn't know about newspapers and photographs and all that. If you'd been tried I could never have hidden my face anywhere."

"And that's why you never told 'im?"

"Well I'm not a fool, am I? Whatever some may think."

"An' I thought it was on my account."

"I wasn't so simple as he thought, was I?"

Dido chuckled. He couldn't help it. He said, "You want to go to Australia?"

"Australia!" She was maternally petulant. "You've got no ambition, have you? You'll be nothing without me. Australia's common. Labouring work, that's all you get there. South Africa is where people get rich. It's the golden land."

He said, "All right."

"You won't just get there by saying all right. It'll cost at least fifty pounds. Besides what I get for the furniture. I shall keep what I can, of course, I love my home. I don't mean to go out there like a pauper. If we want to travel decently and have something to start with when we get there, we shall need every penny of fifty pounds. Well?"

"All right," he said at length. "I told you. I'll borrow it off Blakers."

"Fifty pounds? And you going half across the world? Why should he risk that?"

"I'm a man of my word. He knows."

"We'll, he'd better look sharp," Grace said. "I don't know why I'm giving you a chance. Because we're married, I suppose. And because of baby. But I shan't wait for ever."

Chapter 27

Towards the evening ten days later Blakers lounged in the doorway of his shop. He took in the everyday scene with his everyday casual gaze; but his eyes searching among the scatter of loafers and children missed nothing. They weren't here today. They — the police watchers who had been in evidence day and night for a week after Dido's return. He had kept an eye open at all hours for the last three days. He was not easily fooled; and he hadn't seen them. It was a bit early in his view for them to call off the dogs; too early to take chances.

He turned into the shop. Dido was hanging a glass door on a wall cabinet. It was a nice job, it gave the shop class. Odd fish, Dido. You might almost know by looking at him that anything he turned his hand to he would do well.

Dido said, "Can I 'ave a word with you?"

"Nice work that is. Fire away, friend."

"You said you'd advance me some money."

"That's right. Trustworthy chap."

"I want fifty quid."

Blakers took this in. He had been calculating when to make the next move and Dido had made it. He had not turned the screw any more since their first talk. No need to — Dido was sharp enough to see the situation. He decided to probe. "Lot of money that."

"You'll be paid back."

"I'm not sayin' I wouldn't."

"Well then — long as I'm trustworthy what's the odds how much?"

"What do you want it for?"

"Need it, that's all."

"That much, entitled to ask what for."

"My business."

Blakers sighed. "You don't 'elp. Lot of money. Five, ten, I can whistle that up any time. What you're askin' for ain't so easy."

"Go on, you got it in the bank."

"That's my business, old feller. You don't know what calls I 'ave to meet."

"It's no, is it?"

"Don't rush me, Dido. Gi' me a chance to think." He paced into the shop. He opened the rear door. "Maria, come an' mind the shop."

His wife came out. He said, "In 'ere, Dido. We can talk quiet."

When they were both in the kitchen he closed the door and let down the square of striped linen that was rolled above the lace. "Don't like nosey parkers," he said. He poured beer into two glasses from a bottle. "Cheers."

Dido raised his glass. "Fifty. You know you'll get it back."

"It's like this," Blakers said. "I can't lend fifty. Honest to God, if you knew what calls I got to meet — it's more than I can do. What I'm thinkin' of, though, I might put you in the way of something." He saw Dido's look sharpen with suspicion. He said, "Depends how much you need the money. I'm givin' you work. You can always save up for it."

"I need it quick."

"Well then," Blakers said and sipped his beer.

"What is it? You want some fags nicked for you?"

Blakers chuckled. "With Woods 'olesalin' at fourteen-an'-eight a thousand? Not much in that for a chap that needs fifty quid. Or for me. 'Ow bad do you need it, Dido? Shall I go on?"

"I'm listenin'."

"Spirits."

"Spirits? You don't sell spirits."

"You don't see all my merchandise on my shelves. Wouldn' do, would it? Well, I can see you're not shocked. You're takin' it very calm."

"Is there fifty quid in it?"

"More, I'd say. You're interested, are yer? Well, it's this friend o' mine. 'E 'as very sharp eyes, this friend. 'E gets about. Wonderful nose for an easy job. Now there's this merchant in Mare Street, Jeffery, Wines and Spirits. Near the Town 'All. Got that? Now my frien' says that Jeffery sends a lad out with 'is deliveries every day. With a plain van — no name on it — mark that, I'm tellin' you for a reason. A plain grey box-van with a pony in the shafts, 'ardly bigger than a postman's 'andcart. But there's a fair bobsworth o' liquor in it every mornin' when that boy sets out. Now look, Dido, this is in confidence. I don' wanna go on if it's not your lay."

"Go on."

"I thought you would. Man of spirit, you are. No burglary or breakin' in 'ere. I wouldn' touch that sort of lay. You mustn't be afraid of short cuts if you want ter get on in business. I'm not. I'm glad ter see you're not. Well this lad loads up an' starts off round eleven every mornin', an' this is the point, before 'e gets on with it 'e always runs down to a coffee-shop in 'Ackney Road — Union Jack Dinin' Rooms. There's 'orse-trough outside. 'E ties 'is nag up there, shoves a nosebag on it an' goes inside for 'is own feed. Well then — you can 'andle a nag, can't you? Even one that might jib with a stranger up be'ind?"

"Trust me with 'orseflesh."

"There you are then. You're there. Lad goes inside. You jump up, whip 'er away, turn sharp left into Mansford Street an' arter that there's such a bleed'n' maze o' back streets Sherlock 'Olmes 'isself couldn't find yer. Plain grey van. No one'll notice it goin' by. That's why I mentioned it. Now, you'll be safe in five minutes. My friend's seen ter that. There's some sheds under the railway arches, not four blocks away. Rented out to tradesmen an' costers. You can get one o' them couple o' bob a week. You just trot the van in there, lock up an' walk away like a gentleman."

"This shed — you want me to rent it?"

"Not my affair, Dido. I'm only passin' this on. You get the merchandise an' I'll talk business. I'll see there's no risk taken movin' the stuff."

Dido took a long time to think it over. "Fifty quid in it, you say?"

"Go an' see for yerself. 'Ave a dekko at the shop, reckon up what the van'll 'old. Same time you'll get ter know the driver's face. After that dinner-hours, you can 'ave a stroll round this Union Jack Dinin' Rooms, get the 'ang of 'is 'abits there. Well Dido, what's it to be?"

Dido said, "Fair enough."

"Good feller. There's no 'urry. You wanna box clever for a while yet. Wait till the law's busy somewhere else."

"I reckon they've packed up."

"You wait till you're sure. I'll tip you the wink when it's safe. Ah —" And he could not help chuckling in a friendly way. "I can' 'elp thinkin' o' you. All these years. The chap that wouldn' thieve."

"I'm left no option," Dido said, "am I?"

"I reckon he's taken the hook," Weldon said. "Twice now in the dinner-hour he's been up by the dining-rooms. He loafs around reading a racing edition."

"He never was a racing man," Merry said. "It paid to cancel the street watch." The friend to whom Blakers referred, who had very sharp eyes, got about a lot and had a wonderful nose for an easy job was Albert. He had gone to Blakers with the plan after it had been reported to Merry that Dido was working in Blakers' shop.

"We might get Blakers, too," Weldon said.

"I doubt it," said Merry. "Nice bonus if we do. But the old chap's fly. Myself I don't think he'll let Dido budge for a while. And when he does, you'll find there's no proven connection with Mr Blakers. Unless Dido coughed. Which he wouldn't. No. I'll be satisfied with Dido. Best have both points watched from now on — the wine shop and the dining-rooms. I'll see the Chief. Is everything set up in Rabbit Marsh?"

"It's all ready."

"Right. That's on from now."

There was no-one watching him. Dido was alert in the street and spied for long periods from windows. He was sure that they had gone away. Too busy elsewhere no doubt, as Blakers had forecast. He would wait for months if Blakers had his way. The old fatguts was scared for his skin. Dido could not wait.

Life at home was calm. It was as if the catastrophe a few weeks back had never happened. Grace was tranquil and coolly amiable but Dido felt that at last he knew her. Every hour of her even talk, her long placid silences, the matter-of-factness with which she cooked and sewed for him, made him feel more the cold implacable purpose which looked out through her eyes. He had no illusions that she would get over it if left alone. His heart skipped with relief every time he came home and found that she was still there — she and his daily more beautiful child. Inside him an ultimatum was rapidly running out.

At half-past three one Thursday morning he opened the street door cautiously. Through a narrow aperture he surveyed the street for a long time in the hazy darkness. It was empty. He slipped out, closed the door quietly and set off at a rapid walk.

He strode through the back streets until he reached Hackney Road. He continued through back ways and missed Mare Street; for his destination was not the wine merchant's. He was bound on his own errand. He did not trust Blakers. Blakers had enough on him already and if he did Blakers' dirty work he would be altogether in the man's hands. He continued northwards.

The windows of Rabbit Marsh were all dark. But behind one of them, on the opposite side to Number 34, there were wakeful eyes. The window was so filthy that no-one could see in from the street even by daylight; but there were random smears in it through which those inside could look out.

It was in a house that had access from a builder's yard at the rear. The room had been rented by a group of road labourers who dossed there on a box and cox basis, day and night; not an arrangement to arouse notice in these parts.

There were two men in the room when Dido left. Both were fully dressed, in labourers' garb. The man at the window said, "He's making for Bethnal Green Road."

"Merry's on tonight," the other said. "*I'll* go and report. You stay on watch."

Chapter 28

Mr Owen did not mind getting up in the early hours. It was Thursday, the milkman's payday. He had been getting up early ever since he was a mite of ten in a Welsh village, helping to clean out a cowhouse for a shilling a week. He had got on a bit since then but he still did a full day's work in his own flourishing dairy. It was worth working for, what he had achieved: a house like a mansion with a white portico and grounds all round it, looking out over the common in front and the pretty park behind that sloped down to the River Lea. Like a house in the country. And driving his own Daimler.

He had bought this motor-car which was now speeding him on his way to the dairy a year ago; second-hand but good as new. It was a possession to be proud of, as smart and comfortable as any gentleman's carriage; and inside its high windowed saloon he was warm and sheltered from the weather on this dark winter morning. He didn't have to worry either about the moneybag on the cushions next to him. He could do sixty miles an hour if need be in this motor.

Not that he gave a thought to the money. His routine was long-tried and safe. On Wednesday one of the men accompanied him to the bank. They returned to the car with the stout little gladstone bag full of coins and drove to his home, where the coachhouse was built on to the main structure. He ran in, the door was closed behind him by the dairyman who then left; he entered the house through a connecting door and put the money in his safe. The safe was guarded through the night by his dog Gelert (Mr Owen knew his Welsh history). In the morning all he had to do was drive straight from his coachhouse to the dairy.

The books had been brought almost up to date by yesterday evening; but there was still the last round and the evening skimmed-milk round to be reckoned in for commission; it would take a smart morning's work to have every man's pay ready by midday.

He forked left out of the main road, slowed in the long side turning and drove slowly in between the wide gateposts of the dairy yard. The floats were already away, but fifty yards in front of him the low line of the sheds was broken by squares of dim lantern-light through open half-doors. A few black human figures moved in and out of the light. He could see the coal fire's nest of red through the glass facade of his office on the left.

He turned right into the old stable, his headlamps lighting brilliantly the uneven brick floor still thinly littered with rotten straw and the whitewashed wall in front. He stopped the car as its bonnet almost touched the wall. He turned off the headlamps. He opened the door, took up his bag and stepped out of the motor-car. In comparison with the blinded darkness in which he stood beneath the low hayloft floor the darkness of the yard in front of him was a pallor. He stepped towards it, staggered in terror under the sudden slump of weight that bore him down, felt a burst of brilliant pain in the back of his skull and —

Not a sound. Dido threw away the small sandbag with which he had dropped from the loft, brushed straw off his coat with a gloved hand, picked up the gladstone bag, pulled from his pocket a black oilcloth shopping-bag and dropped the other bag into it. He moved towards the door. From just inside the entrance he peered across the yard. The small, distant figures moved about their affairs. In the other direction, the street was empty and silent.

He slipped out, remaining against the wall, and moved along the wall in the angle of thicker darkness formed by the wall of the stable and that of the entrance. He was almost at the gate. Another rapid glance in each direction, then he stepped out, and walked away down the street, a man with a shopping-bag going about his business.

It was daylight when he approached Rabbit Marsh. This suited him. There was no reason why he should be connected with the robbery; and in the last resort no proof. If there were people astir his presence in the street would be normal at this hour, perhaps even unnoticed. His hiding-place was ready; not in the house of course. He still went in the mornings to harness up Tommy Long's horse for him and he would go to the stable as usual. In the place he had found, the money would be safe as in the Bank of England; until he judged things to be all quiet and, with passages booked, he could just melt away one day with Grace and his baby.

One of the watchers at the window looked round as Inspector Merry came into the room. He noticed that Merry had abandoned his dainty shoes for a pair of massive issue boots. Merry said, "Has he come back yet?"

"Not yet, sir."

"He never showed up at the wine merchant's. I thought he might switch his plan. He's that sort of fellow. But I don't know where he's got to now."

They waited, and after a little while one of the constables said, "There he is."

He walked into the street, a small figure on the opposite pavement. He was carrying a black shopping bag that bulged at the bottom. They watched in silence. He went past his own house and continued on his way. He turned into the stable archway. Merry stood up and the other two rose with him. "You wait here," he said. "I'm going to have a look-see."

One of the constables said, "I wouldn't tackle that chap one-handed."

"You wait," Merry said. "Wait here. Till I blow my whistle."

The stable yard was empty. Dido stepped into Tommy's shed and with sure rapid movements shifted a heap of old furniture. In a few moments a crate stood revealed. He moved this aside. In the brick floor where it had been was a manhole. It was a drains inspection manhole covered with the rust of years except round the rims, where Dido had pried it out. It would just take the moneybag, wedged on top of the drainpipe. With the cover back in place, dirt and rust brushed back over the rims, the crate put back and buried once more by the heap of furniture, Dido had no fear for the money.

He lifted the iron cover and pulled the gladstone bag out of the carrier. A voice came to him from the doorway. "Wakey wakey."

Merry stood there, his lips tucked up in an odd smile. Dido hurled the moneybag at him and dived after it. Merry staggered aside and Dido raced to leap for the back wall. He was not running with any hope or object; it was an animal reflex.

He jumped down into a strange back yard and as he ran for the house he heard Merry's boots land on the flagstones behind him. The back door was closed but he ran at it like a battering-ram with fists clasped to his head and it crashed open.

As he staggered into the passage of the house there were shouts from the stairs, faces gaping at him over the banisters; and Merry was in, and the two men were swinging punches in the narrow passage. Dido stopped Merry with a right to the belly, and while his adversary was still gasping, half-doubled, swung a full slop-bucket at him by its handle.

Out through the front door into Jenner Street, alongside the railway embankment. The babble of voices followed him. People appeared at other doors. He ran for the wall but his fingers missed the top and he was running again, Merry pounding after him. The railway. The yards. Acres of rails, sidings, sheds, thousands of trucks. There must be somewhere he could hide, gain a minute's respite.

The wall was lower ahead. He ran for it and his hands grasped the top, but arms clasped his legs, he thumped to the ground on top of Merry. The men rolled upon each other, striving, their faces strained with effort and the rage to kill. Merry on top, hair spiked, face dripping, clothes soaked with slops, panting, blocked Dido's arms with one elbow and with his free hand clutching Dido's hair banged Dido's head on the pavement. A heave that almost tore Dido's guts and he was half-up, ramming Merry against the wall with all his body's force. He staggered up, Merry clinging to his coat, pulled free of the coat and ran. Merry flung the coat aside and dived after him. Dido was almost at the steps. These steps rose steeply above the level of the wall, giving access to the bridge; and by another flight of steps to the alley which led to Rabbit Marsh.

Dido dashed up the steps. There was only a wire fence between the platform and the railway, over which he could easily swing. But at the top he turned and waited. The money was gone. He was done for, his gamble for life was lost. There was only his rage left; a rage fed by the restraint of months; the lust to grapple with this man who had become his personal enemy, who personified all the enemies, all the inimical forces that had driven him to the slaughter; for slaughter, in his fury, it must be — one of them or the other.

Merry had thrown away coat and jacket. His shirt was torn and blood from his face stained it. He dodged to and fro as Dido above him moved to smash him down, and after a feint leaped the last steps on to the platform, pinned at once to the fence by Dido's assault.

The two men strained together, thumping short punches into each other, their bodies bending like those of two locked dancers. Dido's weight bent Merry back, back, in a pressure that would either break his spine or throw him down on to the railway lines.

Merry butted head to head and Dido's grip weakened for a moment, his face a mess of blood beneath glaring eyes and in the moment Merry wrenched free. They lurched to and fro, punching. People from Jenner Street were running towards the foot of the steps to gather, staring, in a clamour of talk. The two men knew nothing of them.

In a scutter of small steps Merry was driven back towards the far edge of the platform. At the last moment he swung aside, put out his left foot and drove a punch to Dido's face. Dido went over his leg and crashed head down on the steps. Half-stunned he tried to raise himself but Merry was on him and a kick sent him rolling down; and another. He rolled down into the alley like a weighted sack and sprawled on the pavement.

Merry ran down. From both directions footsteps and voices closed in. He had only seconds. He stood over his senseless enemy; the wild beast he had hunted down, for whom locking away was too good, on whom he must inflict his own punishment, who must be made harmless. With all his strength he drove the toe of a police boot into the base of Dido's spine. Then he stamped hard on the back of each limp hand and brought a heel down upon the instep of each ankle, where the small bones were.

People from Jenner Street were on the platform above, gaping down. In the narrow entrance at the Rabbit Marsh end, more people were crowding. Mr Merry leaned against a wall, breathing hard. Only now did he fumble in the fob pocket of his trousers, bring out a police whistle, put it to his lips and blow three shrill blasts.

Chapter 29

At eight o'clock on a Sunday morning in the summer of 1918, a small, bent man rose from a mattress on the floor of one of the hovels in Jaggs Place and put on his creased, stained jacket and trousers. He was Dido Peach.

He had been out of prison on licence for two months. He shared the room with two other derelicts who both still snored on their mattresses.

Even when he stood up his back was bowed. Merry's kick had damaged his spine. He hobbled because the bones of his feet had not healed straight and for the same reasons his hands were like the crooked claws of an advanced arthritic.

With stealthy speed he took a few trifles from under his mattress and stuffed them into his pockets. He could not trust his room-mates. He was alone in the world.

Soon after he had gone to prison Grace had returned to work at the teashop. Two months later she had slipped out of the house early one morning carrying her baby and a bundle. Roley Blakers, who was out riding his bicycle, saw a young man with glasses help her into a taxicab and heard the young man answer to the name of Sidney.

Terrified by the sudden disappearance of the girl and the child Mrs Peach applied to the only representative of authority she knew, P.C. Gaffney. Some time later the police ascertained that the girl and her baby, in company with the young man, had left the country. Perhaps somewhere in a golden climate Dido's daughter grew up to be as he had wished — happy, prosperous, educated and respected; for in the human tangle there are some strands of hope and well-being; but he would never know and nor do we.

Chas went to France with the Expeditionary Force and was blown to pieces within a month. Shonny joined up under age and before he was eighteen he was killed at Ypres, his apple cheeks worm-eaten.

Mrs Peach was said by the women in the shops to be mental, with her wandering eyes and puzzled, private mutterings; and Ada took her away. Ada never wished to see or hear of her brother again and Mrs Peach never again saw her son.

Mr Merry stepped out of Blakers' shop. "Don't you worry," he said.

"A wink is as good as a nod," Blakers said and disappeared inside. After four years of war Stanley Blakers had not been called to the colours and the good offices of Mr Merry had something to do with it. Blakers had not been unwilling to show his appreciation. There were many who would pay large tribute to an influential policeman these days. Merchants avoided the rationing laws. Wealthy foreigners flouted the Aliens Regulations. Publicans and club owners kept late hours in spite of the new Defence of the Realm Act. All were grateful for a blind eye. Mr Merry's principles had not changed. He was always strict to administer the law — the law as he saw it. But petty regulations did not concern him. He was a man of authority. He could do lordly favours, exercise his lordly discretion. If thank-offerings came his way — well, that was no more than his rights. It had nothing to do with bribe-taking, which was a mean and petty business.

He was a Superintendent, his promotion hastened by his past achievements. He was no longer in the Division but his work at the Yard often brought him down here and indeed he came out of inclination as well as duty, for he still looked upon the district as his fief.

He looked these days a prosperous and worldly man; and he was. His children were doing well at their grammar schools. A substantial house was being built in his mother's name which in the course of time would come to him. He had put on weight. It showed in the swell of the smooth, rosy skin over his cheekbones and it made his eyes look smaller, more intimidating for all their mildness. It showed in the increased breadth of his smart summer overcoat with its black velvet collar. He still carried an umbrella. It was furled in its case like a rod of black, its spokes enclosed in a band of chased silver. No one had ever seen him open the umbrella. In a drizzle he kept it rolled and in heavier rain he was somehow never about. With the handle of his umbrella he gripped a rolled pair of new tan gloves. His feet were encased in small, shiny shoes.

He crossed the road and surveyed the street as he strolled. It was quieter these days. The war, of course. It had taken the men away. In fact the war in his view had done a bit of good down here. The roughs had turned out to be a patriotic lot, all rushing to join up at the start of it; and by now most of them were heaps of rags on the plains of France. But there was no doubt, there was also more money about. And there were these Lloyd George insurance things. And most of all the licensing hours, which had closed the pubs for most of the day and almost emptied the streets of the drunks who had once abounded. War or no war, it would never be the same again round here. And some of the change was his doing. That gave him great satisfaction.

Mr Merry paused. Dido Peach came limping out of Barsky's shop. He carried a pair of trestles which he set up in the roadway. While Merry watched he returned to the shop and soon reappeared with the board, posts and tarpaulin cover to set up the stall. He scratched a living doing this and other odd jobs for the traders. Barsky dropped some coins into his claw; he bobbed his hand in acknowledgement and started across the road like a lamed crab towards another shop.

He reached the far pavement near Mr Merry. Merry swung the point of his umbrella up as a sign to Dido, then held it out to keep Dido at its length. He said, "Morning, Dido."

"Mornin'."

"How you keeping?"

Dido's voice was husky. What with those ribs stove in and more than five years in a damp cell, he was a bit bronchial. "Mustn' grumble."

Merry lowered the point of his umbrella to the pavement and leaned on it. His faint, approving smile took in Dido from head to foot; and he noted the way the man bore the inspection, patient as a donkey. Merry said, "They treating you all right?"

"Mustn' grumble." Dido's crookback made him look like a menial, his unrevealing gaze level with the buttons of the detective's coat.

"Well —" Merry spun a shilling into the air. "Behave yourself."

The coin dropped to the pavement. Dido's head came up and for a moment his eyes looked directly at Merry, astonishingly alive and clear. Then he stooped and picked up the coin. Afterwards, "Much oblige."

"Keep your nose clean."

Dido was silent. Only his eyes answered, looking directly into Merry's; clear, grey, unfathomably patient. He had lost everything except the only place he knew, the familiar place in which to die. In silence he would endure anything, from this man and from the others, rather than be driven from it.

The detective strode on as if Dido no longer existed. Dido hobbled rapidly into a shop. Mr Merry went away down the street, tranquil of countenance, brisk of step, swinging his umbrella, making the weekly round of his province.